sophia of silicon valley

sophia of silicon valley

ANNA YEN

wm

WILLIAM MORROW
An Imprint of HarperCollins*Publishers*

SOPHIA OF SILICON VALLEY. Copyright © 2018 by Anna Yen. All rights reserved. Printed in the United States of America. No part of this book may be used or reproduced in any manner whatsoever without written permission except in the case of brief quotations embodied in critical articles and reviews. For information, address HarperCollins Publishers, 195 Broadway, New York, NY 10007.

HarperCollins books may be purchased for educational, business, or sales promotional use. For information, please email the Special Markets Department at SPsales@harpercollins.com.

FIRST EDITION

Designed by Bonni Leon-Berman

Library of Congress Cataloging-in-Publication Data has been applied for.

ISBN 978-0-06-267301-5 (hardcover)
ISBN 978-0-06-287042-1 (international edition)

18 19 20 21 22   LSC   10 9 8 7 6 5 4 3 2 1

For my family

sophia of silicon valley

prologue

MEET SCOTT.

I hear the chanting from two blocks away. *Scott. Scott. Scott.* The voices spilling out of San Francisco's Moscone Center are loud and clear, cheering for the man who was just named *Time* Man of the Year. Or something like that. The same man who, at the moment, is insisting I divert our route *away* from where we are supposed to be, despite already being twenty minutes late. My phone is on the verge of exploding. My heart just might join it. *Welcome to my world.*

"Uh, is he close?" the conference organizer calmly asks in the first of a series of voicemails I would retrieve later, each one sounding more panicked than the last.

I'm not wearing a watch, but I dramatically look at my bony wrist anyway so Scott notices I'm concerned about the time. "Are we there yet? I'm pulling over right now unless you tell me where we're going," I say, trying to sound pleasant because every time I yell at my CEO, I have to give him one dollar. It's not even nine o'clock in the morning and I've already given him three.

"I'd just like to drive along the water," he says.

I'd like you to get out of my car.

As we pass the city's storied Ferry Building, now a lavishly overpriced food and agrarian mecca, my passenger suddenly yells, "Pull over!"

"But the convention—"

"I said *here*, Sophia." Scott directs his rimless glasses at me; his eyes warn me to do as he says.

I hold my breath and squeeze my eyes shut, praying we don't crash as I yank the steering wheel to the right and cut off three cars. My rear end slides across the Yellow Pages directory that helps me see over the steering wheel of my mom's midnight-blue Mercedes—the car I had to borrow because it's been one of those eighty-hour work-weeks that left me with no time to fill my own gas tank. *Ah, the glamorous life of being one of Scott's executives.*

"*What the hell?*" shouts an angry taxi driver as I pull up along-side the red-painted curb. While the man hurls a handful of "bad Chinese driver" insults my way, Scott zips up his black raincoat over his mock turtleneck T-shirt and exits the car. He seems to just glide through the pouring rain untouched by the pelting drops. Maybe he secretly invented an invisible force field. Entirely possible.

No, that's superhero stuff.

Well, he could have.

Focus, Sophia, focus!

I jump out of the car and step directly into a puddle that has formed from the pouring January rain. My feet are soaking now and there's no doubt my new black Prada pumps—the ones that get me two inches over the five-foot mark—are ruined. *Dammit! I'm making the company pay for these.*

A young Ferry Building valet runs over from his umbrella stand to tell me I'm parked illegally, but I cut him off with a twenty-dollar bill and ask him to watch the car. "I'll be *right* back," I say. My plan is to wrangle my CEO back inside before the convention center erupts, so the Mercedes needs to be close. Do I still hear chanting from a mile and a half away, or am I going insane? *Scott. Scott. Scott.*

It's only seconds before I catch sight of his black raincoat making its way through the sea of camera-toting tourists and foodies who have been standing in line for two hours to get a baguette that, to me, tastes the same as the grocery-store brand. As the black coat weaves through the Ferry Building's gorgeous central nave, I realize where my target is headed, so I beeline toward him. Not a small feat for a short shopaholic in heels who noticed a pair of cute rain boots for sale a few stores back; I should be rewarded for not stopping to take a closer look.

"Scott—" I huff, slightly out of breath.

"Chocolate chip cookies," he says, pointing to the glass case in front of us.

I look in the case and all I see are crumbs on the plate with the sign VEGAN, GLUTEN-FREE, ORGANIC CHOCOLATE CHIP. He knows there are no more cookies, but he demands one in a way that reminds me of my completely irrational mother.

"Uh, hi," I say to the blissed-out brunette behind the counter wearing a name tag that says DHARMA. "Listen, Dharma, that's my boss's boss over there, and we need one of your vegan chocolate chip cookies."

"Sure." She smiles. "Those are my favorite. When do you need it?"

"Well, um . . . *now.*" Her eyebrows shoot up. She glances over at Scott, who is pacing back and forth barefoot. When did that happen? Mental note: *Find his shoes.*

"I'm sorry, we can't make them that fast."

"When will the next batch be ready?"

The girl bites her lip and shakes her head. "Not today."

I hear my mother's voice in my head: "*There's no such thing as no.*"

"Are you holding any for another customer?" I cajole. I open my Prada wallet to let her know I have money. "I'll pay five, ten, or even twenty times the retail price." *Just give me the cookie.*

Vegan Chick looks up again at my CEO and I see the recognition light go off in her head. She realizes the barefoot man in her store is *him.* The tech genius whose technology changed the entire landscape of personal computing. She retreats into the back and returns with a pink box with the name *Brennan* scrawled on it. Then, like a moth to the light, Dharma walks slowly toward my CEO. There are some benefits to "being Scott."

"Thank you." I smile, stepping into her path and exchanging the pink box for a hundred-dollar bill. "Oh, can I have a receipt, please?" I ask. I'll need it in order to expense the cookies (along with my shoes).

My passenger is now standing in the corner of the bakery with his eyes closed, hopefully focusing on getting ready for his big speech. I take a terrified peek at his feet. *Yes! Shoes on.* "Okay," I whisper while ushering him back toward the car.

Soon, I'm sitting on the thick telephone book again, but there's a knock—a police officer motions for me to roll down my window.

"You know you're not supposed to park here," he says, tapping his plastic water bottle on the car hood. *Ouch!*

"I know, Officer. I'm really sorry. I just had to run in really fast," I explain, flashing my perfectly straight white teeth, which usually get me out of speeding tickets.

"You people in your Mercedes think the rules don't apply to you," he replies, knocking the water bottle against the hood again. The hairs on my arms stand up and I resist yelling at the cop for banging on the car. *Okay, no flirty smiles? Let's try demure instead, and if that doesn't work, I've got plenty of other tactics, Mr. Policeman! Bring it on!* I soften my voice, pout slightly, and tilt my chin down toward my left shoulder so my almond-shaped eyes look sad and apologetic. "I know. I'm really sorry. I shouldn't have parked here. I'm leaving, though, and I promise I won't do it again."

Mr. Cop raises his voice and taps the water bottle against Mom's car to punctuate each of his words: "Read the sign! It says 'No Parking!'" He is bent over, peering into my window, and I wait for him to recognize the man in my passenger seat. But when there's nothing but uncomfortable silence, I turn to see Scott looking in the opposite direction, absorbing the serenity of the water, meditating, or doing whatever he does to get Zen.

With his head still turned away, Scott mumbles through his mouthful of chocolate chip cookie, "Let's go. I'm going to be late."

Then the policeman barks in my ear, "Are you listening or what?" just as my cell phone rings. I close my eyes, trying to hold it together, but it's too late now.

"LISTEN!" I shout at the policeman in an *I mean business* tone. "I SAID I'M SORRY. I DON'T KNOW WHAT ELSE TO SAY. IF YOU WANT TO GIVE ME A FUCKING TICKET, THEN HURRY THE HELL UP. OTHERWISE, GET OUT OF MY WAY! I'VE GOT TO GET SCOTT KRAFT TO MOSCONE! AND I SWEAR IF YOU TAP THAT BOTTLE AGAINST MY CAR ONE MORE TIME, I WILL—"

I stop screaming when I see the surprised look on the silent cop's face. Then, with a disgusted wave of his hand, he says, "Lady, you need help. Just get out of here."

Scott turns to me and says, "You owe that man a dollar."

As we screech back toward the convention center, the *Scott, Scott, Scott* gets louder. I narrowly miss a few soggy pedestrians before pulling up at the side entrance, where a security team is waiting; one of them opens my door and smiles. The chariot carrying the world's first *cool* geek has arrived. He is a tech genius whom people all over the world—even Vegan Chick—worship. I know by the look on his face that it's happening. Scott is *ready*. That inner god or genius or whatever the hell it is has emerged. When he gets this look, it doesn't matter what Scott Kraft says. He will mesmerize you.

Scott. Scott. Scott. They're still chanting. Sometimes I still can't believe that I've become necessary to this man. Me! The girl who prided herself more on her college nickname ("Party Ball") than on any academic achievement is now Scott's investor relations guru (i.e., the evangelizer of his company to Wall Street). And I'm only twenty-six years old. I'm not sure how it happened. Actually, I know exactly how it happened. Unreasonable immigrant parents, a *life is short* attitude, and a mouth I can't seem to fully control. I've been trained since birth to get what I want; now I use this "skill" to get my bosses whatever *they* want. I've made it into the inner circle.

"Here we go," I say, grabbing a bottle of Smartwater from my purse and offering it to Scott. He waves it off. I fill my lungs with enough air to get through this last obstacle course, then move directly behind him so I can steer him through the backstage door. His stride slows as we approach the greenroom, which is filled with congratulatory flowers and colorful balloon bouquets. I place my hand lightly on his back to make sure he doesn't stop to examine a rose and become distracted by its "intricate design of petals perfectly layered to . . ." *Oh blah blah blah, just keep moving.* The last hurdle is the hallway leading to the stage, which is filled with frantic stagehands and next-up presenters. A gaggle of women rush over to tell Scott how much they love him or to simply wish him good luck, but I stiff-arm each of them until, at last, we reach the wings. I whisper to myself, "Touchdown." Here's where I can relax and hang back. These people don't want me. They want Scott. *Scott! Scott! Scott!* And that is okay, because this is where I'm most comfortable—behind the scenes. *He's the chief, I'm the warrior.*

Scott walks out on the stage and holds up his hands. I can't see past the footlights at first, but I know there's a big crowd out there. The cheering is so loud I can feel it pounding in me and pushing adrenaline through my veins. The floor shakes beneath my pumps, and the audience's energy reverberates off the huge auditorium's walls.

"Hello, San Francisco, I'm back," he croons into the microphone with a voice as calm and smooth as an Alpine lake. The crowd hushes instantly, as if he's flipped a switch. I peer out at the dignitaries in the front row and the blinding flashes coming from photographers' cameras. Everyone is leaning forward, holding their breath. Some people are smiling so wide that it looks like it hurts. Others dab at their wet eyes, overwhelmed by their hero, their savior.

"Well," Scott says. "Are we ready to make history today?"

chapter 1

SCOTT ALWAYS SAYS THAT THERE are no mistakes. Our screwups, he'd lecture me, are intentional moves directed by our inner selves in order to find our true paths. "You are exactly where you are supposed to be, doing exactly what you should be doing." It would have been nice to have this perspective three years ago, when my inner self was having a nightmare of a time navigating life. My outer self wasn't doing much better.

WHEN MY PATENT-LEATHER loafers first stepped inside the plush offices of Global Partners, my nerves gave way to excitement. The investment bank's lobby was furnished with intricately detailed dark-wood tables; low cushioned couches covered in luxurious, rich-hued fabrics; leather chairs; and large arrangements of white orchids tended to by a man in a short-sleeved green polo shirt. The view overlooking San Francisco Bay added to the "top of the world" feeling rushing through me. I'd graduated from Santa Clara University a few weeks earlier, and working here was my silver bullet, the answer to my prayers: a path to the white picket fence, two kids (preferably twins), and the Mrs. Homemaker lifestyle that I'd wanted ever since I could remember. Until I found Prince Charming, I'd spend my time living it up *Sex and the City* style while working at Global Partners—the place that would lead me to parties, cute banker and stock trader boys, and off-site boondoggles. *That* was what I couldn't wait for.

BUT THOSE THINGS never came. Instead, three months passed, filled with long (not *happy*) hours, mind-numbing spreadsheets, and back-stabbing Ivy League coworkers who seemed more interested in either mansplaining to or one-upping me than actually *dating* me.

Worst of all was my boss, Jack Wynn—a man often wrong but never in doubt. The forty-year-old, Harvard-educated East Coaster had devilishly alluring green eyes and a physique that showed how seriously he took his hobby (training for triathlons). He was strikingly attractive in a powerful, rich, Brooks Brothers kind of way. Although Jack was smart, it was his boys' club politics and cunning ability to schmooze that catapulted him into the role of head of technology and media investment banking. In fact, I wouldn't have gotten the job at Global Partners if Jack hadn't pulled one of his classic brown-nose moves: hire the kids of Silicon Valley CEOs to ensure Global Partners would win any of their dads' banking business. The confidence Mr. Wynn exuded made him the perfect investment banker. It also made him a frustrating boss.

My second Tuesday of September had already started out rough after Jack's assistant approached me with the news that his royal highness "doesn't approve of white slacks in the office." But according to *Elle,* "Only an idiot would give up her white clothes because of some outdated rule."

The kind assistant then explained, while trying to hide a smile, that our boss found that few women could wear white slacks without "their crotches smiling" and allayed my horror by assuring me that that didn't apply to me in this case.

"Nonetheless," she continued, "Jack has an unwritten rule that he wants followed."

Later that day, the camel-toe expert himself appeared at my desk for what I feared to be further white-pants discussion.

Instead, he said, "This needs to lead with the fact that they're a dating site," while handing me a marked-up printout of a PowerPoint slideshow. I wanted to scream because this was the same project that had kept me at the office until the late hours the night before, the one that made me miss drinks with my friends, and the one I'd thought I'd finished weeks ago but that each day came back to me with more changes. It was part of the "window dressing" that needed to be done for our client (an online dating service) before we began our search for a potential buyer.

I looked at Jack's edit and took it upon myself to voice my opinion. "But Jack, most of the target buyers already have their own dating properties. The only thing they're going to care about is our client's huge member base—they want more eyeballs on *their* properties."

"Wow. You certainly go against the stereotype of meek Asian girls, don't you?" Jack said, laughing and nudging me as though I should have found humor in his joke.

"Anyway, you're wrong," I said. "We should lead with our fifty million members, because that's the only reason they'd want to buy us."

Jack turned his back to me. "Just make the change, Sophia. Why do you have to make everything so hard?"

"Why do you always have to insist you're right?" I replied, defiant. It irritated me to no end that Jack never made the slightest attempt to consider my perspective, that I might actually be adding some *value*.

Jack said sternly before walking away, "Do it now."

Defeated and angry, I turned around and hissed "Asshole" louder than I'd meant. My heart dropped for a moment, but when Jack didn't react, I returned to my frustrated state. I made the edit he asked for and emailed the new slide to Jack, fully expecting other changes to come back to me within minutes.

IT WAS FIVE thirty the next morning and I was barely awake, having just finished work four hours earlier. While standing at the earth-toned granite counter of my parents' kitchen, I robotically spread butter on a piece of toast and stared out the window that overlooked the landscaped garden. To my chagrin, at age twenty-two, I was living with my parents in the upscale hills of Woodside, California. It was what my traditional Taiwanese parents expected me to do until I married, just as my older sister, Audrey, had done. The difference was that Audrey had actually *wanted* to move home—she was a penny-pincher and did anything to save money. When I argued this and asked my parents to help fund a new apartment in San Francisco—"the city"—they bombarded me with the names of their friends' daughters who "obeyed their parents and lived at home after college."

We all knew that the biggest reason I was forced to stay home wasn't anything we'd discussed. My parents wanted me home so they could watch over their "baby"—the one they always worried about. *Lucky me.* I couldn't fault them, though. They still blamed themselves for not noticing my drastic weight loss, frequent visits to the bathroom, and constant thirst when I was about to turn eight. It wasn't until a month or so after my birthday, when Mom saw me in the bathtub—my ribs sticking through my skin—that she recognized the telltale signs of diabetes. My situation was made worse by the fact that I was diagnosed as a "brittle diabetic"—someone whose blood glucose level swings drastically without warning, despite insulin shots and carefully planned meals. My episodes often landed me in the hospital, and each time it happened, my parents felt they had failed me. Their lifelong goal was to take care of me, and to never let anything happen to me again. But even moms and dads can't control everything, can they?

My parents' ten-thousand-square-foot, two-story, oval-shaped white stucco home sat nestled among huge oak trees and four acres of natural landscaping. *Architectural Digest* had dubbed it "a modern masterpiece"—a place my engineer father built as a gift to Mom after his medical-device company went public (thanks to Jack Wynn). To them, the house embodied the American dream, but to me, it was my childhood home. I couldn't wait to find out what life had in store for me next, outside of the house where I grew up.

Mom's voice snapped me out of my daze. She was seated on one of the kitchen island stools behind me. "Sophia, not so much butter. No one is going to want to marry you if you keep rounding out. Besides, it's not good for your diabetes, you know." She may have missed my weight loss when I was a child, but she certainly noticed every pound I had added to my four-foot, ten-inch frame as an adult. She didn't hesitate to share her opinion about it, either. Sure, my face had rounded out a bit, but my ballet-dancer legs and tight rear end still looked great in a short skirt, so the extra pounds didn't bother me.

"Okay," I answered while wrapping my butter-loaded toast in a paper towel and turning to leave.

"You going to work?" Mom asked, looking at me with a frown. As I leaned in to give her a kiss, she placed her right index finger and thumb on the bridge of my nose and pinched rapidly.

"Mom! Stop it!" I exclaimed, pulling my head back and swatting her away with both hands.

"Mei-Mei, you've got to pinch the bridge of your nose so it becomes taller."

Nice parting words of wisdom, Mom.

I brought my toast to my mouth and had almost escaped the kitchen when Dad called over from the adjoining great room. "We're proud of you, you know, our little Silicon Valley girl." The toast stilled at my lips and I looked over my shoulder to get a view of my beaming father.

"Thank you, Daddy," I said warmly before using my free hand to blow him a kiss.

Mom followed me out of the kitchen all the way to the front door so she could fuss with my hair. "You need to be taller to wear those wide-legged pants! They make you look like a squatty little creature," she jabbed one last time before I practically ran outside. Her "constructive criticisms" rolled easily off my back. *Duck feathers, duck feathers,* I repeated to myself.

I climbed into my black BMW convertible—the one I'd over-indulgently bought using my first Global Partners paycheck and a "little" help from my parents—then cruised down their steep driveway. Before speeding onto the freeway, though, I stopped for a treat that was usually reserved for Sundays: a soy café au lait. *Calorie counting be damned.* At five minutes before six in the morning, the coffee shop was filled with young entrepreneurs who already had adrenaline (and caffeine) seeping from their pores. They passionately pointed to their laptops, each appearing to have a world-changing idea. If *that* failed, it wasn't a problem because they had three or four others waiting. I didn't understand how these "dreamers" could lose millions in venture capital money without blinking an eye, and why the men in button-down shirts lining Silicon Valley's VC row—Sand Hill Road—continued to fund them. What *did* seem clear, though, was that the dreamers all wanted the same things: fame, power, and fortune. This exact scene was unfolding everywhere in Silicon Valley: people inspired by the "unicorns" of their era—the companies founded by daring twenty-year-olds who became billionaires overnight. They were all fighting for their share of the modern-day gold rush, and their hushed voices using trendy phrases like *game-changing, pioneering, viral,* or *best of breed* made my eyes roll.

Best of breed? What is this, a dog show?

I was better than they were. I was off to a *real* job. An investment banking job.

When I arrived at the office on that hot early-fall morning, I marched straight to my desk, hardly noticing the orchids or the bay view anymore. I sat at one of eight particle-board desks lined up along a long, wide yellow-fluorescent-lit hallway, hidden from the clients and anything else glamorous. This is where the analysts sat staring at our computer screens until our legs became numb. When I'd started, the more senior analysts had warned me about falling prey to the dreaded investment banker "gut and ass spread": a gradual widening of one's body parts thanks to too much sitting. *Well, there's something to look forward to.*

Perhaps it was because my numb ass was distracting me, or because my back was turned, but I didn't notice when Jack appeared behind me and called me into his office. This had been a regular occurrence for various reasons, some of which were disciplinary (and in my opinion, unjustified), some of which were purely business. Regardless of the reason, I hated going in there—it smelled of antiques, and the mounted deer head on the wall was always staring at me. *Yikes.*

"Sophia. Please, sit down." I planted myself in one of the nickel-studded leather chairs, then scooted forward slightly so my feet could touch the expensive Turkish rug. Jack paused, folded his hands on the desk, and leaned forward. Suddenly I got a feeling in the pit of my stomach that this wasn't going to be good; Jack hadn't called me here to talk about the slideshow, my white pants, or my software industry summary. I attempted to look serious.

"This isn't working, Sophia," Jack began.

"I know, I'm sorry." I looked down at my hands. What was the professional version of detention? Whiteboards to erase? *I will not argue with my boss* typed ten thousand times into my company-issued BlackBerry? I told myself I'd do what he asked, if only to get him (and that poor deer) to stop staring at me.

"We're going to have to let you go," he continued.

My jaw dropped. *No fucking way.*

"What?" I argued. "But . . . don't you have to give me two weeks' notice or something?"

"No. You're an at-will employee." Jack clapped his hands together once, as though to say *Done deal.* "We're going to have to ask you to clear out your desk right now. Security is already there to take your computer."

"Right *now*?" I protested. "This is a mistake."

I sat there stunned. I couldn't lose my job. This was going to be the answer to my prayers, the sum total Girl Scout badge of Moving Forward with My Life. And whether I liked working at Global Partners or not, I knew I was lucky to have such a good job. Panic rushed through me as I imagined being stuck at home with Mom. She'd spend the next year grooming me into the perfect marriageable specimen, making me feel like I wasn't good enough. This couldn't be happening. No. I wouldn't let it.

I felt my cheeks redden as I slowly got to my feet, my reasonable heels digging into Jack's stupid rug. I looked straight at him. "You can't do this." I wanted to threaten him with a call from my father, but I knew that was the wrong thing to do.

Jack didn't answer. He had already gone back to his emails. He wasn't just waiting me out; he wasn't even seeing me anymore. I was already gone. Invisible.

Damn you, you arrogant bastard.

Furious, I stormed out of the room with tears streaming down my face. *Don't cry,* I scolded myself. *Don't cry.*

I PARKED MY car in my parents' driveway, wondering what the hell I would do with my finance degree and telling myself it was okay that I was fired because I didn't belong with those Ivy League *summa cum laudes* anyway. The banking job was never what I really wanted to do. I'd wanted to turn my twelve years of ballet training into a Golden State Warriors cheerleading career. Dancing was always my greatest joy; I loved how it made me forget—how impossible it was to think about anything and how I'd lose myself in the music and the choreography that went along with it. But one night over dinner I tried discussing my post–high school plan with my parents. Mom had just stood up to retrieve a set of chopsticks from the kitchen drawer, which she would use to serve the chow-fun she'd prepared, and before the word *cheerleader* had even left my mouth, both chopsticks came flying across the kitchen and nailed me in the back of the head. I turned around to see Mom's glare—her warning that I'd better stop this nonsense once and for all. So as always, I did what my parents expected of me, and now I was a diploma-holding, unemployed loser.

My sister, Audrey, was the smart, independent, and reasonable one—the one who would have fit into the investment bank scene just as well as she did the hedge fund world in which she worked. Older by three years, she was blessed with street smarts; perfect physical health; a five-foot-*five* frame; a strong, high-bridged nose; and large, almost Caucasian-like eyes that I envied. She excelled at every sport and academic subject she attempted; she was motivated and aggressive and her beauty was undeniable. She was the perfect Chinese daughter, and it would be too simple to say that I was jealous of her. I was, but I loved her and looked up to her, too. She had it all, the life I thought I wanted: a caring, loving husband; a beautiful home in Palo Alto; and a baby girl named Ava I adored. The first time I'd held my niece, I was certain that if love could be measured, I was the one who loved her the most. Gone was any disappointment that my sister had beaten me yet again. In its place were visions of how I'd be the best aunt in the world.

I was the opposite of Audrey. To start, we looked nothing alike. I was the petite, "cute" one with a small heart-shaped mouth and apple-red cheeks that no amount of foundation could temper. I was also the sick one, the one cursed with diabetes and every side effect that came with it: a lousy immune system, compromised kidneys, high blood pressure, and probably more to come. My poor health history was why my parents coddled me, and why they raised me to be taken care of, to shop and look pretty. They didn't care if I did poorly in school; they just hoped I would live a stress-free, happy life with a husband who loved me. I didn't mind one bit going along with their plan, since their expectations seemed low. But my parents often sent conflicting messages, like telling their daughters to lose weight in the same breath that they insisted we eat more. That they raised us to be barefoot and pregnant while constantly reinforcing the importance of being employed and independent was confusing, but there was no doubt they'd find my termination at the investment bank disappointing. Worse, it would be considered "losing face"— besmirching our family's good name. I was not looking forward to telling them what had happened.

I entered my parents' home and immediately heard the familiar, calming sound of trickling water coming from our koi pond in the center of the foyer. The cool marble floors felt nice compared to the Indian-summer air outside. I dropped my purse, threw off my shoes, and procrastinated by walking to the left side of the pond, where, behind a rock, we hid the fish food. I tossed a few pellets into the water and made a wish, the same way I'd done since I was a kid. *I want to be married.* The bright-colored fish waved themselves toward the surface with open mouths and fought for the food. I said good morning to them before crossing the foyer, walking up three steps, and passing the curved staircase that led to the second floor. I gently pushed on the swinging door and entered my parents' contemporary kitchen.

Bright sun streamed in through the windows, blinding the view of the large landscaped garden outside. It was nearly nine A.M. and the delicious aroma of just-steamed Chinese barbecue pork buns filled my nose. I considered whether I should sit down and enjoy one before saying anything to Mom and Dad about work.

Like a paper clip to a magnet, the voice of Bugs Bunny and the sound of Dad's laughter pulled me through the large opening separating the kitchen from the great room. Dad stood in front of the television, mesmerized by the battling cartoon characters that could entertain him for hours. When I walked up behind him to see which *Looney Tunes* episode he was watching, my pout gave way to a slight chuckle. We both stood there like zombies until we heard Mom yelling from the master bedroom upstairs, "Daddy! Stop watching TV! Breakfast is getting cold!"

"Man! How do her superhuman eyes see you?" I cried.

Dad smiled at the sight of me, then crinkled his brows and looked at his watch. "What are you doing home? I thought you left hours ago for work."

Fearing the wrath of my mother, he quickly headed for the kitchen, expecting me to follow. For a moment, I remained in front of the TV, wondering how I would tell him that I'd been fired from my first job. Well, technically it was my second, my first having been taken from me before it even began. That wasn't because I'd angered a client or made some egregious error. It was because I'd made the mistake of telling the human resources director that I was a diabetic after I'd received an offer letter, but *before* I actually began working. When he asked me, "What if you're in the middle of a meeting when something happens? Like when you need to take a shot or eat something?" I explained to him that I would excuse myself if I was meeting with clients, but that I imagined coworkers would understand. After all, it wasn't as though the crinkling of a granola bar wrapper was a huge disruption. At this point the director said he would call me back, but he never did. In fact, I never heard from him again. *Asshole.* Finally, I threw away the consulting firm's offer letter. They no longer wanted me. I was damaged goods. *Welcome to Silicon Valley.* When I finally told my parents, they had an unsurprisingly unsympathetic response. They had been warning me since I was diagnosed that I should never speak of my health issues, especially to potential suitors. "People won't understand them and will see them as a stigma," they'd said. "They'll use your illness against you, or feel sorry for you." I had thought this was just another one of their traditional Chinese views, but maybe they were right.

Dad called me from the table. "So why are you home? Are you feeling okay?" My parents always asked me that, fearing something had caused my blood sugar to rise or fall.

I sighed deeply and said, "I got fired." My eyes turned red as I held in the tears.

"What? Again?" he asked in a disappointed tone, even after I reminded him I didn't actually get fired from the first job.

"It wasn't my fault!" I declared, fully aware that my high-pitched, cracking voice was the perfect way to soften my father.

Dad shook his head and said more calmly, "Welcome to the real world, Sophia. It doesn't matter whose fault it is. What did you do?"

This wasn't like when I disregarded my parents' advice and lost the consulting job, so I was confused as to why Dad wasn't standing up for me. "I didn't do anything. I just tried to do something right the first time so I wouldn't have to waste my time doing it again."

"Uh-huh. Sure," Dad said with raised, accusing eyebrows. "Jack wouldn't have fired you unless you'd really done something wrong."

"What's wrong? Why are you home?" my mom asked, bounding through the swinging door. She walked past me and stopped at the counter, and although her back was to me, I could see her dusting off crumbs I'd let fall onto the granite earlier that morning. A criminal offense in her book. "Are you feeling okay?"

"I got fired," I said, looking down at my feet to avoid Mom's glare. She was slightly taller than me—a classic beauty with porcelain-white skin, perfectly applied red lipstick, and delicate Asian features—but her looks were deceiving. Underneath the china-doll appearance was an unpredictable temper, a demanding personality, and a propensity for soul-crushing comments that would be devastating had Audrey and I not developed our Teflon coatings.

"What did you do? Did you mess up a spreadsheet or something?" Mom asked, not really caring about the answer but certain it was my fault. She really had no idea what I did at work. Dad and I had tried to explain to her what an investment banker did, but to this day, she tells her friends I was a bank teller.

Mom turned to Dad and blamed him. "Daddy, you shouldn't have pushed her into finance. She can't even balance a checkbook!" Dad was silent. Then, facing me, she filled her lungs with air—fuel for the fire that was about to shoot out of her mouth.

Here we go.

"You've embarrassed our entire family! You're such a disaster. That was the place you were supposed to find a husband. How are you ever going to feed yourself? You were so lucky to even have that job!" she yelled. "I'm sure you were arguing, as usual. I've told you so many times to watch your mouth. You need to listen to people more and talk less, and you really need to be more like your sister."

Mom stopped to take another breath, so I jumped into the split-second break.

"MOTHER!" I screamed as loud as I could. "You're always telling me I'll never be happy if I compare myself to others, so *why* are you comparing me to Audrey? I'm not Audrey!"

Mom closed her mouth, although she remained angry.

Success. For now.

Soon she began mumbling about my incompetence and walked into the other room, where she also threw in a few disapproving comments about my long, wavy, thick black hair. According to Mom, my abundant mane made me look part troll, part wild animal. "*Ai-ya, pi-tou-san-fa!*" She returned minutes later with a bundle of cash, which she stuffed into my hand. "You might as well use the day off to get your hair cut."

"Can I just explain what happened? It wasn't my fault!" I exclaimed. I wanted my parents to feel sorry for me and to understand that a major injustice had just taken place.

Tears welled, then flowed from my eyes. Tears of humiliation and disappointment that I'd messed up, and a little from the relief that Mom hadn't murdered me. But while most parents soften at seeing their children struggle, mine have always had the opposite reaction. We are a family of "chin-ups": Have a problem? Get over it. So even though my mother's chastising was over, she didn't hesitate to rush me along, or "chop-chop" as she would say. She certainly didn't care that I was down in the dumps. "You've stepped into a shit hole," she said. "You'd better dig yourself out of it quickly because it's smelly down there. Go find yourself a new job. It's the best way for you to meet nice boys."

chapter 2

THE ONLY THING MOTIVATING ME to get out of my warm bed one week later was my low blood sugar. And the feeling hanging over my head that I was on a fast track to nowhere. While most of my high school and college friends were making fresh lives for themselves with new careers and their own apartments, I was still waiting for the thing that would kick-start my "real" life: a husband. I was obsessed with finding my better half—a life partner—to prove to my parents, and myself, that someone could love me despite my health problems, my height, and my race. I told myself that *he* would be the key to my happiness and the person who would finally allow me to be just like everyone else.

I could tell by the silence of the house that my dad had already gone to work. Maybe Mom would be gone, too.

No such luck.

I pushed open the kitchen door and bumped directly into her.

"What is your plan today?" she asked.

"Why?" I knew there was something behind her question—errands or her version of Emily Post—so I told her I was spending the day looking for a job.

Survival tactics.

I made myself a cup of coffee, despite Mom's *tsk-tsks* about how Americanized her children were with their coffee instead of green tea. Holding my caffeine in one hand and my old college laptop in the other, I sat on one of the barstools and checked my email. The first message was from my best friend, Kate.

To: Sophia Young
From: Katelyn Grace
Subj: Tonight

Let's meet at the Rosewood for drinks and boy hunting. See you at 7!
Xo Kate

The next email looked equally promising.

To: Sophia Young
From: Audrey Young
Subj: Check out this YouTube video

Sissy,
Thought this would make you smile, but DO NOT try this yourself.
Sister

The link from Audrey brought me to a thumbnail of a video that, according to the YouTube counter, had been viewed nearly twenty million times. The thumbnail showed a man standing next to a treadmill, which immediately diminished my hopes of being entertained. But I clicked on it anyway, and as the video began to play, one of my favorite hip-hop songs started to blare over my laptop's speakers. I watched closely as the man leaped onto the treadmill—while it was moving—and began to dance! My eyes widened and I giggled in surprise as Mr. Cool hopped, skipped, flipped, and spun on the moving conveyor belt, all to the beat of the music. I swayed along with him, my foot and knee bobbing up and down, too. *Ooh, fun!*

Within minutes, I was standing on the treadmill inside my parents' garage, attempting to copy Mr. Cool's amazing routine.

To: Audrey Young
From: David Young
Subj: Your sister

Audrey, your mother called. Please meet us at the Stanford
emergency room. Sophia fell off the treadmill and hit her head.
Did you send her that video? You know better. Please try to do
a better job looking out for your little sister.
Daddy

THAT NIGHT, AFTER a thorough lecture from my entire family that
would forever cause my mother to rebuke, "and for God's sake don't
kill yourself" every time I told her I was going to work out, I handed
my keys to the parking valet and walked into Silicon Valley's place to
be seen: the Rosewood Sand Hill. The sprawling luxury resort was
discreetly tucked into the Santa Cruz Mountains, and its sweeping
terraces overlooked the grassy hills, dry from the summer's above-
average temperatures. I smiled at the sight of Kate standing in the
open-air lobby—a lobby teeming with young, Waspy men wearing
lanyards around their necks. The lanyards could mean only one
thing: a conference had just ended. More important, the bar would
be busy, no doubt filled with investment bankers and power players.
No dreamers in sight.

"Did you hear Andre Stark has a new girlfriend?" Kate gossiped
when I got within earshot. She was referring to the young, handsome
CEO of a space transport company who was standing ten feet away.
The same Mr. Stark was rumored to be working on the world's first
electric car company, which promised to change the entire auto paradigm and the world along with it.

"Oh no! But doesn't he know he's *your* boyfriend?" I joked.

"Well, you know what I always say," Kate said, leaning in close to my ear. "Girlfriends . . ."

". . . are only speed bumps!" I said, finishing her sentence. It was one of the things we always said to each other so we could keep on dreaming about the *what-ifs*. We laughed, officially greeted each other with hugs, and walked into the dim, wood-paneled bar, grabbing a corner table with gray velvet chairs.

"I've been thinking a lot about your predicament, and I know what you should do," Kate said excitedly, as though a bright light had just been lit above her head. "There are lots of openings at Sterling, Rich and I bet you could get a job there, too!" She'd been working for four months as a paralegal for the prominent law firm; our voices shrilled at the idea of spending our days together.

"Wait. I don't have any training."

"Hey, I didn't either, but I did it. They'll teach you. It's easy. They just want smart people."

I can be smart. Sometimes.

"You did two summer internships there and you majored in poli-sci," I said.

"There are lots of hot, young, single guys working there," Kate cajoled. She, like my parents, was hoping I would find a great guy. She'd seen the poor dating choices I'd made in college and probably wanted me to hook up with a nice lawyer like Mark, the first-year associate she'd recently gone out with.

I laughed. "Well, in that case," I told her, "I'll give it a go! Why not? I've got nothing to lose!"

Change of plans: banker husband is now a lawyer husband.

"Awesome. Send me your résumé and I'll get it to the right people."

"Thanks, Kate," I said, promising myself to do better, to be better, this time. If not for myself, for my friend.

Katelyn Grace and I had been inseparable since we were college freshmen, both shunning our Catholic-school upbringings and celebrating our newfound freedom by drinking and making out with every frat boy we could find. She was tall, with wavy light brown hair and an exotic, beauty-queen-worthy look that often caused strangers to ask, "What *are* you?" Her reserved, elegant East Coast manner made her seem mysterious, proper, and regal—on the outside. One would never guess she was the same drunk person who had to be carried out from a restaurant on the night of her twenty-first birthday. The person who spent the night on the floor of our dormitory's bathroom, praying to the porcelain gods. She was loyal, intelligent, fun, and had a very quick wit about her. What I respected most about Kate was that she knew exactly how to get what she wanted. It was time that I did the same.

After we hatched our plan, we left our high-top table and decided to have a little fun with the lanyard guys. As we bellied up to the bar, I smiled with satisfaction: the perfect number of people were standing around it—crowded enough to give me an excuse to tap one of them on the shoulder and use my favorite line. "Hi. Sorry, but could I *please* squeeze in for a moment to get a drink?" I asked bashfully.

"Oh, sure," a cute venture capitalist said as I turned sideways and brushed up against him, arms up in the air, looking straight into his eyes. My shy smile brightened into a big one.

"Here, actually, why don't I get you a drink? What do you want?"

"Oh, that's okay, I need two drinks. One for my friend as well," I said, still inching past Venture Capitalist Guy but slowly turning to face the bar.

"No problem. What do you guys want?"

"Really? Oh gosh! Thank you!" I squealed. "A vodka and soda for me, please. And a glass of house white for my friend."

"Impressive. Hitting the hard stuff on a school night, eh?"

No. But I'm guessing a long explanation about how vodka doesn't raise my blood sugar would be a bit of a turnoff. I shrugged and smiled, then made my way back to Kate.

"Classic," Kate said, laughing. "Well done."

"He's cute! And did you see his friend? I'd say it's a toss-up."

"Hmm. Okay, I get the tall one, then." Kate winked.

"Deal!"

THE FOLLOWING WEEK, I opened the heavy glass doors that led to one of the top law firms in the country. It was tucked into the foothills of Palo Alto, appropriate for Sterling, Rich's reputation as the center of Silicon Valley—the go-to firm offering tech companies a long menu of services that led clients to believe they were going to be billionaires. From first rounds of funding to selling shares on the public stock markets, Sterling, Rich was where the action happened. There was an actual humming coming from inside this fifty-thousand-square-foot compound. Kate had told me people were at the office twenty-four hours a day, seven days a week, working on transactions for some of the world's best-known companies. Based on how tied she was to her BlackBerry and mobile phone, I guessed everyone here was at their clients' beck and call.

But I wasn't wary of that. I ignored the fact that I had few qualifications for this job, swallowed hard, then *click, click, clicked* my way across the gray stone floor, pretending not to be impressed by the dome of the firm's grand entrance. *Fake it till you make it.* I straightened my posture, smoothed out my vivid paisley-print silk skirt, and held my head up high as I passed the expensive-looking white leather chairs and stainless steel tables neatly placed in the reception area. They were flanked by two-story glass staircases and wood-covered walls that rose so high that I wasn't sure they would ever end. I imagined myself belonging in a place like this, and tingled from the idea that I might be the wife of a Sterling, Rich lawyer.

This will do nicely.

I approached the beautiful crescent-shaped reception desk, which nearly stretched around the entire circumference of the lobby. Behind the desk sat a foreboding security guard who was so muscular that I nicknamed him "No Neck." Beside him were three receptionists, each wearing a headset that seemed to float above her heavily shellacked hair. Over this warm and cheery group hung a bronze engraved sign: STERLING, RICH, GOODMAN & ROSENBACH.

The receptionist farthest on the left bared her pearly whites with a warm welcome and asked for my name. Within seconds, she lifted her headset off her head like a beauty queen might lift her crown, stood up, and led me to a conference room just down the hall from the lobby. "Help yourself to the drinks. Grant Vicker will be here in a few minutes," she said as she shut the walnut door. I twiddled my fingers and looked around the room. Hanging from the walls were large, magnified images of blurry objects that I examined for a while before deciding they looked like spinning carousels.

I gingerly pulled out a chair and sat down at the beautiful cherrywood table so I could reread Grant Vicker's *American Lawyer* profile that I'd printed out at home. Grant was *the* hotshot attorney at Sterling, Rich. He'd risen quickly through the ranks of the firm and made partner a full two years earlier than the rest of his entering class of ambitious peers. Grant's quick-thinking negotiation tactics and skillful approach to executing initial public offerings gave him an impressive reputation and attracted an all-star list of clients that probably minted money for this firm. The article highlighted his various Princeton awards and the fact that he'd earned the highest GPA ever recorded from Stanford Law School. I couldn't believe that an accomplished man like Grant Vicker was interviewing me, but the person who'd called me to arrange this meeting had said that apparently he liked my background.

Which background would that be? The fired-from-previous-job background or the slam-dunk ADA lawsuit background?

I was in the middle of applying a layer of lip gloss and examining the artwork when Grant walked into the conference room. I turned around to find a man that looked different from the one I'd seen photographed in the *American Lawyer* article. About six feet tall with thick, tousled hair and a boyish grin, he looked like he could have been a ski instructor during the winter and a rafting guide in the summer. But his bellowing voice and lumbering walk made him appear much more intimidating than he was—at least to me.

"Aren't those artworks pretty?" he asked.

"Pretty ugly," I blurted out with a mischievous smile.

Grant laughed. "That's the thing about art—everyone has a different opinion, and I'm glad to see you're not shy about giving yours."

Did I just score a point?

He sat down across from me, placed a leather-bound folder on the table, and continued, "Kate has raved about you. How long have you two known each other?"

"Over four years. We met as freshmen in college," I replied. The memories of our fun, careless school days were still fresh in my mind.

He looked at my résumé for a moment, nodding his head. *Part-time sales associate at Gap for four years. Marketing intern at IBM, junior year.* His tongue was sticking out of the corner of his mouth, and for a moment, he looked like a kid who was concentrating hard on coloring inside the lines. He didn't appear to be much older than I was, and his casual demeanor made me feel as though I were just talking to a friend.

"Kate mentioned you were at Global Partners. Why did you leave?"

I paused for a moment, wondering if I should use the answer Dad rehearsed with me—*the commute was too long*—but I didn't want to lie to my new friend (if that's what he was). "I—I was fired."

Argh—brain fart! I shouldn't have said that. Rookie maneuver.

"Do you mind if I ask why?" Grant asked.

"I didn't get along with my boss."

"Who was your boss?"

"Jack Wynn."

Grant smiled and said, "Yeah, he's an asshole."

Oooh, I like you!

"So tell me why you're interested in law," Grant said.

I dug deep for a scoop of bullshit and then remembered my dad's advice to look Grant straight in the eye and to seem ambitious by sitting forward in my chair.

"In college I took a class called Law and the Judicial System," I said, which was true, except by "college" I meant "high school." "Since then, I've wanted to be a lawyer, and I think a job at Sterling, Rich would be a really good start."

"A lot of paralegals here are on the law school track, but we'd ask you to commit to two years," Grant responded. "If you make it two years, I will write you a recommendation letter—that *is*, assuming you deserve one. Will that long of a commitment be a problem?"

I shook my head.

Unless Mr. Right finds me.

"So why do you think I should hire you?"

"Well, I'm not going to lie. I clearly don't have any paralegal experience. But I'm organized, hardworking, a quick learner, really fun, and if I must say so myself, everyone *likes* me. That's always good for client relations."

"Well, it's good that people respond positively to you, but actually, your experience is exactly why you're here, so don't sell yourself short. Most of my business revolves around taking companies through their IPOs and—"

"Wait, so do you mean I won't get to sit in court and yell?" I interrupted, sounding genuinely disappointed.

"This is corporate law, Sophia. Not litigation. You won't be in any courtrooms. That is, unless you or I do something terribly wrong and find ourselves being prosecuted."

I nodded and scribbled a note down in my little reporter's note-book: *Don't get prosecuted.*

"I like that you have a nontraditional background. And, even though you weren't at Global Partners that long, you are Series 7 licensed, so you have a good understanding about the stock market and will get up to speed faster," Grant continued, referring to the financial securities test I barely passed when I joined GP. "What is the biggest lesson you think you learned there?"

"Pigs get slaughtered," I said without blinking. It was one of my fa-vorite Jack-isms. I was referring to the old Wall Street saying, "Bulls make money, bears make money, pigs get slaughtered." It counseled against excessive greed and impatience. Ironic that someone like Jack Wynn would appreciate it. *Rat bastard.*

Grant smiled. "Yes, indeed they do. Well, you must have a good work ethic, or you wouldn't have lasted even a month at that bank. Work ethic is the hardest thing to vet when you're interviewing can-didates." He capped his pen and leaned back in his chair. "Any ques-tions?"

"Yes," I said. I capped my pen, too. My dad often told me that professionals respond well to mirroring. No harm in trying. "What did *you* major in?"

Grant smirked. "History."

"*History?* That's interesting. Why history?"

"History is my favorite topic. It's an antidote to our tendency to assume that the way things are today is the way that they've always been and therefore naturally should be. It's like somebody once said: 'The past is a foreign country. They do things differently there.'" Grant laid his well-manicured hands across his leather folder.

Sheesh. A simple "I like history" would have sufficed.

"I read in your bio that you were a Supreme Court clerk before coming to Sterling, Rich."

"Yes. Yes, that is true," he said. He looked as though he missed those days.

"Wow! So you were a do-gooder." I tucked my hair behind my ear. "But you sold out for a paycheck, huh?"

Grant tried not to laugh. "That's right. And right now, this greedy bastard is going to walk you out."

"So do I have the job?" I asked, point-blank. I knew it might be too direct, but I had nothing to lose.

"Are you going to show up if I say yes?"

"Why wouldn't I?"

Grant Vicker just smiled.

"I GOT A job," I said, beaming.

"What? Where?" Dad asked.

"Sterling, Rich!" I responded, proud to say the name of my new employer who had emailed me earlier that day with a formal offer letter.

We were gathered for our weekly Sunday dinner—me, Kate, Audrey, Mom, and Dad. It wasn't uncommon for Kate to join us, so I'd invited her to help celebrate the good news. We were seated on the clear acrylic chairs at the dining table in our great room. Between the kitchen and this room, we had everything we needed: a bathroom, a sunken family room with a large-screen television, a large eating area, and clear views into the garden on one side and over Silicon Valley on the other.

Dad smiled at Kate, certain she'd had something to do with my stroke of good fortune.

"Hey, don't look at me. The only thing I did was submit her résumé," she said, waving both hands in the air.

Dad turned serious. "I'm sure you did more than that. Thank you, Kate. You are a very good friend."

Kate smiled and nodded modestly. "Don't thank me yet. She'll be working long hours and you probably won't like it."

"How much are they paying you?" my mother asked, always the one worrying about money despite the fact that she had been raised with a silver spoon in her mouth and my father had been successful enough to build her her dream home.

"Not as much as the investment bank, but I get paid double time if I work more than eight hours a day," I said.

Audrey was more skeptical. "Yeah, and they'll bill you out for ten times the amount they pay you. Law firms are such rip-offs."

I frowned.

Why don't you go join Ava and your husband at your in-laws?

"Daddy is very proud of you, Sophia," my father said, glowing. Then his face fell. "But please don't work too hard. Your health comes first."

Although I understood how he felt, I winced at his comment and wondered if my health would always overshadow my achievements. It occurred to me long ago that the worst part of having a chronic illness wasn't the illness itself. *Although it royally does suck.* It was the assumption that I couldn't handle things as well as healthy people, or at all. Have you ever noticed that when someone with an illness does something amazing, it's always "despite"? Even when the illness wouldn't actually get in the way of what they're doing whatsoever?

He swam the English Channel, *despite* bipolar disorder!

She won the chess tournament, *despite* breast cancer!

The last time I'd checked, diabetes wasn't directly in conflict with kicking ass in the legal world.

Mom noticed my disturbed expression and changed the subject. "Oh! Maybe you'll go to a top law school and find a nice boy," she said with honest excitement.

Amen!

"We always thought you'd be a great lawyer, given the mouth you have on you," she continued, taking my mind off Dad's comment.

"Let's focus on being thankful I got a job and that I'll get to work with Kate. So back off, Mom," I joked.

Mom raised her shoulders to her ears and chuckled with embarrassment.

"Which group are you in?" Dad asked, turning to my friend.

"I work for Austin Sterling, Mr. Young."

"He's the firm's founder, Dad. A big deal," I added.

Audrey clearly wasn't excited for me. "I guess it's good that you got a job, but this has nothing to do with your finance degree, and you've got to stop thrashing around, Sophia. I mean, who does that? Who just walks into a law firm and says, 'Oh hey. I'm going to be a paralegal, not for any good reason other than I have nothing better to do'?"

Maybe she's jealous.

"That's the one thing your sister does well, Audrey. She doesn't think—she just goes," Mom said.

"The *one* thing, Mom?" I prodded. But Mom was right. I was good at *not* overanalyzing. Sure, in some cases it had gotten me in trouble. But for the most part, my tendency to jump in with both feet had served me well. *Yay for me!*

"Well, that and spending money," Dad said, poking me in the side.

Mom nodded, Audrey shook her head, and I stood up to change the subject and to kiss up a little. "Thanks for dinner, Mom. It was very gourmet! Kate and I are going to meet some friends."

"Now? It's so late," Mom said.

"Mom, it's only eight thirty."

"Oh. It feels later. Probably because it's getting so dark so early," she muttered to herself.

"No drinking, Sophia!" Dad said. "Too much sugar!"

"I know, I know."

Kate stood and followed me as Mom shouted after us, "If you do drink, don't forget to take extra insulin!"

I pretended I didn't hear her because I was too busy feeling thrilled with myself. I was eager to go out and celebrate my next chapter. Maybe with this new job my family would start to take me seriously. Would I?

chapter 3

A FEW DAYS LATER, WEARING my favorite leopard-print shift dress, I opened Sterling, Rich's glass doors and took two steps forward with closed eyes. This was it—my big debut in the legal world. I imagined my name in bright lights on a Sterling, Rich marquee: SUPER PARALE-GAL GIRL: STARRING SOPHIA YOUNG. It wasn't the Warriors or Broadway, of course, but there was an excitement brewing inside of me that felt just as exhilarating, as if I were going onstage. I opened my eyes, expecting to see an audience that was ready to cheer. Instead, a few men in ties and women in boring skirt suits were having conversations, speaking on the phone, or reading documents as they hurried to their next meetings. *What have I signed up for?* Jack Wynn's words rang unbidden in my head and gave me a brief moment of stage fright: *"We're going to have to let you go."*

I didn't have time to dwell on that for too long, though. One of the Beauty Queens at reception was smiling at me pointedly—it was one of those lips-don't-touch-the-teeth kind of smiles. "Can I help you?" she asked.

Within moments, Miss America was walking me up the glass stairs on the right side of the lobby and onto a gray-carpeted landing ad-joining a very large conference room. The "VIP room," as she called it, was centered between two wide hallways; we walked toward the one on the right. I noted a kitchen stocked with coffee and a glass-fronted refrigerator filled with soda, then imagined myself sashaying into the kitchen thrice daily for my gratis Diet Coke pick-me-ups. We'd passed the kitchen and two short pass-throughs when I heard a booming voice screaming expletives. I lowered my head to hide my smile and the fact that, for some reason, I found it hysterical anytime someone strung obscene words together.

The voice was coming from one of the offices toward the end of the hall, thirty feet away. I looked around to see if anyone else noticed, but no one seemed to flinch. People, mostly women, sat at their desks facing the hallway, lined up like ants on a log, either speaking into their telephones or typing away feverishly at their computers. Across from them, on the right side of the hall, were large, windowed offices overlooking a carefully landscaped, full back parking lot. Most had messy, paper-piled desks and shelves filled with books that didn't look very interesting. As the booming voice got louder, I fully expected that when we got close enough, a curtain would be ripped aside to reveal the Great Oz. But within a few feet of the office, I recognized whom the voice belonged to. Not the Wizard: Grant Vicker. Miss America and I stood in his doorway for a moment, then she whispered to me before returning back down the hall, "I'm sure he'll be off in a minute so just wait here."

"Tell those lazy-ass, inanimate fucking objects that we received comments from the SEC again—they're questioning the validity of the company's metrics." Then silence.

"They can't just *make up* metrics that ultimately don't say anything about their company."

Grant lifted his left hand and began to wave it as he continued, "That's like saying, 'Look over here, not over there.' This country would be in a lot of trouble if the SEC was *that* stupid." Then silence again.

"Look, I highly suggest you help your client identify the financials and metrics that accurately reflect the state of their business. Otherwise this thing isn't going public."

No "goodbye" followed; no "take care"; no "thank you." Just the sound of the receiver slamming into the phone cradle. Conversation over.

Grant looked up at me and his face smoothed like a shirt under a hot iron. He smiled warmly, his conversation apparently forgotten.

"You actually showed up."

"Of course I did. Why wouldn't I?" I asked.

"Well, I don't think many people actually believe that they can just say they're going to be a paralegal one day, and then be ballsy enough to do it a few days later. It's nice to see you. Welcome."

Grant stood and walked out the door, not checking to see if I was following. I rushed out behind him, down the same hall through which Miss America had led me just five minutes earlier. But instead of walking toward the stairs, he turned right down a small pass-through that separated one side of the floor from the other. Then, suddenly, he stopped. I was so close on his heels that I nearly slammed into him.

We were standing before an open frosted-glass door, and Grant was gesturing as though he were a tour guide displaying the majesty of the Taj Mahal. "Here we are," he said. "This is your office."

For a split second, mystified by my luck, I allowed myself to imagine the world beyond the doorway as a vast, hill-facing expanse, as impressive as Grant's office.

"Shall we?" He ushered me in.

My hill-facing expanse was in fact a six-foot-wide closet with the ambiance and airiness of a shoe box. The closet's modular desk faced the door, and two matching chairs sat in front of it. A floor-to-ceiling combo bookshelf and file cabinet ran the length of the back wall. Fluorescent lights flickered from the ceiling, and lit by their unpleasant glow sat a woman in her late thirties, her highlighted curly blond hair short. Even though the pale yellow of her silk blouse wasn't doing her any favors, she looked warm and professional. As she rose to introduce herself, she tucked a large binder under one arm and stashed a pen behind her ear.

"Thank you for showing Sophia around today," Grant said stiffly.

Without waiting for so much as a response, he was gone. I made a mental note that the Truly Busy don't need to say goodbye. Maybe someday I'd cut that word out of my vocabulary, too.

"Hi! I'm Grant's former paralegal, Ellen," the woman said. "I'm going to show you the ropes."

"Hi!" I said with a bright smile, not so much because I was happy to meet the woman who used to have my job but more because I recalled Kate's story of how Ellen and Grant had parted ways. She had asked Grant to stop swearing so much, and in response, Grant fired back with "Who died and made you fucking queen?" When Kate shared this with me, I'd laughed and thought, *Now that's the kind of boss I want to work for.*

Ellen and I spent most of the day going through every little piece of minutia, from Grant's current client roster to the ins and outs of what my responsibilities would be during various legal transactions. It all sounded daunting, but I didn't allow myself to worry. I focused on taking copious notes and kept reminding myself that Kate wasn't far away. Ellen also graciously offered her assistance, saying, "I'm just on the other side of this wing so come by anytime. I'm always happy to help." The women at Global Partners were even more cutthroat than the men so my predecessor's offer caught me by surprise. How reassuring it was to have such support. *Women power!*

As the clock approached six thirty, Grant appeared in my doorway. I was learning how to navigate Sterling, Rich's digital client-billing system; its six-minute-increment tracking system translated minutes into tenths of an hour. It confused me. Ellen had given me an old-school, ring-bound Franklin Planner, which had preprinted pages for each day. The hours were separated by ten dotted lines, each representing a six-minute increment that I could use to remember which clients' accounts I worked on that day, and when.

"Come on," Grant said, "you should listen to this call with the banker from GP about our response to the comments from the SEC. You can start to learn how we counterargue."

We. That's nice. I'm a we.

But then I froze. Grant noticed my now-pale face and asked, "What? What's wrong?"

"Who is the call with at GP?" I asked, almost tearing up as I recalled the firing incident.

"Jack Wynn," Grant said.

"Oh, Jesus. I can't be on a call with Jack Wynn!" I responded, feeling clammy and slightly faint.

"Let me explain something to you, Sophia. Bankers are like real estate agents. They don't actually *do* anything, but they make a shit ton of money and, unfortunately, are a necessary evil. I don't care if Jack Wynn fired you. He's an asshole. But he's an asshole we have to work with quite often, so don't worry about him. He can't touch you while you're working here. Well, assuming you don't do anything egregious to him."

Grant and Ellen restored my faith in humanity, or in Silicon Valley at least.

Minutes later, I sat in his office as he dialed into a conference call number. "Just listen in and learn," he advised.

When the call began, I shuddered upon hearing Jack's voice, then took a deep breath and grasped my pen tight. As Jack and Grant went back and forth about the different ways they could respond to the SEC comments, I gathered this call was a follow-up to the one Grant had been having earlier that morning, when I'd arrived. They sorted through the financials and business metrics that our client's peers used, and reasons why those did or didn't apply to "our" company. At the end, Jack and Grant agreed that it was best if they called the SEC the next day, together.

Before we hung up, Jack asked, "Should we have a code word?"

"What do you mean?" Grant asked.

"I mean, if you and I need to talk privately about something during the call, should we have code names for each other so we know if one of us wants to put the SEC examiner on hold?"

Grant looked at me incredulously and rolled his eyes, then leaned closer to the speakerphone to say something. But before he could, I leaned over and whispered in his ear, "How about we give him the code name 'Pig Fucker'?"

Grant dropped his head and shook it slowly, trying very hard not to laugh while he responded to Jack. "Let's just tell the SEC we need a moment if we want to talk on a separate, private line."

As I walked out of the office that evening, a sense of satisfaction washed over me. Watching Grant weave and tackle every angle of a problem could be valuable, although I wasn't sure how. He was a maestro at analyzing situations, negotiating, and predicting results. If I listened to and observed Grant Vicker carefully, maybe I would become skilled at it, too.

I HAD PLANS to meet Kate and her first-year associate, Mark, at the Dutch Goose after work. "I want you to meet his roommates. They're medical school residents!" she'd exclaimed when we met earlier in the day. Like the Rosewood, the Goose was a favorite of ours—one of those wonderful places you walked into and immediately felt its history of countless drinking stories, date nights, and evenings spent with friends seated along its worn wood picnic tables. When I hurried in fifteen minutes late, the buzzing chatter coming from the young hopefuls inside somehow calmed me.

"Hey!" Kate yelled, waving at me. "I came by your office around seven to see if you were ready to go, but you weren't there."

Kate, Mark, and Mark's two roommates were sitting in the far corner booth. The Golden State Warriors game was playing in the background, and as I walked over, the peanut-shell-covered floor crunched under my heels.

"Grant's working on an IPO for a mobile app company, and guess who the banker is?" I asked, smiling.

"Who?" Kate leaned forward as though I were sharing a good bit of gossip.

"Jack Wynn!" Mark shouted out as if he were a game show contestant. When I nodded, Mark continued, "Kate mentioned you used to work at Global Partners. That man is on a lot of IPOs."

I wanted to tell them all about the conference call, but instead, I waved to the two roommates and apologized as I slid into the booth, "Sorry, didn't mean to be rude. Hi, I'm Sophia."

Kate introduced me to the dark-and-stormy-looking roommate, a solid nine who mesmerized me so deeply that I barely waved to the curly-haired, shorter guy.

Kate pointed to Dark and Stormy and said, "He's studying ophthalmology."

"Oh!" I jumped in my seat, reached into my purse, and threw on my new pair of glasses. "I just got new glasses! What do you think?"

The stunned look on Kate's face told me I was making a fool of myself, but only a split second of awkwardness passed before a man's voice saved me. "In that case, did I mention I'm studying urology?"

The voice came from Mark's other roommate—the shorter, curly-haired one whom I'd barely noticed. The table erupted in laughter and I smiled brightly at him. "Peter," he said while extending his hand.

The moment was interrupted by the vibrating phone in my purse, which I answered. It was my dad. I plugged one ear with a finger and held the phone with the other hand as I made my way outside to hear him.

"Hi, Mei-Mei. Where are you?" Based on the echo coming through, Dad was on speakerphone.

"I'm at the Dutch Goose."

"Tell her no drinking!" my mom shouted from the background. In her opinion, drinking establishments were a triple whammy for me: first, proper ladies shouldn't be seen in bars; second, the empty calories did nothing for anyone's waistline; and finally, diabetics really shouldn't drink because it generally messes with their blood sugar levels. Mom was right on the last point, but I wanted to *live* my life.

"Sophia, you're not going to drink, are you?" asked Dad.

"No, I'm not drinking." *You are going to hell for lying to your parents again.* "Why are you calling me?"

"Are you coming home for dinner? It's late and we want to hear about your day."

"My day was really good, Dad. Really good."

"Does that mean you didn't get fired yet?" Dad asked, laughing.

"Very funny. No, I think I'll do really well at Sterling, Rich," I responded.

"Okay. So you're not coming home for dinner?" I knew Dad was hoping I'd return for a healthy meal; he didn't want to seem as though he was babying me, so he said, "You should take it easy, young lady. Why are you always going? You can't seem to sit still."

"I'm going to just eat here. I'll be home in an hour or so, okay?"

Before he hung up, my mom leaned in to the speakerphone so close that I could visualize her practically touching her lips to the phone base. Technology still baffled her and she was always worried people on the other end couldn't hear her. She shouted slowly, "Come home soon, Sophia."

I rolled my eyes but yelled into the phone as I took slow steps back toward the bar, "Okay, Mom. I love you."

DAYS LATER, I walked into my office with a slight bounce in my step, wearing the new pink twinset Mom had bought me. To my surprise, someone was waiting—a cat-sweater-wearing short, round, elderly woman with gray hair and glasses. I thought I had walked into the wrong office, but immediately saw the framed photo of me and Kate on the left corner of my desk.

"Oh, hello," I said. "Are you looking for me?"

I assumed the visitor was a Sterling, Rich employee; I hadn't met anyone outside of Grant's small group.

"Are you Sophia?" the woman asked. When I nodded, wearing a blank look, she said, "I'm Penny Jenkins. I'm your voice coach." Penny clearly enunciated every word, her dropped chin and lips forming facial shapes I'd never seen. I swear she somehow managed a star configuration in there.

"Oh, you must have the wrong person. I don't have a voice coach. Who are you looking for again?"

"Sophia Young."

"Yes, that's me. But I didn't hire a voice coach."

"Grant did." The woman continued to enunciate. "He said your voice is too high. It sounds too young. He'd like for us to work on it." It was clear from her stern expression that this was not a joke. "Let's get started, shall we?"

Somehow, in just a few minutes, I found myself lying flat on the floor, learning how to "breathe from the diaphragm" and *mi-mi-mi-mi* my way into sounding professional. So far I just felt like I was an understudy in *The Sound of Music.* I had no idea what this had to do with law or IPOs, and wondered if it could be considered gender discrimination.

But aren't we past all that yet? That's so eighties!

"Your *problem* is," Penny chided, "you speak from your vocal cords. That's why you sound like you're squeaking. Professional women don't squeak, my dear."

"But . . . don't all people talk from their vocal cords?"

"*No vocal cords for you!*" Penny retorted. I felt as though I were back in elementary school being scolded by my piano teacher. Any minute now, she'd produce a ruler to slap my wrists.

As Penny guided me through my "exercises," she explained that male brains aren't designed to listen to female voices. "It's a fact," she said. "Women have natural melodies in their voices that men can't process, and if you're going to be a successful woman in this valley, you're going to have to avoid the tones they can't make out."

"Stupid men," I grumbled. "How long will we be doing this?"

"If you practice, we should have this *fixed* in a few weeks. Now inhale, and . . ."

You've got to be joking.

"An hour a week?" I asked.

"Every day, honey. Your sound frequencies are particularly high, so we have a lot of work to do." Apparently my voice needed to come from my abdomen. I just hoped my abdomen was hiding a special reserve of professionalism that I didn't know about yet.

One hour later, Penny left my office as I rose from the floor feeling well rested. All the "breathe in, and out . . . hold . . . and in, and out" had relaxed me. But when I had a moment to process what I'd just been subjected to, I became angry that Grant didn't give me advance notice about Penny, and also a bit sad that I didn't get through my first month without him finding a flaw. I marched down the hall and stormed into his office. But I was immediately disarmed when I found him slumped over a document with his face only about three inches above the desk. His tongue was peeking out of the corner of his mouth again while his Montblanc pencil mercilessly marked up the page; his childlike appearance thawed me just before I rapped on the door lightly.

"Hi, do you have a minute?"

"Sure, what's up?"

"So I met Penny Jenkins."

"Who is Penny Jenkins?"

"The voice coach."

"Oh, I didn't know that was her name. The paralegal coordinator found her for me."

"What's wrong with my voice?" I squeaked.

"Well, I figure if at some point you really do call someone 'Pig Fucker,' you'd better sound older than five."

"Oh." I took a deep breath as my mind searched for fighting words. "Well, do you do this for men so they can sound more . . . *manly*?"

Grant narrowed his eyes and grinned suspiciously. "I do not have any knowledge of any man taking voice lessons for this *particular* reason. And, if a man working for me sounded like you do, Penny whatever-her-name-is would have been in his office as well. The voice lessons weren't a knock against feminism or anything. Don't take it so personally. I know a lot of other women have taken voice and presentation lessons, if that makes you feel any better."

My shoulders relaxed as I exhaled. *Fair enough.* "Okay, well, I would very much have appreciated it if you'd just given me a heads-up. I was really caught off guard."

"My bad. Sorry," Grant said.

Wow, he apologizes.

"Yeah, yeah, yeah." I smiled.

"Since you're here, we're having an organizational meeting next week to kick off the Chaussure IPO. Want to join?"

"What's an organizational meeting?"

"It's a meeting that includes management, underwriters or bankers, both sides' counsel, and auditors. Real fun. The company will give the bankers an overview of their business and then we'll talk about the IPO's structure, timing, who does what."

I'd lost interest two seconds ago, but willed my eyes to focus on Grant and pay attention so I could learn.

"Plan to be there at least half the day, if not all day," Grant said.

Will there be lunch? My blood sugar needs lunch.

"They're in Seattle, right?" I made a mental note to bring juice boxes and granola bars from the stash I had inside my desk drawer.

"They *are* a Seattle-based company, but their executives are close by in the South San Francisco Baylands. They thought it was important to have a presence here in Silicon Valley."

I nodded. As my toothless grandmother used to say, "There's always some asshole who wants to move to California."

CHAUSSURE PROMISED CONSUMERS online access to the world's largest selection of shoes. All shoes, all sizes, anytime. Despite all its skeptics, the company had enjoyed skyrocketing growth due to its flawless execution and Nordstrom-like customer service. Chaussure's public promise was to guarantee even the most obscure footwear items at the lowest prices. I loved shoes as much as any woman, but I couldn't help but reflect that Chaussure's goal sounded more evil than good. They wanted to do away with traditional brick-and-mortar stores, crushing every mom-and-pop along the way. In my mind, they'd never succeed. Too many people loved to browse shoe departments, and who was going to buy a pair they couldn't see, feel, and actually try on? How could browsing online compare with holding a four-hundred-dollar Sergio Rossi stiletto and dreaming of one day owning a pair? *This company is going to be a dud.*

Grant walked toward the entrance of the Chaussure office at a pace that I couldn't keep up with, no matter how fast I tried to move my Nine West–clad feet.

"Just a heads-up, it is not a love fest between the bankers and the executive team," Grant said.

"Why did they hire them, then?"

"One of the board members had a pre-existing relationship," Grant answered while he continued racing ahead. "That's how things work in Silicon Valley—they may not be the right person for the job, but if there's a pre-existing relationship . . . well, oh boy, then they're the right person after all," he said sarcastically.

"So what's wrong with them—the bankers?"

"The firm itself sucks, but regardless, it's not uncommon for executives to dislike their investment bankers, because of the huge fees they charge and all the nosing around that they do. Tony Sine is the lead banker on Chaussure, and he's actually quite good."

As we walked through the entrance of the building, Grant continued, "You should also know that the CFO, Aidan, has a thick accent. He's Irish, as in from the city of Cork where the accent is extremely unusual. I'm only now beginning to understand what the fuck he's saying. And he likes to mess with Tony, so he pours it on extra thick and speaks really fast when he's asking questions."

Laughing, I said, "Okay. I'll do the same to you with my new Penny Jenkins voice when you're annoying me."

A chuckle from Grant. "Well played."

I was surprised to find that there was no real lobby but rather just a ramp leading to the black metal door of an elevator. Honestly, I was unimpressed—this dump was a far cry from the polished settings of Sterling, Rich. I questioned how well Chaussure was *really* doing. While looking around the empty nothingness of the poorly lit room with its concrete walls, I saw something out of the corner of my eye. Something metallic that was moving around at the end of the ramp, over by the elevator. It stood there as if waiting. When we approached it, lights turned on, and the robot said, "Hi. I'm Rosie. What is your—"

I reached out to touch it, but Rosie rolled swiftly back a few inches, just out of my reach, without pausing her sentence. A self-security thing?

"—name and who are you here to see?" the robot finished. This was the coolest thing I had ever seen! After Grant gave his name, Rosie asked, "Is Sophia here with you?" Both of us were asked to provide our thumbprints on Rosie's screen, which served not only as an ID but also as an automatic signature to Chaussure's confidentiality agreement. Scratch the whole "dump" thing. Now I was impressed.

"I want to work here," I whispered to myself. But unfortunately, Grant heard me.

"What?"

"Nothing. I was saying, 'Who'd want to work here?'"

Smooth move, Sophia.

Rosie asked us to step into the elevator, then bid us adieu as the doors slid shut. When they opened again at the building's top floor, I got my first-ever glimpse of what a startup really was. Dozens and dozens of twenty-year-olds in hoodies buzzed about on scooters and bikes in organized chaos. There were dogs playing freely, and a Ping-Pong table took up an entire corner of the space; it was surrounded by colorful beanbag chairs where employees lounged with their laptops propped on their thighs. Amid the futuristic scene sat some surprisingly sloppy-looking employee desks, two-by-four plywood planks precariously balanced on top of two black file cabinets, ironically matched with pricey Aeron chairs. A feeling of excitement brewed inside me as I watched the wrestling dogs, saw the relaxed and happy faces of the employees, and felt the sense that there was a deep camaraderie within these walls. *Welcome to the startup world.*

We weren't alone. A guy with thick glasses, black Reebok sneakers, and pants that were slightly too short for him waited outside the elevator, ready to lead us to a steel-framed concrete conference room that sat squarely in the middle of the open floor plan. The concrete cube's small windows had shades drawn over them, and I could hear employees nearby whispering to each other, wondering what was going on inside "the cube."

Lucky me: I was about to find out.

The conference room contained a group of twenty white guys with expensive shoes and sport coats, perusing what appeared to be a *Wall Street Journal* article. When they were finished, one of the guys slid the paper onto the table. I could just make out a pencil sketch of Eric McCabe, the CEO of Chaussure. Beneath his face blazed the headline CHAUSSURE.COM'S GROWTH CONTINUES TO DEFY. What was going on in here? I quickly scanned the room. The air was tense, every white guy completely alert.

Tony Sine, the lead banker and a dead ringer for Clark Kent, rose to speak as Chaussure's CEO paced back and forth with his arms crossed, shaking his head. Tony seemed to be trying really hard to look intense and angry, but I thought he just looked like he was trying to go to the bathroom. Eric's big ears were red and he had this silly grin on his face that he couldn't seem to get rid of. He looked like someone I might have hung out with at Santa Clara: too cute and too young for me to take seriously. He also seemed to be just a bit too full of himself.

"Look, we're supportive that you're trying to increase Chaussure's brand awareness," Tony the banker said. "God knows I'm the one always toeing the line, but even *I* can see why this article would be a problem for the SEC."

Eric stopped his pacing. "Grant said any PR that was in the 'normal course of business' would be fine with the SEC. This is the normal course of business, right?"

No one had noticed we'd arrived, so Grant chimed in. "Hey, let's not misquote me, now. Normal course of business is a television ad highlighting your shoes and fabulous service—not a front-page article in the leading financial journal with your comments about Chaussure's hypergrowth. The SEC will likely view this as trying to create public interest for your upcoming IPO. It could mean a holding period—a delay—before you go public."

"Well." Eric sounded disgusted. Maybe the conversation was over. I prepared my nice-to-meet-you face in case I was about to be introduced. But then he continued: "You're only focusing on one thing! You're completely missing the part where I talk about how great it is to work here. Look!" He pushed the *Wall Street Journal* article toward Grant, pointing to a dense spot in the middle. "'Every day working here is like being in Paris.'" Satisfied, he looked up at the group. No one was responding. I tried desperately not to roll my eyes and laugh.

I slipped out of the room—not because I wasn't enjoying the Silicon Valley drama but because I had to go to the bathroom. Bad. As I passed the elevator bank, I saw Eric McCabe coming my way. I stopped.

"What do *you* think?" he asked me. "Are they right?" He didn't even know who I was—only that I'd come in with Grant Vicker. I'm sure he assumed I was an attorney.

"Are they right about what?"

"Is the *Journal* article bad? I mean, how could that be seen as bad?"

"Well, I'm not a lawyer," I started slowly, "so I won't comment on how the SEC is going to react. Personally, though, I didn't care for the Paris comment."

"You didn't like it?"

"God, no."

"Why not?"

I turned 180 degrees, my arms stretched wide to indicate the hoodied young dudes, the ad hoc desk situation, the giant bowls of chips and Skittles. I asked, "Does this look like the Champs-Élysées?"

To my relief, he burst out laughing. Safe passage to the restroom.

When I returned, the meeting had begun with a mind-numbing discussion over logistics. I kept my eyes on Eric, who was leaning casually against a whiteboard, wearing the calm expression of a man whose confidence never falters.

"Good morning," he was saying now. "I'm going to let the team here do most of the talking, but I want to be clear about something.

You're about to be part of a company that is going to change the entire shopping paradigm." *Unlikely.* "By applying technology to an archaic industry, we are forcing retailers to offer consumers the best selection and the most competitive prices."

Everyone around the table seemed to swallow it hook, line, and sinker. I leaned back in my chair. If you'd asked me, Eric was seriously overstating the importance of his company. *Change the shopping paradigm, ha!* After laying down a few house rules (we were never to omit the *dot com* from the end of *Chaussure*), Eric introduced Aidan, the company's CFO.

"Hiya," he said, followed promptly by a load of gibberish that I couldn't understand.

My eyes opened wide. Was he speaking English? Because he sounded like two Chinese people trying to speak a horrible version of French. Aidan rolled words off his tongue faster than an auctioneer selling methamphetamines to a roomful of rich drug addicts.

The lights dimmed and we turned our attention to rows of numbers projected onto the far wall. With a singsongy brogue, Aidan explained each line item on the income statement, moving his laser pointer from top to bottom quickly. My ears were on full alert, but I could catch only a word here and there.

"Fahrty milloh . . ."

"O'er der tirty-tree baklóige . . ."

Tony interrupted. "Backlog? Did you say backlog? Why would there be backlog in your business?" He was frustrated and everyone could tell.

"Dat yer a lath . . . big fecus . . . boat da tax . . . wallow on tirty-tree," Aidan said, more quickly than before. This is what Grant had meant; Aidan was purposely pouring on his thick brogue to make Tony feel stupid.

"What?" Tony asked.

"Dat yer a la big fecus boat da tax wallow on tirty-tree," Aidan said again, this time not breaking between words and definitely sounding like he was singing.

"What?" Tony asked again.

I looked at Grant, who had his chin tucked into his chest. He was trying not to laugh.

"Wha ken ye Americans nit undahstand me sure dey cin."

"What?!"

"Dat yer a la big fecus boat da tax wallow on tirty-tree."

"Excuse me?"

"Datyeralabigfecusboatdataxwallowontirty-tree!"

Tony's blank face showed that he didn't understand Aidan whatsoever. Still, he nodded his head and said, "Oh. Okay, thanks. That's great." *Poor guy.* This was great entertainment, but even more, it was a world-class lesson in how to use a voice or accent to distract and defeat an opponent. Suddenly I was thankful for Penny Jenkins.

IN JANUARY, AFTER many late-night IPO prospectus—drafting sessions, endless amounts of state-of-this-or-that forms to fill out, and lessons on how to create various legal documents from scratch, we finished the Chaussure *dot com* IPO. It had been four months since I'd started, and in the company of over two hundred lawyers, legal secretaries, and paralegals, I had found independence, confidence, and a sense of peace that was new to me. The learning curve had been more extreme than I'd imagined. Before long, I was clocking eighty-hour weeks doing the same work that first-, second-, and even third-year attorneys were doing. It was an insane boom time in the financial markets; everyone seemed to be making money and operating with a *just get it done* mentality. Investors were especially hungry for technology IPOs and network security was a particularly hot topic, so companies flew out of the gates one after the other, making secretaries millionaires. Sterling, Rich was in the middle of it all; we had become so busy that the firm was known in the Valley as "the meat grinder." I didn't give a second thought to our firm's reputation. I, like everyone else at Sterling, Rich, was burning the candle at both ends, and was managing to keep up, *despite* my diabetes! That is, until the morning I came home after pulling an all-nighter and greeted Mom at our front door by throwing up on her slippers. I was exhausted.

My workload and sleep deprivation brought out an impatient, bossy, and to-the-point manner that made me feel like I was becoming my mother and would have surely gotten me fired from most places. Thankfully, though, it didn't seem to bother Grant, and he continued to demonstrate his trust in and respect for me. He also pointed out that those same qualities in a man would have been rewarded, and fueled my ego further by leading me to believe I was an equal to the JDs from Harvard, Stanford, and Chicago who worked next to me. *I'm finally fitting in.*

When it came time for my six-month review, both Grant and my peers gave me glowing reports. The only comment that made me pause was Grant's response to the question, "Is this person on track to be promoted?"

Sophia is certainly capable of handling the responsibilities of a senior paralegal, Grant wrote, *but I don't believe that's her goal. She's a one-person show.*

What's that supposed to mean?

I asked Kate that evening as we sat at the Dutch Goose celebrating the completion of a particularly long and arduous financing for one of her clients.

"He probably means you like being an individual contributor and that you don't need much help," she said, showing no indication that she'd had only three hours of sleep the night before.

"Well, that's definitely true," I responded, raising my glass and clinking it against hers. "Maybe it was a polite way of saying that I wouldn't be good at mentoring junior paralegals because he knows I don't have the patience for it, and that's what I'd have to do if I was promoted to senior paralegal."

"Well, whatever he meant, it was a compliment I'm sure."

"What about you? Do you want to be a senior paralegal?" I asked my best friend. "You'd be great at it. You are *very* patient. Just look how you handle me!"

"True dat!" Kate declared. Then, with a more serious expression, she said, "I'm fine with being a senior paralegal if it happens, but I *really* want to be a lawyer."

The determination in Kate's eyes told me she definitely would be someday. "You're not going to be just a lawyer. You'll go all the way to making partner!" I cheered. After all, that was the top of the food chain.

I wondered what the future held in store for me. What would *I* be proud to say I did when I looked back on my life fifty years from now? For so long I'd wanted the life my mom had. But now I wondered whether that would be enough.

chapter 4

JUST WEEKS BEFORE MY TWENTY-FOURTH birthday, I found myself standing next to Daniel Weinstein at the funeral reception in Los Angeles
for Kate's grandfather. Daniel was Kate's distant cousin and I found
his confidence and dual-degreed air wildly attractive. Although I
knew it was completely inappropriate and indecorous to flirt with
someone at a *funeral,* I couldn't help but touch his arm gently and
simper when he asked, "Can I get you anything?"

I should have asked for a vodka soda, but to fit in with everyone
else, I asked for a glass of wine.

"Yes, a chardonnay would be great."

Who knows whether it was the alcohol or chemistry, but Daniel
and I spent the next three-quarters of an hour talking about our careers, our love of traveling, and the unbelievable coincidence that he
lived down the hill from my parents. We would have kept going had
Kate not flashed me her "bat signal"—two fingers placed flat against
her collarbone. I excused myself from Daniel and crossed the room
to rescue my best friend; when I approached, Kate whispered in my
ear that she was tired of speaking to "these strangers." I thought that
might be the end of Daniel Weinstein, but I later found him standing
next to me once again, sharing funny old stories about him and Kate
playing together as kids.

I wondered why my friend had never mentioned Daniel before,
but none of that mattered at the moment. I liked this guy and could
tell he felt the same. When the reception room began to empty, his
parents approached.

"Mom, Dad, this is Sophia Young."

"Are you Japanese, Sophia? You look Japanese," said Daniel's mother.

"Actually, I'm Chinese. My parents were born in China and then immigrated to Taiwan."

"Oh! The Jews love the Chinese! They're the Jews of the Pacific!" she said.

Daniel's father agreed. "That's right. That's what Nona always said."

I had no idea who Nona was, but I assumed he was referring to a grandmother or mother.

"I have a Chinese friend named Sophia who lives close to us in Pueblo, Colorado. Her name is Sophia Chu. Do you know her?" asked Daniel's mom.

I pretended to give Mrs. Weinstein's question some serious thought while Daniel rolled his eyes. "Hmm, nope, I don't think I know a Sophia Chu," I responded.

Daniel put his hand on the small of my back and guided me away while turning to tell his parents, "I'm giving Sophia a lift to her hotel, so I'll see you later."

Ooooooh, I like the take-charge type. Maybe he could take care of *me* someday.

A DO NOT DISTURB sign that I'd stolen from my Los Angeles hotel hung on my closed office door, but someone was knocking anyway.

"What?" I barked, turning my attention from my computer.

"Want to get lunch?" Grant asked through the door.

Uh-oh. He never asks me to lunch.

"Sure."

I stood up and opened my door. Grant rarely came into my office, and his booming voice sounded even louder in my small space. "I'm just grabbing something at the place around the corner," he said.

Before we were two steps out of my office, Sterling, Rich's mail courier approached, carrying a large bouquet of red roses. "These are for you," the courier said.

"Wow. Do tell," Grant teased as I handed him the vase so I could read the card. My dad often sent me roses "just because," but I couldn't help but hope:

Please let them be from Daniel. Please.

Happy Birthday, Sophia
—Daniel

I flashed all my teeth at Grant and glowed with glee. "They're from a guy I just started seeing," I said.

"Oh boy! I can't wait to hear about him," Grant said mockingly. "Come on, I'm starving."

"Okay, but you're buying. It's my birthday, you know!"

"July tenth, huh? Well, we can't just go around the corner, then. Come on, I'll drive."

"Where are we going?" I asked.

"One of my favorites," he said.

Fifteen minutes later, we pulled into the parking lot of the best Chinese restaurant in town, Chef Chu's. When we walked inside the crowded foyer, Grant steered me toward the private room on the left, where I saw Kate; my parents; Audrey with her baby, Ava; my brother-in-law, Hank; the rest of Grant's lawyers; and some of the other paralegals I'd become close with. "Happy birthday, Sophia," my boss of nearly a year said.

I threw my arms around him and impersonated Sally Field: "You like me. You really, really like me!" Grant blushed and then nodded toward my beaming parents. I wished Daniel were there to see it, but only Kate knew about him—aside from what I'd mentioned to

Grant. I wasn't ready for my parents and Audrey to scrutinize Daniel as they had the others, always causing family fights. Today was about me—and that's the way I wanted it.

WITH MY PARENTS frequently out of town setting up Dad's new Asia office, it had been easy to practically move into the run-down house Daniel shared with four roommates just weeks after we'd met. It was the only way for us to see each other, if rolling around between the sheets could be called seeing, because Daniel was working hard as an intern for an environmental consulting firm, and I was continuing to burn the midnight oil at Sterling, Rich. Weekends when I wasn't working were what we cherished the most—we socialized with each other's friends, went to the movies, and fell into the comfortable life of a couple, which assured me he was *the one*.

By summer's end, it felt as though Daniel and I were married; I was head over heels in love and tempted to admit my feelings for him, but that wasn't the narrative I wanted. I wanted a declaration, a promise. To be pursued like the women in the fairy tales I'd grown up with. And why not by Daniel? He was attractive in a mad-scientist kind of way, was highly intelligent, and had good earning potential, and the sex was out of this world. What else did I need?

But as fall began and my parents' return was only a few days away, the reality of my situation came to light. Everything was about to change. Summer vacation was over and the ruthless dictators were coming home. My sleepovers at Daniel's would end, except for the times I resorted to using high school tactics like saying I was staying the night at Kate's or making up some other lie.

"You're an adult, Sophia. Why do we have to sneak around?" Daniel would ask, or rather, complain.

I tried to imagine telling my parents that I was crashing at my boyfriend's house, tried to imagine them driving past his house down the hill from theirs, seeing my car parked in front and acting as if they were fine with it. But before I could really even get started, I began to laugh. "Daniel, seriously. They would absolutely shit a brick if they ever found out I was sleeping with you. God, it would kill them. I would never hear the end of it and, well, you just have to know my parents. They have this superhuman power—torture nagging or something. Telling them is just not worth it."

I prefer to lie and sneak around.

Daniel thought this was ridiculous but said he'd play along if I promised to at least tell my parents about us. It was a good compromise, in my opinion, so I agreed.

"I MET HIM at a funeral," I said to Mom a few days after she and Dad returned. I'd thought telling her over the phone while I was at work was the best way to do it, so if the call didn't go well, I could pretend I had some sort of meeting.

"You met him where?"

"A funeral."

"Who died?"

"Kate's grandfather. You know, Papa. So I flew down to L.A. for his funeral."

"Oh no! You didn't tell us Papa passed. Give her family our best. And *please* stop saying you met someone at a funeral. It makes you sound so tacky and desperate," she said. "What does he do?"

"He's in graduate school. At Dad's alma mater, *Stanford.*"

That should make her happy.

"A student? *Tsk, tsk.* I can see how this is going to turn out. You're going to end up supporting him while he starts his career and he'll enjoy living off you, which probably means Daddy, too, until he makes a little money. When there's actually some real money in his bank account, just when you're stuck at home raising his children, he's going to leave you. It's a divorce just waiting to happen."

Nope, not happy. Mom had already sized him up: bad marriage material.

"Jesus, Mom! No one—"

"I tell you!" she interrupted. "It happened to Auntie Anita. Exact same situation. Now what about that nice boy I set you up with? Auntie Helen's son, the accountant?"

"Come on, Mom, you've seen him. He has a middle part in his hair. A butt cut!"

"That's easy. Just take him to your hairdresser."

"And he only wears loud Hawaiian shirts with tight corduroy pants!"

"We can take him to Nordstrom."

"His teeth! They are awful!"

"We'll slap some braces on him, then. What else is wrong?"

I couldn't help but laugh. Mom had an answer for everything, or at least she thought she did.

"Mom, I have to go. I have work to do."

"It's nine o'clock! Aren't you coming home soon? Do you really have work to do or are you going out with . . ."

"The funeral guy." *Snigger.*

"WHAT did I *just* tell you?"

"WEI?" MOM SHOUTED into her mobile phone. "*Wei?*" The sound of cars honking loudly suggested Mom was keeping the "bad Chinese driver" stereotype alive.

"Yes, Mother. I can hear you," I replied quietly in English, picking up my pace past the secretaries' desks so I could reach Kate's office faster. She was in the middle of Sterling, Rich's three wings, and I was almost there.

Mom shot off at least five more *wei*s without taking so much as half a breath; I knew she'd repeat herself less than three more times before she hung up, and I *really* needed to talk to her. *Three, two . . .* I shut Kate's office door behind me, then let loose. "MOM! I CAN HEAR YOU!"

"Oh," Mom replied innocently. "I couldn't hear you. Where are you?" I looked at Kate seated at her desk and waved.

"I'm in Kate's office. She says hello." Kate nodded.

Mom *tee-hee-hee*d shyly before saying hi in English. Then, back in Mandarin, she said, "Invite her and her boyfriend to Thanksgiving dinner."

I turned my eyes to Kate and relayed the message; Kate stood up and took the phone, knowing my mom both loved and was embarrassed by the attention. "Hi, Mrs. Young. Thank you very much for the invitation, but I'm going to my boyfriend's house for Thanksgiving. I'm coming to Sunday dinner this weekend, though, so I'll see you soon," she said before handing me back the phone.

"Mom, I thought maybe I'd invite Daniel to Thanksgiving dinner. What do you think?"

Mom was quiet for a moment, then said, "Mei-Mei. We were gone all summer. It'd be nice for Thanksgiving to be our family time. How about we invite your friend over for dinner another time? Maybe after you two have been *friends* for a little longer. It's only been what? Three months or so?"

Five months, Mother. Five.

What she meant was that she didn't want to upset my father. And when it came to me, boys always upset him. Dad thought of me as his little girl, too naïve and too kindhearted. "They're going to take advantage of you," he'd say, concerned I would kowtow or hand over my paychecks to any no-good guy as long as he was handsome. I thought for a moment and decided Mom was right. *This isn't a good idea.* I could see Dad making a scene, which might cause Daniel to run for the hills. There were less complicated girls to date than me—nondiabetic, all-American, tall ones, with parents who spoke perfect English—and I wasn't ready to lose him.

"I'M TIRED OF holding my head up," I said after work at seven thirty that Tuesday evening as Kate, Mark, and I headed toward our own pre-Thanksgiving dinner.

"I'll drive," said Mark, knowing Kate and I wanted to catch up on the latest law firm gossip. "Where are we meeting Daniel?"

"He took Caltrain up, so he'll meet us at the restaurant and catch a ride home with us," I answered before turning my attention to Kate.

"It's *so* stereotypical," my best friend said. "Rich law partner leaves his wife and kids because he's fallen for his bombshell secretary."

"My mom always says to make sure your husband's secretary is much older than you," I said.

"She's right!"

"Well, my secretary is a man, so we don't have to worry there," Mark offered.

"So evidently the secretary walked away with half his net worth! Like four or five million dollars," Kate said.

"But they were only married for what—nine months?" I protested.

The remaining hour-long drive probably wasn't too fun for Mark because most of it revolved around *stupid man* this and *stupid man* that. When we arrived at the restaurant, he nearly ran up to the entrance, where Daniel was waiting for us. "Hey, man. So good to see you," he said.

San Francisco's newest and trendiest restaurant was a neon-lit warehouse that charged patrons an arm and a leg to sit at a communal table and dine on a prix fixe menu consisting of raw vegetable sticks stacked in *Jenga*-like formations. Grant had overheard a young client raving about it, so he (or rather his secretary) bought me a gift certificate and insisted I give it a try. The reservation wasn't easy to get; the online booking tool essentially told me there were "no tables available during a two-hour window for the rest of your life." But thanks to a new Silicon Valley company that sold secondary market reservations, we managed to secure our seats.

Inside, it was obvious which people were the tacky nouveau riche of Silicon Valley and which were the local city dwellers: the former were dressed, or rather overdressed, in high-priced fashions that probably hadn't even made it into the retail stores yet, and the latter simply wore jeans. Mark, Kate, Daniel, and I fell into the much smaller "we're just working folk" group—people who were in oh-so-passé professions dressed in conservative work attire.

The car conversation was loud on the way home—from the front seats Kate and Mark debated the pros and cons of prenuptial agreements, and in the back seat Daniel waxed poetic on his opinions about globalization. Then, rather suddenly, my boyfriend asked me if I had any vacation time. I wished we were alone because Kate and Mark's voices were loud, making this private moment feel unprivate.

"Yes, of course. Whatcha thinkin'?" I asked. I was trying to sound casual, but my heart was beating fast. *My first romantic getaway!*

While Daniel shared with me his wish list of vacation spots— "Hawaii, Bali, Costa Rica. Oh, what about New Orleans? I've never been there!"—I was overanalyzing. *I think there was something different about his tone just now, although his facial expression didn't seem particularly head-over-heels.* My excitement tempered and Daniel saw it in my face. I wanted this trip to mean something to him— something more than just a vacation, something about *us*.

"What's wrong?" he asked.

"Nothing."

"Sophia, I know you think you hide your feelings well, but you wear your heart on your sleeve. What's wrong?"

"We haven't talked at all about our future!" I complained. "Can you tell me where your head is at?"

Suddenly Kate and Mark stopped debating and the only sound in the car was the humming of the engine. The painfully awkward silence felt like it was dragging on forever, but only a few seconds elapsed before Kate loudly blurted, "Blah, blah, blah, blah . . ."

Kate to the rescue.

I could see in the passenger-side mirror that Kate was wearing a horrified expression and I couldn't help but laugh. "'Blah, blah, blah'? That's the best you can do?"

"Oh my gosh, you guys. I'm so sorry. *We're* so sorry."

"That's okay." Daniel chuckled. "Sophia and I can talk about it later."

But when later came during our phone conversation that night, I wished it never had.

"I'm not looking for a serious relationship," Daniel said.

I sat in my bed looking down at my hands and holding back tears.

"I'll be finishing school this summer and starting a new job in the city. I can't commit to anything right now. I'm really sorry."

"So were we just having fun, then?" I asked as Mom's evaluation of Daniel as bad marriage material passed through my head.

"Well, no. I care deeply for you, but I just want you to know I'm not looking for anything serious."

"Have you been *seeing* other people?" I asked, jealousy already overwhelming me.

"No, of course not. It's not like that. We're exclusive. I'm just telling you that marriage is not in the near future."

"Oh," I said. I looked down at my hands again, my disappointment deepening. "I am ready for that type of commitment, Daniel. I mean, not married with kids right away or anything"—*lie*—"but I'd like to find the person I'm going to spend the rest of my life with. So I need to think about this. Is that okay?"

Daniel's voice sounded sad. "Sure, of course."

A FEW DAYS after Thanksgiving I had created an online dating profile and soon was having lunch with a guy I'd met through an Internet service, a fireman with a young daughter who lived with him.

"But wait, don't you have to work something like thirty-six-hour shifts? Does she stay with your ex-wife when you're working?" I asked.

"Well, my wife lives in the house as well," the fireman said, spearing a french fry with his fork.

"Oh! That's very progressive of you. And you mean your *ex-wife*, right?"

"No, we're still married."

"Separated?"

"No. It's inevitable, though. We're having a lot of issues, and—"

"Well, maybe that's because you're out dating OTHER WOMEN!" I said loudly as I stood up.

Moron.

My next date was with an engineer. I could tell from our first phone call that Mr. Engineer was very socially awkward, which I overlooked because his online profile indicated the man had potential. He suggested we meet the next day at a trendy restaurant-bar in San Carlos called Town, and I agreed to a drink but explained that I had dinner plans. On a scale of one to ten, he was a seven, so not bad at all. But after introducing himself, he asked if I minded paying. "I forgot my wallet."

The guy seemed genuinely embarrassed about it, so I agreed. *After all, I can bring home the bacon and fry it up in a pan.*

When the bartender came to take our drink orders, Mr. Engineer said, "I'll have a glass of the cabernet. And a filet mignon to go."

What?

By the last day of that same week, I'd booked an early December trip to Italy for Daniel and me. After my run of bad dates, I was so thankful for my boyfriend that I decided the trip, or the airfare at least, would be my treat, because the thought of any more online dates horrified me. Besides, I'd hatched a plan: I'd kill Daniel with kindness and *make* him fall in love with me. Kate didn't approve whatsoever, and even threatened to tell Audrey. But *she* hadn't met the guys I'd just gone out with.

The week in Italy flew by without a single argument. It was amazing how much those days changed me; for the first time in my life, I felt like an adult who was making her own decisions, paying her own way, and in a real relationship. It felt great! But more thrilling than the statue of David or the Ponte Vecchio was the comfort of knowing that someone—Daniel—could love me, diabetes and all.

It began to rain on the last afternoon of our romantic holiday; Daniel and I raced through the old cobblestone streets and ducked into a wonderful small restaurant that held only six tables. Unlike the touristy places we'd eaten, the menu here was all written in Italian, and no one in the place spoke a word of English. It was the most memorable day of the trip—we sat there drinking and laughing with the restaurant owner as his brother, the chef, brought us plate after plate of authentic Italian fare. The carbohydrate-filled dishes were diabetic nightmares for sure, but I had insulin for that, so my running mascara became my bigger concern. I remember so clearly Daniel's smiling face as he sat next to me, soaking wet from the rain. We held hands underneath the table and kissed passionately after the owner left to tend to other guests. It was perfect, absolutely perfect.

AS CHRISTMAS APPROACHED, life seemed like it was right on track. I had a boyfriend, first of all. And I'd become a valuable contributor to Grant Vicker's team at Sterling, Rich—something I had never imagined. It had been more than a year since I first walked through those huge glass doors, and I had nearly fifteen IPOs under my belt to prove it, with more lined up thanks to Grant's thriving business.

I remembered my goal on my first day at the firm—to find a husband. *This will do nicely.* Sterling, Rich *was* working out nicely, just
not in the way I'd expected. "Go to college," my mom had always
said. "Make yourself just smart enough so a more successful man will
marry you. A doctor or lawyer, perhaps." Somehow, somewhere, I'd
forgotten that goal.

"DAD, PLEASE BE gentle with him."

"I'm going to shoot him in between the eyes!" Dad joked. It was
the first time Daniel was meeting my parents, and I was racked with
nerves. I would have preferred for Daniel to just honk when he was
outside, but he wanted to introduce himself to Mom and Dad despite
my warnings. I knew this wasn't going to be pleasant—it never was
when it came to my dad and boys.

I looked pleadingly at Mom. "Help me!"

"Your father is very protective, Sophia. You can't fault him for
that," she said with a chuckle.

"Dad, just remember. His name is *Daniel.* Not Brian or Erik
or . . ." My dad liked to call my ex-boyfriends by the wrong name. He
thought it was funny. Anyone else would call it passive-aggressive.

"Got it. Daniel," Dad said to me as the doorbell rang.

Let's get this over with—quick!

We raced to the door, pushing and shoving each other, and were it
not for my tight, long dress, I would have gotten there first.

"Hello! You must be Brian," Dad said.

Shit.

"Hi, Mr. Young, I'm Daniel," he said before awkwardly waving to
my mother.

I was glad my dad's "joke" went unnoticed, but Dad turned to Mom
and said in Mandarin, "Idiot doesn't even realize I just offended him."

Daniel hadn't taken three steps into the foyer when Dad handed him the star for our fifteen-foot Christmas tree, which we'd just finished decorating that morning. It sat squarely in our foyer and was tall enough to almost reach our second-floor skywalk. "Can you please put this on the top of the tree for me? I'm too old to climb up there," Dad said.

"I thought you called the handyman to come do that for us," I said, glaring at Dad.

"Well, I did, but since Daniel is here, and the ladder is out, I figured he could help."

Daniel walked to the base of the ladder and looked up. "Uh, um, sure. Sophia, hold the base for me."

"Please," Dad said to Daniel sternly while Mom stood in the background saying nothing.

"Yes, please, Sophia, will you hold the ladder for me?" Daniel asked, and I swear I heard him gulp. Daniel climbed, or rather shook, up the ladder and did as my father asked. When both of his feet stood firmly on our marble floor again, he said to me, "We'd better go."

Daniel said a quick goodbye and walked—ran—out the door.

Well, that went well.

I spent the duration of the short drive to the law firm's holiday party convincing Daniel that my dad didn't hate him.

"Yes, he does," Daniel insisted.

"No, no. He's just like that. But next time you see my parents, maybe just try to talk to them a little. Compliment my dad on the house—he loves that."

"You want me to kiss his ass?" Daniel hissed.

Yes. Yes, actually I do.

The fact of the matter was that my dad didn't trust any man who was within one hundred feet of me, and the only thing that would change that was Daniel waiting on me hand and foot. My dad wanted me married off but only to a man he knew could handle me and take care of me. He made it his life's mission to test each guy I brought home to make sure he was worthy. But Daniel wasn't raised with Chinese filial piety. I stared out the car window and struggled to reconcile my desire to be with Daniel—to be an adult—with the comfort of being Daddy's girl. What does a woman madly in love do in this situation? A woman who knows that her relationship with her boyfriend could forever alter her relationship with her parents? Which should she choose?

I choose Daniel.

WHEN WE ARRIVED at Sterling, Rich's holiday party, I got my first real glimpse of Daniel in his tuxedo—without a judgmental Young family member in the way, at least. He looked as handsome as ever. "We made it," I said. Daniel's hands were freezing but firm on my bare back.

"By the skin of my teeth," he said, laughing.

"We look prrrrretty amazing," I noted with an air of satisfaction.

"Come on, Ms. Amazing." Daniel lowered his hand down my back to give me a pat, then hooked my arm in his and led me into the party. "Kate and Mark are over there. We have an open bar to investigate."

The alcohol was flowing, but still the lawyers couldn't stop talking about work—or about Scott Kraft's recent visit to the office. "He was in to see Austin Sterling," people whispered, circulating rumors that the firm's founder had hand-selected Grant to work on a secret Scott Kraft project. Daniel and I, however, ignored everyone and sweated through our formalwear, dancing to every song the DJ played. There was no one who navigated the dance floor better, no one who dipped me so effortlessly to the old-timey jazz songs, no one who could anticipate more readily when I needed a drink or a tiny mushroom filled with goat cheese. No one whose hands felt better on my waist when he was guiding me through the crowd. I couldn't believe I'd ever thought of breaking up with Daniel over my need to control the definition of our relationship.

When the DJ ended the evening with Elvis Presley's "Can't Help Falling in Love," Daniel sang every word to me, holding me close, tilting his head back and forth like a Vegas impersonator. I laid my head on his chest and pressed my cheek into his lapel as Elvis crooned.

"*Wise men say,*" he warbled, the bass thumping through the room, "*only fools rush in.*"

That night I lay in my own bed playing over and over the image of Daniel during that last dance. I fell asleep thinking about his eyes. They told a story, but I didn't know which one.

chapter 5

THANKS TO THE MULTIBILLION-DOLLAR VALUATIONS that investors were giving to every smart—and, quite frankly, stupid—idea that came across their desks, the New Year further fueled America's period of "irrational exuberance" (as former Federal Reserve Chairman Alan Greenspan would say). But no one in Silicon Valley complained about the Nasdaq soaring to all-time highs; the stock market created a whole new generation of rich people. Camrys became BMWs and every night was another lavish party with open bars and high-priced entertainment. Being in the San Francisco Bay Area was living what many would consider "the good life."

Don't be such a party pooper, Mr. Federal Reserve!

But by May, people could no longer ignore the signs that this party period wasn't sustainable and that a slowdown was imminent. Sterling, Rich clients rushed to take their companies public before a true stock market correction, while other companies simply crashed and burned. In either case, Sterling, Rich no longer just hummed twenty-four/seven—it throbbed, thundered, and nearly burst at its seams. What little work-life balance I had before now seemed like a distant memory; I survived that summer by feeding off the law firm's adrenaline, free coffee, and the free cafeteria that was added downstairs so employees never needed to leave the premises. Sleep was often defined as a few precious minutes under my desk, I'd missed family dinners and Ava's second birthday, and Daniel had to come to the office if he wanted to see me at all. The stress of being torn between work, my family, my boyfriend, and my health weighed heavily on me, but blood sugars be damned! I was high from the facts that an important man like Grant needed me, that my coworkers respected me, and that for once in my life I wasn't the cute one, the sick one, the Chinese one, or any other "one." I didn't let any of that define me at Sterling, Rich. What defined me was that *I* was Grant Vicker's paralegal. *Super Paralegal* in my own mind.

The setting sun blinded me as I stuck my head into a cocky sixth-year attorney's office. His name was Tyler and he sat three doors down the hall from Grant; he was the most senior attorney on my boss's team, so we'd worked together on a handful of transactions. We were in the middle of one that required his attention, so my dropping in wasn't unusual.

"Nice Chinese haircut number twenty-two," he said, referring to my fresh two-inch trim, compliments of the firm. Someone must have pointed out to Austin Sterling how worn down and grubby his staff looked, because we'd recently received a firm-wide email announcing that masseuses, manicurists, and hairstylists would be on-site every other week and encouraging us all to sign up.

I contorted my face and asked, "What do you mean?"

"I mean there's only so many hairstyles a Chinese person can wear because they all have straw-like hair."

"I don't have straight hair, Tyler. It's wavy. I just blow-dry it."

He wasn't listening, though, and I didn't want to give any further attention to his idiotic comment, so I continued, "Did you review the PacketTrap shareholder agreement I drafted?"

He looked at me, wearing an annoyed expression. "In the future, if you want to speak with me, please make an appointment. I'm very busy."

"Tyler," I said, my tone becoming lower and more serious, "it's a yes-or-no question."

"I'm a sixth-year attorney, Sophia. I went to Harvard Law School and have a dual JD/MBA. You really shouldn't take up my time with those questions, even if it's a quick and simple answer you're looking for. I will get to it when I get to it."

I almost started laughing. "Yeah, well you're also the idiot who maintains lame hair theories and bought a hundred-thousand-dollar car with a manual transmission that you don't know how to drive."

Take that, you shithead.

I walked away before I said anything I might regret.

Later, when Grant asked me about the PacketTrap shareholder agreement, I responded nonchalantly, "I can't be sure because Tyler says I'm not allowed to talk to him."

"What?" Grant chuckled incredulously.

"Oh, sorry. That's not entirely true. He said that if I wanted to ask him anything, I needed to make an appointment. And just to be clear, Grant, I'm not doing any such thing. He has no idea who he's dealing with."

"Obviously not," Grant responded, looking entertained. "Still, I'll talk to him. He's just overwhelmed with work and stressed about making partner."

I walked out of Grant's office, grumbling about Tyler's bit about "Chinese haircut number twenty-two." I wasn't trying to get my co-worker in trouble; I was treating this like a regular bitch session with my boss, whom I was very comfortable with. But I'd forgotten he was also a former law clerk who'd reviewed civil rights cases under Supreme Court Justice Thurgood Marshall.

"What?" Grant asked with obvious anger and concern.

I stopped and turned around, my face hot with alarm that I'd opened a can of worms. "Oh, nothing. It's fine. I just thought it was so moronic."

"That's *not* okay, Sophia. I feel really strongly about that. It's serious and there's no excuse for it. I'll definitely talk to him about *that*."

"Please don't, Grant. I have to work with him, and it's really important *to me* that he feels we can say anything—anything—to each other. I'm sure I've said plenty of inappropriate things to him, too," I said, remembering a few past examples of obnoxious comments I'd thrown Tyler's way. "I need him to see me as one of the guys and not some prissy, thin-skinned girl who will run to the boss when her feelings have been hurt. He won't trust me, then, and that will make things so uncomfortable. Please don't say anything."

Grant's expression was steadfast; the best I could do was getting his promise that he'd limit his comments to Tyler to "that's simply not okay." He studied my face then, and said in a fatherly tone, "I know you were here really late last night, and here again early this morning. You've been working extremely hard and I've never even said thank you. Get done what you can by a decent hour today and then go home, okay?"

I LAY IN bed half-awake noticing the rapid beating of my heart. *Get up, Sophia. Get up.* Although my mind was doing its best to send alert signals through my body, the messages were clouded and too weak to move any of my limbs. I wasn't aware that my blood glucose levels had dropped to a perilous low; I only knew I needed help. *Get up, Sophia. Get up.* Looking as though I'd had too much to drink, I stumbled to my desk and plopped down in my chair. I strained to clear my foggy head but felt nothing except confusion. The only comprehensible thought I had was *Audrey. Help. Audrey.* I pressed the first speed dial number on my phone; when Audrey's voice came over the speaker I tried to say something, but only nonsensical words came shouting out from between my lips. In a panic and no longer able to hear her on the speaker, I picked up the telephone receiver, held it to my ear, and continued to shout—louder and louder.

The next thing I knew, I was seated on the floor, fighting the sugary gel that was being forced down my throat. Minutes passed before I could articulate any words, but I could hear Dad calling my name. Although my eyes were closed, I knew he was holding me upright; it was unclear how much time had gone by before I realized it was Mom squeezing the glucose into my mouth. Slowly, the fog cleared.

"I'm going to throw up if you keep feeding me that stuff," I mumbled to my mom with my mouth full of gel and my eyes still closed. She told me to be quiet. Then she put the gel down before sticking a straw in my mouth and using it to feed me orange juice.

"I'm going to throw up, Mom," I said as I swallowed, unsure of why I could hear Audrey's voice shouting through the telephone receiver that dangled off the edge of my desk.

Mom ignored me.

"Mom, I'm going to throw up," I said more loudly, feeling nauseous from the sudden spike in my blood sugar level.

I opened my eyes and vomited all over my mother, then smiled smugly.

"I told you I was going to throw up!"

THE TO-DO LIST for Red Bean Wireless's IPO was ten pages long, and I was just beginning to dive into it when the telephone rang. "Hello, Mei-Mei. Sweetheart, did you get your blood tests taken this month?" Mom asked over the phone. I glanced at the calendar and realized it was June 25 (i.e., late June—i.e., *shit*). For as long as I could remember, I followed my doctors' orders and had blood samples drawn at the *beginning* of each month so we could catch early warning signs of any diabetic side effects. The last time I remembered being stuck in the veins like that was . . . March? *Bad Sophia!*

I wanted to lie to Mom—to get her off my back—but I didn't. "No, Mom. I haven't gone yet."

She took a deep breath and went from zero to sixty in less than one second. *Oh boy. Here we go.* "What have I always told you? Your health comes first!" she shouted. "Use your *brain*! If you don't have your health, you don't have anything. Daddy and I aren't going to be here forever, you know. You need to learn how to take care of yourself!" She droned on and on, and on, and on. I thought of Penny Jenkins and how men don't hear certain tones in women's voices. *I wonder if I could develop that talent.* I pressed the Mute button and continued typing on my keyboard. *Let her get it all out.* When it was time for me to leave for my meeting, I did what I knew would shut her up for now—an apology.

"Okay, Mom. I'm sorry. I'll go there today."

But I didn't. I just kept working. I knew I needed to go home to shower and change clothes before the next day, though, so I stayed at the office until I was certain my parents would be asleep, then snuck in. And back out to the office.

The next day, I was seated at my desk reviewing a document when Grant appeared in my doorway. I looked up but remained hunched over the papers.

"What do you want?" I snapped, wearing a huge smile. It always entertained me to pretend *he* was working for me; Grant thought it was funny, too.

He laughed at our never-old joke and said, "Nice pants. Going to the derby?" I looked down at my loud blue-gingham pants and tried to think of a clever comeback, but before I could, Grant continued, "Your father came to see me about you."

This was one of those times that the Daddy's-girl role didn't suit me. I put down the pen, sat up straight, and chuckled nervously. "Uh-huh. And what did he say?"

"That man is scary."

I laughed. "No, he's not. Come on."

"I'm not kidding. There's something about him that is intimidating. In fact, I'm afraid of him."

"Don't worry about it. He's a total pushover."

"I'm serious. He's scary. And he's all business. He said I'm working you too hard and that you have something personal to take care of."

"But—"

"But nothing. For God's sake, get your blood tests done! I don't want to see your dad in here again," Grant said. Then, as he turned to go back to his office, he shouted, "Unless he's bringing us business!"

I sat at my desk, frozen by my embarrassment. *How could Dad barge into my work and embarrass me like this? I'll deal with him later.* I dialed Daniel's number to tell him what had happened, but his comments were less than supportive.

"Why *do* you work so much? We never even get to see each other anymore," he complained.

Way to turn this into something about you, Daniel.

"Because people are depending on me," I replied, defensive. "We're *all* working hard."

"Well, you can't keep this up. You won't last. *We* won't last."

His comment took me by surprise. *Is he thinking of breaking up with me?* I changed the subject then, and asked Daniel how his day was going. He had just started a full-time job at the environmental consulting firm he had interned at last summer and was in the midst of moving to an apartment in downtown San Francisco. There was too much happening already for me to engage in any fight, and besides, it wasn't the time for drama. Later, though, when the emails and phone calls had slowed and my Do Not Disturb sign hung from my closed door, I thought about what Daniel had said and wondered whether I really would need to choose between my career and my relationship. *My career.* A few years ago, those words would have seemed ridiculous coming out of my mouth, but now they elicited a sense of satisfaction and pride that surprised me.

If Daniel truly loved me, he wouldn't make me choose.

WHEN A PRIVATE company starts the IPO process, its employees and shareholders imagine the value of their shares soaring; excitement over the millions of dollars that they will collect fills their hearts and faces. That is, until they learn they have to sign a "lock-up"—an agreement that they won't sell a single share for six months after their precious IPO begins trading. The stakeholders' grand illusions fade . . . because everyone knows anything can happen in six months.

Although it was only quarter to two, the glow of the early August morning looked as though the sun were already trying to make its appearance. I quietly closed the door to our house and headed to work, feeling completely exhausted and alone driving through the empty streets of Silicon Valley. But as soon as I turned into Sterling, Rich's parking lot and saw all the lights turned on, my loneliness disappeared. I knew it was business as usual at the firm—meetings were going on and lawyers were hunched over their desks. *Ah, the place that never sleeps.*

The glass doors felt particularly heavy at this oh-dark hour, and I walked through them cursing the person responsible for my late-early day. His name was Ciaran Hayes and he was the trustee of Red Bean's largest shareholder, Peekamoose Family Trust. Mr. Hayes was based in the Isle of Man, a tax haven in the middle of the Irish Sea, and he was ignoring me. *Doesn't he know who I am?!*

I passed the very full VIP conference room at the top of the stairs and slowed my pace so I could rubberneck as I passed by. *Which Silicon Valley hotshot is here now?* Confident I wasn't in the semi-presence of anyone special, I headed down the familiar hallway to my office, where I turned my attention to the first task at hand: hunting down rogue lock-up agreements.

Seated at my desk, I rolled up the sleeves of my white button-down shirt, took off my sensible black ballet flats, and prepared for battle. *Come to me, Mr. Ciaran Hayes!* I put the phone on speaker mode so I could free up my hands to attack the stack of letters and packages that had piled up. As junk mail flew into the recycling bin, a pleasant voice with an English accent said, "Good morning, office of Ciaran Hayes. This is Lorraine. How may I help you?"

Her accent disarmed me and I turned on my friendliest tone. "Good morning. This is Sophia Young and I'm calling from Sterling, Rich in San Francisco. May I please speak to Ciaran?"

"I'm so sorry, but he's in a meeting right now." I quickly analyzed Lorraine's voice to determine how I might get past her. She seemed professional but genuine, and not part of the Ciaran Hayes conspiracy.

"Oh gosh. No problem. When do you expect him to be finished?"

"I really don't know. But I can take your number and have him ring you back if you like." Then, likely realizing the time, the voice on the other end of the phone continued, "Isn't it quite late in San Francisco?"

Here was my chance to soften Lorraine. "It *is* really late—just past two in the morning, in fact. The only thing keeping me at the office is a signature that I need from Mr. Hayes. I won't be able to leave until I speak to him." To sound tired, I spoke softly and quietly and channeled *pathetic* as best I could.

"Oh my," she said with a tinge of concern. "I will pass him the message immediately and ask him to ring you as soon as he's free."

Two hours and another three calls later, Lorraine had lapped up my finest chitchatting and ass-kissing, so when I dialed for the fourth time, she knew my voice.

"Hiya, Sophia. Sorry, no. He's still in the meeting."

"Is this the *same* meeting he's been in?"

"Yes, I'm afraid it is."

"Do you think he'll be coming out soon?"

"Well, I suppose he'll have to come out at some point to use the loo," she said, chuckling.

"Let's hope he had a bran muffin and coffee this morning," I offered sarcastically.

Lorraine burst out in laughter and I enjoyed the fact that I'd warmed up the secretary. Just then I noticed a scruffy head peeking into my office unapologetically, peering right at me. *Who is this weirdo with the rimless glasses and black T-shirt? And how long has he been standing there?* I looked him over uneasily and assumed he was with the late-working group in the VIP conference room. He must be on his way to the bathroom.

I pointed toward the men's bathroom and waved the stranger away. When he didn't leave, I got up to shut my door in his face, but he insisted, "Come talk to me when you're done." Even after I closed the door on him, I could still see the outline of his body through the door's frosted glass.

The sound of Lorraine whispering into the speakerphone brought my attention back to my phone call in progress. "Listen, Sophia. I'll go get him. I'll just tell him I forgot to ask who was on the line."

Score!

Less than a minute later, a male voice came over the phone. "This is Ciaran Hayes." He sounded like someone who got paid a lot for doing whatever his rich clients told him. A yes-man.

I turned on my friendliest *I'm just doing my job* voice. "Mr. Hayes. This is Sophia Young calling from Sterling, Rich. I know you're extremely busy, but I was wondering when I might get the signed Red Bean lock-up agreement returned from you."

Clearly annoyed, Ciaran responded, "I have no idea what you're talking about."

You goddamn liar.

I hid my impatience. "Oh dear. That's my fault and I am so sorry. But would it be all right for me to email it to you *right now*?" I asked, bringing up the soft copy on my computer screen.

"Our email is down, I'm sorry."

"Well, I can fax the document to you," I responded, clicking the Print button on my screen.

"Our fax machine is broken."

That was it. Mr. Hayes had pushed me over the edge. I came out with guns blazing and in full Penny Jenkins mode. "I'd have to be stupid to believe there is no way to get you a two-page document in this day and age, don't you think?"

"Ummm . . ."

"So are you calling me stupid?"

"I, uh . . ."

"Well? Do you really think I'm stupid?"

"Of course not," Ciaran said.

"Okay, then. We both know you're just trying to avoid signing this, and believe me, I understand. I wish we could just forget this whole thing. I really do. But the investment bankers aren't going to let this go, because you—or rather, the trust you manage—are the company's largest shareholder. I'm sure you're a very reasonable person, but the bankers will not take Red Bean public without this document."

Doesn't Ciaran know this? Or does he think he can bamboozle the SEC?

"Well, I'm sorry, Sophia. But I really can't sign the document."

"Why not?"

"That's confidential."

I saw through his ploy to avoid the lock-up. "Okay. Well, Ciaran. The way I see it, you can *not* sign the document, and then *you* explain to your client why his shares are worthless. At least I did everything I could," I said, pausing for dramatic effect. "*Or* you can sign the document, we can get the green light from the bankers, and I can stop harassing you. Trust me, I get no pleasure from it. We're all just trying to live our lives here. That being said, lives are much more enjoyable when there's a roof over our heads."

There was silence on the line. Then, "Okay. Fine. Email the document."

"Thank you! Will you please sign it as soon as you receive it?"

"Yes," he responded, sounding like a broken man.

"Great. And you will email the *signed* document right back to me, with the original to follow by overnight mail?"

"Yes." He sounded annoyed.

"Okay. Thank you very much, Ciaran. You are a true hero."

With a grudging laugh now, he responded, "Good day, Sophia."

Satisfied, I hung up the speakerphone without saying goodbye and opened my door. Minutes had passed, fifteen at least, and the scruffy man was still standing there, peering at me with his eagle eyes.

"I'm sorry. Are you looking for someone?" I needed him out of my way so I could march over to Grant's office and tell him the good news.

"No," the man said. "I heard you talking on the phone." He let an awkward grin cross his face. "Very impressive. You're going to come work for me."

"Oh, I see. Eavesdropping on one phone call and you're sold?" I asked incredulously.

"That's all I ever need."

"Who *are* you?" I demanded.

He looked surprised that I was asking, but not disappointed. Nor did he extend his hand to introduce himself. He just said, "I'm Scott Kraft."

chapter 6

IT WAS NOT THE FIRST time I'd heard his name. He was the genius high school dropout and cofounder of Quince, a maker of revolutionary computers that were known for their simplicity and ease of use. Scott had coined the term *user experience* and redefined the standard for the entire personal computing industry by making technology accessible to the masses. He wasn't just a genius; he was a fixer, solving problems people didn't even know they had yet. I didn't care, though. I just wanted him to get out of my way so I could give Grant the good news about Ciaran Hayes.

As Scott stood there staring at me, I noticed what I hadn't earlier: trademark Levi's, a simple black T-shirt, and Toms organic shoes. He had smudges on his rimless rectangular glasses that made me want to grab them and wipe them clean, but I refrained. Years ago Scott had been publicly humiliated when Quince's board of directors fired him from his own company. At least, those were the rumors. Although I'd heard about him being in a meeting or two with our firm's founder (and my dream crush, yet to even say hello to me), Austin Sterling, Scott had been seen very little in public. I wondered why he was standing here.

"You may not know me, but I'm the CEO of Treehouse. I want you to come work for me." *Treehouse? Never heard of it.*

"You're right," I reminded him. "We don't know each other."

"But I *do* know you," he insisted. "I picked up on your energy from the hallway. You know how to open your valves and vibrate to get exactly what you want." He pushed his glasses up higher on his nose but didn't take his sharp eyes off me for a moment. "You have a holistic way of manipulating people."

What he said sounded halfway between New Age hokiness and a sexual come-on, and I truly had no idea what he was talking about. *Valves? Okay, friend.* I ran through a few possible responses before I decided to be offended. I'd been called manipulative by more than one ex-boyfriend, so that's where my head went first.

"I don't know who you think you are, but you're wrong," I said.

"I'm right. And you know it. I'll talk to Austin Sterling."

"No!" The last thing I wanted was drama in the middle of Red Bean's IPO, or a red flag that I was "manipulating" people, much less clients. Shoot, Austin didn't even know who I was. But then I had another thought: maybe a compliment from Scott Kraft could get me a raise—that is, if "manipulative" was a compliment in this world. "Unless," I added slowly, "you're going to say good things, of course."

Scott started to turn away. "Someone from Treehouse will call you."

"No! Really!" But by now, Scott was halfway down the hall.

"Wait! What's the job?" I asked. Stock administrator, probably. Perhaps even in-house paralegal. Whatever it was, I told myself, I didn't want it.

As he rounded the corner at the end of the hallway, he turned his head to shout back, "Investor relations. We're going public."

I DIDN'T EVEN know what an investor relations person did; all my client communications were directly with CEOs, CFOs, or sometimes in-house general counsels. But Kate certainly knew when she came rushing over later that morning.

"No Neck downstairs said he heard Scott Kraft offering you an IR job last night when he was making his security rounds. Is it true? The rumor is all over the office!"

I leaned back in my desk chair watching her pace as far as she could in my office—two steps back, two steps forward. She seemed very excited.

"It was actually really early this morning. But it doesn't matter. I like where I am," I said.

"Well, then, you're stupid." This adjective was usually applied to me by my family members, not by Kate. When coming from Mom, Dad, or Audrey, *stupid* was something I ignored, but now I was actually listening. "I mean, think about it: you work like a dog, and if you count the number of hours you're here every day, you're getting paid well below minimum wage. I want more for you than senior paralegal, Sophia. Who gives a shit about a senior paralegal?"

I had to admit that this was not a mystery. The answer was a resounding *no one*. Kate was right, and when I called Audrey, she said something similar. But I wanted *someone* to see my point of view— someone to tell me I wasn't crazy. I called Daniel and launched into the story of Scott's offer, leaving out Kate and Audrey's opinions and my commentary on Scott's smudgy glasses. Daniel didn't care about those kinds of details.

"You're kidding me. You're really debating this?" he said. I could hear a hint of jealousy in his voice. "You've got to do it. It's the chance of a lifetime."

"But I'm scared."

"Babe, don't be scared. You'll do great."

"What if they fire me because they don't like me? I've got a good gig going here! And what about Grant? I couldn't leave him."

Laughing, Daniel said, "They won't fire you. Just scope it out. You don't have to decide right now. And we should talk about why you were at work at that hour of the morning." That was three for three on the yeses. Daniel, Audrey, and Kate seemed to think I was sitting on a gold mine.

After fretting for another two-tenths of an hour, I determined not to focus on Scott or Treehouse anymore; I had work to do for Grant and that's all I knew for sure. Anyway, Scott might have just been sleep deprived, drunk, or crazy—it *was* four o'clock in the morning when we spoke. Maybe he would forget about the whole thing.

THREE DAYS LATER, I walked up to my office door to find a Post-it note stuck there waiting for me.

> Please come see me.
> —Austin

I swallowed hard and a knot formed in my stomach. *Shit! They're going to fire me.* I felt like a dead man walking from my office to the firm's middle wing, where Austin held court. I hoped to get a glance of Kate so she could give me some reassuring thoughts, but her office was empty, and Sterling's—across the hall and one door down—was not. His assistant saw me and waved me straight in. *Gulp.*

"I understand you met Scott Kraft the other night," Austin said with a serious look on his face (not that I'd ever seen him have any other look). He was sitting at a simple contemporary desk of tan-colored granite with distressed dark wooden legs. Two tastefully matching vertical silk screens hung on the wall; they complimented the desk and added a je ne sais quoi to the room. A forest-green velvet couch ran along the wall whose windows overlooked Page Mill Road. Perfect. Stylish, but serious.

I had idolized everything about Austin Sterling since I'd arrived at the firm nearly two years ago. His distinguished appearance, complete with perpetual tan, was only part of it. Austin was mysteriously quiet, and his presence was commanding. He dressed almost exclusively in Ralph Lauren Black Label, and not infrequently I'd see his picture in the pages of *San Francisco Magazine*'s About Town section. Unfortunately, he was rarely without his breast-implanted socialite wife, whose puckered mouth always looked as if she had just inhaled a mouthful of lemon juice.

We were in the same meeting once. It was an extremely complicated transaction whose negotiations weren't going well, even for Grant, so Austin had to get involved. When he walked into the room, it was as though all the air was sucked out, and you could almost hear the gasp from the opposing counsel. I remembered biting my top lip to stop myself from smiling at their frightened faces.

That's right. The big guns are here now.

I fumbled to answer Austin's question. "Yes, I met Scott Kraft last night. He seemed pretty ordinary to me, ordinary in a ridiculous sort of way. I'd never want to work for that man."

"I see. That's a very interesting perspective," Austin replied politely. "He was impressed with you, Sophia. Apparently he found you quite capable of navigating around roadblocks and convincing people to do things they don't want to do."

"Ha! Well in that case, how about I convince you I should get a raise?" The compliments from Austin sailed over my head—I was nervous, the perpetual invitation for my stupid wisecracking self to appear.

But Austin only gave me a courteous laugh, then returned to being serious. "He wants you to work for Treehouse. You see, confidentially, we were drafting his company's S-1 registration statement last night. That's why he was here." Austin was referring to the several-hundred-page document full of legalese that outlined a company's basic business, financial history, and all the risks that could impact its operations. It was a required SEC document for any organization wanting to go public, and I was an expert at them, having helped Grant draft so many for the IPOs we'd done. Then Austin continued, "With Scott Kraft's name attached to this S-1, I think it will be a successful transaction."

"I don't know anything about IR, Austin," I murmured. I couldn't imagine leaving the place where I'd grown comfortable. The place where my best friend worked and where I wasn't measured by anything other than how I did my job. Why would I ever leave? For the first time, I was valued and respected. It was hard work here, but it had everything I needed.

Just then, Grant walked in and joked, "Getting into trouble again, Sophia? Austin told me he was planning on talking to you today."

Phew. Grant is here to save me.

"I'm not taking the job," I said, looking straight at Grant, worried he might be angry.

"Are you fucking crazy?"

I was confused. He *wanted* me to go? But why? Shouldn't he fight for me or offer me more money so I would stay . . . or *something*?

"What?" I asked. "But you need me. We have all this stuff to do." I began to pace the length of Austin's office, my mind racing with alternatives. Anything but leaving. "If it's a 'save face' thing, I can go for a little while as a consultant and pretend to test it out."

Austin broke in. "Again, very interesting."

I took that as a sign of encouragement and looked at Grant. "How about that, Grant?"

"He's not *agreeing* with you, you moron. When someone says, 'Oh, that's interesting,' that means you're a fucking idiot!"

"Oh." I turned slowly to Austin, reddening with the realization that he'd used the phrase more than once.

More calmly, Grant continued, "Take the job, Sophia. Scott Kraft is a big deal. This will change your life. Besides, he's one of our biggest clients, and if he wants you to go work for him . . . well, we'd encourage you to go."

I looked at Austin, then at Grant. Then at Austin again. *Who's the decision maker here?*

"Are you firing me?" I asked in a panic.

Austin got up from his desk and walked slowly toward me. When he stood just inches from my face, he said in a proud, fatherly tone, "We'll be very sad to see you go." That was his polite way of answering, "Yes."

Someone else will be in your chair before the seat is cold.

I couldn't bear the thought of being fired again.

"When do I start?" I asked in a defeated tone. I may have been confident, even overly confident, with my peers and with Grant, but standing there in front of Austin Sterling made me timorous.

"Not until early September, so we have plenty of time for you to finish Red Bean and transition the rest of your clients to another paralegal."

And with that, the decision was made. I was pimped out to one of Sterling, Rich's most important clients.

AS THE LEAVES outside started to turn from green to orange, red, and brown, I began tying up loose ends at Sterling, Rich and dreading losing the comfort and safety of my second home. With everything handed off earlier than expected, I spent my last week at the law firm reading the S-1 that Austin had given me. Treehouse was a "new media company" that promised a whole new form of family entertainment; the movie it was about to release was one *I'd* even seen trailers for. It was an animated film called *Treasures,* a story of a grown man's valuable toy collection that comes to life when humans aren't around. I, probably along with every other moviegoing know-nothing, had assumed *Treasures* was a Samba production, since Samba was the eight-hundred-pound gorilla of the animated movie industry. And of theme parks. I tried to think of another company that had succeeded in that niche or even come close to Samba, but I couldn't. Interestingly, Samba and Treehouse were in bed together; they had a formal agreement that required Samba to market and distribute Treehouse films, although the gorilla had creative control. There were also complicated financial royalty and expense schedules that were part of the Samba agreement but not specifically detailed in the S-1.

THE AIRPLANE LANDED at SFO the night before I was to begin my adventure at Treehouse. Daniel and I were freshly tanned from a Labor Day getaway to Kona, Hawaii, and went straight from the airport to meet Mark and Kate for dinner. Over the course of the evening, Kate and I gossiped about our law firm peers, made catty comments about other people in the restaurant, and talked about Kate's hatred of the LSAT exam that she was studying for. We all but ignored the two guys and their conversation about who would make the World Series and their crushing performance in fantasy football.

"What did the Treehouse CFO say when you spoke to him?" Kate asked.

"We didn't talk for long, but he sounds really cool. It sounds like some of what I'll be doing is similar to the stuff I did for Grant, since they're going public. But after the IPO I'll be responsible for the Wall Street communications."

After a game of four-person credit card roulette (which I lost), Kate asked, "Are you excited about it?"

"I'm getting there," I said as I swirled the ice cubes in my drink. "Animated movies are fun, right? At least more than the paper pushing we've been doing at Sterling, Rich."

"Oh, come on, you love it!" Kate said.

She was right.

I looked away dramatically as though I were acting out a Shakespearean play. "I know, I know. I do. Don't—"

"—listen to me!" Kate said, finishing my sentence. We giggled while I paid the check, and then it was time to leave. I loved that we knew each other so well, and I held on desperately to the hope that our friendship would always, always be just like this.

Daniel drove me home, and when we pulled into the driveway, he asked, "What are you thinking about? You're so quiet."

I turned my head toward him and responded, with a contented grin, "I just love the four of us. I never want any of it to change."

IN THE BLEAK morning light, a September drizzle coated the East Bay in a thin film of blah, which matched the feeling in my stomach. It was my first day at Treehouse, and as I drove up to the tan-colored single-story office, the sight was anything but inspiring. The building was shaped like a blocky U, and at 8:45 A.M., the parking lot was nearly empty. There was no need to circle for a parking spot and no buzz of gardeners tending to the lush landscape like they did every morning at Sterling, Rich. No crisp-suited men making haste toward the building entrance. No gilded sign over the lobby.

Inside, behind an unimpressive desk in an even less impressive entrance bay, the Hawaiian-shirt- and lei-wearing receptionist was disarmingly cheery. His name was A.J., and he looked like a huge teddy bear of a cartoon character. *I guess I'm not in Kansas anymore.*

"You must be Sophia," A.J. said. "Weeeeeelcome to Treehouse!" I recognized his unmistakable voice as the one on the company's automated telephone system. He sounded like a ringmaster announcing the circus acts of "Press 1 for Directions!" and "Press 2 for a Company Directory!" He probably had a caffeine drip somewhere.

"Yes, how did you know?" I asked, gently putting down the box of office items and mementos I'd brought from Sterling, Rich to scratch my neck. *Damn wool sweaters!* I was wearing a cabernet-colored twinset with a matching pleated plaid miniskirt. Thanks to my mom, I looked as though I'd stepped straight out of a J.Crew catalogue.

"We don't get many visitors. And Ashley keeps running over here asking whether you've arrived yet or not. God, I hope you do better than the last six people who tried to do this IR job," A.J. said.

I must have looked confused, because he added confidingly, "Ashley is Scott's assistant."

But I wasn't confused. I was stuck on "the last six people." My palms began to sweat.

Suddenly, I heard a crisp, snappy voice coming from behind me. "Sophia! It's a crazy morning, but I am so happy you're here." I turned around to see the voice's owner walking toward me. Petite and in her early forties, Ashley looked like a Japanese anime character: thick brown pixie-cut hair, enormous brown eyes, and impossibly long lashes. She looked hip yet professional in her blue fitted blazer and matching tapered pants, even with the telephone headset wrapped around her ears. The black patent platform lace-up loafers she wore made her a few inches taller than me, causing me to stand up as straight as I could. Ashley wore round, John Lennon–style glasses. She peered at me through the frames, evaluating but friendly.

"Scott won't be in today, but that's good because we'll need to get you set up," she said in a professional tone as she led me through a door on the left side of the lobby, rattling off my first day's agenda. I had never heard anyone talk that fast; had she not been enunciating every consonant and vowel so clearly, I wouldn't have understood her. Her brisk pace kept up with her mouth, as though she were an Olympic speed walker racing for a gold medal. Ashley held her key card up to a security sensor and the door unlocked with a *click*. On the other side, I suddenly stopped; I couldn't see a thing.

"Your eyes need to adjust, but just keep walking. There's nothing to run into," Ashley said.

I blinked several times and then walked gingerly ahead. A long hallway dimly lit with fairy lights came into view; the caverns of the open doors of the screening rooms on either side were mysterious and dark. I could tell from the distant sound of Ashley's voice that she'd walked quite a bit farther ahead. Holding my box tightly, I shuffled toward her words' staccato rhythm. Finally, after about twenty steps, I felt the hallway walls open up into a large room. At least fifty cubicles snaked through the space, and as my eyes adjusted, I gasped in delight at how each one was painstakingly decorated. Treasure troves of paraphernalia—from small plastic toy figures to human-size Tyrannosaurus rexes, movie posters to monster masks— were draped, stacked, pinned, or somehow mounted in ways that surrounded each cubicle owner with their own form of inspiration. At first I thought perhaps it was all set up for Halloween, but that wasn't for another month and the cubes were too intricately detailed to be temporary. Water and food dishes for dogs were everywhere. *Oh, there are dogs here!* There was even one plywood shack complete with a crooked, hand-carved sign that read GONE FISHING. The whole structure had been built around the existing cubicle like a rickety disguise. I felt like I was inside an amusement park.

The large dream-like room was lit by more fairy lights, but brighter: small, twinkling pods that had been strung above each row of cubicles, patterned like waves on a moonlit night. On the walls hung colorful storyboards outlining the story of *Treasures*. I was so entranced by this wonderland that I lost track of Ashley.

As I spun around looking for any sign of her, she came speeding back toward me from a hallway behind the sea of cubicles. "Oh, sorry. I forgot—a tour. This crazy area is where our creative team sits. Can't you tell? Pretty cool, isn't it?" *It's certainly different.* Ashley took me by the elbow and led me to the other end of the wonderland. We walked through a heavy metal door into a curved hallway and passed a modest kitchen area before landing on the other side of the U.

"This," Ashley explained, "is the noncreative side." She then pointed to the closest office and continued, "Our CTO, Matteo, is here." I peeked inside the office and noticed its walls were covered with framed posters of Italian motorcycles. "And our CFO, Jonathan, is there. You spoke with him already, didn't you?"

I nodded.

"Good. He's a great guy. You'll enjoy reporting to him," Ashley said. Then, turning her attention back to the tour, she pointed to the offices again and said, "You sit there next to Jonathan. I'm across from you there, and Scott is across from Jonathan, right there. The rest of the offices and desks at that end are accounting and human resources." The rooms all looked the same: tiny, dreary, and dated. They had flimsy doors and sliding windows that, instead of facing outward, faced inward toward the hall. I felt as though I'd left the amusement park and was now inside a boring low- or no-tech company. It couldn't have been more different from the cubicles in creative. Fluorescent lights glowed on the low ceilings; ugly, textured, dull wallpaper covered the lifeless walls. The drab carpet looked like it had been trodden by hundreds of sad, overworked feet. I wanted to go back to the fairy cubicles, but no such luck.

"Who sits in that 'Gone Fishing' shack?" I asked.

"That's Dylan, our chief creative officer," Ashley responded before changing the subject entirely. "Where do you live? Just wondering how far you have to commute."

"In Woodside."

"Oh, I'm in Woodside! My husband and I live in a little cottage way up in the hills. Which street are you on?"

"We live on Fernside," I said, wondering if maybe someday Ashley and I would be carpool buddies.

"Fernside . . . Fernside . . . wait, do you live near that modern white house on the hill that you can see from virtually everywhere? I love that house," she said.

My face turned hot. "Um, it's my parents', actually, and I live at home with them."

"Really? You're joking. We saw that place in *Architectural Digest* a while back. That's amazing. You're so lucky!"

Hearing Ashley gush about my house made me proud of my immigrant parents and my dad's vision of our family home. It didn't seem to faze her that I, a grown woman, still lived with my parents. *Maybe it's not so uncool after all.*

Ashley parked me in a lonely, plain office that had a metal chair with worn-down puke-green upholstery and a seventies-looking desk with three metal drawers and a honeycomb-colored acrylic enamel top. I noted the absence of a Quince device; fortunately for me, in its place was the desktop I was accustomed to. Next to it, I recognized a copy of the thick legal-size document that was Treehouse's S-1.

I felt like a new kid at school, and was beginning to get homesick when suddenly my cell phone rang: Mom. Of course. I knew I'd face her wrath if I didn't pick up, so I pushed the Answer button surreptitiously and timidly said to Ashley, "I'm so sorry, but it's my mom. Do you mind if I take this really quickly? I just like to be sure nothing is wrong. Will you be in your office?"

"Sure, no problem. We're finished anyway. Get settled and check in with Jonathan when you're ready. He should be here soon."

I nodded and turned my attention to my mom, who was shouting into the phone.

"Hello, Mother," I said in an annoyed tone, but I was secretly happy to hear her familiar voice.

"Sophia? Is that you?"

"Yes," I answered impatiently. After all, *she* was the one who had called *me*.

"They left a notice on our front door," she said, sounding exasperated.

"Who is 'they,' Mom?"

"I don't know. There's a notice on our door. It's white and purple."

"Mom, that's FedEx. See on the front? It says, 'FedEx,'" I said, trying to keep my temper in check.

"Oh. Well, I don't know what it is, but what should I do?"

"Just sign the back of it—there's a long square where you sign. Then just hang it back on the door and they'll leave the package." Silence. "Mom? Do you see the long square on the back?"

"What long square? How can a square be long? I don't see it. Can you just come home and take care of this?"

Oh so high maintenance. I could be the president of the United States and it wouldn't matter. I'd be getting this very same call.

I responded with an incredulous chuckle because I'd learned long ago that when it came to my mother, I had to laugh or I'd cry. "No, Mom! I can't. I just started my job. Where's Dad?"

"He just left for that conference in Chicago. Well, I'll just leave this here and you do it when you get home."

"No, Mom! It's really easy. Please just sign the back of the slip and hang it on the door," I pleaded. When I'd left the house this morn-ing I'd lied and told her I would be staying at Kate's house tonight, "since it's closer to work." The truth was, I planned to spend the next night or two at Daniel's in San Francisco and I didn't want to ruin our plans by having to haul my ass all the way to my parents' for this ridiculous task that my mom could very well take care of herself.

"No, I don't know how. Please just help your mother."

"Don't you want me to save the commute time and get an extra few hours of sleep?"

"Oh, fine," she said as I sighed with relief. "I'll just leave it here and your father can deal with it when he gets home later this week."

"But Mom, they'll only try to deliver it two more times and then you'll have to drive down to FedEx and get it yourself."

Upon hearing this, she began to stress out, which then caused her temper to rise. "Well, I don't know what you want me to do! Why do you guys order this online stuff anyway? Neither of my daughters were raised right. My friend Helen's kids are always helping their parents." Before she could digress into a ten-year lecture about how she hated when we ordered things online, causing total strangers to appear at our door, or how she guessed she just wasn't important enough, I interrupted, "Okay, Mom. I'll come straight home after work."

Click. She hung up. Typical of my mother—and to be honest, not totally unlike Grant, either. I seemed to attract these types: no *thank you* or *goodbye*. I shook my head, knowing Mom was mad. *I wonder if I'll have to deal with her later.*

I stood in my office, motionless and overwhelmed, unsure of what to do (other than be frustrated with my mom). I texted Daniel: Classic Mom story. Can't wait to tell you, but I won't be able to come over tonight. Then, remembering what I did at the law firm when I felt like my wheels were spinning, I thought about my time in six-minute increments and began to unpack my things. At the top of the cardboard box was the framed menu from my going-away party at Sterling, Rich. I picked it up and read, then reread, all of the *goodbye* and *we'll miss you* messages my coworkers had written me, making me miss the place where I'd gained my professional sea legs. I placed the frame on my desk, unsure whether I wanted to cry or smile at the Sterling, Rich memories that raced through my head.

MY NEW BOSS, Jonathan, had an accent I couldn't place when I'd spoken to him on the phone: an odd combination of New York and London that gave him a very professional, no-nonsense air. But he looked nothing like I'd expected when I appeared at his office door later that morning.

"Hi! You must be Sophia," he said, standing up from his chair and giving me a big bear hug that immediately felt natural and comfortable. Jonathan had thick, wavy dark hair, and his large brown eyes and wide grin reminded me of the *Sesame Street* character Ernie. He was slender, just shy of six feet tall, and bizarrely dressed in a wizard costume. Nothing about him suggested he was *the* Jonathan Larsen, star CFO whom Scott had recruited away from the world's most successful gaming company. Jonathan was both a CPA and a former lawyer at Sterling, Rich. He was no dummy.

He motioned to an ugly chair in front of his desk that had a wizard hat and fake beard on it. "Just throw those on the floor," he said. "Nice to meet you in person. I hope you brought a costume—we're having a Halloween party this afternoon."

"Really? It's September. I didn't come prepared." I felt like a foreigner once again.

"No problem. It *is* indeed September. But as I'm sure you can imagine, Halloween is one of the company's favorite holidays and we're really kicking into crunch time with the movie, so we wanted to celebrate now just in case there isn't time next month. You'll get a laugh out of it—there's a costume contest with prizes. I just saw one of the animators on my way in and he's dressed like—like a newborn baby. Completely buck naked except for a homemade diaper and a light blue knit beanie on his head." Jonathan laughed, but it wasn't until later that I realized why. Naked-baby guy was about six foot four with a full-grown beard.

Wanting to make a good impression, I dove right into my comfort zone: business. "I read the first draft of the S-1, and when we spoke you said you expect the IPO to be just after Thanksgiving?"

"That's right. Since Thanksgiving kicks off one of the most important movie seasons of the year, our plan is to release *Treasures* just before the holiday in order to get our name out there before the roadshow the following week. We'll have to file a few amendments before then, but we should be ready to go in less than twelve weeks. Speaking of which, I think the best way for you to learn is to join us on the trip." Jonathan stopped talking and turned his chin up as though listening for something. It sounded like an old, loud air-conditioning unit, or maybe a helicopter. "Scott is here," he said to himself, then continued. "Anyway, the roadshow. Scott and I will be telling the story over and over, so it will be good for you to listen in to the Treehouse messaging and hear all the questions from the investors. After that, you'll be the one telling our story and building relationships with the investors and analysts. Scott has great confidence that you'll do well at that."

I didn't hear what Jonathan said for the next few minutes because I was too excited about the fact that I was actually going on the roadshow. *Who cares that I don't know anything about IR?* Flying to fourteen cities in ten days and staying in fancy hotels sounded thrilling! A man's shouting voice brought my attention back to Jonathan's office, though.

"ASHLEY! WHAT IS THAT SMELL IN MY OFFICE?"

I looked at Jonathan. He raised his eyebrows and cracked a sinister smile.

From down the hall, Ashley's calm voice could be heard meeting the assault. "They sprayed for ants today, Scott."

"*What?!* You sprayed those chemicals in *my* office? Why on earth would you do that?"

Jonathan got up and shut his door. He wasn't the only one. I looked out his open interior window; other office doors were shuffling closed, copy machines were stopping, people from accounting and human resources were scurrying toward the kitchen. A flood was coming, and the animals were fleeing for the ark.

"Well, Scott. You have an ant problem. I know you know this because you complain about it all the time. So unless you want ants crawling all over your keyboard, we decided to spray your office on a day that you're not here. Which brings me to the question of why you're here," she asked.

There was a long silence. Then, "FUCK! YOU'RE GOING TO KILL ME WITH THAT SHIT!"

"Again, why are you here? I called you an hour ago and you confirmed you were not coming in."

More quietly now, but I could still hear him through the open window, he said to Ashley, "Christine kicked me out of the house. It was her opinion that I was driving her crazy, so I took the helicopter up."

"Uh-huh. Well, that's not my fault."

I pulled my head back from Jonathan's window. I didn't want to be spotted, or hit with some unpleasant verbal debris.

"FUCK," Scott said. With that, he stormed back out toward the kitchen.

I felt remarkably calm and almost wanted to laugh. It was familiar in a way, like a yelling match I might have with my mother. I knew I would like this Scott Kraft guy.

Suddenly, Scott's voice was back. "Is the new girl here?"

"Sophia," Ashley responded, reminding him that I actually had a name. "She's with Jonathan."

I braced myself and glanced at Jonathan for guidance, but he was busy rolling his chair to the farthest corner of his office just as the flimsy door flew open, almost sailing off its hinges.

chapter 7

"NEW GIRL. WHAT ARE YOU doing?" Scott stood right in front of me, looking me over from head to toe. Once again, his glasses could have used a polish. It seemed safe to assume that unlike Jonathan, he wasn't about to give me a big, welcoming bear hug.

Jonathan interjected, "We were just talking about the roadshow. I thought she should come with us."

Scott didn't say a word. He just nodded.

Then, he began speaking to Jonathan as though I weren't in the room, which didn't matter to me since I had no idea what they were talking about anyway. The two men discussed sliding scales for merchandising receipts and whether someone would be paying someone else royalties, and how Treehouse's commercials division should receive revenue for licensing its proprietary animation-rendering software to Samba. Just when I thought my brain might explode over their ongoing conversation, a jovial-looking man entered the room, whom Jonathan introduced as the chief creative officer, Dylan. *So this is the cubicle-shack dweller.* He had a round face with rosy cheeks, and wore loud, radically colored patterned shorts with a gray T-shirt that read GENIUS AT WORK. He was also wearing a red cape and superhero boots that I assumed were part of his Halloween costume. *At least I hope they are.*

"Sorry to interrupt, but there's an issue. We previewed the recent cut of *Treasures* to Samba last night and they want us to make serious revisions."

"What do you mean? Which part?" Scott asked.

"The *entire movie*!" replied Dylan. "They said it's not going to work the way it is. But if we do what they're asking, we'll never make the Thanksgiving release."

The four of us were squeezed inside Jonathan's small office, but somehow Scott managed to take a step closer to Dylan. "No. We can't delay the release. How did this happen? We've been showing them our progress since the beginning and they've given their feedback the entire way through."

"Yes. But as you know, we didn't incorporate all of those ideas. Sure, some of them were good and we used those. But not all," Dylan explained. "My concern here is that, ultimately, they have to give their final sign-off before we can release."

Scott stuck his chin out. "The fuck they do."

"You know they do."

There was a long, intense silence in the room while Dylan, Jonathan, and I watched Scott pace back and forth, at least as far as he could inside the office's confines. I listened carefully as my brain did its best to decipher what was going on. It was one of the things my parents had brainwashed into Audrey and me: "Listen, don't talk. You'll learn more."

"What do *you* think, Dylan? Does it work the way it is?" Scott asked.

Dylan dropped his head slightly and brought his fist to his lips. *A man in serious thought.* Not a minute later, he flipped his head up and said, "It works. It does. It's great and I'm really proud of it."

"Then keep going."

"But . . ."

"Just go."

Dylan looked at Jonathan and Jonathan looked at Scott. The CCO's tone was serious. "What about the Samba agreement?"

"Let me worry about Samba. I don't care what you have to do. Just get that movie out for Thanksgiving."

Dylan had an idea. "So hold off on the IPO—even just one week. We don't need the cash. Do we?" Dylan asked.

"We do, and we don't. The issue is timing. There's a very small window—the Monday after Thanksgiving through the first week of December—when we are still safe to go out. If we miss it, we run the risk of losing important investors to early holiday vacations or not being able to go at all until spring, when investors are settled into the new year. And who knows if the stock market will be receptive to unprofitable startups like ours by then. If we can go now, we should," Jonathan explained.

I wanted to contribute to this important conversation, to prove my worth on my very first day, but the intensity in the room told me I should keep my mouth shut.

Scott added, "And to answer your question, we *do* need the cash if we're going to grow our team—yours in particular, Dylan—so we can work on movies in parallel. That's critical because we'll only survive for so long making a movie every three years. We've got to narrow the gap between releases. You want to build your digital animation school, Treehouse University? We need money for that. And if we're going to be in any position to renegotiate this fucking Samba deal like I intend, we're going to need a war chest."

Scott took off his glasses and laser-focused on Dylan. "You finish the movie. I'll talk to Samba," he said before gliding out of the room, then shouting, "Ashley! Get me Samba!"

It seemed to me that Scott had a clear vision of what he wanted and how the Treehouse IPO was all going to go down. I enjoyed seeing *this* side of a business; at Sterling, Rich and Global Partners, my jobs revolved around reacting to wheels already set in motion by conversations like this one. I hadn't thought Scott and I would have *anything* in common. But maybe we did. Maybe that's what he saw in me that night at Sterling, Rich; he called it "manipulating people," but perhaps "persistence" was more accurate. I didn't know how to be any other way, after all. My mom would never have allowed it.

Thanks, Mom.

At the time, I also didn't know how valuable, or rare, this character trait was. Clearly it came in handy at fast-paced startups.

TWO WEEKS LATER, I'd emerged into a routine of sorts that was exhilarating and exhausting at the same time. Each morning, Ashley would ring me at five thirty sharp, just as I'd be standing at our kitchen counter pouring coffee into a commuter mug and getting ready to leave the house. Mom, who arose when I did so she could make me breakfast while I showered, noticed the pattern and began keeping a pen and paper next to our Breville Barista so I could write down the list of people Ashley gave me to call back. At first I found the list *interesting,* to say the least, because there was always some non-IR-related item on it. People asking Scott Kraft for a financial donation, for example. But I soon figured out that there was no one else at Treehouse to answer these random queries, so they were left to me; I'd become a de facto Treehouse and Scott Kraft spokesperson.

The hour-long commute never bothered me; I spent the time returning phone calls and checking them off my call log.

"Yes, I am definitely interested in using your stock surveillance software. Our CTO, Matteo, is reviewing your documentation, and since his team would be responsible for implementing your software, I can't sign your contract until I get his approval." Then, "No, I'm sorry. I can't give you Matteo's contact information." By six thirty, my morning coffee was usually squeezing my small bladder, forcing me to fumble for my keys so I could let myself into Treehouse and run for the bathroom. Unlike Sterling, Rich, the building was always quiet, with just me and Ashley in at this hour; it was the perfect setting for us to get work done. For those first two weeks, I spent the time learning everything there was to know about Treehouse—its financials, its relationship with Samba, and how our business model would work once we released *Treasures*. At seven thirty or so, the receptionist would arrive and turn on the building's overhead lights, cuing me to turn my attention to my email and the eternally blinking red voicemail light on my phone.

There was, of course, a stray predawn call from time to time—when Ashley felt a matter needed immediate attention. The first time it happened, she must have caught me in the midst of deep sleep because I didn't hear the ringing until she called a third time (as she impatiently informed me).

"Hello?" I answered, trying my best to sound awake and alert.

"Listen, the *New York Times* just called for a response to something Scott said while he was out to dinner with his wife. Someone must have overheard him and it's causing a lot of hysteria. Can you handle it, please?"

I'm not sure what "handle" means, but sure. I'll give it a go.

"Okay," I said. Not like there was an option to say no. I rubbed my eyes awake. "What did he say?"

"Oh, you know Scott."

Not really.

"What did he say?"

"He said that if Bill Filac dropped more acid, his products would be more creative."

I sat up, now fully awake and trying not to burst out laughing. Bill was the CEO of Filac Software, Quince's biggest competitor. I didn't have any experience dropping acid myself, but I knew Scott's words were fighting words and I loved good office drama. "What? He did? Oops!"

"I'm sure you'll handle it with grace. We just don't want the *New*

York Times to print it. *Valleywag* already wrote something on their blog last night, but Scott's not worried about that. They're a gossip blog. The *New York Times* is one he *does* care about. For them to publish this quote would be a terrible and distracting headline for us and our IPO."

"Isn't it time we hire a PR person?" I asked. After all, this wasn't just someone asking for a charitable donation. This was the *New York Times*!

"Ha! You'd think. But we haven't. Not yet, anyway. Scott said this is what you're good at," Ashley said.

I am?

"The emails and voicemails have already started to come in—I forwarded those to you. I'd start with the *New York Times* reporter, though. His contact info is in your email."

I flipped back my warm, peach-colored down comforter and rolled off my queen-size bed. Hunched over and dragging myself to the other end of my childhood room, I walked past the two large windows that faced the valley. It was three o'clock in the morning—pitch-dark outside with just the dim glare from the streetlights below. Being awake at that hour made me feel lonely, but I shook it off as soon as it came. *No time for loneliness. Time to work your magic.* I wiggled onto the white upholstered cushion of my polished nickel-finished chair—the one that matched my wall-to-wall white lacquered desk. I turned on the lamp and squinted to shield my eyes from its brightness. My fingers pulled out a Bic from the blue-and-white ceramic pen holder that I made when I was twelve, then reached for the Post-it pad next to the telephone. I dialed into my Treehouse voicemail, but when the first message was from a livid woman calling from Mothers Against Drunk Driving, I hung up. *Can't deal with that now—it's too early.* It wasn't until later that day that I heard the other messages from Alcoholics Anonymous, Al-Anon, and every other antidrug organization out there, all rallying a cry to boycott anything related to Scott Kraft, because they had heard about his acid comment and felt the need to share their opinions about his "lack of morals" and "poor role model" actions. *Rumors travel fast.*

On my BlackBerry was the email that Ashley said she'd sent— the contact information for the *New York Times* reporter who had called for a comment about the *Valleywag* blog post. I opened my ThinkPad, did a quick search on the reporter's most recently published articles—everything from network security breaches to the last-mile connectivity problem. *What the hell is that?* A quick scan of the article explained that the term referred to something about telecommunication companies and their challenges around providing high-speed Internet service to remote geographic areas. *Yawn.* I took a slow, deep breath, the same way I would if I were trying to calm down my quick-tempered mother, then dialed the reporter's number.

"Hi," I said, trying to sound cute and flirty and ditching any voice-coach-of-yore influence that remained. "This is Sophia from Treehouse. I understand you had some questions for Scott? Isn't it a little early for you over there? I hear East Coasters don't get to work until ten A.M.!"

"Well, I don't know about ten o'clock, but we're certainly not early risers in this town," the reporter said. He sounded deflated, dorky, and older, perhaps married with high school–age children. Probably someone who didn't get a lot of attention at home because his wife was too busy carting the kids around.

"That's right. The town that never sleeps, right?"

"The *city* that never sleeps," he said.

I laughed harder than I needed to. "Oh, sorry. English is not my first language."

"Oh, really? What is your first language? You speak English very well."

"Mandarin. I didn't speak English until I was about six years old."

A big exaggeration. More like three.

I crossed my fingers and hoped that this guy was on the Orient Express, or at least had a bit of yellow fever. *This is where being Chinese comes in handy.*

"Oh, really? My wife is Chinese! Were you born there?"

Bingo!

I spent the next few minutes recounting the personal story that always fascinated people: How Dad escaped from China by swimming two and a half miles to Hong Kong with his eight siblings when he was a teenager, and how two of them drowned. Then, after immigrating to Taiwan and graduating from high school there, he snuck onto a cargo ship that was on its way to America. And how he earned his Ph.D. from Stanford. The *oohs* and *aahs* coming from the reporter told me now was a strategically wise time to bring up the rumor. A personal connection had been established.

"Anyway, I'm so sorry I've taken us off the subject. You'd asked about Scott?"

"Oh, right. Yes. I was hoping to speak to him about his comment that Bill Filac should drop acid to make his products more interesting. There's always been a rivalry between them, and, well, we'd like to know if he'd care to comment."

"What? No, I don't think Scott would ever say something like that. He's got young kids. Besides, you and I both know that the rumor of a rivalry between Quince and Mr. Filac's company is more likely something made up by less seasoned reporters than yourself. Both companies serve completely different audiences and markets."

"Well, you're right on that point."

"Look, all boats rise with the tide. So what I know Scott wants to do, and am sure Mr. Filac does as well, is to empower people with technology, don't you agree? But then, there's the issue of the last mile, which is an entirely different problem."

Distract, distract, distract. Might as well use that boring article to my advantage.

"Ha. Isn't that the truth?"

"And that issue isn't up to Scott *or* Mr. Filac. Regardless, Scott has the utmost respect for Mr. Filac. Who wouldn't? It's a huge market and for every Coke, there's always a Pepsi."

God, spending too much time with Jonathan. "All boats rise," "For every Coke there's a Pepsi." Vomit!

"Respect, huh?"

"Well, sure," I said before fake giggling. "Other than *maybe* having some opinions about how uncreative it is to name a company after yourself. I mean, can you blame him? Who does that?"

"People with huge egos. That's who," said Mr. *New York Times* Reporter. "Hmm. So are you saying it's not true—what Scott said?"

"Well, look. It certainly doesn't sound like him—he's vegan, you know. And lives a *really* healthy lifestyle. The guy meditates every morning and has a spiritual yogi and everything. We even now have one at Treehouse. I can't imagine him condoning any sort of illegal drug use. The man won't even take an aspirin," I said, trying to interest him in these other details. *That's called deflecting.*

"Treehouse has its own yogi?"

"Well, not like a full-time employee or anything. Just a spiritual adviser."

"And vegan—what is that? Like vegetarian but only raw food, right?"

"No. Vegetarian but also no dairy—no animal products whatsoever. I mean, he doesn't even eat cheese! I love cheese!" I squealed.

"I do too," he admitted.

"Oh! Well, I hear there's a lovely cheese store in Chelsea—let me take you there the next time I'm in New York!"

"That would be great," he said.

"Great! It's a date! So did I answer your question?" I asked.

"Well, I'd still like to talk to him, but if that's not possible, I'm not comfortable writing anything about the *Valleywag* article. The *New York Times* doesn't print rumors."

"Well, that's just what it is," I said. "Okay, well, here's my cell phone number in case you need anything. Anything at all." I wished him well and hung up. *God, I wish Mom were that easy!* Then, after letting Ashley know I'd taken care of the reporter, I dragged myself back to bed, feeling slightly dirty for being such a flirt but forgetting about it quickly as I drifted back to sleep.

DESPITE ALL THE interruptions, which usually had something to do with "so-and-so calling," I made good progress on completing the last items that needed to be addressed before we left for the roadshow: negotiating "what will we get if we list our stock on *your* exchange" proposals with the Nasdaq or NYSE; working with Jonathan on the "teach-in" for our research analysts, who we hoped would be supportive mouthpieces to Wall Street as soon as we went public; coordinating between Treehouse's finance team and the Sterling, Rich lawyers to provide the financial information they requested so they could update our S-1 filing; and helping Jonathan prepare the investor presentation we would use on the roadshow. I'd had little interaction with Scott since I walked through the Treehouse doors six weeks ago; it seemed as though Jonathan might be shielding me from our fearless leader. *Maybe he's afraid I'll turn into former IR person number seven.* I asked Ashley about the six that came before me. She began by saying rather loudly, "I'm no gossip," then leaned toward me and whispered, "Scott fired them."

"Anything I can learn from?" I asked.

"Well, you're already at an advantage because Scott hired you himself, and I'll bet he's more likely to keep you on just so he doesn't have to say that he was wrong," she said with a laugh.

"Thanks a lot," I mumbled.

"No sense of humor this morning? Fine. The others had been sent by a recruiting company Jonathan hired about six months before you started. Let me think," she said, tucking her short hair behind her ear and tilting her head slightly. "The first one was a longtime IR executive, and on her first day here you could tell she just wasn't going to fit in."

"What do you mean?"

"I think she was just too rigid. She had a process that probably had worked for her in the past, but Scott felt like she was treating this job like a template that had been created and that wasn't what he wanted."

"Can you give me an example?"

"Well, for example, she didn't think there was any point in considering Nasdaq because she swore up and down that the New York Stock Exchange was the better platform. And when Scott pressed her on why, the only thing she said was that she always went with the NYSE. She was out the door by the third day, if I recall correctly."

Ashley went through numbers two, three, four, and five rather quickly before she came to the last one. "Number six was here the longest," she said.

"How long was that?"

"He was here about one week before he had a complete breakdown." Ashley chuckled unsympathetically.

I laughed nervously and changed the subject.

"GOOD MORNING, MATTEO," I said, walking into Treehouse's kitchen to get a glass of water. Our CTO was standing in front of the seven-thousand-dollar Italian espresso machine he'd demanded—the same espresso machine that no one except him could figure out how to use. "Jonathan and I were just saying we should get trained on Shareholder.com soon. Did you review the technical documentation I sent? Is it okay for Jonathan to go ahead and sign the contract?"

"I looked at it," he said, straight-faced. "It's such a simple piece of software. I can't believe you want to use that. I'm going to build you something better."

"I don't need anything better. Besides, a lot of companies use their stock surveillance tool," I said, confident in the research I'd done. "Even Samba uses it, and they're a multibillion-dollar business."

"Ha. Don't just follow what other people are doing, little lady. Think of *new* solutions. I'll build us something in-house."

"How long will *that* take?" I asked, deciding that now wasn't the time for me to take issue with Matteo's "little lady" comment. *I need his help.*

"Eh, a few months."

"I don't have a few months. This has to be done before the IPO. Is this a budget thing? Or is there something you *don't* like about Shareholder.com?"

"Why don't you go back to your IR stuff and let me take care of the technical matters of our company," Matteo said, shooing me away with his hand.

"What I don't understand is why you want to reinvent the wheel. Stock surveillance isn't our business, so I'm handing you a perfectly good solution."

Then I realized what this was probably about. Matteo wanted *credit* for our stock surveillance; he wanted everyone in the company to be aware of his extraordinary talents. But I knew that under no circumstances would Jonathan and Scott agree to let Matteo touch this project; his priority was finishing the technical renderings of the *Treasures* characters. So I told myself to back down. *Let Scott and Jonathan fight this one.*

Matteo was too busy stirring sugar into his espresso to respond to me, so I exited the kitchen—without my water.

Two days later, an email from Jonathan appeared in my inbox.

To: Sophia Young
From: Jonathan Larsen
Subj: Shareholder.com

Scott took care of it. Please schedule us for training this week. I'll assume someone comes here.

I'D BEEN TOLD that Scott didn't like meetings.

"He thinks email is one of the best mediums for sharing status updates and that meetings should be saved for problem solving," Ashley had explained. Which is why I was surprised, and nervous, when the following week, she IM'd me.

Ashley: Scott wants to see you.
Sophia: When? Why?
Ashley: Now.

My hands became a bit clammy. I wasn't sure I was ready for Scott. I had suddenly become afraid of him, although I really didn't know why.

Scott was on a phone call but Ashley waved me through. "He's just finishing up."

I crept into Scott's office carrying my pen and notepad. Unsure of whether to sit or stand, I fidgeted a little before settling on staying right where I was: near the door.

"How much would it be?" Scott said. Then, after the person on the other end of the line finished speaking, Scott asked, "What kind of permits? And how long would it take? Okay. Let me get back to you."

Scott hung up the phone and turned his attention to me.

"Nice haircut," he said.

My right hand shot up to touch my hair and I realized Scott was referring to the three-inch-shorter, flat-ironed A-line bob hairstyle I'd adopted a few days ago.

"Thanks!" I said, surprised that he'd noticed.

"We're going to announce *Treasures'* release date. Can you please write a press release?"

I've never written a press release before, but sure. Why not? How hard can it be? Copy the Samba format.

"Yep, no problem. But doesn't everyone know it's coming out the day before Thanksgiving?"

"Yes. But what they don't know is that this is a Treehouse production. You'll have to do some coordinating with Samba's PR team, but I want you to draft it to emphasize that *Treehouse* is the creative force behind the movie."

"Okay, no problem."

"And a quote from me. Draft it and email it over."

"But won't this be viewed by the SEC as pre-marketing the stock before our IPO?" I wanted to seem important and knowledgeable, but I just ended up stating the obvious.

Jonathan entered the room. "No, it's the same thing as a product announcement. Normal course of business."

Then a light went off in my head. "Oh! Brilliant! You're putting out the release now so you can do a bunch of media interviews just before the IPO! It will build investor momentum just like you said, all under the guise of 'normal course of business.'"

Scott began tugging at the hem of his jeans as though he was pulling up his socks. I could tell he was agitated. He stood up suddenly, sending his chair sliding back on the thinly carpeted floor. "This is the only time I'll explain myself." Scott began to pace. "No one knows our name or who we are. They all assume *Treasures* is a Samba film. We need to start building our own brand, and the sooner Treehouse becomes a household name, the better. I don't want us to be dependent on Samba forever."

"So should I set up interviews for you or something?" I asked.

"I want you to personally email a copy of the release to every journalist, editor, and news desk you can find," Scott said.

I scribbled notes on my legal pad and began listing the news outlets that *I* was familiar with: *People, InStyle, Us Weekly, Enter-*

tainment Tonight, Vanity Fair, Mercury News, the *San Francisco Chronicle,* KTVU News, *USA Today.* Then my pen stopped as it dawned on me how horribly unqualified I was for this job. I was certain Scott didn't mean for me to focus my efforts on *People,* but that's about all I knew! *Fake it till you make it. Say something, stupid.*

"Uh, so should I coordinate with Ashley to find time in your schedule for these interviews?"

Scott turned around to face me. He took a deep breath and then asked, "Are you stupid or fucking stupid?"

I contemplated his question for a moment, smiled, and answered what Audrey had called me many times before. "Fucking stupid."

Jonathan eyed me and tilted his chin down so he could hide his wide grin. Then Scott leaned in close to me as though he wanted to tell me a big secret. "The key is to make them want you. Not to have to spend hours speaking to every fucking reporter out there."

> To: Scott Kraft
> From: Sophia Young
> Subj: Treasures Press Release
>
> Scott,
> Hope you're having a good morning. Per your request, please find attached a draft press release announcing *Treasures.* I've included information about the plot, a list of the voice actors, and the movie's release date, and listed Dylan as the director. I also included an embellished version of the Treehouse company description that was included in the S-1, and added my name as "Contact."
>
> Please let me know if you need anything else.
>
> Thanks and regards,
> Sophia

I hit the Send button and leaned back in my chair. *My first email to Scott Kraft.* It felt exciting and satisfying. I was certain he'd approve.

"WHAT DO YOU mean Scott isn't available for an interview?" It was only the next day, and already an angry reporter named Pat was shouting at me after seeing the press release on the news wires.

I held the handset away from my ear. "I'm sorry, Pat. He's not available."

"Listen to me. You seem new to all this. I am a reporter from the *Wall Street Journal* and I'm telling you, you don't just put a press release over the wire if you're not willing to speak to the press."

"It's just that his schedule is completely booked," I said.

"You can't find TEN FUCKING MINUTES on his calendar?" he screamed.

"Um." I pretended to scan Scott's calendar, which I didn't even have access to. "Nope. Sorry."

"What about when he's driving to the office?" Pat asked.

Ugh, this guy is relentless.

"No, he has a call at that time already." Then, realizing I could try the ol' IPO-quiet-period stunt, I said, "And we're in the quiet period, so there's really very little he can say."

"Don't try that bullshit with me. I know he can talk about this. He just issued a goddamn press release about it!" Pat was screaming again.

I scratched my head. My mobile phone was ringing, the red message light on my voicemail was blinking, and I had to get off the phone. "Pat, I'm really sorry, but he's just not available."

I could hear Pat inhale deeply as though he needed full lungs for the stream of expletives he was about to let rip. I deliberately increased the pitch of my voice so I could sound young and sweet. "Please don't shoot the messenger."

Pat stopped screaming. "I'm sorry. Just call me if you find some time in his schedule. Thanks."

The next three days were filled with a stream of calls, all with the same outcome, including my *New York Times* "friend" from the acid incident. Scott was nowhere to be found, leaving me feeling cornered and battered.

"Where is he?" I asked Ashley.

"At home," she said.

"What is he doing?"

It was after ten o'clock and I wanted to strangle the jackass for making me take the fallout from his strategic press stunt.

"His trainer was late this morning."

"He has a personal trainer every morning? Is that why he doesn't get in until ten o'clock?"

It must suck to be him.

"You didn't hear it from me. Anyway, he waits until traffic has cleared before he hits the road, unless he takes the helicopter," Ashley responded.

My cell phone rang again, reminding me of the chaos that the press release had created. I was totally unprepared and inexperienced, but no one in the company seemed to care. I didn't know what else Scott and Jonathan expected—Samba's marketing engine had been publicizing *Treasures* across every conceivable media and print outlet for weeks, and although studio names are never mentioned in those instances, Samba was the behemoth and the public expected it to be a Samba production. But when people—journalists in this case—realized it was a *Treehouse* production and that Scott Kraft was behind Treehouse, it was as though every Scott fan (and nonfan, quite frankly) wanted to know more. They'd been waiting for years to see his next venture after Quince, and our press release announced that their messiah had reappeared.

My cell phone rang again.

I shouldn't have tried to be so important. Now everyone and their mother has my cell phone number.

"JUST TURN OFF the phone," Daniel said.

"I can't just *turn off* my phone, Daniel," I said. As soon as I saw the hurt look on his face, I regretted my tone. It was past midnight and we were naked in bed and had just had *I haven't seen you in so long* sex, which wasn't as good as *you're so sexy when you're making dinner* sex, but it did the job. I reached for my BlackBerry on the nightstand when suddenly Daniel said, "I feel like I'm just your joystick."

"Huh?"

"I mean, you just come over, climb on, do your thing, snap at me, and then go back to work."

I put down the BlackBerry and giggled. "Oh, Daniel. I'm sorry!"

"It's not funny."

"But it is! You're not my joystick. I'm really sorry. I'm just completely in over my head." I turned to Daniel and tried to kiss him, but he pushed me away.

"Forget it." He stretched for the lamp on his nightstand and turned it off, then rolled over and showed me his back.

I sighed. *You big baby!* Then I considered how Daniel (or his ego) felt about my job. I was working with an incredibly important person and making more money than he was, while he was doing entry-level consulting work with a salary that just barely covered his rent and school loans. I switched out of my turbo-work mode and softened, then gently placed my hand on Daniel's shoulder, feeling nothing but love—mad, desperate love. No other man ever cared about me enough to have this sort of reaction, and although we were fighting, I smiled. Sick of me, I know. But it felt good to know I could affect someone this deeply. I wanted to try to make up, but I had a lot more work to do for Jonathan. So I let Daniel stew and began emailing the list of reporters and publications that had called for interviews earlier that day, just as Jonathan had requested. *I thought Scott didn't want to do interviews!*

Scott said I was to email him straightaway if *Time, Hollywood Reporter,* or *Newsweek* called, but I'd emailed him about them two days ago, and he hadn't responded. *Is this an ego thing or something?* I felt offended that he didn't reply to any emails or even acknowledge anything I'd done since my first day at Treehouse.

The next morning at work, Jonathan appeared in my doorway.

"You need to stop emailing Scott."

"But, he said to—"

"Sorry, I meant you need to limit the number of emails you send him."

"What did he say?"

"Let me just put it this way: you're giving him too many details, and he finds statements like 'hope you have a good night' terribly annoying."

I crinkled my eyebrows. I'd always fancied myself as someone who was good—no, great—at crafting emails. So Jonathan's warning was like a hard slap to my face, especially given how hard I'd been trying. I did my best to hold back my tears, but they welled up at the lower rims of my eyes anyway.

"That's so mean!"

Jonathan let his surprise flash over his face, then laughed quietly. "You pretend like you have such a hard shell. But you're really a softie!"

"I know. It's awful, I'm sorry," I said, embarrassed at my breakdown and dabbing away at my damp eyes with my index fingers.

"Don't worry about it! Just use the information and fix it."

What Jonathan said explained why I hadn't heard from Scott. *Okay, fine, God forbid you strain yourself and type a few words. I'll give you something that only requires two or three characters,* I thought bitterly. I drafted, then redrafted, and redrafted for ten more minutes my next email to him. It had only two sentences and required a simple yes or no.

> To: Scott Kraft
> From: Sophia Young
> Subj: Time
>
> Time magazine called. Keri Boot wants to speak to you.
> Yes/No?

Within minutes, an email appeared in my inbox.

> To: Sophia Young
> From: Scott Kraft
> Subj: Re: Time
>
> Only if she guarantees the cover.

The phone call to Keri didn't go well, at least not when I asked her to guarantee the cover. We hung up, and within minutes, her editor called.

"Sophia, you know I can't do that," he said.

"Well, I'm sorry, truly I have no idea what's possible and what's not, because, to be honest, this is my first press release," I said, hoping to disarm him.

A moment of silence went by and I was certain Mr. Editor would cave in about the cover topic.

"Well, let me tell you. I can*not* guarantee the cover. There are lots of things that can happen between the time Keri does the interview and the time we go to print."

Shit! "Well, you're the editor so I assume you're the boss. If there's someone else you think I should speak to, please have him or her call me. Otherwise, blame yourself when you see an article about Scott and Treehouse *on the cover* of *Newsweek*!" I hung up.

An hour later, a call from Keri sealed the deal for the only interview Scott granted after all that press release craziness.

"Okay," she said, sounding surprised. "He'll be on the cover."

chapter 8

"'INSTANT CLASSIC' WRITTEN ALL OVER IT," wrote the *Hollywood Reporter*. "Just perfect. Script, characters, animation . . . ," said *Empire*. "[*Treasures*] is both an aural and visual delight," raved the *New York Times*.

Well, they did it. The dream that Scott, Dylan, Matteo, and the entire Treehouse creative team had worked so long and hard to achieve finally came true. *Treasures* had the most successful Thanksgiving opening ever, earning rave reviews nationwide. That Sunday, I enthusiastically waved goodbye to my parents and climbed into the spacious back seat of a chauffeured black sedan. *My first business trip*. I felt like such a grown-up, an *important* grown-up, as I was shuttled to the airport. It truly only dawned on me then that I was flying with Scott Kraft. For insurance reasons, Jonathan took a separate flight to New York that had left earlier that balmy morning—it was standard protocol at Treehouse that executives not fly together, and I shuddered thinking about the reasons why the insurance company enforced this. Between the insurance policy and the fact (according to Ashley) that Scott never traveled alone, I was the one stuck flying with him. *A five-hour flight with Mom sharing her "wisdom" with me would be more fun.* But no one was going to kill my buzz this morning.

The day's printed-out agenda from Ashley read *Scott and Sophia meet at United Airlines Gate 82,* so I waited there until I heard "Last boarding call for flight 6 to JFK" before stepping onto the Jetway, dragging my suitcase behind me.

"He's not here, Ashley," I said into my cell phone, panicked that I had done something wrong.

"Dammit! Why can't he stick to the schedule? Let me find him."
Click.

Then, lo and behold, when I stepped into the Boeing 777's aisle not fifteen seconds later, there was Scott Kraft seated in 1A. The flight attendant offered to take my coat and whispered as she placed a glass of champagne on my seat's wide armrest, "He seems really nervous."

I nodded, sat down next to Scott, and happily wiggled around in the fancy leather first-class seat before texting Ashley, I got him.

"Hi!" I said cheerfully, hoping to distract Scott from whatever was freaking him out. "I was waiting outside."

"Don't speak to me," Scott said.

That was so incredibly rude that I found it hilarious. *Pure comedy! I love this guy!*

The airplane began taxiing down the runway, and I watched Scott squeeze his eyes. He made such snug fists with his hands that blue veins bulged. His back was glued against the dark navy seat and his breathing was even and deliberate. Had he been a friend and not my boss, I would have tried to talk him down. But Scott didn't seem to be one for chitchat or comforting, so I sat silent, sipping the champagne that the flight attendant offered earlier. I noticed the man seated across the aisle push some buttons on his armrest to recline his seat and raise his footrest. I examined the various buttons on *my* armrest and, after pushing a few that I shouldn't have (including the flight attendant call button), raised my own footrest to a level that suited me. *Ah, that's better. Now my feet don't have to dangle off the floor.*

When the pilot announced we'd reached cruising altitude and turned off the seat belt signs, Scott opened his eyes, relaxed his fists, and laid each hand on an armrest. Not a half a second later, though, the airplane vibrated and Scott gripped the armrests tightly, his knuckles white. I referred once again to Ashley's Day 1 schedule (detailed in fifteen-minute increments) for some indication of how I might comfort Scott, but she'd written only *By the way, Scott is a bit skittish on the airplane.* I'd call this a flat-out phobia! The other thing Ashley had fitted me with was a tote bag full of applesauce made by Scott's personal chef, two bottles of Smartwater, and some sort of homemade trail mix. I looked at my watch—*Maybe he wants a snack?* But before I could ask, Scott began to speak.

"The most dangerous time periods during a commercial flight are the ten minutes after takeoff and the ten minutes before landing," he said in an unnaturally high voice. I wasn't sure how to respond, so I reached over for the tote bag as well as my purse.

"Do you want a snack?" I asked, pulling out a small mason jar full of applesauce with one hand and a raffia-tied parchment-paper bag that held his trail mix with the other.

Scott shook his head.

I put the snacks back in the tote and dug around in my purse. Then I pulled a pill out of my pillbox.

"What about the helicopter? You fly in that. Isn't it the same thing?"

"No. A pilot doesn't have as much control in a large commercial aircraft like this," Scott said before adding, "That really smells. What is that?"

"It's for high blood pressure," I responded.

Scott looked surprised. "You're so young."

I raised my eyebrows and shrugged, not wanting to get into the whole "diabetes side effect" thing.

"High blood pressure at your age? That's a bad sign," he said.

"What are you talking about?"

"High blood pressure is the beginning of cardiovascular disease. You should learn how to meditate. Besides, manufactured medications wreak havoc on your cells—there's always some side effect or chain reaction that happens in your body when you take one, so you should avoid them at all cost."

I didn't care for Scott's prediction and tried hard to push it out of my head. It wasn't my nature to research my various ailments because I simply didn't want to know. If the doctor told me to take a pill, I'd take a pill. That was all there was to it.

Scott turned to get a closer look at me and said, "At least you don't look like you have any signs of cardiovascular issues."

Oh, so now you think you're an M.D. "Oh yeah? What's that supposed to look like, Doctor?"

"Well, people with high blood pressure are often overweight. If they're not, then it's likely something genetic so you'd be screwed regardless. Others look bloated—they have edema. They're puffy."

I nodded as though I understood, but really I was just egging him on. "Uh-huh. Puffy like the Pillsbury Doughboy? You see cardiac patients often?"

"I like to sit in on medical school classes at Stanford," Scott said, completely missing my Pillsbury joke.

Ugh, that sounds awful. "Why would you do that?"

"I'm just learning. It's always good to expand one's brain." Something about the way he answered suggested there was a lot more to Scott's medical curiosity, but I didn't feel comfortable prying.

I would have changed the subject, but Scott continued his prior line of questioning. "Are you supposed to work the hours you're working? You're not going to have a heart attack on us or anything, are you?"

A+ on the social skills, Scott.

"I am healthy. But thank you for your concern."

"I wasn't concerned."

"Oh. Anyway, I work those hours because you don't seem to think we need to get any help."

"Why do we need help? Samba does all the marketing and PR and you handle all the IR. If our teams are effective and productive, then, in my eyes, we're fully staffed. Besides, I don't trust people," he said, looking down and pulling at his socks through the bottom of his jeans where there were small, noticeable holes. By now I knew that's what Scott did—tugged at his socks through his jeans—when he was stressed, anxious, or simply frustrated.

"There's a lot of 'stuff' that comes up, though, that has nothing to do with Treehouse and *that* takes up a lot of time. The acid debacle, for example." I noted Scott pulling at his pants again, so I left it alone.

The delicious aroma of baking bread filled the cabin, signaling that our meals would be served soon. My CEO stood up and mumbled something about washing his hands, then moved past me and into the aisle. A flight attendant came by with a tray of warm mixed nuts and asked me for my drink order before moving on to the next row.

I removed a long, thin cosmetic case from my purse, retrieved my glucose monitoring kit from inside, and used it to test the level of sugar in my blood. *Normal.* Then I reached inside the cosmetic case again and withdrew a syringe, which I used to inject my pre-meal insulin. The woman across the aisle eyed me suspiciously, but I ignored her and went about my business. Over the years I'd become accustomed to the stares. With the left sleeve of my fall-colored cashmere sweater pushed up to my shoulder, I jabbed the small-gauge needle into my bicep and pressed down the plunger, then capped the syringe and placed it back inside my purse. The whole thing took twenty seconds. When Scott returned and hastened to buckle his seat belt, the suspicious woman leaned over and said to him in a condemning tone, "She was shooting drugs over there while you were in the bathroom."

Scott turned to me with a confused look.

"I saw it myself," the woman said, pointing at me. "She shot something into her arm."

"I assume she's joking?" Scott asked, unsure if the woman and I were colluding on some trick he wasn't finding funny.

"Yes, I shot up."

"Seriously?"

"Yes."

"What? What did you shoot up?" Scott seemed almost excited.

"Insulin," I answered while turning to face the nosy woman, who said nothing but suddenly busied herself with a book.

"You're diabetic?"

"Yep."

"God, that shit will kill you. I know someone who just died from that. Terrible disease."

Scott's insensitive comment should have upset me, but it was *so* shockingly rude that this time I laughed out loud.

"Well, it hasn't killed me so far," I said. "But life is short and anything can happen, so . . ."

"That's probably why you're the way you are."

"How exactly am I?" I asked.

"You emit a *get it done* attitude."

"Yep," I declared proudly. "Chop-chop! That, and let bygones be bygones! Those are some of my life mantras." Also *fat, dumb, and happy*, but I decided not to include that this time.

Scott cracked a grin. "I'd have to agree with some of those. If you're so chop-chop, why aren't you married?" he asked.

"Really? You don't have anything else to ask me?"

Scott shook his head.

"I have a boyfriend," I answered.

"That's not what I asked. How long have you been together?"

"About a year and a half."

Four hundred and eighty-five days, actually. But who's counting?

"What does he do?"

"He's an environmental consultant."

"So why hasn't he married you yet?"

I frowned. "I don't know."

"Like you said, life is short, Sophia. You've got to reach out and grab what you want." It was the first time he'd said my name.

"Yeah, but in this case, it's not up to me."

"Sure it is. Does he know this is what you want?"

"No."

"Then tell him straight out," Scott said. "But for the record, I don't like him. If a guy that age is dating a woman for that long, it means he's afraid of commitment, he's selfish, or he'll never marry her. I'm old-fashioned that way and you deserve better."

"You don't even know him."

"I don't care."

I would have stood up for my future husband more ferociously, but my heart softened at the image of Scott sitting there like a pouting child—crossed arms, tousled hair, and holey jeans.

"Enough about me. What do *you* think about my hair?" I asked jokingly, hoping to make Scott laugh. *Bingo!* He chuckled, so I took the chance to ask him, "Why are you doing this?"

"What?"

"This. This roadshow. This company. You don't need the money. At least, I don't think you do. So why Treehouse?"

"It's about legacy," Scott said, but quietly, looking down as though he were talking to himself.

"Legacy? You've already got a great legacy. Everyone already knows what you did at Quince."

"That's unfinished," he said. "Anyway, Treehouse is a chance for me to leave something behind that touches the hearts of my children—forever. And not just my children or even my grandchildren, but all generations to come. Computers are replaceable, but stories are not. And this is an opportunity for us to make the quality of animated films dramatically better—the animated film industry hasn't been touched in decades. What we're doing is raising the bar. And we're starting this Treehouse University, the training program for all the young talent we've hired—it'll teach them how to tell stories, to de-sign and create, in a whole new way."

Scott's passion moved me. It touched my heart. Through all his brashness, there was a very sensitive person inside. *Just like me.*

WHEN WE LANDED in New York, a driver in a black suit was waiting for us, holding a sign with my name printed on it. *Wow, that's cool.* An hour later, the limousine pulled up to the hotel that the bankers had arranged, much to Scott's disdain.

"I'm not staying in that stodgy hotel," he said as he picked up the phone. After a few minutes of yelling at Ashley for doing a poor job overseeing the itinerary that the bankers had arranged, he got back in the limousine, and I followed. As we pulled out onto the avenue and headed farther downtown, I looked longingly out the car window at the hotel's ornate gold awning and admittedly gaudy but wonderful Corinthian columns. But when we pulled up at the contemporary Four Seasons Hotel on Fifty-Seventh Street, I thought, *Even better.* We were greeted by two doting bellmen and the hotel's general manager, who escorted us through the lobby and straight past hotel registration. The manager was overly chatty—*He must be nervous*—telling us several times how welcome we were and reminding us that if we needed any-thing at all we should call him directly. When we reached the fifty-first floor, one bellman said to me, "This way, Ms. Young." He directed me to the left, and as I followed him, I turned to make sure Scott co-operated by following the general manager and the other bellman to the opposite end of the floor. I waited until they disappeared into his room.

He didn't even say good night.

I turned my attention to *my* bellman, who stood holding open a door that he must have unlocked while I was making sure Scott was taken care of. "Welcome to the Presidential Suite."

My eyes widened with surprise. *Oooh, come to Mama!* The room that I'd get to enjoy for only eight or so hours was as big as a small house. It had floor-to-ceiling bay windows and two balconies, a large sitting area, and an expensive-looking white leather couch. Most jaw-dropping of all was the view of Manhattan laid out below, but I didn't examine it for long, because out of the corner of my eye, I spotted a personalized welcome note and gift basket. I walked toward the gift basket, passing a polished-wood television console with two closed cabinet doors. *That's where the minibar must be!* The bellman unobtrusively placed my suitcase inside the closet to the left by the door. He was about to put Scott's snack bag inside as well, but I stopped him midreach.

"Oh! Do you mind taking this to Mr. Kraft's room, please?"

Better you than me.

"Of course! Is there anything else, Ms. Young?"

How much do I tip in a place like this?

"No, thank you," I said as I handed him a five-dollar bill. Then I came to my senses. "Oh, I assume Scott has an equally nice room, right? It wouldn't be right for me to have the nicer room."

"He's staying in the other Presidential Suite, Ms. Young."

Seconds later, with the bellman gone, I walked farther into the suite and saw a door on the far left that led to a luxurious bedroom and en suite bathroom. I leaped onto the king-size bed, ran my hand along the softest white sheets I'd ever felt, and called Audrey.

"You won't believe where I'm staying," I said.

"Where?"

"The Four Seasons! In the Presidential Suite! And we flew here first class! And a chauffeur, who had a placard with *my* name on it, was waiting for us when we landed!"

"Don't get used to it unless you're paying for it yourself," she said. *Such a buzzkill.* The sound of my niece, Ava, suddenly crying in the background sent knives through my heart and interrupted the conversation.

"Awww, let me talk to her!" I demanded.

"She's just tired. I need to put her down."

"Just put her on speaker. Tell her Auntie Sophia wants to speak with her."

Ava was halfway through a blood-curdling scream when I barked loudly like a dog several times. The screaming stopped, so I barked again, even changing the pitch of my barks to make them seem more realistic. *Probably not what Penny Jenkins imagined.* After nearly a minute of hearing Ava giggling, I shouted out to Audrey, "And *that's* how it's done!"

"Yeah, yeah, yeah. Thanks. I'd better get her down for her nap. Remember what I said about that hotel."

I rolled my eyes, then stood up so I could help myself to the suite's minibar while dialing Daniel next. *He'll be more excited.*

I spent the next three minutes gushing to Daniel about the airplane ride, the chauffeur, and best of all, the Presidential Suite. He was mostly quiet on the other end, except for the occasional "uh-huh," and "wow." But when I started describing my view of the Empire State Building, Daniel interrupted and said, "Babe, that's all really nice and everything, but I've got to go."

Okay, not so excited. Who should I call next? Kate!

"*Hola, chica!*" I exclaimed when I heard her voice on the other end of the phone and the sound of her keyboard, which meant she was at work. It was how we used to greet each other in college, but somewhere along the way we'd forgotten about it. Until now.

"*Hola!*" she said enthusiastically. "Where are you?" When I told her, she said, "I grew up in New York and I've never even stepped foot into that hotel." I grinned and thought how wonderful it would be if someday we could take a girls' trip here together—just the two of us. Like old times. Except we'd be in a luxury hotel instead of a youth hostel.

"How is work?" I asked, knowing it couldn't be that good since it should have been a quiet Thanksgiving weekend, but this was one of the first questions Silicon Valley people asked each other. I made a mental note to stop doing it. *Shouldn't we all have something more interesting to talk about? Nothing better to say than "How's work?" or "What do you do?"*

Kate answered the way she always did—"It's crazy"—before launching into a long and complicated story about an unreasonable client. Somehow, the topic segued into something more interesting for both of us: the dress she'd bought for the Sterling, Rich holiday party.

"Mark's going to love that!" I said after hearing about her elegant purchase.

"Ha. Not so much. I showed him and he said he didn't like it." Kate's tone was that of someone who didn't care. She had a hard shell, rarely showing her emotions, but I knew Mark had hurt her feelings. I also knew Kate hadn't said a thing to him about it.

Oh Mark. Mark, Mark, Mark.

I did my best to convince Kate to share her feelings with her boyfriend, then changed the subject, knowing she didn't like it when I tried to solve her problems. *But I'm a problem solver!*

"Oh, and while you're Miss Important on your roadshow, guess where I'll be tomorrow? The Red Bean launch party."

"Hey! That's *my* client."

"Your *old* client," she said. "They closed four entire streets in downtown San Francisco and built three stages to feature different musical performances by U2, Sting, and Jimmy Buffett."

"What?! That's insane!" I said, not hiding my jealousy. Then, thinking about it further, I asked, "Is that how they're spending that IPO money? Shit, that's just over and beyond."

It was also so typical of what happens in Silicon Valley.

When it was approaching eleven o'clock, Kate and I finally hung up. I ordered room service and then forced myself to sleep, knowing the East Coast time change would make my morning wake-up call particularly painful.

At 7:15 A.M. the next day, 4:15 A.M. Pacific time, my eyes burned from exhaustion as I rolled my suitcase out of the elevator and stepped into the quiet, grand hotel lobby. It faced a large lounge where professionals were seated two by two, having early meetings and coffee. Next to an older man stood a cute (an eight, maybe nine), well-groomed junior investment banker named Sendur, whom I recognized from the S-1 drafting sessions back home. He was holding a tray of drinks with Starbucks logos printed on them as he approached me, leaving the older gentleman to his BlackBerry.

"You found us," I said.

Sendur handed me my soy au lait, and when he noticed the happy but surprised look on my face, he said, "Ashley made sure we knew what the team wanted to drink each morning."

I smiled. "Is that one for Jonathan? He'll want a mocha."

"Yeah, Ashley told us. But nothing for Scott, right?"

"Nope. Yoga and meditation are his morning caffeine," I said.

When the elevator's double doors opened again, Jonathan and Scott stepped out, looking as handsome as ever, exuding confidence, intelligence, money, and power. *Scott, a solid ten, and Jonathan a ten, too!* I almost didn't recognize them in their dark suits, ties, and polished shoes.

"Well, you look very nice," I said.

Jonathan smiled and reached for his mocha. "Thanks."

When the compliment wasn't returned—yes, I was fishing—I suddenly felt like a dowdy old woman dressed in my houndstooth-patterned sweater, matching skirt, and reasonable heels. *I shouldn't let Mom buy my clothes anymore.*

The older banker, who was later introduced as Ric, briefed Scott,

Jonathan, and me about the people and asset management firms we'd be meeting that day, then Sendur collected each of our driver's licenses. "So I can run ahead and check us in at lobby security before each meeting," he said before pointing toward the limousine and black SUV parked outside the revolving doors that led to Fifty-Seventh Street. "We're ready to go."

Jonathan waved his hand ahead toward the waiting cars. "After you," he insisted.

I did my best to play it cool, as though it were perfectly normal for me to be escorted into a limousine by influential bankers and two powerful technology executives. But my feet wanted to skip. Skip, skip, skip along toward this next adventure. *Control yourself, Sophia.* Instead, I walked to the car with a new, confident stride.

AT EIGHT O'CLOCK, even though it was only one block away from the Four Seasons, our small caravan pulled up to the curb outside the iconic General Motors Building. Sendur checked us in at the security desk, gave us each a visitor badge, then led us into an elevator. When the doors opened twenty or so floors later, we entered the lobby of Baron Capital, a multibillion-dollar asset management firm with the most beautiful offices I'd ever seen. The walls were stark white and an expensive-looking lighting fixture hung over the reception area, which had an unobstructed view overlooking Central Park. The receptionist, a twentysomething woman with dark hair and heavy makeup, directed us to the waiting area, where at least two dozen stunning modern art paintings were displayed.

Jonathan took his time moving from one painting to the other; I turned around and saw Scott standing in front of a breathtaking floor-to-ceiling glass fish tank. It was jaw-dropping—incredibly clear, dark blue water, and exotic, colorful fish swimming happily inside: clown fish, puffer fish, a blue angelfish, and even a starfish. I'd never been scuba diving, but this is what I imagined it to be like. As my eyes followed the orange clown fish that glided to the right, Scott crouched down to examine the intricate, glowing sandy bed toward the bottom of the tank. Upon close inspection, I could see that a single glass panel separated the bottom third of the tank from the top. Scott brought his face closer to the glass and I peered to see what he was looking at. At first I couldn't make it out, but then it came into view—a small octopus nestled between two rocks. I heard Scott whisper as he cracked a smile: "My spirit animal."

"What's a spirit animal? Is it like your horoscope?" I asked.

"No. It has nothing to do with birthdates. It's an animal that comes to you in some form or another, like in a dream or in some other more physical way," Scott said.

"Mmm," I said, but it all sounded like hocus-pocus to me.

"Everyone has their own spirit animal that most closely represents them—their traits or skills, or what they're supposed to learn or become."

We watched the octopus undulate toward us, drawing ever closer to the glass. Scott seemed to be sharing some sort of telepathic moment with it. The serenity was interrupted by an obnoxious chewing sound coming from behind us. I turned around to see Jonathan shoving a(nother) handful of peanut M&M's in his mouth.

"Look! They have peanut M&M's!" He smiled broadly.

Before I could respond, a man called out Jonathan's name and asked us to follow him to the conference room. I tapped Scott on the shoulder, sorry to break up the spirit animal staring contest. It was show time.

"I'm Mitch." A friendly-looking man with smiling eyes and a slight underbite reached to shake Jonathan's hand. "Thank you for coming in." Mitch turned to repeat this exchange with Scott, except Scott kept his hands behind his back, awkwardly put me between himself and the investor, and said, "Hi, I'm Scott."

Ashley had warned me Scott didn't like to shake people's hands.

I could tell by Mitch's expression that he found Scott's behavior odd, so to get past the uncomfortable moment, I chimed in and introduced myself as the head of IR.

"Ah, the gatekeeper," Mitch said with a nod and a grin.

The gatekeeper. I like that.

I knew from the banker briefing this morning that Mitch was the young portfolio manager of a $400 billion technology fund at Baron Capital, and he tended to be a solid, long-term holder. It occurred to me that I should have reminded Scott and Jonathan about the who and what of this meeting while we were all still in the limousine. *Too bad we didn't have code words.*

Mitch led us into a packed conference room just on the other side of the fish tank. When we entered, three professionally dressed men and a woman stood from their seats at the large oval table, and it was standing room only for the other dozen or so suits. Mitch joined his colleagues on the far side of the room and motioned Team Treehouse and the bankers to take the remaining five chairs. I wondered if the people who were left standing were going to remain that way for the entire duration of the meeting.

"So, I've seen the commercials," Mitch began. "In fact, my kids are really excited about seeing your movie," he continued as he sat down in one of the black leather chairs. "Now, are those ad trailers all created and paid for by Samba?"

Ric chimed in. "We can certainly get into that, but we have a prepared deck that explains everything." He was referring to the investor presentation I'd helped Jonathan prepare. "So should we start there? Feel free to break in with questions, though." The banker's tone suggested Mitch didn't really have a choice, and I was suddenly thankful for the role he played controlling the conversation. *Maybe Jack Wynn isn't that bad.*

As if on cue, Sendur passed out bound copies of our slideshow, opened his laptop, and projected our twenty-slide presentation onto the conference room screen.

The first image in the deck was the safe-harbor slide. The young banker flashed it onto the screen, displaying a dizzying array of legal jargon meant to protect companies from lawsuits by warning investors to do their research before investing. He then clicked to the next slide in the deck, which outlined the financial details of the IPO: number of shares offered, per-share price range, etc.

Ric addressed the group as if everyone in the room understood the safe-harbor information was simply a formality. "With that out of the way, let me hand it over to Scott Kraft," he said.

Scott stood in front of the screen, which showed the Treehouse logo modified to incorporate several of the *Treasures* characters.

"There is only one significant brand in the animated film industry today," Scott began. "Samba. Our goal is to establish Treehouse as the second. A brand's success is earned over time if a company has the right mix of trust, experience, and, in our case, story. For example, Samba pioneered the animated feature-film industry in the mid-1930s and since then has been the trusted brand to provide appropriate family entertainment. Their track record of hiring the storytellers and animators to create this type of entertainment gives them undisputed experience in making wonderful animated films. This in turn gives movie audiences a viewing experience that no other brand has been able to surpass. Until now. At Treehouse, we believe we have recruited the industry's best talent—that is, animators and storytellers—and equipped them with the most advanced computer-generated imagery technology to give audiences an entirely new, mind-blowing, heartwarming viewing experience. It's an experience that starts with *Treasures*."

The Baron Capital guys, Jonathan, and I listened intently as Scott explained the points of the next ten slides: the experience of our management team, our proprietary software, and our other revenue-generating businesses. When the title slide showing *Jonathan Larsen, Office of the President and Chief Financial Officer,* appeared, Scott said, "Now Jonathan will review the financials, including the business relationship with Samba."

After Jonathan finished, Mitch and his colleagues used the remaining time to fire off questions. They weren't trying to be difficult; they were trying to weigh the risks of investing in Treehouse.

"So this Samba deal—can you give us more details other than sharing box office receipts after their marketing expenses are recouped? That's not enough detail for us to build our internal models."

"How important is the technology here? Will it speed up the time between movies?"

"How do I know Treehouse isn't a one-trick pony with *Treasures*?"

"Why the name Treehouse?"

"How are you planning on using the proceeds from the offering?"

Throughout the entire meeting, I didn't say a word. There was nothing for me *to* say. It was up to Jonathan and Scott to sell these people on our company, and I knew they had this covered. I also knew I was there to hear *them* tell the story. To learn. I sat at the end of the table memorizing Scott's and Jonathan's cadences and writing down everything they said; I was exhilarated by the thought that one day soon I'd sound as polished, knowledgeable, and passionate as they did.

Approximately two minutes before our meeting was scheduled to end, I waited for Jonathan to finish answering a question, then said while looking at my watch, "We need to wrap things up." Mitch, who'd greeted me so warmly just forty minutes ago, glared at me as though I'd duped him out of a winning lottery ticket. "Just a few more minutes," he shot back.

"I think our time is up," Jonathan broke in as he and Scott stood from their seats. "If you have any follow-up questions, perhaps Sophia can find some time for Scott or me to ring you later."

Yeah, take that, Mitch!

Once we were back inside the car, Jonathan said, "It'd be a good idea to sound the bell five minutes earlier next time."

I nodded. Inside I felt much more than that. Jonathan's support in that meeting and his acknowledgment of my role made me feel like part of the team; I wanted to impress him even more.

Minus the M&M's and fish tank, almost the exact same scenario played out seven more times a day for eight more business days. Forty-five-minute meetings (thirty minutes for presentation and fifteen minutes of Q&A) and thirty minutes to travel to check in at security and start the next meeting.

In the big cities like New York, Boston, and San Francisco, our schedules often included catered lunch meetings where we presented to larger groups of fifty to one hundred people. *Who knew there were so many institutional investors in the world?* They packed themselves into the ballroom of the local five-star hotel and sat patiently, intently, listening to Scott and Jonathan pitch Treehouse's investment opportunity. Scott hated those meetings the most—the clinking of knives and forks against plates made it hard for him to concentrate. He also was bothered by the "stalkers": well-dressed women who approached him for autographs or asked to take photos with him, neither of which Scott ever agreed to because he despised doing both. These women sat front and center pretending to be potential investors— and maybe they were—but they paid more attention to their lipstick and hair than anything else. Their softball questions and their way of slinking around afterward, trying to get close enough to snap a selfie with Scott in the background, gave them away. These stalkers gained access through their large bank accounts at the investment firms. I kept noticing one blond helmet-haired, Chanel-suited woman in particular. *Am I imagining it, or is she following us from city to city?* Despite her efforts, she never managed to lock eyes with Scott while he was presenting; she also never succeeded at getting in front of all the aggressive investors, mostly men, who circled Scott as soon as he left the stage. By the fourth city, I had become annoyed with Ms. Chanel and intercepted her while she scurried toward Scott. I gave her a *we both know what's going on here* smile and handed her my card before saying, "If you have any questions, don't hesitate to contact me directly." I never saw her again.

The car rides in between meetings were the most exciting for me. As soon as the limo pulled away from the curb, Ric would call us from the SUV and give us his thoughts on the investor response to our presentation. Midway through the roadshow, I began adding my feedback as well, reminding Scott if he'd forgotten to say something important or suggesting Jonathan consider answering a specific question differently. We were constantly refining our messaging, making adjustments to the presentation on the fly, and if an investor asked Jonathan a financial question that he couldn't answer, he'd call his finance team when we got into the car so he could get the answer for next time. The end of the day rarely involved dinner but rather planes, trains, and automobiles to race to the next city—Boston, Chicago, Baltimore, Dallas, Denver, Los Angeles, San Francisco, Kansas City, London, and back to New York, where most companies make their last push toward the finish line. When we checked in to each hotel, a fresh delivery of Scott's applesauce and trail mix would be waiting in my room with a print-out of the next day's agenda and the never-ending call log, which I did my best to keep up with while I was on the road.

At first I felt an odd sense of power, from my association with Scott and Jonathan (the dynamic duo), from the banker entourage, and from usually being one of the few women in the room. It was the only time I didn't mind not being "normal." But by the fifth day on the road, none of it mattered anymore: the views and luxury hotels didn't impress me and I could have cared less that I was in the presence of the great Scott and Jonathan team—they were old hat. I'd already memorized their monologues and answers verbatim and I was getting bored. *Been there, done that.* Add that to my exhaustion and I just wanted to go home and stuff my face with Mom's ma po tofu.

OUR FLIGHT FROM San Francisco landed in Kansas City just past midnight, and by the time I rolled my suitcase into my hotel room, it was well after one o'clock Monday morning. *Three more days to go.*

"Hello," Daniel said, his voice sounding raspy with sleep.

"Hi. Sorry to wake you," I said tenderly. "I already miss you."

"Hi, babe. I miss you, too. Where are you?"

The weekend break at home with Daniel and my parents hadn't been enough to erase the feeling of dread when I left for the airport again Sunday evening. Hearing Daniel's voice made me teary and homesick; my dreams of becoming a Mrs. came flooding back. It just seemed so much easier.

"I'm in my room now. Go back to bed. I just wanted to say good night."

"You okay?" he asked.

"Yeah. I'm just ready to finish this whole thing."

"Home stretch, babe. Home stretch. I love you. Sleep tight."

Click.

When the telephone rang loudly the next morning, I had no idea which city I was in. I picked up the receiver assuming it was my wake-up call, but instead, I heard Sendur's voice on the other end of the phone.

"Hi, Sophia. We're all waiting for you in the lobby. Are you on your way down?"

Holy shit, holy shit, holy shit.

"Yes! I'll be right down. Give me two minutes!"

I leaped out of bed, ran to the bathroom while stripping off my pajamas, then fumbled for the toothpaste in my cosmetic bag. As

I used my tongue to rub around a glob of Colgate in my mouth, I applied mascara while I peed. It was a miracle, but five minutes later I grabbed a banana out of the fruit basket and ran down the empty hotel hallway. Suddenly, I stopped. *Where in the hell is the elevator?* The hallways all looked the same by now, and I had no recollection of even arriving last night. I quickly looked both ways and saw an exit sign in the direction I'd just come from, so I turned around and ran that way.

I was breathless when I reached the lobby; my eyes were swollen, my hair was in a disheveled ponytail, and I was carrying my shoes. *Mom would be so proud.*

"Sorry I'm late," I said.

Scott looked at me. "You have banana on your face."

I could feel a smudge of it on the corner of my mouth and tried to play it cool. "I know."

"You *know* you have banana on your forehead?" he asked, wearing a quizzical look.

I couldn't help but burst out laughing; my unruly, undisciplined manner caught Scott off guard and the corners of his mouth turned up ever so slightly.

Ric ruined my fun. "I hope you get used to this. You'll be leading this show the next time," he said.

I'd rather eat glass. Amazing how quickly the novelty of it all had worn off.

Jonathan handed me the napkin that was wrapped around his mocha and Sendur passed me my morning soy au lait. "How often do companies do these things?" I practically whimpered.

"A few times a year—they're called nondeal roadshows. Your investors like to see you in person every once in a while, and it's good to give them face time and remind them why they invested. It's a way to keep the shareholders loyal and engaged," said the young banker.

Jesus flipping Christ!

"Anyway, where were we?" Ric asked. "Oh yeah, the book. Let me tell you how we're doing and I'll ride with you guys to the next meeting so I can brief you on today's meetings."

The book was the list of investors who'd contacted our bankers and placed "indications of interest" in Treehouse stock. These forms detailed the number of shares each investor wanted to buy and the price he or she was willing to pay, which usually fell within the price range that was set by bankers before the roadshow started. The point of the roadshow was to build as much demand from investors as possible; the more demand, the higher the price. On occasion, if an IPO was really hot, the bankers would "raise the range," and that's what Jonathan and Scott were hoping for.

The first meeting of the day started like every other, except I noticed something I hadn't before. Perhaps because I wasn't so busy trying to listen, I had a chance to *observe,* and what I saw was fascinating: Scott scanned each batch of new investors we met, reading each one of them to figure out what he needed to say to make the entire room tick. He had an incredible gift—the gift of human observation—even though he seemed to be living in his own world. Based on the investors' body language, questions, and other things that I hadn't quite figured out yet (not for lack of trying), Scott ever-so-slightly adjusted his comments for each slide and his responses to each investor question so that his audience's eyes would almost glaze over in awe. I tried to make the connections he was making—*What does he see in that person to make him answer that question that way?* And there was a tone to Jonathan's voice that I noticed; it made people think, *Of course I should invest.* That was another talent I knew I needed to acquire.

"*No, Mr. Investor. We don't make any money, we have no experience doing what we're doing, and, by the way, our hands are tied by the eight-hundred-pound gorilla in the industry. But of course you should invest millions in our business. You'd be stupid not to.*"

After our last meeting the next day, we had enough time for an early dinner at a trendy sushi restaurant that Scott wanted to try. Sendur said, "I doubt we can get in. They only take four or five reservations a night, so there's like a two-month wait at that place. The rest is walk-in."

"It's only five fifteen," I said. "We'll get in."

Minutes later, Team Treehouse pulled up to the restaurant, which had a line wrapped around the corner. *Uh-oh. We're not getting in.* We all got out of the car and I led the way toward the front of the line.

"How long have you been standing here?" I asked the hungry-looking couple who were waiting patiently just outside the restaurant doors.

"We got here three hours ago," the woman said matter-of-factly.

I laughed, then realized the woman was serious. And she *didn't* think it was funny.

Jonathan opened the door and we all stepped inside the dimly lit hot spot. It was a suave vision of cerused oak, brass, and a combination of teal leather couches and zebra-patterned chairs. I stepped up to the hostess, who looked as though she were made of plastic and had a stick permanently installed up her rear. "Good evening. We don't have a reservation, but I was hoping there was *some* way we could get a table for five? We just flew in."

She guffawed, then said with a horrified look on her face, "If you don't have a reservation, I can't help you. You'll have to wait like all the others."

"There's no way you can seat us?"

"Did you see the line out there?" asked Barbie Doll.

"Your manager may be able to help us. The name is Kraft. Scott Kraft."

The name didn't seem to register with Barbie, but she left her station and told me to hold on. I turned to see Scott's reaction, but he was staring at the floor, deep in thought. He'd done this a few times over the last two weeks, looking as though the world weighed heavily on his shoulders. He seemed tired and vulnerable when he had this look, and it concerned me. *Or maybe I should offer him some apple-sauce.*

Barbie returned with a large man wearing a baseball cap.

Mr. Manager, I assume?

"Hi! Welcome! Come with me, I'll take you to your seat," the man said.

"One of us is vegan. Will you be able to accommodate him?" I asked as I sat down and pointed my chin toward Scott.

The manager turned to look at my CEO, and he nodded as though my request was no big deal. Twenty minutes later, five different white-gloved waiters carrying beautiful trays of sushi stood before our table.

"The vegan plate goes to . . . ?" one of the waiters asked.

"Me. That's me," said Scott, staring at the plate of brightly colored vegetable skewers with three different dipping sauces and tightly wrapped vegetable rolls.

"We made these just for you, Mr. Kraft," said the owner, who had returned to wish us a "lovely dinner."

I picked up my fork and reached over to Scott's plate to taste one of his sauces.

"What are you doing?" Scott asked in a cold, quizzical tone that made me freeze for a second.

"What?" I asked innocently. *Friends and family share!*

"Eat your own food," Scott said, sounding flustered and frazzled.

Licking my fork, I shrugged my shoulders and said, "Jeez. Relax. It was a clean fork! I just wanted to try one of your sauces."

With two fingers Scott picked up the dipping sauce I'd just tasted and placed it in front of me. "Here, you can have it." I rolled my eyes and waved my hand for the waiter so I could ask him to bring another.

I HAD NEVER spent that much time traveling with people outside of my family, Kate, and Daniel. There was always the possibility that Scott, Jonathan, and I would tire of one another and become irritated with each other's idiosyncrasies. But Team Treehouse seemed to fit, and by the end, Jonathan's and Scott's language cadences, nervous tics, overuse of idioms, mood predictors, and common phrases felt natural to me.

On our last night of the roadshow—the night we would set a final stock price based on the book, the night before Treehouse shares would begin to trade publicly—Scott, Jonathan, and I were inside United Airlines' Red Carpet Club waiting to board our flight home. *Finally!* Ashley had reserved a conference room for us, which paled in comparison to some of the fancy meeting rooms we'd sat in over the last two weeks. In ten minutes, Team Treehouse was to dial in to a conference line to speak to the head of equity trading at the investment bank, who would give us the final book tally and his pricing recommendation. I looked at my watch.

"Why are you always looking at your watch?" Scott asked.

"I'm not."

"Yes, you are. It's very distracting."

I looked at Jonathan, who said, "I didn't notice."

I looked back at Scott, ready to remind him that it was my responsibility to keep us, and our meetings, on schedule.

"Let me see that watch."

I took off the knock-off Gucci bracelet watch I'd bought myself two years ago—it had a black ring around the face for this trip, but I had nine other colors tucked away at home.

Scott examined the watch, made a face, then put it in his pocket.

"What are you doing?"

"You're going to drive yourself insane being so concerned with the time. From today on, you are not to wear a watch. At least not in my presence," he said.

"How am I going to tell the time?" I asked, wondering if I was ever going to get my watch back.

"You'll figure it out."

Jonathan broke in, "It's time to call in. You have the number, Sophia?"

On the phone were representatives from our three investment banks, one of our board members, and lawyers from both sides. The head of equity trading spoke first.

"You're nine times oversubscribed," he said.

I threw my hands up in the air as though we'd collectively scored a touchdown. Then, seeing how calm and quiet Scott was, I slowly dropped my arms to my sides.

Did I miss something?

"That's good, right?" I asked.

"Yes, it's good. It means there's nine times as many shares requested as we have available for the IPO," Jonathan explained.

"But ten times would have been great. It would have meant we could raise the range," Scott said, looking disappointed.

I wondered if Scott premeditated everything, and everyone, making sure everything lined up so that, in his mind, he had the best odds of achieving the results he wanted. His disappointed face told me that "nine times oversubscribed" didn't fit Scott's grand plan, but I found his reaction ridiculous. There was a discussion about whether we should fly back overseas to London to see if we could inspire more investor interest so we could raise the price of the IPO shares. I realized I wasn't terribly experienced in any of this, but we'd been traveling for eight business days and the thought of flying back to London for one or two more meetings made me physically ill. I wondered if I could slyly point out how ridiculous they were being.

"You guys want more orders so you can raise the offering price, right?"

The banker's voice came over the phone and said, "It sends a message to the Street that this is a hot IPO."

"And it would give us a little more padding in our coffers if we raised the per-share price," Jonathan added.

I furrowed my brows. "But it *is* a hot offering. It's a nine-times hot offering." Then I repeated something Jack Wynn used to say: "And pigs get slaughtered."

Jonathan didn't hear me, but Scott did.

"What did you say?"

Uh-oh.

"Nothing," I whispered.

"What did you say, Sophia?" Scott asked.

"I said, 'Pigs get slaughtered.'"

Scott half grinned for the first time since we'd left for the second leg of the roadshow. "I suppose she's right. We should take what investors are willing to pay now and have confidence we'll make up the rest in the public markets after we get a few quarters under our belts. Something isn't resonating with them, and I'm not sure a trip to London will change that. It could work against us if people are expecting us to price tonight. Besides, this was our plan and I'd like to stick to it."

"Okay, then. Let's do it," Jonathan instructed the bankers. Scott nodded approvingly at me.

That was the first time I really felt like I was no longer a tagalong or just a vague presence. I'd become a contributor. My confidence surged as I realized Scott and Jonathan valued my opinion. I couldn't wait to tell everyone at home.

THE NEXT MORNING was our first day of trading: Friday. I awoke *in my own bed* to headlines that read: TREEHOUSE SHARES SOAR: STOCK MORE THAN DOUBLES and TREASURES CONTINUES TO BREAK BOX OFFICE RECORDS. Adding to the excitement were entertainment industry whispers about *Treasures'* good chances of an Oscar nomination. At the office, congratulatory emails and phone calls from friends poured in; Grant sent a bottle of Veuve Clicquot, and flowers from Kate arrived at my door. But when I opened the email from Keri Boot, my heart stopped. She'd included a digital copy of the *Time* issue that included Scott's interview. It would be published on Monday, and Scott was not on the cover. *Oh, shit!* That week's edition wasn't what the editor had agreed to. And I knew it was wrong, but I was actually consoled by the fact that a major overseas conflict was the reason the cover was snatched from us: WAR BREAKS OUT IN THE MIDDLE EAST, it said. I forwarded the email to Scott and shut my computer quickly, since Daniel and I had planned to play half-day hooky until we met Mark and Kate for celebratory drinks at the Rosewood hotel bar. It had felt like forever since we'd had any quality time together, and I missed everyone terribly.

Minutes later, my phone rang. I knew it was Scott calling about the *Time* cover, so I hesitated to answer—one ring, two rings, three. I knew if I didn't pick up the phone, though, forcing Scott to hold in his anger, he would really blow an epic gasket when the inevitable happened. Better to let him yell now. As I slowly brought the cell phone up to my ear, I could already hear him screaming.

chapter 9

THE MONDAY AFTER THE ROADSHOW, I pulled into Treehouse's parking lot and, as usual, saw Ashley's sparkling-clean silver Honda sedan. I was about to let myself into the building and lock the door behind me, just as Ashley had done at zero dark thirty. But today would be different—today was the first *real* day I'd be head of investor relations for a real, public company. *Wow. Me.*

Despite Scott's tantrum about the *Time* cover, I was still high on the IPO headlines and expected it to be a rather relaxed day, especially compared to the months leading up to the IPO. But my joy quickly gave way to a shudder when I looked at the number of messages showing on the telephone display. At 6:15 A.M., there were 256 voicemails on the investor relations line, about eight times more than the day we'd announced the *Treasures* premiere. The investors we'd met on the roadshow and any journalist would know that IPOs had a mandated quiet period between the day of their first trade and the company's first earnings release. *Who could be calling?*

I turned on my computer and logged in to the stock surveillance service's website that I'd learned how to navigate before we went on the roadshow. The same one that Matteo had wanted to build from scratch. *Idiot.* Then the hair I'd spent nearly thirty minutes blow-drying that morning went immediately up into a ponytail, as though I were about to take on a full day of scrubbing toilets. With a notepad in hand and the speakerphone on, I listened to each message while scribbling down the name, and phone number or email address of the caller, smiling almost the entire time. The voicemails were from people all over the world—from London to Lisbon, Nevada to Florida—but they shared the same message: *We love you.*

"Hi, Investor Relations. This is Mr. Charles Stewart calling from Amarillo, Texas. That's right. *Amarillo.* I saw that there movie of yours, *Treasures,* and I couldn't believe my eyes. Y'all did that with just computers? 'Course I don't regularly see those types of movies, what with the grandkids grown and all. But my wife, Mary, and I, well, we thought we'd go down and see what those computers could do. Ha! She was bawling like a baby by the end—she really enjoyed the story. Sure, I liked it, too, but darn it if you guys aren't going to be the next Samba! And that Scott Kraft you got over there? Well, he's just done it again, hasn't he? When y'all went public, Mary and I went and bought some shares. We believe in y'all Cali-fornians and want to know when the next movie is comin'. Please call us back."

The two hundred fifty-sixth voicemail that I listened to, hours later, was from a man with a deep, serious voice. He wasn't effusive like most of the others. He simply said, "Your CEO has changed the world."

I glowed with pride and saved the message. All that hard work, by Scott and Jonathan especially, was worth it. *We did it! I can't believe we did it!* I knew we weren't actually changing the world, at least not at Treehouse. But what we were doing felt really important, and I remembered what Scott had said that day on the airplane about his legacy. Slightly emotional, I whispered to myself, "There's your legacy, Scott."

It was late morning when I realized that the stock market had opened. I looked at my computer screen and was pleased to see Tree-house's stock was still on an upward trend, but something looked strange. The real-time stock trade volumes weren't moving in large blocks; instead the trade numbers were moving in increments of tens or hundreds. *Does that mean it's the retail investors buying shares? Must be!* The same retail investors that the bankers told Scott, Jonathan, and me to ignore were currently the reason Treehouse's stock was slowly and steadily moving up.

"You don't want retail investors. The institutions are the ones who have the buying power," the banker had said. "Individual investors aren't sophisticated and don't tend to be long-term focused. They also have a herd mentality, which is really tough if, God forbid, you get into a rough patch."

I sent a note to Scott and Jonathan about the voicemails and the stock price movements. It was information they'd want to know. For the rest of the day I returned every phone message left on my voicemail, not to mention answering the people who called and actually caught me live. The retail investors exuded an energy and excitement that I fed off of, and I wished I could have bottled it up and shared it with the guys. Although the quiet period prevented me from saying anything meaningful about Treehouse's business, I did my best to chitchat with each caller for at least a few minutes. They deserved that, and so did I.

That night, as Daniel lay in bed reading a boring business book, I rested beside him, staring at his bedroom ceiling. I let out a loud sigh and noticed my stomach felt funny. I told myself it was because of work.

Or maybe it's just the Chinese takeout I ordered.

I knew it was more than that, though. It bothered me that I felt lonely, even though my boyfriend was right next to me.

Don't be so dramatic, Sophia.

"What's wrong, babe?" Daniel asked.

I kept my eyes focused on the grooves of the drywall above. *One thing at a time.* "Nothing. I'm still digesting the fact that I'm working for Scott Kraft." My voice was hoarse from talking all day.

"Is that a problem?"

"No, no. But there were so many calls today that really drove home the reality of my situation," I said. Then, forcing myself to stop analyzing my relationship with Daniel, I brought up something else that was overwhelming. "*I'm working for Scott fucking Kraft!* If I think about it too much, I get a little intimidated." This was the honest truth.

"That's the best part of you. You don't think," he joked.

I punched Daniel in the arm, which I'm sure he barely felt, but he squirmed and yelped. He put down his book and rolled onto his side to face me. With one hand, he reached over and rolled me on my side so I faced him as well. Looking me straight in the eyes, Daniel said, "Babe, he puts his pants on one leg at a time, just like everyone else. Remember that."

I tried to push the voicemails out of my head, rolled onto Daniel, and touched my forehead to his. "Thank you."

Then back to my flat position staring at the ceiling, I forced myself to stop thinking about any doubts I had about Daniel. *Six minutes at a time, Sophia. Six minutes at a time.*

ONE WEEK AFTER the IPO, *Treasures* was on track to be the most successful movie of the year and Treehouse's stock price was holding steady. The better the film did, the longer my call log got; every day my voicemail inbox was besieged by so many enthusiastic supporters that Jonathan agreed to approve a dedicated telephone number with a prerecorded list of the top ten questions people were asking, along with their respective answers, of course. There was no way for them to leave me a voicemail. When I heard A.J.'s ringmaster voice announce on Treehouse's main phone line, "Preeeeeess 8 for our General Investor Relations line," I squealed with delight. It proved to me that what I was doing was important, and cemented in stone that all of this was real.

On Thursday I was preparing for my last meeting of the day—a weekly session with Jonathan—when Ashley walked in.

"Hey, we need to take our waltz lessons. Do you think we can do it at your house?"

"What waltz lessons?" I asked.

"Didn't you read the holiday party email? The whole company will be waltzing at the party next weekend."

The truth was that I'd stopped reading intra-office emails long ago. There were too many of them going around, and I could barely keep up with emails as it was. So I answered Ashley's question with another one. "Why are we waltzing?"

"It's what Scott wants. I brought in dance instructors while you guys were on the roadshow, so now everyone knows how to waltz but us. It's mandatory."

I hung my head. "Really? Seriously? Everyone took lessons? How many did you guys take?"

"The instructors came four times but I couldn't go because, well, you know Scott's schedule. Anyway, I ordered lunch and heat lamps and everyone had a blast taking lessons together in the parking lot."

Only at Treehouse.

"So what are you thinking?"

"How about two hours tomorrow night? Are your parents in town? Do you think they'll mind?"

Knowing my parents would understand if I asked them to stay upstairs, I told Ashley it would be fine.

"Great. I'll bring the instructors. Just make sure Daniel is there, too."

"Okay," I said unenthusiastically, making a mental note to tell Mom and Dad.

"I'll send you a calendar invite," Ashley said as she raced down the hall.

My meeting with Jonathan went smoothly; we discussed the stock performance, institutional investors we didn't have that we'd like to target in the new year, and the upcoming travel plans he'd made for his family during Treehouse's weeklong holiday break.

"Oh, also, what would be a great help is if you researched when Samba and other public media companies are releasing their earnings. We're hoping to do ours the second week of February, and we don't want to get lost in those companies' noise. Also, I'd like you to draft the earnings script for Scott and me. I'll email you some preliminary financial information, but it won't be final until we get confirmed figures from Samba and close the books. Still, you can get started," Jonathan said.

I noted my new tasks and then stood up to leave, but Jonathan continued. "Scott's going to want to officially announce the new Treehouse University we started. And . . . and . . . and . . ."

I sat back down and scribbled down Jonathan's words as fast as I could. The floodgates had opened.

ON FRIDAY NIGHT, our doorbell rang as the clock struck eight, and on our front doorstep stood Ashley and her husband, Jonathan and his wife, plus two strangers dressed in full formal attire who were introduced as our instructors.

I tried to be gracious and sound welcoming as I ushered everyone inside, out of the cold, dark winter night, but the only thought going through my head was, *Shit, I forgot to tell Mom and Dad!*

Ashley looked past my black leggings and red turtleneck and stared directly at my feet. "Put on some heels. Scott and Christine are right behind us."

"What?" I asked, looking back at Daniel, who was making his way from the kitchen to the front door. *Scott and Christine are coming?*

"Shoes on," Ashley repeated as she slid out of her sneakers and slipped on the high heels she was carrying.

I didn't mind hosting the Larsens, but my CEO and his wife were a different story. Suddenly I felt nervous about having them over, although at that point I didn't have much of a choice because leaving them outside was likely out of the question.

My anxiety gave way to the terrible, almost painful sound of metal scraping against a surface. I opened the front door wider and saw the underside of Scott's Porsche Carrera dragging along the bottom of my parents' steep driveway.

Eeeek.

Scott seemed oblivious as he zipped up to the flat, circular portion of the driveway in front of our house. Christine stepped out of the car and yelled out to Ashley, who had appeared next to me just outside the front door, "Ashley, can you please see to it that Scott gets rid of this car? He drives like a maniac and is a danger to himself and everyone else on the road."

Scott laughed. He was lighter and more relaxed than I'd ever seen. It was clear how smitten he was with his wife. He didn't mind her being the boss.

I looked at Daniel, but he didn't make eye contact with me. He was mesmerized, overcome by the Scott Spell. I turned my attention to Christine. It was the first time I had ever seen her. She looked like a supermodel plucked out of the wilds of Scandinavia, and, as if her beauty wasn't enough, she had brains as well. Christine was an Ivy Leaguer who was "changing the world" in her own way, through the tremendous education programs she ran.

"Hello. You must be Sophia. Thank you for hosting us tonight." Christine extended her hand gracefully toward me as she entered the house. "I'm sorry we're late. Scott was helping one of the kids with his homework." *Smart, beautiful, four kids, and a husband who helps with the homework—I want your life.*

I looked like the Cheshire Cat as I nodded at Christine, acting as though I could relate to what she said. An awkward moment of silence passed before I spoke: "Let me get this straight. We're learning how to waltz tonight?"

"It's always been a dream of Scott's to host a party with guests Viennese Waltzing around a Christmas tree," Christine explained, looking elegant even as she took off a camel cashmere coat that was the same color as her perfectly tailored trousers.

The visual of everyone doing some terrible version of *The Nutcracker*'s opening scene made me want to laugh, but I held myself together and introduced Daniel instead. Suddenly I saw movement out of the corner of my eye; Scott was heading up the three steps that led from the foyer to the living room on the left. *And he's off!*

"That's the living room, Scott."

"Forgive him," Christine said.

We walked together toward Scott, who was standing in the center of our stark white living room next to the two puzzle-piece-shaped stainless steel coffee tables. Except for the twinkling lights that shone from Silicon Valley, the floor-to-ceiling windows were dark from the night sky. Christine, Ashley, and the rest of the guests commented on the view—something I hardly appreciated anymore, but it *was* a sight to see. Scott looked deep in thought. He was always observing and storing things in his mind so that he could use them later. I knew his observations affected the way he wanted our slideshows to look, or how he wanted to phrase certain things. *But how? And when?* I wanted to learn, too, so I could be like him. *And like Christine.* I followed his gaze to see if I could figure it out now.

"What do your parents do?" Scott asked. He was wearing his usual outfit: jeans and a black T-shirt.

"My mom doesn't work. Her job is to torture me," I said, grinning. "Dad was an aeronautical engineer, but now he runs a medical device company. They design and manufacture commercial-grade electronic thermometers."

Scott nodded.

The peaceful moment was interrupted by Mom yelling from up-stairs.

"Who's at the door?"

I felt awkward saying, "Scott Kraft is here," so I answered, "It's me, Mom."

"Audrey?"

"No, me!"

"Which me?"

"Sophia!"

"Sophia, I thought you were home."

"I *am* home, Mom."

"Then why did you say Audrey?"

"I didn't. You did."

"Oh. Well, clean up your room if you're home. Messy rooms lead to messy minds. How many times do I have to tell you that?"

"Okay, Mom," I shouted back, fearing if I didn't acknowledge her, she'd yell even louder. I was mortified, but accustomed to this type of exchange happening in front of my friends. We were a loud, direct family, and there was nothing I could do about it.

My guests started laughing and I nervously joined them. Dad must have heard our voices because I heard his den door open up-stairs, then his footsteps crossing to the middle of the floating glass bridge so that he stood directly over our foyer.

"Sophia, do you have some friends here?" he called down.

"Yes, Dad." I felt like a teenager whose parents were intruding. Still, I was happy that my coworkers were here to meet my dad. He was impressive, after all.

I heard Dad's slippers shuffle the rest of the way across the bridge, then down to the landing in front of the kitchen. The shuffle got louder as they made their way through the marble foyer and up to-ward the living room, where we stood.

"Dad, this is my boss, Jonathan."

Dad stood there in his pajamas and bathrobe. He secured the navy robe with its terry-cloth belt and chuckled. "Oh! Excuse me. I didn't know she was having guests."

"That's okay, Mr. Young. Sorry for the intrusion. I'm Jonathan. This is my wife, Helena; Ashley and her husband, Chuck; Scott Kraft and his wife, Christine; and our two dance instructors."

Thankfully Dad remembered me telling him that Scott didn't like to shake people's hands, so he just nodded politely toward everyone and said, "We love having young people in the house."

You're not that much older, Dad.

"You have a lovely home, Mr. Young," Scott said.

"Did you decorate it yourself?" Christine added. "We've been try- ing to decorate our home for years, but Scott is quite particular so it still looks like it belongs in the seventies."

"Ha. No. We have terrible taste. A decorator was recommended to us—Franck Falls. He did it. Isn't it nice? Although I was shocked at the price of these couches."

"Golly, it's wonderful," Scott said.

"Golly"? "Golly"? When did he start saying "Golly"?

"Here, let me show you guys around," Dad said as he put his hand on Christine's shoulder and guided her toward the other side of the house. I stayed put with Daniel, and as the guests walked away, I heard Dad say, "You know, I designed this myself for my wife, Mrs. Young. There's a view from every single room in the house."

TWO WEEKS LATER, Daniel and I stepped out of a limousine and into the crisp December San Francisco air. We tilted our heads back so we could fully capture the sight of the three enormous wreaths that hung from the Edwardian pillars of the historic Palace Hotel. They were intricately decorated with hundreds of lights and rippling red ribbon; the sight of them nudged me into the spirit of the holidays—a

spirit that had eluded me up to now, thanks to the whirlwind of the
roadshow and ensuing post-IPO madness. Treehouse had become
a Wall Street darling, though, and I spent every minute of my day
doing everything I could to keep it that way.

Standing there curbside, Daniel looked handsome in a rented tuxedo, and I felt very elegant in a flowing, long black velvet dress. *Not
that Daniel has even noticed.* He'd barely said a word to me during
our hour-long drive. The twinkling white lights and bright red poin-
settias that filled the impressive, bustling lobby put the pile of work
on my desk and my hundreds of unanswered emails out of my mind
for a moment. I followed Daniel as best as I could in my four-inch
spike heels, but I couldn't keep up. Daniel didn't turn around, but
clearly he knew I was falling behind because he slapped the back of
his thigh twice, wiggled his fingers at me, then began snapping as
though he were calling a dog. "Come on, Sophia."

I stopped walking. *Who do you think you are?*

Daniel turned around, rolled his eyes, and rag-dolled his upper
body in frustration.

"You know I hate it when you walk in front of me," I said. "You've
been doing that a lot."

"Well, then walk faster," he said.

"I can't," I complained as I lifted up my long dress to my ankles
and showed him my heels.

Daniel held out his hand but didn't move any closer to me. It wasn't
the time to take a stand and pout, so I shuffled toward him, annoyed.

The beautiful Parisian-style glass dome of the Garden Court came
into view, but that wasn't what caught my eye. In the center of the
room, beneath the dome, was a fifty-foot-tall Christmas tree that I
would have assumed was fake had it not been for the scent of Doug-
las fir that filled the air. It was adorned with hundreds of unique
Swarovski crystal ornaments. They magnified the light radiating from
the rows of bulbs strung around and around the tree. A twelve-piece

orchestra softly played classical music from the corner of the room, and my coworkers, usually dressed in crazy T-shirts and jeans, wore tuxes and floor-length gowns as they socialized with fancy drinks in their hands and nibbled on passed hors d'oeuvres.

Daniel led me toward the party. "Introduce me to your friends," he said.

"You met almost all the people I know when we were learning how to waltz. I haven't really met anyone else," I said, grasping his hand tighter.

"What do you mean you don't know anyone?"

"I mean I'm always stuck on my side of the office. Most of the company is creative and there's no reason for me to mingle with them. Besides, I haven't had time to meet anyone. I've been on the road for weeks, and the only people I really talk to are Jonathan and Ashley," I said shyly. The insecurities I'd felt all my life—about not being interesting enough, about being damaged goods, about not being tall and blond—all came flooding back. All I could focus on was the large group of strangers in front of me engaged in animated conversations; they seemed so familiar and comfortable with one another. I was certain they were discussing topics I couldn't contribute to—world affairs, politics. Their marriages and their children. *What do I know?* I'd spent the last two years of my life engrossed in legal transactions and then Treehouse's IPO. That was all I'd had time for, all that I knew.

"What about the CTO, Matteo?"

"He's not my favorite. And I don't have much to talk to him about."

"You know nothing about him at all?"

"I know he's married with three kids."

"Okay, that's good. You're great at talking to people about that stuff. What about Dylan, the creative guy? He seems interesting."

"The only thing I know about him is that he's a big supporter of the Juvenile Diabetes Association, but I don't know why."

"Well, that's something to talk about! Does he know you're a diabetic?"

"No."

"Oh, come on, Sophia. Tell him you're a diabetic! Let's get a drink and then we'll go talk to some people, okay?"

Daniel dragged me to the bar, where I gladly gulped down a martini. As I sipped on my second drink, absorbing my surroundings, I overheard Daniel talking to the stranger on the other side of him.

"Yeah, I have an idea. I think it's going to be really hot. And listen, if you know anyone who might be interested in investing, let me know."

I rolled my eyes and tugged on Daniel's sleeve. When he turned to me, I glared at him and said, "Dude. Not cool."

"What?" Daniel asked defensively.

Just then, waiters started ringing dinner bell chimes, politely asking the Treehouse group to kindly take their seats. And saving Daniel and me from a fight.

Just after dessert was served, the orchestra began to play louder—Mozart, Strauss, and Beethoven—and two by two, couples began gliding around the Christmas tree. It was such a memorable, breathtaking sight to see—not at all the bad version of *The Nutcracker* that I'd envisioned. Scott had such great vision, though, didn't he? It was exactly as he'd dreamed so he wasn't at all surprised that we looked like professional extras on the set of some costume drama, or that everyone was enjoying themselves as they quick-quick-slowed their way through the Viennese Waltz. His creativity and imagination were inspiring and mind-blowing. *Who else would think of this?* As Daniel led me toward the tree, I searched for Scott in the crowd and finally caught a glimpse of him standing by himself in the back corner. *Ah, he looks so handsome in a tux.* For a moment I felt angry with Christine for leaving him alone—wasn't he *her* responsibility right now? But Scott didn't have that sad, concerned look on his face that I'd seen so many times during the roadshow. Or his cerebral look, for that matter. Instead, he beamed as his employees waltzed past him wearing their finest attire. I could tell he was pleased with himself for orchestrating such a unique holiday affair; I was pleased with him, too.

The sound of Daniel quietly chanting "Om-pa-paah, om-pa-paah" helped me glide back in step as we twirled around the tree. We *looked* like the perfect couple, but I couldn't help but notice how different we felt now compared to our first Sterling, Rich holiday party together. *We're just in a rut. An eighteen-month rut.* I closed my eyes and forced myself to focus on the now.

chapter 10

"YOU'RE A TERRIBLE WRITER!" SCOTT grunted as he sat at his desk furiously flipping through the conference call script that Jonathan had asked me to draft. Treehouse's inaugural earnings announcement as a public company was scheduled for February 17, and I knew Scott wanted it to be special. But "terrible"? That seemed a bit extreme. I was a lot of things, but a terrible writer wasn't one of them.

"No, I'm not," I insisted.

"Yes, you are."

"Even the bit about—"

"I hate the whole script."

The two of us sounded like fighting children.

"I'm sorry," I said, even though I wasn't, "but can you please be a bit more specific?"

"I just don't like it."

"Wow. That helps a lot. Such a man of details," I said sarcastically, shaking my head.

"Just send me some bullet points."

Jonathan broke in. "It may not be a good idea to wing it this first time, Scott. There will be hundreds of people and press listening in, and we'll want to be sure to stay on message. We've still got two weeks. Let us take another stab at it."

"No. I'm going to sound scripted." Scott pulled at his socks through his jeans for the fifth time, then turned to address me. "Give me four bullet points you want me to hit, Sophia. Also, I don't want the call to sound all muffled and scratchy like everyone else's. You'd better check on that."

Ugh. Such a perfectionist.

In those few seconds I was demoted from drafting one of Scott Kraft's most important public speeches to checking the sound quality of the conference call lines. Excellent.

"Which teleconference service are we using?" Scott asked.

"Bridge," I answered.

"No, use InterCall. Their sound quality is best. But even *they* aren't that good. There's got to be a better way," Scott said as he struck the *Thinker* pose.

And we're off on a tangent.

"InterCall can't handle that many lines." Then I had an idea. "How about I see if we can use the sound studio at KQED?" Our local National Public Radio station—Scott's favorite.

"Great suggestion," Scott said, his face lighting up.

Note to self: weasel our way into KQED.

This, of course, was before any of us realized our call wouldn't sound any better unless we broadcast it over KQED's radio waves. In retrospect, that should have been obvious, and I later felt like an idiot for even making the suggestion.

"Bullet points, eh?" I asked.

"Yes. That's all I want," he said. Then, earnestly, as though to make sure I wouldn't forget this crucial detail, he added, "Trust me: you are not a good writer."

Scott's words ignited a ball of fire in my stomach. *I'll show you.*

ON MY WAY home that evening, I stopped at San Francisco's Ferry Building for a quick bite to eat with Daniel. "I have some great news! Let's meet at the Mediterranean place," he'd said just a few hours earlier. Given the day I was having, great news was just what I needed.

When I arrived at the eatery, I was relieved to see that it wasn't completely full—just a lot of suits who probably worked in the offices upstairs enjoying happy hour cocktails and appetizers. A hostess led me to one of the communal tables overlooking the open kitchen and disappeared behind a silver beaded curtain. I felt as though I'd been holding my breath all day, so I closed my eyes and inhaled deeply through my nose before slowly and gently letting the air out. *Ahhhh.* I opened my eyes again—no sign of Daniel, so I reached in my purse and pulled out the "terrible" earnings call script that had ruined my day. *Might as well be productive while I'm waiting.*

"Whatcha reading?" Daniel asked ten minutes later when he appeared at the table and bent over to give me a kiss.

"Oh, nothing. Just this earnings script I gave Scott earlier," I said, putting the document back in my purse.

"Wow, you're writing stuff for him, huh?"

"Not exactly. He hated it."

It really was a piece of crap, I realized. It had a defensive tone and no spark; I knew I could do better.

"Ah," Daniel said without prodding any further. I wanted him to be sympathetic, but he didn't seem to care. Instead, he declared, "I have good news!"

Thoughts of work disappeared immediately. I sat forward, put my elbows on the table, and smiled with anticipation. "Very exciting! What is it?"

"I gave notice today. I'm quitting my job."

I leaned back and picked up my water glass.

"Seriously? Why?" I asked, trying to hide my concern.

"I want to start my own company," he said. "A tech company."

It took everything I had to stop myself from rolling my eyes.

"That's great, babe. But most people don't just quit their jobs to do that. They do it *while* they're working. Isn't that the smarter approach? You have student debt, don't you?"

Daniel locked his eyes on mine. "I just feel like the train is passing me by and everyone else is on it but me." I could see how serious he was about this and how badly he wanted it, but Daniel wasn't startup material. He was too honest, not a salesman, and thought too much in black and white. He'd get eaten alive.

I tried to muster up a flicker of enthusiasm. "What's the idea?"

"It's called Clicktone."

"Clicktone? That's pretty catchy. What does Clicktone do?"

"It's an online exchange where people can trade their unwanted gift cards."

I weighed Daniel's idea and asked myself whether I'd use such an exchange. *They don't expire. They're becoming more and more popular. But here's the wrench—how many gift cards do people get every year? Not that many.*

"How will you make *money*?"

"Advertising. And a small fee for every gift card trade."

"Okay, well before you can sell advertising, you need users, don't you? Users are really expensive to acquire. So where are you going to get funding?"

"I don't want funding. That just gives investors a chunk of *my* ownership."

Pigs get slaughtered.

Daniel opened his menu and glanced through the appetizers as he continued, "Anyway, getting users won't be a problem. I'm going to use my Stanford alumni network. This is going to be a viral thing. Friends will tell friends."

He's been reading too much Wired *magazine.*

"Who's going to build the technology for this online exchange?"

"I'm going to teach myself to code software," Daniel replied. He never questioned his intelligence or skills—you had to give him that—but still, that was the stupidest thing he'd said yet.

"Are you sure about this? You're going to give up your job right now?"

"If not now, when? What am I doing that's so important, anyway? It's not what I'd imagined."

"You're saving the environment!"

"Wellllll . . ." Daniel waved his hand as though the environment wasn't so important after all.

There was something more behind this new life plan, and I needed to know what it was. I remembered Daniel's expression a few weeks ago when he saw my paycheck stub in my purse. He was looking for my car keys, but his raised eyebrows and pursed lips told me he got a blow to his ego instead.

"Why are you doing this, really? For the money?"

"Ha, no, of course not. It's just way more appealing to me than being wrapped up in the red tape of environmental politics."

Daniel was still looking at the menu as though his new life plan weren't a big deal. For the first time I saw the child that he was. I wanted to protect him from what I knew would be a failure, but it was clear that he'd made up his mind. My only option was to accept his decision and help him—*For better or for worse, right?* But my heart sank like a rock as I heard my mom's voice in my head:

"Men need to have their ducks in a row before they're ready for marriage, dear."

"Daniel," I said in an effort to get his attention. "At least let me introduce you to—"

"I don't want your help. I want to do it myself."

"But—"

"Sophia, I know more about this than you do," Daniel declared.

"Ha! Okay, right. Sorry, I forgot," I said sarcastically. A few years ago I might have actually believed Daniel, but now I knew better.

Mom's voice came into my head again:

"Men don't want women who are smarter than them. They need their egos stroked."

If Scott were here he'd stand up and dismiss Daniel with just a look. But Scott didn't want the things I wanted. He hadn't spent a lifetime looking for Prince Charming, waiting for the person who would make her half a whole. I could crush Daniel under one stiletto with the force of what I knew, but did I want to?

Pick your battles, Sophia. Bite your tongue, Sophia.

But I couldn't.

"Except you don't," I said.

"What's that, babe?" Daniel was sipping a glass of wine that had just been placed in front of him. He peered at me innocently over the rim.

"You *don't* know more than I do. Least of all about running a startup. I've watched the best, and worst, in action."

I waited for this to escalate into a fight. But Daniel didn't seem to have heard me at all. He was buried in the menu, finger trailing along the offerings. Suddenly he looked up brightly.

"Oysters?" he asked. "I feel like celebrating."

LATER, AS I drove home to my parents' house, I called Audrey whimpering.

"What's wrong? You okay, Sissy?" she asked. "Are you sick?"

"No!" I snapped. "Stop asking me that. You guys always think I'm sick, and I'm fine!"

"Okay. Jeez."

I began to cry. I could barely hear Audrey through the phone as she asked me again to tell her what was wrong.

"Daniel," I managed. "He's going to try to start his own company, which means he's never going to ask me to marry him! You know what Mom says about men and their stupid ducks! Marriage is totally off his radar."

"Oh, Jesus, Sophia. Are you still on that? You haven't talked about wanting to get married for months, *thank God*! Besides, isn't it too soon to be thinking about marriage? How long have you two been together?"

"Over a year and a half!"

"Oh," she said, sounding disappointed. "Well, have you guys discussed marriage?"

No.

Audrey read my silence and responded appropriately. "Look, you may want to get married, but I think you like the *idea* of it more than the man you're dating."

I knew Audrey was being protective. She hated seeing me hurt or upset. Still, it felt good to argue. I could always count on my big sister for that. "That's easy for *you* to say! You're married and you have Ava!" I shouted. "You're such a hypocrite. Of course I want to be married. I'm just not in such a hurry anymore."

"The grass is always greener," she said.

Audrey would never understand why I wanted to get married so badly. I didn't blame her—I couldn't really explain it, either, other than that marriage was the next "thing" to do, and Daniel was the closest way there. Besides, the thought of life without him seemed unbearable. Health problems, long hours, even Scott Kraft I could handle. But heartache and loneliness were a different story.

IT WAS AUDREY'S idea for me to take the day off. "Tomorrow your eyes will be swollen from crying," she'd said the night before. "Come up to the city and have lunch with me at the office." Between the conference call script debacle and Daniel, I felt like I was following in

IR person number six's footsteps, so Audrey's suggestion sounded like a good one. Besides, I had been thinking about getting a new look—a smarter, sleeker one rather than the country-club fashion that Mom filled my closet with—so the next morning I headed to Union Square. A couple of hours later I arrived at Audrey's office on the nineteenth floor of the Transamerica Pyramid still pouting a little despite a new, short bob-style haircut, two shopping bags full of on-sale winter clothes from Saks Fifth Avenue, and a less full one representing my jump on a new spring wardrobe from Neiman Marcus. Audrey was on the phone barking at someone, likely one of her traders, so I sat down. Without getting off the phone, she slid an unmistakable robin's-egg blue box across her desk, which I caught with my right hand and an excited smile. There was a small enclosure card that read: *Never wait for a man to buy you a diamond. Love, Audrey.*

I opened the trademark Tiffany & Co. box to find a three-carat pear-shaped diamond solitaire that hung from a simple eighteen-inch white-gold chain.

Gasp!

All thoughts of Daniel fell away as I unclasped the necklace and pulled each end around my neck. When I looked up at Audrey, she was shaking her head in disgust, shooing me out of her office so she could finish her phone call. It was so typical of her, of our family. *Have a problem? Fix it and get over it.*

ALTHOUGH JONATHAN, DANIEL, and even Kate had counseled me to "just give Scott the bullet points like he asked," I was determined to rewrite the Treehouse earnings call script because if I didn't, I'd be forever known as a "terrible writer." So over the next weekend I spent hours reviewing my old roadshow notes, trying to remember the cadence of Scott's voice, the exact words that he'd used, and the topics he seemed passionate about; those were the ones he'd want in the script. Then, channeling Scott, I began to type, delete, and then re-type for two days straight.

On Monday, three days before our earnings call, I waited until Ashley gave me the okay before I went to see Scott. When she did, my new spike heels snagged on the fibers of the commercial-grade carpet and I could hear them whisper *prick, prick, prick* as they carried me into his office holding a newly revised conference call script.

"Nice dress," Scott said. I was wearing a new, simple black Armani sheath dress and sleek Manolo Blahnik sling-back heels, both purchased the day Audrey gave me my diamond.

"Oh, thanks. I was wondering if you'd look at this new draft of your script."

"You already sent me the bullets."

"Yeah, but I took another shot at it."

"I don't have time to review it," he said without looking up from his computer.

"I worked hard on this, Scott. You don't have to read it now, but promise you'll take a look at it before the call."

His eyes turned toward me, narrowed and glaring. "You're upsetting me, Sophia."

"*You* are upsetting *me!*" I said. Despite my better judgment, I could feel my voice rising. "Help me help you."

"You're yelling."

"Scott, you don't know real yelling until you've met my mother. I can really yell, and this isn't it." There it was, my best Penny Jenkins–approved, from-the-abdomen voice. I wanted him to know I meant business.

"Hmmph. I'll believe it when I see it," he said before reaching out for the document. He spent a few minutes scanning my work as I stood there; his face showed no expression. When he looked up again, his silence made me want to run and hide. *I'll just be in my office looking at the job listings, thanks.* But then Scott gave me a nod and said, "Better. Much better. It works. Has Jonathan seen this already?"

"No."

"Okay. I'll make some edits, but it looks pretty good. Send it to me and please cc Ashley and Jonathan."

I did nothing to hide my huge smile. *He said please.*

Ashley walked in as I strutted out of the office. "Doesn't she look great today, Scott? That bob and black dress suit you," she said. My mom had said the same thing earlier that morning—it was the first time she hadn't picked at me before I left the house.

"She does look good. That's a great look for you, Sophia. Simple black outfits are always in style. But kill the costume jewelry."

Scott might know a lot of things, but he sure doesn't know a real rock when he sees one.

"Got it," I said, embarrassed at the attention. But there were worse things in life than being styled by Scott Kraft.

I LET MYSELF into Daniel's apartment after work, planning to make a quiet dinner for two after I kicked off my shoes. Even hearing about Daniel's progress on his startup—as minimal as it was—sounded good to me. The whole *I know more than you about everything* nonsense still nagged at me, but I had been trying hard to put it out of my mind. Because if I couldn't forget it, maybe he wasn't so charming after all. I could hear my mother now: *I told you so.*

"Wait until you hear what happened today with Scott and Dylan," I called out. I put my purse down on a strange shoe box with my name on it, then found Daniel in his room.

"What's up with that box by the door?" I asked.

Daniel shook his head and sat down on the bed. "This isn't going to work, Sophia. I can't be just some bit player in *The Sophia Show.* That's not what I want. I packed your stuff up for you."

My thoughts immediately went to my insecurities—did he want someone taller? A blonde? Someone smarter? "Did you meet someone else?" I asked.

It would have been easier for me to hear if another woman were the reason this was all happening, but instead Daniel said, "I'm tired of living in your shadow."

"What? That's ridiculous." Even as I said it, though, it felt untrue.

"Every time we're with our friends, or your family, we spend the whole time talking about what *you're* doing," Daniel continued. "Or what Scott Kraft is doing. It's as though I'm just along for the ride. No one seems interested in Clicktone, not our friends or even my own family."

That's because it's a stupid idea, you moron.

Daniel was referring to our recent dinner with Mr. and Mrs. Weinstein. The same dinner where his mom had handed me her copies of *The Joy Luck Club* and *Wild Swans* and said, "Oh, you'll love these." I envisioned adding them to the stack of other unread Chinese-themed books she'd given me. Thankfully, before she could corner me into a discussion about them, Daniel had changed the subject.

"I've got Clicktone's shopping cart built," he'd said very enthusiastically while our appetizers were being served. But Mr. Weinstein had only nodded politely at his son before changing the subject: "Can you give us a hint about which actors will be the voices for the new characters in your next movie?"

The truth was that my life *was* more interesting than Daniel's. At that moment, anyway. There was no doubt he was book-smart and hardworking, but I was savvy and even more hardworking. Let's face it—I was also just plain more entertaining than he was. But none of that meant we couldn't be together. Did it?

"How long have you felt this way?" I asked.

"It doesn't matter," he mumbled, looking at the floor. Then, with tears welling in his eyes, he said loud and clear, "We don't have a future together."

I stared at my bare feet; I couldn't look at Daniel's face. Couldn't believe the words I was hearing. Had I done this? Mom's lifelong words of advice entered my thoughts:

Men need their egos stroked, dear.

You need to let the man be the man, dear.

You can be right without letting him know you're right, dear.

But how was I to play that role *and* be the woman who could bring home the bacon and fry it up in a pan? That was the person my parents raised me to be, but they never actually told me how I was supposed to pull it off.

I left without the box. He could have my things. I didn't need them anymore.

I CRIED UNABASHEDLY for two weeks. Straight. At work, at home, in restaurants. With anyone that would listen. My heart was filled with grief, pure grief, and I couldn't believe how badly I hurt. I couldn't sleep, eat, or drink, and my blood sugar levels were all over the map. I felt all alone even though my parents were on the other side of the house; I knew I couldn't talk to them. They were certainly not disappointed at Daniel's absence and didn't understand why I was. It was almost one o'clock in the morning when I rang Kate.

"I wasted all that time. Almost *two* years! I thought he loved me," I sobbed.

My best friend whispered ever so quietly into the phone, "Hang on. Let me go into the other room so I don't wake up Mark." Then, seconds later, in a more audible tone, she said, "Oh, Sophia, I'm so sorry you're going through this. You just have to dive through it. Just take a deep breath and jump."

"I'm trying. I really am," I said. I knew I'd have to pull it together soon because even *I* was tired of hearing myself talk about the demise of my relationship with Daniel.

"You just weren't ready to say goodbye, so you're upset that he was the one to say it," Kate reassured me. "But you would have done it when you were ready. I know you would have."

That all made sense, but it didn't help at all. The worst part was that I couldn't pinpoint why I was so devastated. I bought a journal to write down my thoughts: *Dear Daniel* letters that told him how much I missed him, simple statements like *I hate you,* and pages and pages of all the things I might have done to drive away my boyfriend.

If it really was because of my career, will all Prince Charmings have the same view? Can't I be a great girlfriend and *have a career?*

The following week, whether it was because of the lack of sleep or the bad breakup diet I'd adopted, my stomach began to ache.

"What's wrong with you?" Scott asked one morning as he and Jonathan passed me in the hallway outside our offices.

"What do you mean?"

"You're all hunched over. And your eyes—they're all puffy."

"Daniel broke up with me." My eyes began to tear.

"Oh, Jesus," Scott said, rolling his eyes.

"Look! I'm allowed to be upset. And if you don't like it, then fire me!" I said, knowing he wouldn't.

"Don't mind him, Sophia. You are always welcome to express your emotions here," Jonathan said as he gave me a hug. "The world would be a better place if *everyone* were more sensitive."

Scott was less sympathetic. "I told you," he snapped. "I told you I didn't like that guy. You're partly to blame, though. You are putting out the wrong energy, Sophia. If you don't reflect on that, you will continue to attract the wrong people."

I furrowed my brow. At least being angry at Scott was one way to make my tears stop. "Oh, come on, Scott. What energy am I transmitting? You seemed to *like* my energy when you met me."

"You transmit a very transactional energy. Very get-things-done."

"What does that mean?"

"You heard me. Energy is like a magnet. Whatever you transmit attracts that very thing back. So Daniel was never going to be the one for you because you weren't putting that vibration out there."

"Excuse me, but how do you know?" I asked.

"I just know. You have to feel what you *expect to have*, not what you *want*. Otherwise, you're just focusing on what's missing—and that's negative energy. Make a list of the three most important elements you want your relationship to have, then visualize you and your future partner living as *that* couple. Actually try to *feel* what it will be like to be with the right person who loves you unconditionally. Focus on that and you'll start to vibrate. And when you vibrate, the energy you emit will attract whatever it is that you're looking for."

"And meditate," Jonathan added. "It opens a new dimension to our lives and is a means to tap into a deep source of positive energy and joy. Just try two minutes at a time, Sophia."

"Yes, meditate. I've told you that before," Scott said.

Well, bring in the circus of experts.

I recalled the meditation workshop they'd forced me to attend shortly after the holidays—it was held at the meditation center that Scott and Jonathan personally funded, then opened to the public. The center was in a beautiful building in a beautiful setting . . . and yet I couldn't wait to get out of there. *Bunch of yogis. Sitting still and focusing on my breath . . . when there was so much I could be getting done.* But it had been three weeks since the breakup, and I'd been thinking a lot about how other people got through things like this. There were the sweatpants-and-ice-cream people, the gym-till-midnight people, the bury-yourself-in-work people, the vibrating yogis. Who was to say that the yogis were any more or less effective than the rest of us?

I didn't have a method. Self-help just wasn't my style. Journaling was as far as I could push that approach. For me, it just took time. Slowly, I allowed myself to mourn the loss of Daniel and the possibility that he brought to me. He had been my evidence that I was doing what I was supposed to be doing: creating the life that Audrey had. But I reminded myself I wasn't Audrey, and I certainly wasn't the same person whom Daniel fell in love with. The person I was "supposed" to be—sweet, happy-go-lucky, giggling at my boyfriend's jokes. Everything that the stereotypical rules of "How to Catch a Man" evangelized. I had become more than that. Something inside me had shifted and I had found the part of myself that felt most natural to me. I still wasn't sure what I really wanted, but I knew that I deserved more. Someone who would love all of me.

chapter 11

MORE THAN A YEAR LATER, I stood in front of Legoland's snack pavilion on a scorching San Diego day, trying to remember why I used to love places like this so much. There was something about the "Lands"— Legoland, Sambaland, all those types of Lands—that filled kids with pure joy, but as an adult without children, their attraction escaped me. I realized these theme parks were all the same: kids running amok as though they were on Red Bull IV drips, the frenetic *pings* and *pongs* of overpriced boardwalk-style games, loud rides, long lines, and jumbo sticky snacks that were a diabetic's worst nightmare. I would have gladly been somewhere else, but a few months earlier, as casually as I might say, "I'd like to try this in a size four," Scott beckoned me into his office and told me to "do some research on amusement parks." *Amusement parks.*

"Ha! Oh, right. I'll get on that straightaway," I said sarcastically. I held my pen to my yellow notepad then, and waited for Scott to tell me what he *really* wanted. But he was silent and seemed puzzled by my tone.

My chin tilted down toward my shoulder and I frowned. "You can't be serious. I wouldn't even know how to get started on something like that."

"You'll figure it out," Scott said confidently before turning to his computer to check his email.

"Do you have any idea what happens when you ask me to do something?" I huffed, feeling the weight of the work I already had piling up. Scott didn't answer, so I continued, "Let me show you."

I stood and took two steps to his whiteboard, then pushed up the long sleeves of my gray silk dress. Using a dry-erase pen, I listed all the projects that were on my plate, none of which included what I was actually hired to do—manage Treehouse's relationship with existing and potential investors and analysts. Next I scrawled various internal and external resources—marketing, PR, graphic design, engineering, finance, Samba—in the shape of a hexagon and shouted while drawing circles around each of them, "When you *casually* tell me to do something, all these wheels get set into motion." I stopped and took a breath, noticing that Scott still didn't understand what the big deal was, so I turned back to the whiteboard and drew lines connecting the projects to the various departments, but more dramatically and furiously this time. When I was finished, my masterpiece looked like the diagram of a molecule. "You are distracting me from my day job *and* forcing me to send teams of people off on tangents! Yet I can't tell them exactly what's going on because God forbid it gets out to Wall Street. So my coworkers think I'm an insane pain in the ass! You have to understand that there's a snowball effect every time you open your mouth!"

Scott tried to say something, but I interrupted.

"You didn't hire me for any of this. I'm not qualified to study the overindulged children at Legoland."

Scott was trying not to laugh, which made me even angrier.

"Oh, yes. This is really funny. Send me on wild goose chases just for yucks. Clearly you overestimate me."

Scott looked at me impatiently, which meant I'd pushed far enough and he wasn't going to change his mind. "Don't give me that shit, Sophia. You're *under*estimating yourself. Instead of being so focused on the to-do lists, take a moment to ask yourself what I'm teaching you."

I opened my mouth to say something, but found myself with no words. Defeated, I stormed out of his office, wishing I weren't wearing the dark stiletto pumps that slowed me down. I could hear Scott laughing behind me, shouting, "Hey, take it easy." Then, louder, "And don't be mad, but I forgot to tell you that we're building a brand-new campus. I'll need a press release, but give as little detail as possible." I stopped in my tracks, turned around, and walked back.

"What did you *forget* to tell me?" I asked, using my hands to make air quotation marks as I said the word *forget*. It was actually Jonathan's job to tell me these things so I should have directed my anger at him.

"We're building a new campus," he said. The smile on his face told me this was something he was really excited about. It also explained why he'd never bothered to make his office nicer; he knew this would happen someday. It was another milestone in his grand plan—whatever *that* was.

"Are you *sure*?"

"Yes."

"Does Jonathan know?" I sneered.

"Yes, of course. We've been working on it for a while."

A while? Thanks for keeping me in the loop.

"You know what will happen when Wall Street hears about this new, enormous expense, right?"

He shrugged, sending me storming out of his office once again.

IN LATE MAY I found myself wandering around the Lands estimating park attendance, number of employees, property costs, average number of times people rode each ride, average concession and merchandise spend per park attendee, etc. All while remotely juggling the day-to-day demands of my IR role. Maybe it was just in my head, but I was actually getting a stomachache observing the massive amounts of money being spent on unhealthy food and cheap plastic toys that I knew would end up in a landfill. My prolonged loitering around the Big Shop in Legoland very likely convinced the hoodied guy manning the cash register that I was either stalking him or planning the world's largest heist of toy sets. I knew I should have been honored and flattered that Scott trusted me with these projects. But it was hard to feel that way while standing in the middle of the chaos, sweating like a pig in my black capris and cashmere-silk-blend T-shirt.

The mind-numbing work was getting old, so I let my thoughts wander to Kate and to our outing just before I'd left for the theme parks. It was the first we'd had in weeks; I was becoming a terrible friend, and I knew it.

"Why the rush to get your lip and brows waxed?" she'd asked as I pulled her toward the pink-and-white Benefit Cosmetics store on Chestnut Street. Her pursed lips told me she wasn't particularly excited about spending her Saturday afternoon running *my* errands.

"I need to get this done before family dinner tomorrow, and then I'm leaving for San Diego," I responded. Then, pointing at my furry lip, I added, "Last time Audrey saw me, she asked whether I thought I was a cat."

Kate laughed. "Love your sister! Hey, how's Ava?"

Ava was nearly four years old now, and although I often spoke to her on the phone, we had spent very little quality time together over the past few months. I kept telling myself I'd see my family and friends more often, but the truth was that Treehouse satisfied something deep within me, so I began to neglect everyone and everything else that I loved. I felt guilty that work had become my priority, guilty that it had kept me from conversations like this one.

"I suck. I'm a terrible aunt, and a terrible friend."

"No, you're not. You're just busy," Kate said, but there was something in her tone that told me she was trying to convince *herself* of this just as much as she was me.

While we waited for the cosmetologist to help me, I pushed work out of my mind and did my best to make up for all the time Kate and

I had lost. She updated me about her law school applications and her family back east.

"What about work? How's it going there?"

"It's slowed down a lot," she answered.

"Or you're just getting better at it."

"What about you? What's going on at Treehouse?" Kate asked.

"Where do I even start? Jonathan and Scott just blurt things out at me and expect me to be able to figure them out. Things that are totally unrelated to investor relations!"

"Like what?" Kate seemed fascinated by my job, which made it all that much more fun for me to talk about.

"Like Friday, for example. Scott picked out these extremely expensive modern chairs for our new theater, and Jonathan said they were too pricey, so he asked me to find other options to show Scott. Who do I look like? Ty fucking Pennington?"

"He's a contractor." Kate laughed heartily, correcting my reference to the home-improvement star and dissolving my rabid expression immediately. *I do love to entertain.* "How's the new building coming? When will it be finished?"

"I don't know, but the planning, permits, and designs had been secretly in the works long before our IPO, so evidently it's moving along in record time. That is, unless Scott discovers *something* that isn't quite right and makes the team tear it all down and start over again." I laughed.

"Who won on the chairs? Scott or Jonathan?"

"Scott, of course. I went and sat in one yesterday and told him they were uncomfortable, but he didn't seem to care. With him, it's all about the design. Since he didn't like any of the ones I picked, we bought the expensive ones."

I'd hated this construction project because as soon as we announced it, Wall Street complained about the budget and worried that Treehouse management would be distracted. I did my best to address their concerns and to hold the hands of a lot of investors. But to no avail, because our stock took a hit anyway, which was made worse when a rumor began circulating that Scott had hired the famous (read: outrageously expensive) I. M. Pei as an architect. To pick up all the pieces, I went on my own version of a roadshow, meeting with institutional investors to quell their concerns. "No, no. That's ridiculous! It's not going to cost a hundred million dollars!" *Just ninety-nine million!* "Yes, the building is on schedule." *Give or take a few quarters.* "Yes, our next film is progressing as expected. See? I have a clip here for you." *Forget that we have no idea what the ending will be.*

Didn't I say there was a snowball effect?

But as the building came together, I marveled at Scott's vision and understood why it was so important to him. At least, I *thought* I did. The building itself was *huge*—about five or six times what our 150-person company needed. I couldn't see why or how we'd ever get that big, but *he* did, and I had to respect him, and his confidence, for that. From what I could tell, the building was going to be the very essence of Scott: simple, creative, and elegant. It was *his* contribution to Treehouse, and I couldn't wait for it to be finished.

With my brows neatly shaped and the skin above my lip bare and smooth as silk (and stinging), I could finally focus on what Kate and I originally intended to do—shop. We ducked into our neighborhood favorites: first Dress, and then Intermix, before hopping into a cab to treat ourselves to sushi in Cole Valley.

A twinge of guilt hit me as I brought a tako roll to my watering mouth. *Scott wouldn't approve of this nonvegan meal.* But one bite was all it took to make me forget about Scott, Jonathan, Treehouse, and Wall Street. We were laughing over my latest dating nightmare.

"Do you remember the guy who approached us the last time we were at Balboa Cafe having burgers?" I asked.

"Yes. The cute one?"

"Exactly! So, evidently, I had my Treehouse badge on that night, so he found me by guessing my email," I said.

"Well, it's not rocket science. Sophia@treehouse.com. Not too creepy. Go on."

"So he asked me out to dinner the following night. He took me to that really good place in the Castro that's impossible to get a reservation for."

"Wait, what does he do?" Kate asked.

"He's a venture capitalist. And you know I love my venture capitalists!"

"Yes. You do. Okay, so what happened?"

"Well, during dinner he reached across the table and took my hand." I reached across Kate's sushi-filled plate and grabbed her hand. "He had this really serious look in his eyes and said, 'I really like you and would love to see you again, but I want to be clear about something that's really important.' Then he says, 'You'd need to wear a kimono when we have sex. It's the only way I can have an orgasm. Is that going to be a problem for you?'"

Kate's eyes widened. "You're joking! Please say you're joking. No way! What did you do?"

"I stood up and shouted, 'I'm Chinese, dammit!'"

"That's it? That was the best you could do?"

"Hey, I was under pressure." I laughed. Then I added, "All us Asians look the same." My best friend laughed heartily as I continued. "Trust me, you're so lucky to have Mark!"

Suddenly, Kate stopped laughing and her expression changed from happy to glowing. "Well . . . that's a great segue. Mark and I are engaged!"

I felt like such a narcissist. *Me, me, me.* "What! When? Gosh, have I been so busy that I didn't know?"

"No. No. Just last night! We went to Blue Line Pizza for a quick dinner and he asked me! It wasn't romantic or anything," she said. "But actually, it was. It was perfect!"

"Okay, so tell me everything. What did he say?"

"Well, we ordered—you know how I like the thin crust but he always insists on their deep dish," she said. "So we ordered both, then after the server left, Mark said, 'It's funny. I used to think I wanted to be with someone who was *just* like me. Someone who wanted to do the same things, talk about the same things, and even eat the same things. But even though you're thin crust and I'm thick, even though you hate big events and I love them, I love you. And I want to spend my whole life with you.' Can you believe it? It's *so* dorky but *so* Mark. Anyway, at first I thought he was breaking up with me—the whole 'just like me' bit—but when I realized that wasn't what was happening, I just started bawling."

I said all the right things with glee: *so happy for you, so exciting.* Inside, though, a different tape was playing: *Oh, shit. I'm going to lose her forever.*

"And of course you'll be my maid of honor," she said.

"Yes! I'd love to! This is going to be great! I'll do a shower, and the bachelorette for sure!"

Kate looked happier than I'd ever seen her. "We want to have a small destination wedding, but we aren't sure where yet," she said.

"Where's your ring?" I asked, looking at her bare left ring finger.

"Oh, he doesn't have it yet. He wants us to go shopping together," she said.

"Are you going to show him that one in the store on Union Street? The one you stare at every time we walk by?" It was a simple platinum band with three modest-sized diamonds, and it fit Kate's understated style perfectly.

Kate smiled. "No. I wish. But it's too expensive, and I don't want to make him feel bad if he can't afford it." I knew Mark could afford it, and Kate must have known, too. She was being considerate of Mark, though. *That's true love.*

I was happy for her, but it forced me to take stock of where my own life was going. Once again, all my friends were moving on— new husbands instead of new jobs this time—and here I was, still single and still dedicating my life to evangelizing the virtues of animated characters.

But as the roller coaster operator's voice snapped me out of my reverie, I remembered that I was doing a lot more than that. I was helping Scott Kraft build his legacy. While I'd been daydreaming, it had gotten dark at the Legoland snack pavilion, and the toddler crowd was slowly changing to rowdy teenagers who were out on dates or roaming free from their parents.

It was time for me to go.

I weaved my way through the children, the parents chasing the children, and the adult children, the ones who surely spent the most here by buying special edition Lego sets in the Big Shop. I exited through the turnstile, hoping not to return. Until Ava was old enough, that is.

AFTER FIVE DAYS at Legoland and Sambaland, I finally met Scott and Jonathan at the place they believed most closely resembled their Treehouse-theme-park vision: Universal Studios. Scott made his way through the property like a private investigator, stopping often to absorb whatever caught his eye. Sometimes he stared almost too long at a woman with a camera around her neck interacting with her telephone; other times I could tell he was comparing the lines for two rides, trying to gauge which one attendees preferred. I'd provided him with pages of analyst reports and industry reports, both of which highlighted the most popular attractions, but he wanted to see it all himself. At every moment, Scott seemed to be asking himself, *What is working, and what would make that better?*

Toward the end of our trip, it was clear Scott and Jonathan had found the attraction that *they* liked the most: *Back to the Future: The Ride.*

"Let's go again," Scott said with a smile.

Ugh. It would be the eighth time on that same ride.

"Hell to the no!" I said. It was the most polite response I could muster and a phrase I'd picked up from spending so much time eavesdropping on groups of obnoxious teens.

"Sophia, live in the moment. Enjoy it," Scott said, not noticing the small Japanese woman staring at us. She had circled us once already at an extremely slow pace and was on round two at a closer distance while holding out her camera. Knowing Scott didn't like talking to fans, I purposely boxed her out without missing a beat in our conversation.

"Oh, come on. Don't be such a downer."

"Seriously. I'll wait right here. And don't use work as an excuse to get me on there, because by now I bet I know everything there is to know about the stupid ride. Speaking of which, we're not really going to do this, are we?" As I spoke I took a few steps toward the stalker woman—her face had glazed over with the Scott effect—and gently turned her around before giving her a very soft send-off. Scott locked eyes with me and smiled.

"Do what?" Jonathan asked.

"A theme park," I responded.

"If we can do it well, I'd like to do it," Scott said, his cheerfulness gone. "You're worrying about something that isn't even a worry yet. Again, live in the moment."

"Oh, believe me," I snapped, "I *do* live in the moment. I live in the moment of five thirty A.M., when my cell phone rings and an investor asks me why you two are here at Universal Studios. It's gotten back to the Street, you know!"

"Oh, that's ridiculous," Jonathan said as he motioned for Scott to join him again on *Back to the Future.* "How would they know?"

"It's summer break! Investors take their families places, and you're not exactly invisible."

"Our stock is stable—we're fine."

"Really?" I asked. "You don't think they read into this? They read into everything, even the timing of your vacations. Did you know that? Last quarter they started calling a week before we announced earnings to ask a very innocent-sounding question: 'Is Scott or Jonathan in the office?'"

"So? Who cares?" Scott asked.

I was about to lose my temper, but just then, a man's voice called out from behind me, "Excuse me, but are you as stupid as you are good-looking? Wait, no! That's not what I meant. I meant . . ."

Scott, Jonathan, and I turned around to see who the babbling idiot was; my anger-filled eyes turned soft as I caught sight of Mark's roommate—the curly-haired, witty one, Peter. He was laughing nervously; his face was bright red. I hadn't seen him since that night at the Dutch Goose.

"Oh my gosh, it's you!" I exclaimed, completely surprised by the random run-in and also relieved to see someone friendly, someone from *home.* "*Very* 'Rico Suave' of you. Do they teach you that in urology class?" Without breaking eye contact with Peter, I waved Scott and Jonathan into the line.

"You know I didn't mean that! I heard someone use that line in a bar the other day and I thought it was funny, especially because it was a woman saying it to a man."

"What were her *exact* words?"

"Well, it was the end of the night, in all fairness, and she'd clearly been drinking. She walked up to a guy and said, 'Are you as smart as you are good-looking? Or are you just dumb?'"

We both laughed, probably harder than the joke deserved, but it was good to see his face in the sea of insanity that I'd been in the middle of all day.

"What are you doing here?" I asked. Out of the corner of my eye I could see Jonathan and Scott staring.

"I took a few days off. My sister and nephew are in town and wanted to see Universal Studios."

"Where are they? Have you guys been here before?"

"They ran to the bathroom. And no, we didn't have that kind of money growing up," he explained. "Too many kids—there were six of us."

There was something about Peter—his matter-of-factness, his humility, his warmth—that drew me comfortably to him. It had been almost four years since that night we'd met at the Goose. He was probably in his third year of residency by now.

"What are *you* doing here?" he asked.

"It's confidential, but I'm here for work." I turned to look at Jonathan and Scott and glared at them for still standing there; Peter's eyes followed mine.

"Oh yeah, Mark said you're working at Treehouse. Congrats!"

"Thanks. This is Scott and Jonathan, and they're just leaving to get in line," I said as I shoved the two men off toward the ride.

As my bosses left, I expected Peter to ask me about the legendary Scott Kraft. Everyone else did. But he just stood there and looked happy. It was refreshing.

"Thanks, it feels like I've been there forever, but I really like it. So you're finished with medical school? Where are you doing your residency?"

"At Stanford. It's hard to leave that place," he said.

For the first time, I noticed Peter's huge, beautiful blue eyes and impossibly long eyelashes. He looked like a cherub, a fit one at that.

"I know. I should have moved out of my parents' house a while ago, but who doesn't love the 'no rent' thing?" The truth was that living with my parents didn't bother me anymore; they weren't in town that often, and being at home meant I could save for my own apartment. In fact, I had begun looking through the Sunday open house listings, but stopped when I saw what my money could actually buy—a dilapidated studio with no parking, if I was lucky.

Peter and I talked about Kate and Mark's engagement a little, about which part of medicine he enjoyed the most so far and why. Him talking about his work made him even more handsome than he already was. *A ten. A definite ten.*

"Listen, I don't want to keep you—looks like your bosses are waiting for you over there. But let's get dinner when you're back," he said, then gave me a hug and walked away.

I watched Peter for a moment, and then turned back to glare at Scott and Jonathan, who had only made it a few steps away. Without missing a beat, I continued our earlier conversation trying to be stern, but probably sounding giddy. "I care! Some sneaky, or stupid, investors assumed if you and Jonathan were out gallivanting around that it meant we had the quarter in the bag. If I said you were in meetings, they interpreted that as it was a tight quarter."

"Wait, who was that guy?" Jonathan asked.

"He likes you. He's got good energy. You should date him," Scott added.

"Yeah, yeah. Let's just finish this conversation," I said. "If investors begin to whisper their expectations to their other investor buddies, a rumor on the Street takes on a life of its own—expectations that I can't manage. So can we please go home?" I felt like I was nagging a husband or a child or something. I deserved to be somewhere sipping a glass of wine and reflecting on the hotness of various men in my vicinity, not cajoling executives out of an amusement-park ride. *Is this what marriage is going to be like?*

"Since you're already in a bad mood, I should tell you that I'm not going to participate in our next earnings call," Scott said.

I stopped walking, closed my eyes, took a deep breath, and counted to ten.

I'm going to kill him.

Then I turned around to face Scott and said very quietly, "Why?"

"I hate those things—you and Jonathan can do it on your own. It's been over a year now. That's enough."

I turned and looked at Jonathan. He was just as stunned as I was. Scott could be difficult, but he usually agreed to what little I asked of him when it came to IR matters. I knew something was going on. What was it?

TWO DAYS LATER, I was finally (and happily) back in the civilized world of healthy foods and *adult* madness when I received a text message from Kate: Just gave your email address to Peter. OMG. Call me asap!

Shortly after, an email appeared in my inbox that made my heart flutter.

> To: Sophia Young
> From: Peter Bruce
> Subj: Next weekend
>
> Sophia,
> Hope you don't mind that I asked Kate for your email. It was great running into you.
>   I'm not sure if you have plans this weekend, but I'm going to the internal medicine department's year-end formal, and I was wondering if you'd want to go with me? The fancy invitation attached includes all the details.
>   Regardless, I look forward to seeing you sometime soon.
> —Peter

I opened the attachment and laughed. The invitation was hand-drawn, I assumed by Peter, on the back of what looked like a pink

While You Were Out note. It included fancy curlicue lines along the border of the paper and was personalized with my name. It read:

DOCTOR PETER BRUCE, M.D.

Hereby Extends a Most Welcome and Warm Invitation to

Ms. Sophia Young

for

Stanford Medical's "We Made It Through Another Year" Celebration

This Saturday at Seven O'Clock in the Evening

Transportation Provided

P.S. Formal attire requested

To: Peter Bruce
From: Sophia Young
Subj: Re: Next weekend

Peter,
I'd love to join you on Saturday. Are we talking tuxedos and floor-length dresses? Please help a girl out. ☺
    Thank you for the invitation.

I PEEKED OUT my bedroom window just as Peter pulled up in a boxy Honda Accord that looked similar to the one my mom drove when I was two. Thank God my parents were out of the country; they would have added to my anxiety. *Do I look okay? Am I dressed appropriately?* I fumbled with my simple floor-length red silk dress, the only detail being a thigh-high slit. I tousled my hair one more time before opening the door. As soon as I saw Peter's approving smile, a comfortable feeling warmed me over. Peter took three steps into the foyer, then kissed me gently on my cheek and whispered, "You look beautiful." The corners of my mouth nearly touched my ears.

The Rosewood's lobby was quiet, but when Peter and I approached the entrance to the ballroom, it was clear that a party was under way. Inside, the lights were dim and Top Forty music was blaring over the conversations of a young, jovial crowd. Their discussions seemed to stop suddenly, though; their eyes turned toward Peter and me. I looked down at my dress to see if I'd spilled something earlier, but the crowd wasn't looking at me. They were looking at Peter.

"Well, well, well. You've finally brought someone to meet the family," said a tuxedo-wearing man with glasses. He walked over and put his arm around Peter. "Hi, I'm Jared. You're the first girl he's brought to one of our many social functions. Seems our boy is a bit shy with the ladies."

"Jared, this is Sophia," Peter said, doing his best to hide his embarrassment.

"Nice to meet you, Sophia. Which department are you in?" Jared nosed.

"Oh, none of them. I work at a tech company."

"Well, we welcome money-hungry tech people," Jared joked before turning his comments to Peter in a more serious tone. "And congratulations, buddy. Well done. No one deserves it more and no one will do as good of a job. I'm glad you're going to be our fearless leader." Jared raised both hands above his head and made bowing gestures as though worshipping Peter.

Peter blushed and humbly changed the subject. "Thanks, Jared. How about you buy me a drink?"

"Yeah, you need one after the day you've had. That patient was a tough one. It's an open bar, so sure, I'll get you all the drinks you want."

We followed Jared into the dense crowd. As though he was testing to see if I would hold his hand, Peter brushed two of his fingers against my palm. I grinned and interlaced my fingers with his, appreciating how strong and large his hand felt against mine. His lips turned upward and he leaned down to whisper in my ear in a commanding but joking tone, "You're coming with me, woman!"

I laughed and asked, "What was Jared congratulating you about?"

"Oh, nothing. It was announced today that I'll be chief resident next year."

A chill ran up my spine. "Wow, chief. Impressive! Congratulations. Are you sure you want to be seen with me? I mean, you're the big man here."

Peter chuckled and squeezed my hand tighter. "It is a true pleasure. I'm glad you could come."

As the party went on into the evening, I knew something special was happening, although I couldn't quite figure out what it was. Perhaps it was the wine, or the heady aroma of the large stargazer lily arrangements. Or maybe it was the way Peter maintained incredible modesty while his peers showered him with praise. But when I saw Dr. Peter Bruce step onto the dance floor and bust some moves like a Madonna backup dancer, I immediately realized what was so special. It was *him*. I was drawn to his silliness and carefree attitude and the fact that he didn't take himself too seriously. He knew exactly where his life was going—he'd always known—*and* was excited about it. I felt giddy in a way that I had never felt before. So much so that it scared me. But I put it all in the back of my mind and strutted my way onto the dance floor with moves of my own.

chapter 12

PETER'S NEW APARTMENT WAS LOCATED across the street from the Palo Alto train station and within biking distance of Stanford Hospital. It was a dated one-bedroom sparsely decorated with dark IKEA furniture, the only exception being an old pink wooden desk that someone had left on a curb. "This is yours," Peter announced one day while proudly setting up the desk next to his. "You can use it when you're here." We both knew our respective long work hours meant the pink desk wouldn't get much use, but it showed how much he supported my career, so I loved every nick and pen mark on it.

The desk was the first thing that caught my eye when I walked into his kitchen early one October morning after taking full advantage of my parents being out of the country. The layer of dust on top of it was the second. But I fought the urge to start cleaning and to be the woman my mom raised me to be. *It's not your house, Sophia.* Instead, I let my boyfriend's voice grab my attention. The night before, he had fallen asleep next to me still wearing his pale blue scrubs and holding a yellow highlighter pen, which wound up on the floor next to the copy of the *New England Journal of Medicine* that he'd been reading.

"Well hello, Sophia," Peter said, trying to act aloof but knowing I knew better. It was a game he played to evoke a smile from me, and I never failed to respond.

I walked over and nuzzled his neck. "Hi. Good morning. What's on your agenda today?"

"Let's talk about something else. I hate how sick people make you so sad," Peter said. "How about I make breakfast for us?"

I grinned. "What's on the menu?"

THE SUN HAD not yet risen as I drove across the Bay Bridge, which took me from Woodside to the East Bay. When I arrived at Treehouse thirty minutes later, light streamed through the crack under Jonathan's door and into the still-dark hallway. I hadn't recalled him *ever* arriving before me, so I stopped in to see if everything was okay. When I saw his face, I could tell there would be no good-morning hug coming from him today.

"Scott is taking over as temporary CEO of his former company, Quince. We need to issue a press release after the stock markets close." I couldn't believe the way he was just blurting it out like that, so calmly.

"What?" I asked, completely confused. *How could he choose boring computers over animated films? Over us?*

"He's going to be spending half his time at Quince," Jonathan explained. Quince had been floundering since Scott had "resigned" more than ten years ago, and its board had recently fired the company's fifth CEO since Scott's departure.

"What does that mean? Exactly?" I asked, feeling slightly panicked. I knew Wall Street would punish our stock for this and that it would take me weeks, even months, to calm down investors.

"He'll still be involved in the things he needs to be involved in here, but you know that the office of the president—Dylan, Matteo, and I—really runs the day-to-day." I assumed this would somehow turn out to mean more work for me, and I couldn't imagine taking on another ounce. I felt scared for myself and for Treehouse. I worried that we'd be nothing without Scott.

Ashley's car wasn't in the parking lot, so I tracked her down on her cell phone.

"This is Ashley," she answered, her *don't mess with me* tone at its finest. Her phone was probably blowing up.

"It's me."

"Hi." Ashley's voice softened.

"Can you have him call me when you hear from him?" I asked.

"Hang on, he's actually right here. Let me get him." *Here? Where's here?*

"What's up?" Scott asked.

"Where are you?"

"We're at Quince."

Shit, it's already happening.

"Please don't do this. Please don't leave me," I begged into the end of the telephone receiver.

"This is important, Sophia. I'll still spend quality time on Treehouse, but the company really doesn't need me anymore. Not day to day, anyway, and that will be what we tell the Street."

"But how can you go back?"

"Listen. It does no good for me to feel any sort of negative energy about the past. That doesn't help me. It doesn't help anyone."

Goddamn Scott and his Zen theories!

I thought of my dad and repeated one of his many sayings: "Baggage only hurts us."

"That's right! I have a chance to restart Quince, and they are at rock bottom, so I have nothing to lose. I can take a lot of risk and be totally innovative," he replied.

"Wait, what do you mean, 'restart Quince'? I thought you were just doing this temporarily. You can't do it forever, Scott. I'm telling you, you will never be able to turn that ship around."

"Thanks for the confidence, Sophia. Now draft the damn press release and move on—and send me my quote the minute you have something. Say I'm taking the interim-CEO role. That will be more accurate until we get everything sorted out." *Click.*

First of all, what the hell is "interim CEO"? He can't just coin his own terms. And second, there goes my date with Peter.

It was our four-month anniversary, and he'd gone to great lengths to plan a special night. I paged him at the hospital, not only to cancel our plans but also because I wanted, needed, to hear his calming voice. Peter had been a steady rock in the midst of the choppy Treehouse seas, and when he called me back, his genuinely understanding "We'll celebrate tomorrow" was all I needed to inspire me to turn to my computer and do as Scott had asked.

The loud ringing of the phone startled me. "Look, I'm downgrading your stock to a 'hold' and I just wanted to give you a heads-up," said the Goldman Sachs analyst on the other end of the phone. *Shit! How did he find out?* His name was Darren Derman and he was a sharp, talented young man just out of Tuck School of Business. I had the other fifteen analysts under pretty good control, and their research reports fell within the range of the earnings estimates we provided. To my knowledge, they were good advocates for us to the thousands of institutional investors in the world of Wall Street. But there were a few like Darren who caught on to even the smallest of details during the earnings calls; the Darrens of the world didn't hesitate to put me, Scott, or Jonathan on the spot. They seemed to particularly enjoy doing it when they asked for comments about rumors, knowing very well we couldn't say anything, even though most of the rumors were true. Damn, I hated the smart ones.

"You can do what you want, Darren. Go ahead and downgrade us. But you don't even know if this Quince news is just a rumor, and you're going to look really stupid if you're wrong." I spoke calmly but emphasized *stupid* and *wrong* for dramatic effect.

"Are you saying it's not true?"

"You know I can't comment."

"My source is reliable and I know this is happening. There is no way Scott can be CEO of Treehouse *and* Quince," Darren declared. I agreed in my head, but of course couldn't say as much.

Before I hung up, I said, "Just make sure you're not doing this to make a name for yourself, Darren. I know you're a hotshot on the Street, but please don't use Treehouse to showboat."

I WAS BOMBARDED by news headlines such as THE RETURN OF THE PRODI-GAL SON when I arrived at the office earlier than usual the next morning. Numerous analyst reports had been published overnight, each one of them downgrading Treehouse's stock to a "hold." Everyone except Darren. I typed a simple email to Jonathan and Scott and attached all the analyst reports that were out thus far.

> To: Scott Kraft; Jonathan Larsen
> From: Sophia Young
> Subj: Analyst reports
>
> Interim-CEO news is out. My guess is stock will drop 20% at open.
> Brace yourselves.

When the opening bell rang thirty minutes later, Treehouse's stock plummeted. A merciful call from Nasdaq Surveillance came in two minutes later.

"There is a lot of activity going on in H-O-U-S," the Nasdaq representative announced, spelling out our stock ticker symbol. "We're temporarily suspending trading."

"*Thank God!*" I declared as I leaned back in my chair and looked up at the ugly, asbestos-filled ceiling.

chapter 13

I WAS STARTLED AWAKE BY the sound of a honking car and looked up to see that the stoplight ahead of me had turned green. I had fallen asleep at the wheel. A quick glance in my rearview mirror didn't show any beaming headlights, so I tilted my head back and closed my eyes again. *Just a few more seconds.*

The intersection of Woodside Road and Alameda de las Pulgas was silent and deserted at eleven o'clock at night. It was located on the border separating the two tony towns of Woodside and Atherton, where the sidewalks roll up at dusk and the cars carrying Silicon Valley's elite disappear shortly thereafter. It was a cold January night, but my convertible top was down in an (unsuccessful) attempt to keep me awake.

"Hey! Are you okay?" a voice shouted at me.

My head shot up from its relaxed position against the headrest and I looked to my left. It was Jonathan in his car. "Hi!" I yelled back. "Yeah, I'm okay. I'm just tired."

Jonathan sounded more awake than I'd been in months. "You must be! I pulled up next to you and you were dead asleep, mouth open and everything."

It was the time of year when the accountants were closing the fourth-quarter "books"; Jonathan and I stayed late so we could begin reviewing them and had slumped out of the Treehouse offices only an hour earlier. These results would symbolize something more than they usually did—three months had passed since Scott's Quince news, and I hoped that when we announced them in February, the news would prove to the world that Treehouse was still thriving, despite the new arrangement.

Although the transition had gone smoothly, I felt as though I'd been through the wringer. On top of my investor relations and other responsibilities at Treehouse, Scott saw to it that I was "lucky enough" (his words) to work on Quince projects as well. Just yesterday he'd delivered the speech I'd written for his first public appearance as Quince's interim CEO. The day had started out rocky, very rocky, due to the infamous cookie episode, but I'd managed to get him to Moscone Center just in time. That day he made history by addressing the largest Quince World audience that had ever gathered since the event's founding twenty years ago. The three-day conference attracted developers, enthusiasts, and Quince vendors who spent the day listening to presentations from Quince experts and visited the thousands of booths that were set up by companies whose businesses were built upon the Quince technology platform. It was a day to remember; I could still see the wings of the convention center's stage and the profile of Scott's face with the stage lights reflecting off his glasses. The roar of the crowd and the rush of excitement I felt for him, because of him. *A true hero's welcome.*

"What are you doing here?" I asked, realizing Jonathan lived one town south of Atherton.

"I'm following you. I knew you were tired, so I wanted to be sure you got home okay. I'll follow you the rest of the way home. We're almost there, aren't we?" Jonathan asked as the stoplight turned green again.

I placed my hand to my heart and pushed down gently on my car's gas pedal. As my BMW edged slowly forward, I said, "You are sooooo good to me. Thank you, but I'll be fine. Go home!"

When I pulled up in front of my parents' house, Peter was standing on the doorstep, wearing his blue hospital scrubs and holding seven red roses. "One for each month we've been together," he said as he handed me the flowers. I could tell he was going to say something else, but I cut him off because I wanted to say it first. I wanted to allow myself to be vulnerable. "I love you, Peter. I truly do."

My boyfriend gently tossed the roses inside our foyer, took my hand, and pulled me close. He stared at me with his big blue eyes, surrounded by incredible eyelashes—those eyes emitted a calm demeanor and confidence that made me feel safe and sure. "You make me happy, Sophia. Every time I leave you I can't wait to see you again." His words were sweet and thoughtful. I couldn't help but notice, though, that he didn't say *I love you* back. Peter leaned in to kiss me, but just before his lips reached mine, he said softly, "So I guess that means that I love you more." We both stood there staring at each other, grinning like two people sharing a delightful secret. But our romantic moment was cut short by a text message from Kate that read: Important. Call me.

It was one of those messages that gave me the feeling that something was terribly wrong. A 911 text would have sent the same chills up my spine. I told Peter something was up with Kate and that I needed to call her immediately. Before the phone even finished its first ring, Kate picked up.

"I know I shouldn't care about this so much, but I'm really disappointed I don't have an engagement ring yet," she said, sounding stressed and worried. It was uncharacteristic of Kate to be overly emotional, so I didn't want to discount how she was feeling.

"You'll find something. It's not for lack of trying. You guys have been looking, right?"

"Yes."

"Well?"

"We just can't find anything we like."

"*You* can't find anything *you* like is probably more accurate. Why don't you just show him the ring you *love*? The one on Union Street?" *Don't make life so hard!*

"I don't want to be one of those people," she said.

"You're not! He's *asking you* to pick something out. And you know very well that he can afford that ring. For goodness' sake, *you* can afford that ring, and he makes three times what you do. *You* have the ability to easily solve this problem, Kate."

"I know," she admitted, then continued to stress for a few minutes more. When it got to the point where she and I were both just repeating ourselves, I evangelized a classic Life According to Sophia Young–ism. "Stop whining. *Do* something about it and move on. Show him the ring, Kate."

"Well, that's awfully empathetic of you," she said, clearly not responding well to my bluntness. "I'll let you go. You sound busy." Then all I heard was a *click*. I decided I would fix things with Kate later or that Bridezilla would come to her senses. Right now, it was time for just Peter and me.

ALL HE SAID was hi, but I knew immediately that the person on the other end of the line was Scott.

"What's wrong? And good morning," I said as I rolled over onto my back and yawned rudely in his ear. The winter sunrise was still hours away, so there was no light coming through the vertical window blinds in my room. But I didn't care. I was still thinking about my evening with Peter and wishing his pager hadn't gone off three hours earlier.

"I saw the latest draft of the shareholder letter. You removed my reference to *This American Life*. Why did you do that?"

"Because most people don't listen to NPR, Scott."

And please don't make me do a focus group to prove it.

"That's bullshit! NPR?"

"NPR does not generally serve the masses. You taught me that when we do something, it needs to be accessible to the everyday

American. And I'm telling you, *This American Life* is *not* everyday America."

"Yes, it is!"

"No, it's not," I argued. "I know you love that program, but *People* magazine and *USA Today*—*those* are everyday America."

Scott was silent for a moment, a sign that I could keep pushing. "Look it up yourself. What's the Nielsen rating for NPR versus Howard Stern or public television versus the *Oprah Winfrey Show*?"

I heard the sound of Scott typing. "Fuck!"

Before I could say anything to rub it in, he added, "I'm not going to comment on this letter until I really understand our investor base." I closed my eyes because I knew his *I want a focus group* command was coming, and all I wanted to do was go back to bed. Scott's frustrated, annoyed mad-genius routine wasn't exactly new, and as if on cue, he said, "I want a focus group that produces statistically relevant data so I can understand the demographics of our shareholder base."

I should have respected Scott for insisting on perfection and "understanding your target." Obviously, if he wanted this, we'd have to do it.

But for God's sake, why can't he just listen to me for once?

I rolled toward the nightstand and grabbed my notepad and pen. Inevitably, Scott wasn't finished. "I also want to see samples from the graphic design agency you're suggesting. Oh, and please reschedule that bus tour visit with Goldman Sachs."

"Scott, we can't just reschedule the bus tour. They're bringing twenty investors from Boston to see other companies—not just us."

"Just make it all happen, Sophia," Scott said.

"I only have two tits," I responded angrily. I could almost hear him smile through the phone, and felt a slight high knowing I could still entertain him.

Scott suddenly changed the subject. "Goddammit. Have you seen the cover of *Rolling Stone*? Andre Stark is front and center."

Ah. That's why you're so grumpy.

My CEO didn't care for Andre Stark, although I wasn't sure why. Perhaps he was jealous of the younger, up-and-coming technology genius, or judging Andre's ladies'-man lifestyle and showy presence. Or maybe it was because Andre was always being compared to Scott by the press even though he was the exact opposite: 100 percent Hollywood, complete with six divorces and a home in the Malibu hills.

"Oh, and Ashley needs your social security number. Can you call her, please?"

"Why does she need my social security number?" I asked.

He responded as though we'd been discussing it for weeks. "The president's dinner. That's tonight. Our chef is preparing now."

"The president? Of the United States?"

Silence. *I'll take that as a yes.*

"I didn't know the president was coming for dinner," I replied, slightly suspicious. "Why do you want me there?"

"Christine and I thought you might enjoy meeting him," Scott said. His tone was innocent, but I read through it immediately.

"What do you want?"

"Nothing. What do you mean?"

"I've been working for you for a long time and you've never invited me to dinner. What do you want?"

Then he came out with it: the real reason. "I want you to help Ashley serve the dinner. Christine hired a catering staff, but you know how I feel about strangers."

I considered his "offer" for a moment—he was right, it *would* be cool to meet the president. But certainly not in the way Scott was suggesting. So I said, "Yes. Well, too bad for you. I'm not a servant."

"But it's the president!"

"I don't care. What you're asking me to do is rude, you know. This is one of your weak points, Scott. Let's start to work on our social skills—your filter. It will be a goal of ours in the coming year," I said through my chuckle. "Besides, I'm having dinner with my family."

Scott blew me off with a disgusted "Ugh" before continuing, "I respect your family time, but this is a unique situation. Anyway, you really should get some distance from your parents. You're twenty-six! Why are you still living at home?"

"First of all, I see a lot less of my family since I started working for you. Second, telling my parents I'm moving out would not go over so well. Chinese parents have a death grip on their kids. And finally, I'll move out as soon as I can afford a place."

"What are you talking about? We pay you plenty. You *can* get a place. A *nice* place."

"Maybe to rent, but not to buy! Pay me enough to do that and I'll move out tomorrow!" I joked.

"Buy? What is it with women and feeling the need to *buy* places?"

"What do you mean? It's a great investment."

"That's not true. That's not true at all. I went through this same discussion over and over with Christine when she wanted to buy."

"Yeah, and you *bought* a place!"

"Against my will! It's insane—the prices in Silicon Valley. I built an entire spreadsheet that proves that economically, buying does not make sense. But women want to nest. They like to nest."

I didn't feel like arguing about this with him, so I stayed silent.

"What time is dinner?" Scott asked.

"Five thirty."

"Okay, come over after."

"No, I'm going to help Kate's fiancé pick out her ring. They're getting married in May. I know exactly the one she wants and he wants me to show him."

"Oh, Jesus. Why do you always stick your nose into everyone's business?" Scott asked, now sounding more annoyed. "It's simply not a good use of your time. You could be doing something so much more important, interesting, valuable."

"What, like serving dinner to people?"

"Don't deflect the discussion," Scott said.

I sat up in bed, ready to defend myself. "I'm not sticking my nose anywhere. I know the exact ring she wants, so why wouldn't I want her to have it?"

"You need to really reflect on why you always worry about other people and not yourself." By the sound of Scott's voice, I could imagine his face—it softened. His tone was slightly condescending, but I didn't mind. It showed that he cared.

"You never stop. Not for one minute. You're either working or trying to fix other people's problems. You couldn't even sit through two minutes of meditation. Those things you do aren't ever going to make you happy. You have to find your happiness and passion from within. I know it sounds trite, but it's true."

"You Americans and your obsession with happiness!" I said, sounding disgusted.

"You're American, Sophia. You don't get to just claim you're Chinese when you feel like it."

Fair enough.

"I'm just saying you should reflect upon your actions more. Understand why you do the things you do. Don't get me wrong, if you're always sticking your nose into people's business *because* it gives you joy, then I'm all for it. But I think you do it for other reasons."

I was pacing beside my bed now, not enjoying this conversation *at all.* I knew Scott was right but refused to let him win this battle. "Oh, so you don't call coming to serve dinner 'wasting time'? What is your point, Scott? I'm having fun. That matters to me." I looked toward the tan cork of my bulletin board, where I'd pinned dozens of photos that reminded me of all the laughter I shared with friends and family, times when demanding bosses weren't calling me at the crack of dawn.

Scott's voice interrupted my thoughts. "First of all, it's not just serving dinner. It could be a *learning* experience with the president, and you're passing that up to go *ring* shopping for *someone else!* I'm saying that you occupy yourself with these small things because you don't want to think about your own life. Why not?"

"I don't have to justify anything to you!" I yelled.

"Okay, okay. I'm just saying . . ."

My voice strained to reach a higher octave. "Stop being so critical of the way I live. You want me to learn things? Then hire some people to help me! I barely have time to go to the bathroom, thanks to the totally unreasonable amount of work you pile on my plate. Speaking of which, I'm ending this conversation so I can get my ass out of bed and into the shower so I can go do what *you* pay me to do." I hung up the phone and wished that I had been on a landline. That would have allowed me to slam the receiver in his ear.

Melancholy washed heavily over me and took the place of my anger as I stepped into the shower. Unfortunately, Scott had broken through, and the words that had haunted me since I was diagnosed with diabetes came flooding back into my head. "Her life span will be considerably shorter," the pediatrician had said to my parents, unaware that I could hear him from my seat in the hall. That's when everything became so urgent—the day I began doing things that didn't allow my mind to dwell on my longevity, or lack thereof. During my younger years, dance was my escape. In high school and college, I added alcohol to the mix. Then my focus was consumed with finding a husband. I was so relieved when work proved it could fill most of this void; solving friends' problems took care of the rest. If I gave myself the time to think about my own life, or even to relax the way Scott suggested, I would go straight to a dark place and I'd never want to get out of bed. *If I stop, I will die.*

chapter 14

IT WAS 6:15 A.M., FIFTEEN minutes before the stock market opened, and I was watching the round rainbow-colored circle spin on my screen, waiting for my computer to access the Treehouse network. When my *MarketWatch* home screen finally appeared, I scanned the headlines and my eyes caught one in particular that was buried toward the bottom of my news feed. I blinked, then blinked again, to make sure I was reading the headline correctly.

TREEHOUSE RAISES Q2 ESTIMATES, Associated Press *(Tue 2:38 A.M. EDT)*.

I clicked on the link and skimmed the article while saying to no one but myself, "Shit, shit, shit! We didn't raise our numbers! How did this happen?" My fingers rapidly crafted an email to the AP reporter, which less than politely demanded a correction to her story. I mentioned something about the reporter being "irresponsible for starting this rumor just weeks before we announce our June earnings results." But then I looked more closely at a quote in the article and saw a name that I knew well. *Matteo.* Our chief technology officer was in India doing press interviews to announce the upcoming release of our second movie, *The Amazings,* and he'd delivered a talk about Treehouse at the local university while he was there. I wondered what could have come over Matteo to make him say something like the headline suggested. *He knows better.* He must have included a financial snapshot slide about us and either misspoke or was misquoted. I looked at the clock on the top-right corner of my screen; the market would be open in two minutes. I pictured our stock price skyrocketing on the AP news and then crashing down when we reported our actual earnings a few weeks later—earnings that would be below what the article said.

I sighed, knowing my dinner with Peter would need to be rescheduled—again—and picked up the phone to call Jonathan. I wanted to show him and Scott that I could handle things on my own now, but then thought twice of it, knowing the consequences would be huge if I didn't handle this one right. A sharp pain stabbed me in the stomach—*shit, this stress is giving me an ulcer*—as I dialed Jonathan's number, but I focused on the article on my screen, which *MarketWatch* had now listed as one of the top stories for the day.

"Good morning, Sophia. You're calling early." Captain Obvious was trying to be polite but was probably wondering why on earth I was bothering him at this ungodly hour.

"Hi, Jonathan. Sorry to bother you, but I'm really not sure what to do," I said, and then explained the AP article debacle.

"What's the stock doing?" Jonathan asked.

I looked at the HOUS ticker symbol. "We're up over fifteen percent on high volume and trading large blocks."

"Have the analysts called?"

"Not yet. But I'll call them—maybe they can issue flash reports that the article is wrong."

"Good idea, Sophia, but any response to this needs to be disseminated publicly."

"After all this time, I'm still learning from you," I said to Jonathan. "I wish I could stay as calm as you under pressure."

"Meditate, my dear. Meditate. As for the learning, my job is to help you grow. That is my primary responsibility." He seemed too good to be real, but I knew he meant it.

Jonathan was quiet for a moment before he said, "Let me call you back."

I hung up the phone, and for a split second, I forgot about the AP story and focused on my stomach pain instead. *Hungry? Gas? Constipation?*

My thoughts were interrupted by the ring of my desk phone.

"Ashley?" I asked as I picked up.

"I have Scott for you. Let me transfer you."

"Scott."

"WHAT THE FUCK HAPPENED?" he shouted. I wondered if this was the pre- or post-personal-spiritual-trainer-session Scott, because if it was the latter, I thought he should get his money back.

"I assume Jonathan told you. Maybe we should see if the reporter is willing to retract?"

"Get Matteo on the phone. I don't care what time it is over there. Tell him to call me immediately," Scott said before hanging up.

The phones began to ring, sporadically at first, but then constantly. I decided to ignore them and dialed Matteo's cell phone instead.

"Hello?" Matteo answered groggily.

"Matteo? You need to call Scott right now. Get up, get yourself a cup of coffee, and then call him."

"What? Why? What's wrong?"

"You were quoted in the press. Did you say something about our upcoming earnings estimates?"

"No. I gave a presentation yesterday that included a slide about our . . . oh shit."

"Uh-huh. Well, whatever slide you showed has us in a lot of hot water. You know you're not supposed to talk about *any* Treehouse numbers. Period. And certainly not the *wrong* ones!"

I wondered if Matteo had been trying to play big man again by commenting on matters outside his scope of work.

"Oh, fuck."

"Yeah. What the hell were you thinking?" I asked, getting angrier and angrier by the minute.

Before I could launch into an all-out lecture about confidentiality, though, I imagined Matteo running his fingers through his wild, curly brown hair the way he did when he was frustrated or deep in thought. I was certain he was already out of bed and freaking out in his hotel room, the slight bulge of his belly protruding from his T-shirt. It wasn't uncommon for Matteo and me to clash, mostly because of his macho personality. But I felt sorry for him at this moment, so I stopped myself and then more calmly said, "I'll do what I can on this end. Just call Scott, please."

THE SOUND OF the helicopter got louder and louder; minutes later Scott was pacing back and forth in my office, his hands behind his back, eerily quiet. I stared at my computer screen and watched our stock erupt.

"Shit!" Scott finally shouted before kicking my filing cabinet. I could see how livid he was by the fire in his eyes. "LET HIM GO!"

Bemused, I asked, "Let who go?"

"Matteo."

I raised my eyebrows. "You're overreacting, Scott. No one's firing Matteo. But if anyone is, it's sure as hell not going to be me."

"I am not in the right state of mind to do it. But it needs to be done. An example needs to be set. We've said this over and over again to employees: ONLY APPROVED SPOKESPEOPLE—that's you, me, Jonathan—" he screamed, poking his finger at me, "are allowed to make any sort of statement about the business side of our company. EVER! I'm not upset over what Wall Street thinks; I couldn't give a shit about that. What I care about is that in one fell swoop, Matteo's *accidental* comment affects our long-term credibility and he's single-handedly fucked all our employees, whose morale will drop when our stock comes crashing down. ISN'T THAT CAUSE FOR TERMINATION?"

He had a point. But the key to our success was, and would continue to be, the synergy between the three people in Scott's office of the president: Jonathan, Matteo, and Dylan. If we lost one of them, we'd be done, so I tried again to calm Scott down.

"It was a mistake. He didn't mean to do it. Did you speak with him?" I asked.

"Yes," Scott answered somberly.

I imagined myself in Matteo's shoes. *God, it sucks to be you.*

"What did you say?"

"Nothing particularly productive for the situation at hand," he admitted.

Scott continued to pace in my office, walk out for a few minutes, only to return screaming creative expletives before exiting again. This went on for an hour until Jonathan walked in. *Thank God.*

"Where's the stock?" Jonathan asked.

"We're still up—well, down slightly from open, but up almost twenty percent now since yesterday. Where did Matteo get those figures, anyway?" I asked.

"He was remembering our internal targets, Sophia. There's a slight chance we could make those, but we certainly don't want expectations to be set there," Jonathan said.

"We should fire Matteo," Scott broke in.

"Well, that would certainly cause a distraction," Jonathan said, "but we're not firing him, Scott, and you know it."

As I considered what *I* would need to do if we fired Matteo, the thought of a press release gave me an idea.

"What about issuing a press release simply reiterating our original Q2 guidance? We could word it in a way so we're highlighting the old figures, not the ones in the AP story," I suggested.

Scott stopped pacing and Jonathan smiled. "Draft it up and send it to me after Jonathan reviews it," Scott commanded before stomping out the door.

TWO HOURS AND a press release later, Treehouse's share price was only slightly higher than it had been before all this Matteo madness began. I read that as a sign that everything was as it should be.

With the crisis averted, I allowed myself to admit that something was wrong with my body. The stomach pain that had begun this morning had become constant, and worse. I texted Peter to cancel dinner anyway, then called my mom in Taiwan. *She'll know what to do.*

"*Wei?*" she answered. Her raspy voice suggested I had woken her from a deep sleep.

"Mom," I whimpered.

"Audrey or Sophia?" she asked, still unable to distinguish our voices after all these years.

"It's Sophia. Mom, my stomach hurts."

Mom was alarmed, and she did nothing to hide it in her voice, "*Ai-ya.* What kind of pain? Did you try sitting on the toilet? You always hold it until you're about to burst. I've told you so many times not to do that." My mother was obsessed with bowel movements, and I managed a smile at her unsurprising reaction.

I answered her list of questions, but stopped short of telling her I'd had a low-grade stomachache for weeks, maybe months. Mom decided the only thing to do was to go home. "Lie down and drink some ginger tea. I will call your sister and have her pick up some clear broth and apple juice. You probably just have a stomach bug."

"Mom, the stock market is open here. She can't leave the office right now."

"Family first, Sophia. Isn't that what we've always taught you girls? She'll be there soon. Just get yourself home, can you do that?"

MY BREATHING WAS shallow and I could barely move when I heard the sound of keys turning inside the front-door lock. *Audrey.* I was propped up on our family room couch because lying down hurt too much. The television was off and I was just staring out the window, trying to remain calm. Audrey's footsteps got louder and I struggled to draw another breath—one of relief at knowing my sister was here to save me, again. I knew she was going to be angry and would blame me for interrupting her day. But I told myself not to worry; this wasn't like the time I snuck out at night and rolled my parents' car down into the creek. I had a feeling this was a real emergency.

Audrey's shouts echoed through our parents' large, empty house and I did my best to respond, but any attempt at exhaling seemed to set my stomach on fire.

"What's wrong now?" she yelled as she came bursting through the kitchen door. I could still hear tiny traces of the hostile teenager she once was, resentful that her sick, coddled little sister took up so much of her parents' attention. Then her voice came from behind me, her irritation barely disguised: "Hello? Are you going to answer me?"

"I have a stomachache," I responded quietly. There were only two stairs down into our family room, but Audrey stomped loud enough to make them count.

"What? Mom called me because you have a stomachache? Go sit on a toilet or take Gas-X or something."

"I tried all those things," I said. "I even took the prescription antacid the doctor gave me last week."

Now she looked slightly concerned. My sister perched next to me on the couch. I could see that she was trying to decide whether to believe me and how worried she should be. "This has been going on for a week? What did the doctor say?"

"It's been around for months, really. But I went to the general practitioner last week. She took X-rays and said it might be scar tissue from something and that it's around my kidneys."

"You'd better call Dr. Levin and see what he thinks about the scar tissue," Audrey said, referring to my favorite MD. He was a nephrologist who began monitoring me when I was in high school because my labs showed I had the beginnings of kidney disease. *Thanks, diabetes!* Although I had been stable for years, Dr. Levin (or "Steve" as he asked me to call him) still kept tabs on me and made himself available whenever I had any questions or concerns about my health. He always went above and beyond for me, and I often wondered if it was because I was so young compared to his waiting room full of elderly patients.

When I reached Steve on his mobile phone, he asked about the pain (stabbing, twisting knife, hurts-so-so-bad) and wanted to know where it ranked on a scale from one to ten (TEN!). I expected him to reply with something helpful, something doctorly and reassuring. Instead, he just asked, "Can you come up to see me right now?"

"Why? Are you worried?"

"A little bit," he replied.

I was surprised at his reaction. "Do you really want me to come all the way up there?" Steve's office was at California Pacific Medical Center in San Francisco—forty-five minutes or more away.

"Yes. I do. I'll let the ER know you're coming and I'll meet you there."

"The ER? Why the ER?"

"Stop asking questions and just meet me there." He hung up.

Seconds later, as I struggled to stand up even with Audrey's help, Steve called back. "Have you left yet?" I cracked a grin because he knew me too well, but the urgency in his voice told me he was really concerned.

"I'm dying," I said. I didn't truly believe it, but there was a small part of me that thought this feeling could be death—the kind of pain you would feel on your last day. Either way, I took advantage of the chance to be dramatic.

"We're all dying, Sophia," he said. "Just get up here."

THE PURPLE RUBBER tourniquet was tight around my arm; my forearm throbbed while the nurse tried to find my vein. It was incredibly uncomfortable, but I was thankful for the pain, as it distracted me from what was actually happening. The nurse was dressed in baggy, seafoam-colored hospital scrubs, the kind that the *ER* actors wore on set. But she wasn't an actor and this was not prime-time television. This was my life.

For the fourth time, the nurse tried to insert a needle into one of my tiny, child-size veins, which were scarred from years of monthly labs ordered by my endocrinologist, nephrologist, and every other ologist. My veins didn't want to cooperate today, rolling away from the sharp metal needle each time it was inserted. Honestly, I didn't blame them; I'd had enough, too. I shuddered slightly and began to hyperventilate as she dug the needle in deeper, angled it to the left, then to the right. My head was turned away, but the aching pain in my arm painted the scene for me, blurred by the tears that rolled down my face. As soon as the needle was set, the nurse could start my painkillers, and it was clear she was desperate to do so, if only to quell my whimpering.

At last, I heard the snap of the IV's flashback chamber signal that the catheter was in. "Got it!" the nurse said as she let out a sigh of relief. I disciplined myself to take as deep a breath as possible, and prayed for the morphine to kick in. *Breathe, Sophia. Breathe.* There was a frenzied tension in the room, but no one moved; the doctor and my sister stared at an X-ray of my abdomen that had been taken when I first arrived. My pain continued to increase, and when Audrey turned back to check on me, somehow she saw it in my eyes. Without taking her gaze off me, she cried to anyone who would listen, "The morphine isn't working!"

Dr. Levin turned to look. When our eyes met, I knew he saw it, too. I licked my lips slowly and tried to gather enough saliva in my dry mouth to whisper over the metal taste on my tongue. "Help me,

Steve," I managed. It was dramatic, yes, but desperate times called for dramatic entreaties. His downward-sloping eyebrows suggested he was considering his next step—would he be risking an overdose if he gave me more, or should he try a different painkiller? Finally, unable to ignore my writhing on the gurney, he told the nurse to administer an opiate three to four times stronger than morphine, and faster acting. "Give her the Dilaudid."

Moments later a nurse raced through the wide, bright hospital halls holding on to my gurney and heading toward radiology. Dr. Levin followed us and I heard Audrey say "ultrasound" but nothing else. Although I was delirious, I was alert enough to know that two technicians were trying to ease me into a horizontal position. But the weight of my stomach's skin was too heavy for whatever was inside me and made the pressure unbearable. I let out a scream, cursing and yelling like Satan's child as they forced me to lie flat and tied me down. Finally, mercifully, my eyes rolled into the back of my head and I felt nothing.

AUDREY STOOD IN front of the room's large picture window, seeming lost in her thoughts as she stared at the fog that ominously enveloped the Golden Gate Bridge. The mauve walls of the hospital room reminded me of the 1980s; I wondered about the dated paint color—the same one often found in dentists', doctors', and OB-GYN offices—and whether it was supposed to be soothing. *It's not soothing to me. It's just ugly.* I noticed Audrey was now wearing jeans, which likely meant it was the next day, and then made a brief attempt to eavesdrop on the conversation going on in the hall. My attention then turned to the low-thread-count hospital sheets that were chafing the hell out of my bare ass. Anything to distract myself from reality.

"Notify the press, Audrey is not on her BlackBerry," I managed, hoping she would engage in some sisterly bickering. Instead, Audrey turned around at the sound of my voice and, wearing a fake smile, asked, "How long have you been awake? Are you still in pain?"

"Much better," I said, avoiding any movement or deep breaths. I could tell the pain was skimming the surface, waiting to erupt once again.

"Mom and Dad got home yesterday and are downstairs getting something to eat," she said.

"They're going to drive me nuts," I responded grumpily.

Audrey smiled and nodded in agreement, but I could tell she was relieved to have our parents home. I considered how little had changed since we were young—I was still a burden. But gone was the anger that used to reside in her eyes; it had been replaced by a softer look: she was older, more tired, more patient perhaps—and had the fine wrinkles to prove it.

My thoughts were disrupted by the sound of Audrey asking, "Do you need anything, Sophia?"

"Peter. Get my BlackBerry and send him an email from me. Just tell him . . ."

"Sophia, don't worry about Peter. I'll let him know."

"No, I don't want him to know," I said as fears of being "damaged goods" came flooding back into my head. *What if this is something really bad? Will Peter run away?* "Just, just tell him something. Anything. Tell him I had to take a last-minute trip to Australia—for work—and that I'll be home in a few weeks."

"Australia? Why Australia?"

"I don't know. It's the farthest place I could think of just now."

"Are you *sure* you don't want me to tell him you're in the hospital? He could be really helpful."

I thought about Audrey being right, but then drifted back to sleep.

MY EYES OPENED at the sound of the door opening. It was Dr. Levin, and he didn't look as though he'd come to shoot the shit. Audrey sat in a recliner-style chair in the corner of the small room; she dropped her *Wall Street Journal* and stood up so she could be near me.

"We've gotten the results of your CT scan and the biopsy," he said grimly. I wasn't ready to hear bad news, so I tried to get Dr. Levin to laugh. He was a handsome man, maybe fifteen years older than me, and had a healthy outdoor-guy appearance. Steve Levin's eyes could charm anyone, and his smile was honest and genuine—it was exactly what I needed.

"Who needs CT results? I just needed a vacation, Dr. Levin," I joked, but my doctor didn't laugh or smile.

Maybe it was because I was terribly tired, but I couldn't bring myself to feel the fear that should have been running through me as I connected the dots—the doctor's concerned expression, CT scan, biopsy. He was there to tell me what I already knew.

I said the words as though I were playing a casual round of pub trivia: "It's cancer."

Dr. Levin lowered his head to hide his disappointment. "Yes. It is. And *please,* call me Steve."

I closed my eyes and searched for panic. It didn't come, though. Only an eerie calm and a blank mind. Then came the fear, but it revolved around having to give my parents the news. *This is going to kill them.*

"Do you think we can hide this from Mom and Dad?" I turned to ask Audrey.

Her expression changed from concern to one I knew well. "Are you fucking insane?"

I tried hard to hold it back, but somehow, my laugh escaped and *Steve* chuckled as well. With the laughter came shooting pain that caused me to wrap both my arms around my torso, but Audrey seemed relieved to hear me laugh, and she wasn't the only one.

"I'm not afraid. I'm not. It's not my time," I said, convincing her and Dr. Levin as much as I was myself. If I didn't stay strong, I knew I'd sink deep into self-pity, and that wasn't going to help me one bit.

Audrey's expression softened once again, and for the first time I could remember, she took my hand and squeezed it tight.

"Anyway, of course it's cancer. If it isn't one thing, it's another," I said, managing a smile.

Dr. Levin stared at me, probably wondering if I'd lost my marbles. "It's a large mass—we think about six centimeters—and it's made your stomach rock hard. Shit, Sophia, couldn't you feel it?"

Dr. Levin's expletive somehow put me more at ease. I shrugged innocently and said, "I've been doing a lot of stomach crunches!"

"We'll need to determine how to get it out—it's complicated because we're not sure if it's on your intestine or your kidney and whether an oncology or possibly a transplant surgeon should operate. Until then, I think you should finally be comfortable. I'm sorry it took us so long to find the right level of pain medications." I studied his face, unsure of the message it now sent. Concern, of course, but not as much as I'd expected. Dr. Levin was a *what's next* kind of a person and not one to lament, so I followed his lead and reminded myself that I knew how to do this, how to stay focused on the now. I drew upon my Sterling, Rich days—the days of tracking my billing hours—and how that practice prevented me from spinning my wheels.

Bill in six-minute increments.

chapter 15

ON THE FOURTH DAY OF my hospitalization, the nurses moved me into my own room. Although floral bouquets from Scott and Christine, Ashley, Jonathan, Kate, and my family cheered up the small space and added a pleasant, fresh fragrance, I couldn't help but find it a cruel irony that the big move of my twenties was not into a charming apartment but into a plain hospital room. When Audrey and Kate came to visit that morning, I was struggling to get comfortable in the very *uncomfortable* hospital bed. A rerun of *Seinfeld* ran in the background, and while the television blared, I concentrated on my laptop, thankful I had plenty of work to keep my brain cells occupied.

"Good morning," they said in perfect harmony.

"Hello!" I smiled.

"Have you spoken with Peter? He keeps calling me," Audrey said as she laid down a stack of magazines on my bed.

"Didn't you tell him I was in Australia?"

"I didn't *tell* him anything. I sent him that lame email you told me to send and can guarantee he doesn't believe a word of it. You really need to tell him, Sophia. Tell your friends! You can't keep this bottled up inside."

"I told people! Who do you think all these flowers are from?"

"At least consider that support group that Dr. Levin mentioned," Kate added, making me feel as though I was being ganged up on.

"Now *that's* ridiculous. I'm not like those people! What is this, an intervention or something?"

"We're just trying to get you some support. Mom and Dad agree."

I argued that I knew what would happen if people beyond my inner circle found out. They would make *my* illness about *them*. They would be angry I didn't tell them sooner and make me feel guilty. I explained to Audrey and Kate that everyday *how are you*s would suddenly be asked in sympathetic tones—tones that fuel self-pity—and that I'd already sensed it from Dr. Levin.

"You're just imagining that," said Kate.

"So what if I am? Does it have any less of an effect?"

But to put an end to Kate and Audrey's pestering, I agreed to call Peter—and only Peter—as soon as they left. "Fine, okay already. If he breaks up with me, it's your guys' fault," I warned.

"I WASN'T REALLY in Australia," I said through the phone while lying in my hospital bed.

"Seriously? I had no idea," Peter responded, uncharacteristically sarcastic in an angry way. "Where have you been? What's going on? Is everything okay?"

Here it goes.

"They found a tumor," I muttered, unable to say the word *cancer*.

I shared with Peter what little I knew of the "friend" in my abdomen, and expected him to respond with a slew of questions that I hadn't dared to ask Dr. Levin, the answers to which I didn't want to know. But my boyfriend surprised me with his reaction:

"It's going to be okay, Sophia. Shit happens, but we'll figure it out. *We'll* deal with it."

My lip quivered with emotion and I was thankful for Peter's supportive, less-than-dramatic response. *That's exactly what I needed to hear.* A few minutes later, I said goodbye to my boyfriend, but not before telling him that I loved him. Then I looked up to see my father. *Oh shit, he must have heard everything.*

I waited for Dad to freak out over me saying the *L* word to a man, but his face didn't suggest that was going to happen. It made me wonder if he knew I'd been talking with Peter, and I decided I'd hold my breath and let Dad make the first move.

"What did he say?" Dad asked.

I smiled. "He said that *we'll* figure it out."

Dad nodded and seemed relieved. "I like that response. I like it a lot. Especially coming from a doctor. When are you going to finally introduce us?"

That evening, I made a decision that was uncharacteristic for me: I emailed a few coworkers and close friends from college I'd kept in touch with, sharing my news with them. Although I'd asked them to keep it private, I knew word of my illness would spread. I didn't know why I lifted the curtain when I'd been so secretive in the past; maybe it was because of Peter's response, or the fact that I could already feel a certain badge of honor as I imagined myself announcing to unsuspecting people, "I am a cancer survivor." Although my friends responded by calling and asking to visit, I told everyone (and instructed my family and nurses to do the same), "No visitors." I wasn't ready to see expressions of sympathy. *Sympathy makes me weak.*

The next morning, hospital carts filled with flowers and gifts arrived; they were from friends and coworkers and threatened to fill every square inch of my room. Instead of making me feel weak, the flowers and get-well cards reminded me that I was loved. *Maybe this is enough love,* I told myself as I reconsidered my goals about having my own family. *Maybe,* I allowed myself to think for a moment, *I already have one.*

THE NEXT DAY, Dad sat in the corner, working on his laptop while my china-doll mom picked up four or five flower-filled vases and balanced them in her arms. "Let's give some of these to the nurses. I'm sure they'll be thrilled. Besides, it helps build goodwill," she said.

"But Mom! I like those flowers," I argued, eyeing the beautiful pink peonies she had in her hand.

Mom put on her *I thought I taught you better* look. "These flowers are not from your friends, Sophia. They're from your *acquaintances*." Without waiting for me to respond, she walked out the door with her arms full.

A ringing telephone interrupted my pouting. "Hello?" I answered.

"Hi," Scott whispered.

"Why are you whispering?"

"Oh. I didn't realize . . ."

I spoke loudly and slowly, as though I were ordering at a drive-through McDonald's. "YOU DON'T NEED TO WHISPER."

He responded with an extremely rare apology—"Oh, oh, sorry"—and I pictured him pulling at his socks nervously, wearing yet another hole in his jeans.

"Stop tiptoeing, Scott. I'm fine. No worries here," I said.

"Do they know anything else? What's the plan?"

"Well, it doesn't look like anything has spread, which is great news, but they won't know until they open me up tomorrow. So until then, I can't eat. I can't wait to get this thing out! I'm starving!"

"I'd want it out, too." I heard people talking in the background, although they were speaking a language I didn't understand. "How large is the growth?"

"Where are you?" I asked, not answering his question.

"South America."

"What? Why? How is it that I didn't know about this?"

"It was a last-minute decision."

No way. You, the control freak?

Mom burst back into the room with emptied arms, looking as though she'd achieved world peace. She then sat down next to Dad with her reading glasses and Chinese newspaper.

"What are you doing there?" I asked, knowing full well that Scott orchestrated everyone, every event, and every "thing" in his life, and never did *anything* last minute. His trips took more planning than a state dinner, and this one—with the food planning and whatnot— would have taken Ashley weeks to organize.

No more chitchat from Scott, though; he didn't have the attention span. "I have to go," he said. Even though it was a quick call, I was touched. Tearful even. But my emotions turned toward the door as Peter casually entered my room, looking as though he were there to pick me up for any ol' dinner. All thoughts of Scott and work faded away, as did the worry about having him meet my parents for the first time. *Peter is here.*

THE LOUD RING of my cell phone woke me from my nap. *How long have I been asleep?* If this clock was right—and there was no guarantee it was—two hours. The late-afternoon sun was beating through the window, and as I shaded my eyes from it, I saw a notepad by my bedside with messages written in my mom's handwriting and several that looked like they came from the nurse's station. All of the messages were from Grant, and that didn't include the two he'd left that morning. *What does he want?*

As I studied the notepad, my cell phone rang again. Certain that it was Grant and reveling slightly in the attention he was giving me, I happily assumed my old grumpy Sterling, Rich tone: "What!"

"That's not very ladylike," my mother said as she entered my room and pushed her way past the most recent delivery of bouquets, balancing her hospital cafeteria dinner. "I hope you don't speak to Peter that way. Dad actually likes this one." She settled into the corner chair and unwrapped the chopsticks she pulled from her purse.

"Hi, Mom," I responded while putting my hand over the phone

receiver, half expecting her to tell me to apply some lipstick. I was amused by the sight of her eating the mashed potatoes and roasted chicken with chopsticks as I returned to my conversation with Grant.

"Where have you been?" Grant asked. "I've sent you at least a dozen emails."

"Why? What do you want?"

"Nice to talk to you, too, Sophia. It's been ages," flowed Grant's sarcasm.

I chuckled gently, careful not to disturb my belly. "Hi, Grant. We just spoke, like, last week. You told me you got that offer to go in-house at that silly Internet search company, remember? So what is it that you want?"

"You're right. I want something," he said with a laugh. "Well, sort of. You've heard of Andre Stark, no doubt. His company is looking for an IR person."

"*The* Andre Stark? The one with the electric cars?"

"Yes. Ion. I'd like to put your name in the hat, if that's okay with you. There's no doubt it's going to be hard to convince investors that Andre can do what he says, but I think it's going to be a winner and a great opportunity for you."

"I don't know, Grant. I'm happy and comfortable at Treehouse."

"This could be your crowning glory, Sophia. *You'd* be the one shaping the story this time and helping them through the entire IPO. It's what Treehouse prepared you to do."

Okay. Keep talking, keep talking. I let Grant float several more compliments my way—how great I was at my job and how uniquely qualified I was for the Ion role.

"Why have they had a hard time filling the position? I would imagine people are jumping at the opportunity."

Grant confessed. "Let's just say Andre Stark is . . . particular." That's code for *a nightmare*.

"Are you trying to pimp me out to another one of your clients?"

I joked, forgetting completely about the *C* word. "You've done that once already. Don't you think that's enough?"

"Yes, but look how well it turned out for you," Grant said seriously. I knew he was right. Grant was an exceptional mentor and I trusted him. *He wouldn't steer me wrong.*

"Your timing isn't great," I said.

"What better timing than now? You'll get stock options that are still very reasonably priced."

"That's not what I mean, Grant. I'm in the hospital," I said before explaining my predicament.

Grant, being Grant, responded with an eloquent "oh shit," but didn't dig for more.

"Ha! Yep, that just about sums it up."

Still, he was relentless. "Ion is going to inspire not just the stock market, but the entire nation. Financially, this could be a life-changing event for you. And selfishly, I'd look good for helping him fill the role." He'd clearly thought this through, and I reminded my-self that I trusted him. He wasn't one to exaggerate, and to make it about himself.

As my dad always said, "It never hurts to try." I asked Grant to give me a few days to think about the Ion job, though, because there were many reasons why I should have been wary: the risk (which had never been my thing), the lackluster IPO market, the turmoil of the auto industry, Andre Stark's reputation, and my health.

After assuring Grant that I was going to be fine and hanging up the phone, I sighed loudly. Mom looked up from her dinner. "Every-thing okay?"

"All good, thanks, Mom. For everything," I said with a nod and a grin. "I love you, you crazy bat!"

She shrugged and giggled like a schoolgirl.

I turned on the television and searched for a show my mom would like, but my mind was elsewhere: how far I had strayed from my original plan to be a happy housewife with a handsome, loving husband, adorable kids, and a beautiful home. But I reasoned that much of that was beyond my control, and that continuing to chase that original dream could be selfish, not to mention burdensome to anyone who got too close to me. I glanced over at my mother, still chopsticking her way through her hospital cafeteria chicken. *Is it right to allow someone to fall in love with me, for me to have children that I could end up leaving motherless? To consign them to a life of hospital cafeteria chicken and worry, of needles and late-night phone calls from doctors?* After all, even if I beat the cancer, I couldn't deny the fact that my life expectancy was shorter than average. I began convincing myself that I should strive for something else. My thoughts turned to Peter.

Run, Peter, Run.

chapter 16

THE TUGGING AT MY ARMS woke me from a heavy slumber just as a woman's voice said, "Let's try to sit you up." My brain registered that she was speaking to me, but my body ignored her; it behaved listlessly and flopped around like a lightweight cotton summer hat. I crinkled my nose and mumbled as though inebriated: "Are we there yet?"

Audrey's laughter cut through some of my fuzziness and gave me just enough strength to crack open my eyes. I grinned at the sound of her cackling, pleased that I entertained her. Seconds later, my head fell forward, then rolled side to side as I grumbled, "I'm tired of holding up my head." Audrey laughed again, this time louder and harder. The woman tried to hold it in, but her giggles eventually joined my sister's.

"Stop laughing at her!" barked my mother. The sound of her scolding my sister induced a satisfied, sibling-in-the-right grin to spread on my face and lulled me back to my daze. Just as I was about to fall asleep, the woman's loud voice counted—"One, two, three"—as two sets of hands hoisted me from the operating room gurney and back onto my hospital bed.

It took a few moments for things to register in my anesthesia-riddled brain as I broke through my daze again: the rancid odor of something rotten filled my nostrils. I frowned and muttered, "What is that smell?" before realizing in a semiconscious state that the surgery was over. *I made it.*

"It's herbal medicine, sweetheart," my dad responded, sounding cheerier than the father of a cancer patient should. I narrowed my eyes to focus better on Dad, who stood slightly back from the women and sipped his afternoon mocha from a plastic-lidded cup.

I managed to turn my head so I could scan the room. Peter was standing there silently in the corner, respectful of our family time, and I knew Dad appreciated it. He was somewhat hidden behind stacks and stacks of brown-paper-wrapped bundles that I recognized all too well. They and the dubious smells they emitted reminded me of the many years I spent resisting my father's well-meaning attempts to cure my diabetes through his natural methods. I hated that period in my life and his interventions in it. All I'd wanted to do was fit in. But how could a child put on a bathing suit and swim with her friends when her back was covered with bruises caused by Chinese cupping therapy? What could a teenager say when friends asked about the smelly brown herbal tonic that she drank during lunch? One day in high school, I'd exploded at my father because I was embarrassed about these therapies, tired of being "sick" in his eyes when I felt fine day to day, and done with being different. That was what I'd planned to say to him, but instead, what came out in a tearful, screaming rush that woke him from his pipe dream was "DIABETES IS NOT CURABLE! LEAVE ME ALONE!"

As I lay there in the hospital bed, I was still certain that I wasn't up for anything "alternative."

"Dad! I am not taking any of that." I turned my gaze and looked for more support. "Mom, please tell him."

Audrey broke in. "It's not him, Sophia. Scott sent all of it."

Dad looked exceptionally pleased as my head wobbled back toward him. I told myself I would fight that battle later. Nothing mattered at that moment except my surgery. "What did the surgeon say?"

Mom and Dad stood on either side of my bed wearing smiles that didn't appear to be strictly due to the pop-up herbal pharmacy that my room had become.

"He said it went *very* well," Dad said. "They said the disease doesn't seem to have . . ."

Dad's voice trailed off and he couldn't bear to finish his sentence. Before either of us could get sentimental, a familiar face walked into my room.

"Well, good morning," the surgeon said, trying nonchalantly to wave his hand in front of his nose as the "natural remedies" hit his nostrils—hard to imagine how anyone could ignore them. He was handsome, tall, Middle Eastern, and exuded an arrogant confidence that went along with his reputation as a "cowboy" surgeon—a risk taker who would do anything to conquer the task at hand. After asking how I felt, he relayed in almost too much detail what he'd accomplished during the surgery. I listened for his tone as he spoke. *He sounds optimistic.*

"We are hoping the pathology report and the lymph nodes show clear margins. That would mean that we extracted everything and that there's no more cancer in your body."

"Did you give me a tummy tuck while you were at it?" I asked, doing my best to charm the surgeon. I was sore and stiff, but my sense of humor hadn't waned.

My mother glared at me to show her disapproval of my flirting, then bowed her head slightly and handed the surgeon a fancy bottle of Veuve Clicquot champagne. *Oh so Chinese.* "Thank you for taking care of Sophia," she said without making eye contact.

"Let's assume the pathology report will be good, and plan to open this for a champagne toast then," the surgeon said just before the black pager attached to his hip started to vibrate. "Get some rest; I'll check in on you tomorrow."

With almost too much enthusiasm, Dad shook the surgeon's hand. "Thank you, Doctor," he said. "Really. Thank you."

THE PHONE WOKE me from my deep, restful sleep, but before I could open my eyes I heard someone scramble to answer it.

"Hello," Peter said.

"Who is it?" I asked.

My boyfriend spoke into the receiver and then asked me, "Do you want to speak to Tony?"

Since the only Tony I knew was the banker from Chaussure.com, and prioritizing work was a complete habit, I reached my arm out to take the receiver while feeling the pull of my abdominal incision. The voice on the other end of the phone was not Tony's—it was Scott's.

"Why are you giving a fake name? What's this 'Tony' business?"

"I don't know. I don't like people knowing it's me."

"Why not?"

Scott didn't answer my question but preferred to focus on what *he* wanted to discuss: the herbs. "Did you get the herbal medicines?" he asked. "Some of them can only be collected by monkeys in Brazil."

Oh Lord. Here we go.

"First of all, were those monkeys well taken care of? They weren't abused or chained down or anything, were they?" I asked softly.

Scott sighed impatiently. "No, Sophia. There were no chains. They gave 'free range' a whole new meaning."

Then it occurred to me. "Is *that* why you were in South America? You didn't go for *me*, did you?"

Instead of answering the question, he continued, "I'm telling you. You have the best herbal medicines from all over the world. I've had them blended with a special root from Nicoya, Costa Rica. That region has incredibly low rates of cancer, and I'm certain the root is the secret to their longevity."

"They're stinking up my room," I told him as I grinned at Peter, who plugged his nose and pretended to choke.

"There's also a blend from India. Those are the anti-inflammatories and—"

"Why do I need anti-inflammatories?" I asked.

"That's what causes cancer. Inflammation," he explained. "There's also digestive enzymes to help you build up the immunity in your abdomen . . ." I wanted to ask which mountain yogi he tracked down to get all this information, if only to egg him on and fluster him, purely for my own entertainment.

Scott continued to ramble about the herbal concoctions, and while I had no interest in trying them, I couldn't help but be grateful that he went to all this trouble. I slowly enunciated each of my next words to emphasize how serious and heartfelt my comments were. "Thank you very much, Scott. I appreciate all the trouble you've gone through. I'll ask Dr. Levin if I can take them."

"Of course you can take them!" he barked. "I would choose those over chemo any day. Are they suggesting chemo?"

"I haven't asked yet."

"Oh," Scott responded, seemingly surprised. "When are you getting out?"

I let out a deep sigh. "I don't know." Then I added, "Just call or email me if you need anything." It was one of our old patterns. I always offered. I didn't even ask myself if I meant it.

I turned to Peter after hanging up with Scott. "So, Mr. Western Medicine, what is *your* professional opinion about all these alternative ways? I bet you didn't study any of *this* in medical school."

Peter shrugged and his expression looked as though he didn't have an opinion. So I was surprised when he said, "I hate to admit it, but I'm a believer. There was an integrative medicine rotation at Stanford and the results were impressive, so I read a lot more about it. There are a lot of cases that prove it works."

"Not you, too. What specifically did you read?"

"Well, take the simplest thing like diet. You know how sugar and carbs affect your blood sugar levels. And some cancer tumors can feed off of sugar and fat."

I frowned. *Oh dear, I love fat.*

"Um, well, there are certain foods that are anti-inflammatory as well, right? You've heard of that."

I nodded.

"So there are herbs that indigenous people have used for years, and Asian cultures, too, that carry ten times the anti-inflammatory properties of something like a blueberry. Turmeric is one example."

Defeated.

ON THE FOURTEENTH day of my hospitalization, Audrey, Mom, and Dad arrived earlier than usual because the pathology report was due back and they were anxious to hear the results. I, too, was nervous, and had spent the better part of the previous few days meditating, visualizing, humming, and doing my best to emit positive energy like Jonathan and Scott taught me after my breakup with Daniel. *Feel what it will feel like when Dr. Levin and the surgeon give me good news.* To make sure I had all my bases covered, I even prayed. *God, please let it be good news.*

Kate was visiting and stood as my family entered. Everyone exchanged hellos before my dad stepped back into the hall with the boxes of donuts he had purchased earlier that morning. I could hear him talking to the nurses, telling them to enjoy the donuts and thanking them for taking such good care of me.

"Don't I get one of those?" Kate asked jokingly as Dad reentered my room.

I shook my head. "They bring food for the nurses and doctors every day. Masters of kissing ass." Dad grinned.

I was happy to see my old friend and thankful for her nonchalant calm. She'd brought a stack of my favorite magazines, tucked inside a green felt satchel she knew I had been admiring for months. Kate wasn't one for mushy speeches or big displays of emotion—this stack of magazines and trendy purse were about as sentimental as she got. She knew I understood. I would have given her one of those donuts if I could have.

"Is Peter coming today?" she asked.

"He was here yesterday. My dad talked his ear off. But I told him not to come today because if he hears the pathology report results, he'll ask all sorts of questions that I may not want to hear the answers to."

"But I thought you guys were cool."

"We are. We are for sure." *I think.*

When Dr. Levin and the surgeon appeared in my doorway, they were both holding the fried and sugar-coated diabetic nightmares that my parents had brought. With his donut-free hand, the surgeon handed me a document that was about six or seven pages long. I saw my name on the front and didn't dare look down any farther. "Well?" I asked.

"They confirmed you had a gastrointestinal stromal tumor. It's an extremely rare cancer." Then, donning a huge smile, he continued, "But the margins and lymph nodes were clear and *that is great news!* That's the best thing we could hope for!"

I was so busy hugging both doctors, my mom, my sister, and Kate that I almost didn't notice my dad. When I turned to look at him, Mom was shoving tissues into his hand. His shoulders were slumped over and he was shaking. I was afraid something was wrong with him—but when he looked up he was smiling from ear to ear. Dad, who never cried (except in the presence of the most pungent onions), and who eschewed any emotion other than optimism and good cheer, was laughing and crying as though no one were watching. But I was.

"My baby girl," he said as he leaned over to hug me. "That is the best news in the world."

Once I allowed myself the full excitement of the report—*Here we come, cancer survivor badge!*—I turned my attention to Dr. Levin and got right to business. "Wow, that wasn't so bad," I said. "Now what?"

My dad leaned in with his good ear so he could hear clearly.

"Well." Levin cleared his throat. "Even though we got everything, and you technically no longer have *traceable* cancer cells, the GI oncologist here recommends chemotherapy, just to make sure the cancer doesn't return. There's one oral chemo that has minimal side effects, the most common of which is severe swelling."

Nope. Don't like that option.

"There's another chemo pill, but that will turn you yellow."

Definitely don't want that.

"We could also try—"

"Let me get this straight. This oncologist wants to fill me with toxins *just because?*"

"It's not *just because.* I'm sure he's trying to prevent it from coming back."

So my options are to look like the Pillsbury Doughboy or Bart Simpson?

"How long would I have to take this chemo?"

"It'd be an ongoing thing, just like your insulin."

"So daily?"

"Yep. It's protocol," Levin said.

"But you don't know if the cancer is going to come back."

Steve Levin didn't say anything, but the look on his face—grim, uncomfortable, and definitely not worthy of Veuve Clicquot—told me all I needed to know. It told me nothing is for sure. That was an answer I never liked, and cancer made it even worse.

I straightened up and changed the tone of my voice so it sounded strong and authoritative, just like the voice coach had taught me years ago. "It's not coming back and I am certainly not going to be a patient of your negative GI oncologist friend."

Dr. Levin gave me a reassuring touch and said, "He's not my

friend. And don't shoot me! I'm just the messenger. What do I look like, a cancer doctor?"

We laughed for a moment, but then I looked at Audrey and my eyes began to dampen. I tried to maintain my composure—*It's okay. It's not your time. It's not your time*—and took a deep breath.

Audrey handed me a tissue from behind her, reassuring me, "We'll get a second opinion."

I nodded and turned to my rock, my dad. "Nothing to worry about, right, Dad?" I asked, my voice cracking.

"My sweet, sweet Sophia. This is just a bump in the road, it's no big deal," he said, reaching for my hand.

Then I turned back to Dr. Levin and asked, "How did this happen? There's no cancer in my family."

"We don't know. It just happens," he said before quietly leaving the room.

LATER THAT EVENING, everything was quiet and everyone had left me to rest. *Sex and the City* played on my laptop—the episode where Mr. Big comes to find Carrie in Paris. I'd seen this one dozens of times before, and I never failed to sigh and tear up when Carrie was crouched in the hotel lobby picking up her broken necklace after leaving the Russian artist. She cried until she saw Mr. Big. The series always sent me dreaming about my own Mr. Right, but this time, I daydreamed about something different. I focused on the beautiful hotel, Carrie's unbelievably amazing dress, and the day that I would *finally* have the opportunity to visit Paris. *I'd better hurry. There's a lot left for me to do in this world.* But I was living at home, making great money for someone my age although not enough to allow me to *do* much of anything. I was on a fast track to steady and stable. It wasn't what I was looking for, or what I wanted out of life.

My thoughts turned to Ion—an opportunity that, if all went well with its stock price, could make me wealthy enough to live a life on my *own* terms. Even though I made a nice salary at Treehouse, I'd been hired too late in the game for my stock options to give me the life that Ion *could*. If Ion worked out, I would never have to worry about being fired, saying the wrong thing, or being at someone's beck and call. Importantly, in a worst-case scenario, Ion could also potentially give me the means to take care of myself if the cancer came back someday. I wouldn't have to be a burden to my family, to Peter, or to anyone else—I could pay people to take care of me. If Ion's valuation went as high as Grant thought it would, I could make sure that, finally, my life would be in *my* control. I picked up the phone to call Grant, and told myself it was the right thing to do.

I am going to be rich, but not just boring old rich.

I'm going to be fucking rich.

chapter 17

A TERRIBLE MALODOR JOLTED ME awake from a deep, blissful sleep on my own Tempur-Pedic mattress. The stench was so strong that I was certain it could stir even a hibernating bear. I knew the smell—it had been polluting our home since I returned from the hospital four weeks ago; an "immune-boosting, cancer-challenging" herbal concoction that Mom brewed downstairs in the kitchen. I wondered which mix of syrupy soup, brown pellets, and powdery phytochemicals was on that morning's menu. More important, how long did my parents (and Scott and Peter, too) expect me to carry on with all the mumbo-jumbo? I'd fought them at first, but their joined forces were too powerful to overcome.

Still sore from the surgery, I turned to my side, pushed myself up with both arms, and made my way toward the kitchen. When I heard the muted sound of Audrey's voice through the swinging door, I picked up my pace because I assumed Ava was with her.

"Where's Ava?" I asked as I stood barefoot in the kitchen.

"Hi!" Audrey said from the family room. "She's not here."

"Good morning, Sophia!" yelled Dad, who was at his station in front of the television.

"Why not?" I asked.

"You have no idea how many germs kids carry. They're like petri dishes. It wouldn't be good for you to get sick *right now.*"

"Good morning, Sophia!" Dad happily yelled again.

"Good morning," I snapped back at Dad. Then to Audrey, "Is she sick *now?*"

"No."

"Well, then why didn't you bring her?" I asked.

"I just told you why. What's the big deal?" Audrey argued.

She thought she was protecting me and that I was making a big deal out of nothing. Except Audrey's cautiousness signaled she was already treating me differently, and *that* is what I reacted to. Anyway, there was something about my sister's daughter that lit me up inside and that could help me forget about everything that had happened—everything that might come. Ava made me smile, which happened less and less during those days, and a niece sighting was just what I needed.

"Don't baby me, Audrey. You know I hate that."

"She's just worried you'll get sick," Mom chimed in.

"You guys are driving me fucking crazy!"

"You're a f—"

"Girls! Girls! Language! No four-letter words in this house," Dad shouted.

My eyes teared up and I whimpered, "It's my last chance to see Ava before I'm buried in work again."

"What's wrong with you?" Audrey asked. "Why are you so emotional?"

"I don't know," I said as I slumped over and used the back of my hand to wipe away a stray tear. This wasn't the first time I had become weepy over nothing. Last week I'd sobbed when Dad told me to put on some socks. When I asked Dr. Levin about my weepiness, he responded, "Your body has been hit by an eighteen-wheeler. Just give it some time to settle down."

If I have to settle down one more minute in this house, I'm going to go batshit crazy.

"You're not ready to go back to work. The doctor said eight weeks," Audrey said.

"That's bullshit. Oh, sorry, Dad."

"Sophia!" Dad exclaimed as he tore through the kitchen.

"Hey, where are you going? Breakfast is almost ready," Mom shouted after him.

"Those damn squirrels are in my trees again!"

Mom looked at me and shook her head. "Your father is crazy." She handed me a mug full of sludge with one hand while she flipped a fried egg with the other.

"Oh God," I said as I looked at the contents of the mug.

"Drink it," Mom demanded, droning on and on about its antiviral and antibacterial properties.

Audrey cringed as she watched me take a deep breath, plug my nose, and slam the lukewarm liquid down my throat. She looked as relieved as I was when I finished the sludge and exhaled loudly through my mouth.

"Ugh!" I exclaimed.

"That's pretty fucked up." Audrey grimaced.

"LANGUAGE!" Dad shouted into the house from his squirrel-watching station outside. Audrey and I laughed.

"It's a good thing I taught you to slam a beer. You're getting some good use out of those skills."

Mom's slipper came flying across the kitchen, barely missed me, and nailed Audrey in the shoulder. "Ouch!" she exclaimed.

There was no need to say anything. My grin and raised eyebrows said it all, so I grabbed a banana and walked toward the door. "I've got to get ready."

Rubbing her shoulder, Audrey said, "I'm heading out, too."

"Why are you even here?" I asked.

"Mom and Dad called—"

I held up my hand to stop her. "Enough said."

I STOPPED AT the gray console table just outside the kitchen door and rifled through the first drawer to find my car keys, left untouched for six weeks. Between Mom's shouting, the clinking of keys in the drawer, and my high heels, Dad must have heard me from upstairs. When I finally found my keys and turned toward the door, Dad was standing in front of it.

"I'm afraid you'll catch germs," he said. "You need your immune system to spend all its energy recovering from your surgery."

"Dad! What are you talking about?" I said, frantically trying to push past him, but he was blocking the front door. "There are germs everywhere, *including* in this house."

"Can't you work at home just a few more days?" he pleaded. "Daddy wants you to stay home. Why go to work? You have that appointment with the new oncologist this afternoon anyway."

I chuckled at the scene unfolding in front of me: Dad parked in the doorway, his arms outstretched high and his legs spread out wide, still wearing his pajamas. When he pleaded like this, it was hard to imagine him as the tough businessman he was known to be. Then again, I must have learned my negotiation tactics from somewhere.

It was then that I noticed that he still had toothpaste in his mouth. *Jesus H. Christ!*

As much as it pained my incision—sternum-to-pelvis, no small nick—I couldn't help but laugh at his foamy lips. I regained control quickly, though, as my desire to escape the house outweighed Dad's shenanigans. I also knew I needed to be in the car so I could speak privately with Ion's CFO—a call that I'd arranged days ago. *No need for Mom and Dad to start butting in.* Within seconds I switched from laughing to yelling over Dad's toothpaste-mouthed pleas. "DAD! Please!"

"I'm begging you, Sophia. Do this for your poor, poor daddy. Stay home just one more day," he said, gargling a bit from the toothpaste. "Mom and Dad are going back to Taiwan tomorrow. Don't you want to spend time with your daddy?"

Drastic measures were in order. As loudly as I could, so that

Mom could hear me from the kitchen, I said, "No! Dad, I'm late! If you don't move, I'm going to start looking for my own apartment!" Toothpaste drooled from Dad's mouth; a disappointed look crossed his face and he dropped his arms. My dad knew my antics too well, and we both looked toward the kitchen door as Mom flew through it. She was on a crash course with the front door, where we were still parked.

"What? Apartment? You aren't moving, Sophia." I felt guilty for a moment, having just put this woman through hell with my cancer and now manipulating her with the threat of moving. God forbid she be forced to explain to her friends that her daughter disobeyed her and actually moved out. But then I wondered what it would be like to live on my own, away from the care and comfort of my parents. I smiled at the thought of my own San Francisco apartment, and of buying my first couch. Of throwing dinner parties with Peter, just like real adults. As Mom rushed over, my hand lightly ran along the ten-inch scar on my abdomen.

Someday, Sophia. But not now. Not yet.

When Dad saw the look of determination on my face and the death grip I had on my keys, he knew he had been defeated. Slowly, reluctantly, he slid out of the doorframe. "I don't like this," he noted as he made way. I could see his eyes tearing a little, but I wasn't sure if it was because the toothpaste was burning his mouth. I chuckled in triumph and pecked both parents on their cheeks before walking outside and down the paved steps toward my car. I was aware of the silence where my mother's parting comments once had been. Where she used to call, "Suck in your belly," or "That outfit doesn't do you any favors," there was just a reminder about my late-afternoon appointment with the new oncologist and her silent approval of the weight I'd lost because of the surgery. I was relieved not to hear her usual commentary, but hated the price I'd paid to avoid it.

I POSITIONED MYSELF in my leather bucket seat, pressed the button to lower the convertible top to let the summer's UV rays warm my skin, and ran my hands over the smooth, padded steering wheel. *Ahhh.* The roar of the engine sounded more intimidating than I remembered, and the tight grip of the low-profile tires around our circular driveway caught me, and my still sore stomach muscles, off guard. But I enjoyed every second of my regained independence as the car eased forward.

The sound of the wind rushing past me and of the crowded freeway fueled my adrenaline. *No coffee needed today.* Surprisingly, Ion was the farthest thing from my mind; instead I imagined walking into Treehouse and the warm welcome back I was soon to receive. I ignored the traffic and acknowledged how good it felt returning to my old routine as I sang along with the radio. When later the ringing of my mobile phone interrupted my blissful state of mind, I fumbled to plug in my headset. In the moments that passed during the phone's first, then second, ring, my nerves began to rattle. Weeks earlier I'd already spoken with (read: been interrogated by) two other Ion executives, and I knew this call with the CFO, Rajesh Patel, would seal the deal.

When the phone rang a third time, my hand hovered above it; my hesitation to answer surprised me. *What about Scott?* I owed him so much. The phone vibrated and rang a fourth time; I picked it up half a second later, but it was too late—the phone had fallen silent. I told myself I would call Rajesh back when I figured out what I wanted to do, then hit one of my phone's speed-dial buttons. "Hi, Peter, it's me."

SHUFFLING IN HIGH heels and a black drop-waist embroidered silk dress toward the new Treehouse building made me feel like Minnie Mouse. My feet had been blissfully bare during my recovery, and it was as though they'd forgotten how to walk in heels. I looked around me to see if anyone had witnessed my less-than-graceful approach, but the coast seemed to be clear. I reached for the vertical steel bar that would open the glass door, but another hand came up from behind me and pulled the bar for me.

Jonathan's eyes sparkled as we both stepped inside and he gave me the warm hug I was expecting. "Hey, welcome back. It's been a while."

Hey, where'd you come from?

"Thanks. But I was never really gone. Just recovering. We spoke every day," I said, trying to downplay how ill I'd been.

"We prefer you here, safe and sound where we can see you. Six weeks is a long time," he said with a grin. "How are you feeling?"

I tried not to read into his question and answered as though it were any given precancer day. "Great. How are you?"

"Glad to see you," Jonathan returned. He noticed me looking around at the new office—I hadn't seen it completely finished. "Pretty cool, eh?"

"Amazing."

"Listen, get settled and then come talk to me about our upcoming shareholder meeting. I'd show you around, but I have to get to a nine o'clock. Oh, and Ashley's booked something in your calendar at eleven, in case you hadn't noticed."

Jonathan left me standing just inside the entrance and I tilted my head way back, feeling as though our new office's ceiling were as high as the sky.

"What do you think?"

I looked left and saw Scott standing there with crossed arms.

"New outfit?" I asked jokingly, referring to his black shirt and worn jeans and noticing his too-thin frame.

Scott shook his head, making it clear my sarcasm didn't register, then said, "Come on, let me give you a tour."

There was a controlled madness happening in front of us—ebbs and flows of people stopped to talk to one another while holding their morning coffees. I followed Scott as he waved his arms like Vanna White.

"The architect had originally put the cafeteria and gym on the opposite ends of the building, but I wanted this courtyard to be the heart of the company. A place where the magic happens—where discussions and brainstorms take place organically because *everyone* at the company will have a reason to come here at some point during the day—to collect their mail, get something to eat, go to the bathroom, whatever," Scott explained.

"Hmm. Very clever. What else is down here?" I asked.

"Well, the gym, theater, and company store to name a few more," he answered as though stating the obvious. "They're all here. This is the place that will inspire and encourage creative thought. It will ensure everyone still feels cohesive even though all the departments are very spread out now."

Wow. Leave it to Scott to think of that stuff.

The building almost felt like a huge airplane hangar framed by lightly tinted glass and beams that were made of gently blasted steel. It emitted a warm and friendly vibe, just as I knew Scott intended. I tilted my head back. My eyes ran along the second-floor offices that overlooked the grand courtyard; I became slightly emotional about its enveloping beauty.

I followed Scott up a broad, steel staircase, then across an arched glass-and-steel skywalk that crossed over the courtyard and connected the right side of the building to the left. We walked through a wide, naturally lit hallway, then through double doors that led to the animators' dimly lit fairyland—an area at least four or five times the size of their old space. I was surprised to see there were no more decorated cubicles; instead there was an entire neighborhood of twenty-by-twenty "homes"—each gloriously custom designed and built by its owner. "It was Dylan's idea to give each animator a budget that they could use to build and decorate whatever they wanted," Scott said as we passed by one complete with faux-stone walls and a turret. "I think it worked out well."

"Did the engineers downstairs get as creative?" I asked.

Scott's look told me I'd asked a stupid question, but he answered it just the same. "No."

A man of many words.

We exited the animators' mecca and crossed the bridge once again, then passed life-size statues of Treehouse characters lined up along the wide walkway that led to a row of offices. Inside the first one was a wall-to-wall fish tank, about eight feet tall and just like the one at Baron Capital. Scott waved toward it and said, "This is me, and on the other side of the fish tank is Ashley," before he continued ahead. But I stopped, turned into his office, and walked up to the humongous tank. It looked like a seafloor, with sand and rocks lining the bottom and starfish and sea urchins clinging to them. I stepped closer to make sure my eyes weren't deceiving me—an octopus stretching almost a foot wide swam happily to an opening between two rocks where it could hide. For a moment I was lost in the tank, staring dazedly into its undulating water. But Scott's voice snapped me to attention; I turned around and rushed to catch up.

We proceeded down the hallway, where framed *Treasures* storyboards hung on the walls. Scott stopped at the fifth office and said before disappearing, "This is you. Jonathan is next door. I'll see you at eleven."

My office was a huge improvement on the old one. A glass wall faced the courtyard and gave the room the feeling that it was much bigger than it actually was. A monitor, keyboard, and mouse were arranged on a simple, drawerless pine desk facing the door, not the great view. I considered flipping the desk and ergonomic chair arrangement around so I could look out upon the courtyard, but remembered that Scott had a feng shui expert place every single piece of furniture and décor in the building. This particular arrangement followed one of his key rules: "Never put your back to the door."

I assumed it was Ashley who'd hung beautifully framed letters and hand-drawn pictures on two of the three walls, each addressed to Treehouse Investor Relations. *I bought ten shares of Treehouse stock,* said one that was written in blue crayon. It was signed, *Sincerely, Ben,* and included his first grade school portrait taped to the bottom. A large, framed *Treasures* poster hung alone on the third wall. In black Sharpie ink on the bottom-right corner was a note in Jonathan's handwriting: *Thank you for all your effort.* When I saw two signatures on the bottom—his and Scott's—I imagined the wrangling that must have taken place and Scott's complaining, "I don't give my autograph."

I exited my office and stood on the glass bridge, then looked down into the courtyard. The artists, engineers, storytellers, and production managers that were there all seemed to be charging in one direction or another as though they couldn't wait to start their day. It was how I felt at that moment, too. I thought of Ion again and questioned whether I could really leave this behind: Scott, Jonathan, and our movie that had entertained so many. Then Scott's words of wisdom came to mind: "Nothing is forever if you don't want it to be."

AT ELEVEN O'CLOCK, I stepped into the new Treehouse theater, where Jonathan and Scott waited for me seated in red-cushioned bamboo seats. These were the same seats Scott had insisted on purchasing months ago, the ones that had caused me so much grief when it somehow got out how much we'd paid for them—worse when word spread that we'd bought three hundred.

I observed Scott wiggling around in one of the infamous chairs and said, "I told you so."

He frowned and responded with something he knew would upset me. "Okay, then find me new chairs."

Jonathan replied with a nervous twitch before he turned to me. "Don't go blabbing this to investors yet, but we finished *The Amazings*. You're one of the first to get a preview."

Just then, Scott waved his arm above his head and the theater lights went dark; the ceiling turned the midnight blue color of a clear Hawaiian night sky. Twinkling stars appeared and I gasped in delight when a comet flew by. *Ahhh.*

Jonathan whispered to me, "Another one of Scott's personal touches."

Seconds later the movie began and I clapped, hooted, and hollered when I saw Treehouse's logo and my coworkers' names on the big screen. I couldn't imagine how proud Scott and Jonathan must have felt knowing that the movie, and the company, wouldn't have existed without their business acumen and prowess.

From the second the movie started, I was transported to a different world. Each of the characters were *Amazing*—and the story was exciting, touching, and funny all the same. When the closing credits began to roll, I stood up cheering, even though I wished the movie weren't over. Tears fell down my face. *Damn cartoons!* The lights turned back on and Jonathan asked if I liked it.

"I *loved* it," I said.

"Which was your favorite character?"

"Oh, by far the little gadget woman! She was hysterical!"

"Did she look familiar?" Scott asked, winking at Jonathan.

I envisioned the character in my head: A-line bob, Asian, black dress and heels that didn't do much to hide her vertically challenged frame, bossy and stomping around all the time telling the heroes of the movie to "chop-chop." It took me a moment, but I put it all together and then frowned, uncertain of whether I wanted to know the answer to my next question.

"Was that character supposed to be me?" I asked.

Scott and Jonathan just grinned and shrugged. I considered this for a moment longer—*Should I be offended?*—then exclaimed, "I don't care. I loved it! I know you always say it's about the story, but the animation is amazing!"

IN THE EARLY afternoon, my fingers were dancing along my keyboard when I noticed Scott standing in my doorway. I turned back to my computer and said, "I'm drafting an email. Sit, I need two seconds."

Just as he took a step into my office, my mobile phone vibrated loudly on top of my desk and Rajesh's name appeared on the screen. *Shit!* I froze my eyes on Scott, hoping he would catch my gaze and not see the name of the person calling. My entire body was still, except for my hand that reached for the phone to turn it facedown. I blindly pressed buttons in an effort to send the call to voicemail.

"Your two seconds are always two minutes, and tardiness is a character flaw," Scott said, speaking into the palms of his pressed-together hands.

"Then *you* are deeply flawed," I joked, secretly trying to ruffle Scott's feathers so he wouldn't focus on my phone.

"I'm not always late," he whined as he brought his hands down to his sides.

Phew. He didn't notice the caller ID.

Like a teenager, I rolled my eyes and returned to the computer, then exhaled a sigh of relief.

Scott continued, "I see those medicinal herbs worked wonders. You're back to your ornery self."

"Wonders. They worked wonders," I responded, turning to Scott with a huge ear-to-ear smile. "I am still going to see the oncologist this afternoon, though."

"Didn't you say you weren't—" He was interrupted by the sound of my phone roaring again. "Does your phone ever stop?" he asked, watching me fumble around with the phone, which I accidentally let land on the floor.

Scott's eyes looked down at the phone. "Hey, it's your dad. Answer it."

"That's okay. I'll call him later," I said as the phone fell silent.

"How are you feeling?"

I glared at Scott and said, "You know I hate when people ask me that."

"Yes, I know. I also know I don't agree with it. It shouldn't bother you."

"It's worse coming from you. You never used to ask me how I was. So now that you ask, it's almost as if you're expecting something to be wrong."

"Do you really want to argue about this?" he asked. "Remember, if you shout you owe me a dollar."

"We're not arguing." I bit my bottom lip and smiled, then changed the subject before I angered Scott.

The phone on the floor began vibrating again, giving me the heads-up it was about to ring. We both looked down at it and I picked it up quickly. *Damn this phone!*

"Hello?"

"I need your health insurance information, please," said Dad.

I braced the phone between my ear and right shoulder so I could rifle through my purse to get the information my father asked for. As I was doing so, the phone slipped and fell to the floor, sending its thin metal battery cover flying across my office.

Scott leaned over to pick up the device, but instead of giving it back to me, he examined the front, then the back. I grabbed it and apologized to Dad, but just as soon as I began relaying my insurance ID number to him, the phone slipped again and crashed on the floor, this time disconnecting the call. *I give up!*

Scott leaned over and picked up the phone. "This looks like a pile of gravel," he said, referring to my device's dents and chipped paint. "Didn't you just get it?"

"Yes, I did, and I know. It looks awful," I said. "But I love it."

"Let me see it again."

I turned my shoulder and held the phone close to me, then nar-rowed my eyes to glare at him. "Why?"

"Just let me see it."

"No," I cried, turning my shoulder as if to block Scott's outreached hand.

"Just give it to me,"

"Why do you want it?"

"Sophia, just give me the goddamn phone."

I reluctantly handed over the device, hoping he wouldn't see any-thing he wasn't supposed to see.

"Why do you love this phone?" Scott asked.

"It's light and text messages are really easy—way easier than my flip phone," I responded.

"Ashley drops the phone all the time, too. Why do you guys prop it on your shoulder like that?"

"Because we're usually multitasking," I responded.

"There are studies about that, you know. It's totally inefficient," Scott said.

"Again, you're one to talk, Mr. CEO of too many companies."

"That's different," he returned. "What about your BlackBerry? You carry that around with you, too, right?"

"Yes, I love my BlackBerry! I'd never give that up." I wondered why he was asking me all these questions. I assumed they had nothing to do with me, so I tried to change the subject. But Scott continued to ask me about my phone:

Wasn't it a hassle to carry a cell phone *and* a BlackBerry? *Yes, they're heavy in my purse.*

How often did I hold the phone on my shoulder? *Almost always.*

Was this why I was always dropping the phone when speaking with him? *Yes.*

How easy was it to use the phone's speaker mode? *It's a four-step process.*

Scott sat down in the chair facing my desk, held my phone in the palm of his hand, and turned it around to consider every angle. He lifted it up toward the ceiling, and then moved his hand up and down as though weighing it. Then he began to press buttons, which should have made me panic, but I knew the look on his face: his lips were pursed, his head was tilted slightly to the left, and his laser-focused eyes were on the beat-up Panasonic phone. Scott shut me and the rest of the world out and thought of nothing else except how he could make a better phone. I left him sitting there while I finished my email, knowing he would find a way. He always did.

chapter 18

THE AFTERNOON OF MY PERSONAL *Amazings* premiere, I went to get that second opinion from the oncologist that Peter referred me to, Dr. Alan Madden. Peter had warned me Dr. Madden was known to be opinionated and skewed heavily toward the blunt side, so when he introduced himself that afternoon, I raised my hand to stop him from saying another word.

"Before we get started, please refrain from saying *anything* negative. I don't want to know about statistics or *what if*s. No offense, but I don't even really want your opinions—unless there's something you feel very strongly about. The only things we should ever talk about are the things you are absolutely certain of and the things that I need to do to stay healthy. I'm a *next steps* kind of a person. You have no idea who you're dealing with."

Dr. Madden's stunned expression told me he wasn't accustomed to people speaking to him that way. In that moment I wondered if I'd crossed a line—*He is the head of the department, after all.* But when he raised both of his hands in the air as though to surrender and said, "I understand," I knew he was the right oncologist for me.

Dr. Madden was medium height, wore tinted round glasses, and had a mustache. A few strands of his close-cut brown hair were standing straight up, and his white coat over his blue shirt and tie made him look as though he belonged in a lab.

After the doctor reviewed my medical records, including the scans and pathology report, he said, "You have quite the medical history."

"That's right. A walking medical wonder," I said proudly.

Madden asked me a bunch of questions: did I still take these medications, how were my blood sugar levels, how was my blood pressure. He stood up from his computer. "You're really going to make me work for my money here, aren't you?"

"Yep!" I tilted up my chin and grinned.

The appointment lasted only fifteen minutes, and in the end, Madden agreed with my self-prescribed treatment—that because I showed no signs of cancer, I didn't need chemotherapy. "Doctors don't have crystal balls, and none of this is exact science," he said. "Let's just watch you really closely, because—"

"Because you don't have any idea who you're dealing with," I interrupted mischievously.

AS I SAT across the table from the CFO of Ion, Rajesh Patel, I provided the same answer when he asked me his first question: "What makes you think you can handle Andre Stark?"

Feeling confident in my abilities, I winked. "You don't have any idea who you're dealing with."

My interview with Rajesh took place in Ion's uninspiring round, mustard-colored conference room, which fit perfectly with the depressing tone of the entire building. Only fluorescent lights glowed above and it felt like a dungeon—no windows or natural sunlight. I'd seen Rajesh's photo on the website—he looked friendly enough. But there seated right in front of me, he wore a stiff smirk that made him look vaguely snakelike and untrustworthy.

"How did you get in here?" Rajesh asked.

"Your assistant brought me in," I answered matter-of-factly, wondering if that was a trick question.

"That's not what I mean," he said.

"Oh, sorry. What do you mean?"

Rajesh's tone remained calm, but his words were biting. "I looked at your CV, and nothing on it suggests you're the right person for this role."

Clearly he didn't find my earlier response witty.

His stare and smug expression told me that he really expected me to take the bait. My face turned bright red, but my silence was deafening. Rajesh must have been uncomfortable, so he asked again, "How did you get in here? You must know someone."

I did my best to sound confident in my answer. "Grant Vicker recommended me."

"Oh, that's right." He nodded and looked at my résumé. "Didn't we have a call scheduled last week?"

"Yes, but we weren't able to connect. Something came up at Treehouse and I had to manage it. Thank you for your understanding."

Or maybe not.

"I see here that you didn't go to an Ivy League school," he said.

"Well actually, Santa Clara is—"

"We only hire people who graduated from Ivy League schools. It's a natural filter," Rajesh said smugly. "Correction: we hire only the top *one* percent from Ivy League schools."

Is this guy trying to unsettle me, or is he really an asshole?

I started to doubt I had any shot at the job, so I dropped any pretense of being polite. "So where did you go to school?" Rajesh Patel might have held the key to my future career, but I knew that he wasn't an Ivy Leaguer, either. From what I could find online, prior to joining Ion he was just a cog in the wheel of a large Japanese automobile manufacturer. He'd left his controller job in India to become CFO of Ion—a *huge* stretch, if you asked me—and when I looked at his poorly populated LinkedIn profile, I wondered why Ion didn't have someone with more experience. Someone who had at least lived through an IPO, or someone who had been a public-company CFO before.

Rajesh didn't respond to my question but instead said, "I didn't think you were a good candidate, but Grant spoke highly of you and your phone interviews a few weeks ago with our VP of communications and VP of finance were positively received, so let's get started. What are your strengths and weaknesses?"

"I'm a people person and have strong communication skills— people feel at ease around me and trust me because I feel familiar to them for some reason. I'm told it's a unique skill set, one that can't be learned."

There was absolutely no reaction from Rajesh, just another question. "And what about your weaknesses?"

"I'm not good with spreadsheets," I said, once again dropping any pretenses.

"What was your major again?"

"Finance. I can read a financial statement and spin a story from it, but no one should trust me to create those documents from scratch."

Rajesh uncrossed his legs and said very softly, "We've interviewed a lot of terrific candidates, and I am personally of the opinion that someone with investment banking or research experience is the best fit."

"Then why are we wasting each other's time?"

Rajesh seemed surprised by that, but continued with his interview anyway. "How is it working for Scott Kraft?"

"Can you be more specific?" I asked. "And just to be clear, I don't work *for* Scott. I actually report to the CFO, Jonathan Larsen."

Rajesh ignored the Jonathan part and went straight to Scott. "Scott Kraft is notoriously hard to manage. So how is it that you've survived for almost three years?"

"I didn't find him challenging at all," I said, pleased that I both answered his question *and* defended Scott.

For nearly an hour, Rajesh peppered me with questions. Each one felt like a bullet shooting through my confidence. Then, abruptly, he stood up and told me that I would hear from someone in the next few weeks. To me, that sounded like code for *when hell freezes over,* but at that point, I didn't care. *I didn't want to work here anyway.* I left Ion's office totally humiliated, and as soon as I sat in my car, my tears flowed.

I SLUMPED DOWN next to Peter in the back booth at the Dutch Goose and did little to hide my red and swollen eyes. Kate, who sat across from me, noticed my puffy appearance and asked with alarm, "What's wrong?"

"Sorry I'm late."

"Why are you crying?" Peter inquired as he put his arm around me and pulled me close. "No one cares if you're late."

"That's not why I'm upset," I snapped before I reined it in and continued, "although I *am* sorry I'm late."

"So what's wrong?" Peter asked.

"They were mean to me."

"Who was mean to you?" Kate frowned.

"Ion's CFO—Rajesh. What an asshole! He had the nerve to ask me how I even got into the building! The whole thing was humiliating."

"No. Come on, he couldn't have been serious," Mark said. "I bet he was just testing you."

Ugh. Just like a man to assume the woman is overreacting!

"That's what I thought. But he wasn't. He really was surprised that I got an interview!" I said. "He was such an unbelievable jerk! He told me Ion only hires Ivy Leaguers and that I don't have the background or experience to do the job."

Kate looked angry, as though she might slam her fist against the table. "What a fucking asshole! You don't want that job anyway, then! You can stay at Treehouse!"

"That's true," I responded, trying to convince myself I was way better off staying put while teardrops continued to roll down my face. But my family had made sure I had skin more than thick enough to

handle what Rajesh Patel could dish out! *Duck feathers, duck feathers.*
It occurred to me that maybe my tears were a sign of mourning—
sadness that I'd failed to reach my next milestone, and that I actually
really did want the Ion job.

My ringing telephone interrupted our conversation and I picked it
up without looking at the caller ID.

"Hello?"

"May I speak to Sophia?"

"This is she," I shouted over the loud music playing in the background.

"Sophia, this is Rajesh from Ion. I've spoken with Andre and he
would like to meet you in person."

Guess you got over that Ivy League shit pretty quick, eh?

Rajesh didn't give me many options regarding dates or times—he
only said, "Andre is very busy but he can speak with you in two
weeks—Labor Day weekend—at ten o'clock A.M. Otherwise it could
be months before another window opens up. My assistant will send
you the specific date and details. You'll be interviewing with him
during a short flight to Reno, but the jet will bring you back after
dropping him off."

Strange, but okay.

Barely thirty seconds after I hung up with Rajesh, the cell phone
rang again. I glanced at the screen: SCOTT KRAFT.

Peter must have noticed my petrified look because he asked with
alarm, "What is it?" Upon seeing my phone, he said, "Oh."

Barring a major world catastrophe, I never missed a call from my
CEO. So I picked up the phone and began walking outside.

Sound normal, Sophia. Just sound normal.

"Hi. What's up?"

"We didn't get to finish our talk the other day."

"I think you got sidetracked by my . . . what did you call it? My
'pebble' phone?"

"Gravel. I said gravel."

"Oh, okay. Gravel. So what's wrong? Why are you calling me?"

"That conference—did you get me an invitation?"

Sadly, no.

"I'm still working on it, Scott."

"The event is next weekend."

"Yes, it is." It hurt me to break the news to Scott that once again he couldn't seem to get one of the few things that he wanted—an invitation to the Sundance Conference, which brought media and entertainment, political, and philanthropic leaders (and their private jets) descending on Park City, Utah, at the end of August. These powerhouses would spend the coming weekend talking about God knows what, and it drove Scott crazy that every single year he was excluded.

In the blink of an eye, Scott's voice went from soft to eardrum-bursting loud. "THAT'S IT! THIS IS AN ACT OF WAR!"

Scott went on shouting combinations of expletives that were, candidly, very creatively strung together. He screamed so loud I had to hold the phone away from my ear; I closed my eyes and waited until he was finished, knowing he probably felt like the kid who didn't get picked for a team. I had done everything I could to get Scott into that damn conference—even tried my (usually) fail-proof plan B, the ol' "send a bottle of wine with a note that says, *Are you ever going to call me back?*" trick. I tried dangling Treehouse's banking business in front of the Sundance bankers—people who would probably sell their souls for any sort of banking fee. The only thing that might have worked was if Scott called the conference owner himself. But his ego was too big for that, so there we were without an invitation. I wanted to tell Scott to screw them all. He didn't need to be part of their hoity-toity conference. None of that would have made Scott feel better, though, so I deflected his attention to another topic.

"I think those herbs are really doing a great job. I've got more energy than I had even before the surgery," I said.

Silence.

"Just forget the conference," Scott said, and I could tell he was doing his best to calm down. "Listen, I want you to know I'm inspired by you and how you've handled the cancer thing. You just plowed through it and didn't miss a beat."

"What choice did I have? It was either get better or be forced to suffer through more of that herbal stuff you sent. Anyway, it's all mind over matter, as you say."

"Well, I think you're just built that way. Welcome back, Sophia."

I hung up the phone and felt a pit in my stomach. It was as though something, or someone, were tugging at me. I questioned my decision to meet Andre and then remembered something my parents always said: "You've got to be riding a horse to find a horse." I told myself I was just keeping my options open, but then fear and indecision nagged at me again. I wondered if I had become one of those Silicon Valley dreamers—the ones hanging out at Starbucks whom I used to make fun of. The ones who spouted off terms and phrases coined by some slick venture capitalist, the ones who couldn't have normal conversations because every thought in their heads, every word out of their mouths, had something to do with the modern-day gold rush.

Have I become so shallow that the real reason for leaving the people and place I love is that I want to make more money? Or is it something else? What is it that I'm chasing?

chapter 19

THE TWO-BEDROOM FLAT ON GREENWICH Street was within walking distance of San Francisco's trendiest restaurants, shops, and exciting
nightlife. Although it had only one bathroom (pink-and-green tiled),
and the furniture belonging to the current tenant was not well suited
to my taste (bright and floral), the place was perfect for me: sunny,
charming, with Victorian-style details and just enough living and
dining space for the parties I imagined hosting. Since the day Scott
and I had our buying versus renting discussion more than seven
months ago, I'd been scouring Craigslist's Apartments for Rent section. This one was the twenty-second apartment I'd looked at, but
the first that felt like home. A nervous feeling took over my stomach
as I imagined moving fifty miles from Peter, but I began to pace and
wring my hands as I realized that telling my parents would be an
even greater challenge. *Yikes.* Still, I took a deep breath and jumped
in with both feet.

"I have a completed rental application here," I said, handing the
three-page document to the husky landlord, who had been tailing me
while I self-toured the apartment. Kate had warned me about the city's
competitive rental market and suggested I arrive prepared: professionally dressed, bearing a completed application and a blank check.

Mr. Landlord looked impressed and said in a thick Russian accent,
"You know there are many people interested in this place."

"I'm sure there are. It is a beautiful flat and I would take very good
care of it."

"Do you have family? Children?"

"No, no. It's just me. I plan to live alone," I answered, hoping Mr. Landlord would view my solo occupancy as less wear and tear on his property.

The man nodded, then glanced through the application. "I rent to you. I like the Chinese. They're very quiet."

You've never met my mother.

The landlord continued, "Very responsible people. You'll pay your rent on time, I know."

I did nothing to temper the wide, teeth-showing smile that had taken over my face as I pulled my checkbook out of my purse and asked, "How much is the deposit and when can I move in?"

IT FELT ODD waking up to a duvet cover scattered with red rose petals. My first reaction was *This is not my bed!* But then I slowly, suspiciously turned my head to look at Peter, who, by some miracle, had Labor Day weekend off. He was fast asleep next to me, so I didn't move any farther—I just happily watched him breathe in and out, in and out. When he stirred, I said, "Good morning, sunshine."

"Good morning," he said groggily but with a contented smile.

"When did you have time to do all this?"

"Do you like it? You fell asleep really early and I was bored so I went and clipped a bunch of roses from your mom's garden."

I snuggled deeper into the sheets as the flowers' fragrance filled my senses. Then, rather suddenly, I exclaimed, "Oh shit, I hope you didn't damage those rose bushes. She loves those."

Peter looked alarmed and threw back the covers to hop out of bed—he was terrified of my mother, mostly because she spoke to him *through* me because she wasn't confident in her English. "Shit! I just wanted to celebrate your new apartment."

"I'm just joking. She won't be back for a few months. They'll grow back," I said reassuringly, pulling him back into bed.

My boyfriend sighed in relief and plopped his head back down on the soft feather pillow. "Just think. By the end of this month, you'll be in your own place. I'm so happy for you." He sounded genuine, which meant a lot because my move to San Francisco would make seeing each other very inconvenient. But to me it was just logistics. Being an hour away from each other didn't have to be forever. Peter still had to do his fellowship before we had to decide on anything permanent, so I wasn't concerned.

"I assume you realize that if you get the job at Ion, you'll be creating a long commute for yourself? You'd have, like, a ten-minute commute if you stayed at your parents'."

I kissed Peter tenderly and said, "Let's not think about any of that right now," moving my hand down his thigh. But he stopped me.

"I don't think we should be messing around yet," he said, looking very, very grim.

"Why not? What's wrong?"

"It's just that your scar is still very raw, and—"

"It's okay, Dr. Peter. I'm fine," I whispered as I brought my lips close to his again. But Peter put both hands on my shoulders and pushed me gently away.

"I'm serious, Sophia. Let's just wait a little longer."

"Like how long?" I asked, feeling somewhat humiliated and rejected. "You're sort of ruining the romantic rose moment here."

"It's just not fair. You got so sick, so fast, and then you just bounce back like nothing ever happened. I'm still reeling over here. I need time to recover."

I threw my arms around my boyfriend, but pulled my head back so I could get a full view of his face. He was definitely serious.

"Peter, I'm fine. Really. I am. What's bringing this on? The cancer? I thought we agreed we'd leave my medical care to my doctors. Fat, dumb, and happy, remember?"

"No, that's not it," he answered.

"Well, then what's wrong?"

"I just told you."

I wanted to downplay my health risks, not only for him, but for me as well. *Don't worry about something unless there's actually something to worry about.* Wasn't that what Scott always said?

"Look, I'm fine. And I have to leave soon to meet Andre. So do you want to sit here and be worried, or should we enjoy our morning and roll around in these rose petals? I assume you picked them because you were being romantic, but you certainly don't seem very romantic right now."

Peter softened. "I picked them because I love you and I wanted to talk about our future. What is it that you want from us, Sophia?"

"What do you mean?"

"I mean, what is it that you want? We've been together over a year now, and we really should talk about our next steps."

I laid my head on Peter's shoulder, incredibly surprised by my lack of enthusiasm to have this discussion. I was deeply, madly in love with Peter, but the timing for this conversation didn't feel right. There was part of me that wondered whether he was bringing this up now because he felt sorry for me. It was that nagging feeling inside of me again. *Damaged goods.*

"I don't know what to say. You celebrate every one of our month anniversaries, and it's very sweet of you, but I've been trying really hard to not put pressure on this relationship. Isn't that what men want?"

"You're stereotyping, Sophia."

"Well, I think also because I got burned so bad last time."

"I understand that, but I think that's unfair. I am *not* Daniel and you know it. What we have is different—special—and I need to know what you want for us long term."

"Well, I just assumed we'd wait until you finished your fellowship to talk about it. Lots of people date for years before they get married!

And what does this have to do with us having sex anyway?" I asked, trying to lighten things up and make Peter laugh.

Peter sat up and leaned over me; his big blue eyes looked uncharacteristically frustrated. "I need to know if you're looking for the same long-term relationship that I am."

Aha! How's that for putting out the right kind of energy, Scott?

"I am. Peter, I am. I want to get married. I've always wanted to, ever since I was a kid."

"To me?" Peter asked.

A year ago I would have jumped on Peter and screamed, "Yes!" It's what my parents raised me to do. And while I knew my own insecurity was partly what was weighing on me, something else brewed inside my head—I was afraid of what yes would mean. An end to my career? *I'm not ready for that.*

"Can you see us spending the rest of our lives together?" Peter asked, staring at me for an answer. But no answer came out of my mouth. Instead, questions flew through my head: Would my job cause constant disappointments for Peter? Would he "turn," just like Daniel had? If I got the job at Ion, would it be possible for me to maintain my relationship *and* have my career? Could women really have it all? What if I got sick again? Would that be fair to Peter?

"I just can't answer that right now. I think we have to have a longer discussion about it. I mean, what time frame are you talking about here?"

"Forget it, Sophia."

"No! No. I just think we should talk about it when we have more time. I should get ready soon to meet Andre for an interview, for God's sake."

"You'll be back tonight, right? We can talk then?"

"We're going to family dinner night—we're barbecuing with Audrey, Ava, and Hank," I reminded him. "But we can talk about it after, okay?"

Wearing an angry and hurt look, Peter climbed out of bed, which sent more rose petals falling to the floor. "I'm going to go make us coffee."

A BLACK SEDAN was parked in our driveway when I walked out the front door. I was five minutes late because it took me way too long to decide on a dark gray Alexander Wang jersey dress, jean jacket, and strappy black sandals. *Very appropriate for my interview.* As I headed toward the waiting car, there was a knot in my stomach, a feeling of sadness and nervousness. The image of Peter silently drinking his cup of coffee in the kitchen, then mumbling, "See you later," before shutting the door behind him. *He didn't even kiss me goodbye.*

"Good morning, Ms. Young. I assume you don't have any luggage?"

"Hi. No, I don't," I said before adding a "thank you" as he opened my door.

It wasn't until we pulled into San Jose International Airport that I noticed my cell phone ringer was on mute and there were five voice messages. My heart beat faster. *Please, please, let there be one from Peter.*

Message 1 (8:34 A.M.): "Hi, Mei-Mei, this is Mommy. We're calling from Taiwan. It's really late and Daddy is still sleeping, but I haven't heard from you in a few days. Are you okay? Please call me back."

Message 2 (8:39 A.M.): "Sophia. It's Mom. Where are you?"

Message 3 (8:47 A.M.): "Hey, Sophia! It's Kate. Your mom called me, but I missed the call because Mark and I were trying to figure out the waffle maker you gave us for our wedding. Her message said she's looking for you. Oh, and Mark says hi. Call us back."

Message 4 (8:55 A.M.): "Sophia, it's Daddy. Mommy is very worried. Please don't make us worry and call us back."

Message 5 (9:02 A.M.): "Sister, it's Sister. Mom wants you to call her right away. I told her you were flying somewhere for an interview today and that you are fine, but now she's mad that you didn't tell her you're flying somewhere. Call her as soon as you can. And good luck today!"

Jesus H. Christ!

THE BLACK SEDAN pulled into a side area of the airport and through a security gate. Behind it was a private jet.

Wow.

The driver stopped the car and in a confident, smooth rhythm climbed out of his seat and opened my door. There was no one on the tarmac, so I stood there alone for a moment, unsure of what to do. The airplane was an impressive eighty or so feet long and the jet bridge was down, inviting me to step inside. A handsome, sandy-blond-haired, blue-eyed man with a boyish grin and slightly slouched posture appeared at the top of the stairs. Although he was dressed simply, in a leather jacket and jeans, his confident energy was magnetic and I was immediately drawn to him. This was the CEO of Ion, Andre Stark, and as he stood up there in the door of the jet, he looked like a superhero ready to conquer the world. "Welcome, Sophia. It's time to leave," he said in a slight South African accent that was so sexy that my knees wobbled for a moment.

Andre's private jet and save-the-world persona added to his attractiveness and intimidated me for a split second. As I stepped up into the aircraft, I reminded myself that he put his pants on one leg at a time and that no matter what, I had a job to go back to.

A flat-screen television showing CNN Headline News was mounted on the glossy walnut divider separating the cockpit from the main cabin, which was flanked by two pairs of cream-colored leather recliner chairs, and matching long leather couches placed directly opposite each other. Even their seat belts looked fancy. A small galley kitchen was tucked toward the rear of the plane, just big enough to hold a sink, fridge, and compact espresso machine. On the counter were two large platters wrapped in cling wrap— one filled with sushi and the other with exotic-looking fruits and cheeses. Another partition separated the kitchen from the "private" area: a double bed and a bathroom stocked with individually wrapped miniature toothbrushes, toothpastes, earplugs, *and* sleeping masks.

Andre instructed me to have a seat in one of the white leather recliners. "It will be easier for us to talk that way," he said. I buckled myself into the one closest to me and assumed Andre would sit facing me. Instead, he strapped himself into the left-hand pilot's seat and began flipping all sorts of levers on the cockpit dashboard. *Holy shit, he's going to fly this plane?* Another, more professional-looking pilot was seated to his right, but it was clear that Andre was the one in command. I watched as the two of them ran through various safety checks and suddenly understood why Andre was such a woman magnet. His voice was quiet, not loud like mine, but it was confident and demanding of respect at the same time.

"We're going to Burning Man," he said matter-of-factly.

"What's Burning Man?" I asked loudly, twisting awkwardly in my seat and leaning closer to the cockpit so I could hear his response. He was approximately four feet away from me, and although the luxury jet's engines were quiet, it was hard to hear him when the two of us were basically seated back to back.

"You've never heard of it?" Andre asked, contorting his face to express his disbelief. And disgust.

No, jackass. I've never heard of it!

"Nope. Can't say that I have," I replied.

"It's a crazy tent camp in the middle of the desert. Money is no good there—it's all about sharing what you have with others: water, drugs, sleeping bags, everything. You should come."

"Oh yeah? You going to share this jet of yours? Because if you are, I'm in!"

Andre grinned with embarrassment. "No. We're flying to Reno and then I'm driving to the campsite just for the day."

"Aha! So you're *cheating*?" I exclaimed, forgetting for a moment whom I was speaking with. *Filter, Sophia!* I contemplated going with Andre, but when he said he planned to be naked the entire time, I burst out laughing and turned bright red.

"I can't go hang out with you while you're naked! I'd never again be able to look at you with a straight face."

"Well, you could go naked, too," he said so matter-of-factly that I couldn't even have taken it as suggestive or offensive.

"It's all sounding a bit orgy-ish now. Thanks, but no thanks."

Andre tried to sway me by promising ten-foot-high art installations made entirely out of Popsicle sticks, but it didn't do any good. He even offered to set me up with a few of his single friends. "They just cofounded new search engine technology that's going to make them rich," he said.

Once we were at altitude, the copilot unbuckled his seat belt and took a few steps toward me. "Can I get you anything?" he asked.

"Um, a Pellegrino would be terrific, thank you."

Seems appropriate for a private jet.

Seconds later, I heard the sound of ice in a glass, the crack of a bottle cap seal breaking, and a hissing sound that I assumed was the espresso machine. Mr. Pilot returned with my Pellegrino and a glass of ice with a slice of lime in it. He made one more trip to the galley, but this time he walked past me to the cockpit holding a Diet Coke in one hand and a tall mug of something in the other.

Before I could unbuckle my seat belt, I heard Andre's voice.

"I asked for *two* yellow ones, *one* blue one, and *one* pink one," he said, referring to the sweeteners in his latte.

I guess I won't be getting organic, vegan, non-GMO here.

As I stood up, the pilot walked past me holding the same steaming mug as he had before. Then Andre said as he unbuckled his own seat belt, "Sophia, come to the cockpit. Let's talk shop."

During the hour-long flight, Andre asked me about my strategy for investor presentations, managing Wall Street analysts and investors, my past experience, and how that related to what he was doing with Ion.

"You and Treehouse have a lot in common, even though you're in two entirely different industries," I responded. "Investors doubt that there will be a market for your products. You're both using the newest technologies to create your products for industries that haven't changed in decades. And most people don't believe that you can actually manufacture the products that you plan to sell. Those are really strong headwinds for investors, but I know how to tell the stories that will convince them to buy your stock."

Two nods from Andre, who didn't seem to care that I had to stand to speak with him.

Fifteen minutes before we landed, Andre said, "I've met Scott Kraft once. Really interesting guy. I'd like to call him and ask him about you, if that's okay."

My stomach felt as though Andre's jet had dropped several thousand feet.

"Scott doesn't give recommendations. And he doesn't know I'm here, so I'd appreciate it if we keep this all confidential," I said.

Andre nodded as though he was making a mental note that he would no longer give recommendations, either. He then reached toward the dashboard and flipped several switches before he said, "One of my board members knows Scott, so he can casually ask Scott about you for me. Your boss won't know you were here."

He strapped on his seat belt again and told me to sit down and do the same. Then he asked one last question. "What would be your primary responsibility if you were my IR person?"

Without batting an eyelash, I responded, "To make you look good."

EARLY THAT EVENING, as I drove *alone* to meet Audrey and her family for dinner, I kept playing Peter's message over and over in my head. He had left it for me while Mr. Pilot flew me home from Reno; when I listened to it, I felt as though I'd been punched in the gut.

"Hello, Sophia. It's Peter. I'm going to pass on dinner tonight. I'm just not up for it. I was thinking—I'm going to be really busy for the next three months welcoming the new residents and playing a big role in getting them trained, so I'll call you when things get settled. Hope your interview with Andre went well. Take care."

Take care? Talk to you in a few months? Is this how every man is going to react to my career? Such babies! Part of me knew I wasn't being fair and that I'd hurt the man I loved. *Give him time to lick his wounds.* But the other part of me was ready to label all relationships impossible, and I wondered if I would ever be able to live up to what my parents—and society—expected of me.

AUDREY'S HOME WAS a stone's throw away from downtown Burlingame, a bustling area filled with young mothers wearing overpriced yoga pants and pushing strollers. She and her husband, Hank, lived in a white Craftsman with a wraparound covered porch and forest-green shutters with a matching front door. Two bright yellow rocking chairs added the perfect amount of character to the house, which looked very modest from the outside. But inside, the twelve-foot ceilings, dove-white walls, and black-trimmed farmhouse windows gave the home an impressive yet relaxed and airy feel. It was like stepping into a Diane Keaton movie set in the Hamptons—bright, modern, and warm. A wall of French doors along the back of the house opened onto a landscaped courtyard where teak furniture and bright Marimekko cushions drew me outside. When I arrived, my sister was playing with Ava on the grass just past the courtyard while my brother-in-law manned the grill.

I can't wait to tell them about the interview.

"Hey! Look, Ava! Look who it is," Audrey exclaimed. "It's Auntie Sophia!"

Ava looked up and donned a smile that could melt any heart. She ran toward me with her mouth open so she could breathe and giggle at the same time. I could tell she was very pleased with herself when she reached me and I whisked her up into my arms, hugging her close. Ava reached for my diamond necklace—the one that Audrey had given me—and said, "Ooooh, that's shiny and pretty. Can I wear it?"

Audrey and I laughed while Hank rolled his eyes. "Oh no. Don't be teaching her about diamonds just yet. She'll learn about those on her own," he said before asking, "Hey, where's Peter? I'm not being invaded by women tonight, am I?"

"Something came up at the hospital," I said, my heart aching slightly as I told the lie.

"How did your interview with Ion go?" Audrey inquired. I was thankful my sister changed the subject by staying true to her *let's get down to business* self.

"Oh yeah, how did it go?" asked Hank.

The excitement of my interview with Andre was overshadowed by the idea of leaving my hardworking but comfortable life for Ion, an unknown.

"I *think* I got the job," I said without much enthusiasm. "At least it seems like Andre liked me."

"Why aren't you more excited?" Audrey asked as I twirled Ava around in circles.

"I am," I responded over my niece's giggles.

Audrey looked at me with a doubtful expression; I knew she sensed my hesitation, so I stopped twirling and explained, "I'm just stressing over leaving Treehouse. A new place, new people. I don't want to leave Scott and Jonathan. They've been so good to me. I'm just getting back on my feet, so I'm wondering if *now* is a good time to take on a bunch of stress."

My brother-in-law chimed in with one of his many statistics. "They say changing jobs is one of the top five most stressful things a person can face—that and death, marriage, moving, and having children."

Audrey glared at Hank, then scolded me. "Why are you stressing, you idiot? There's absolutely *nothing* to stress about. All you know *right now* is that you have a job and you explored another opportunity. Period. That's it."

I nodded.

Fair enough. Why worry about a decision when there's no decision to be made?

Audrey continued with some sisterly advice. "Well, I think you should take it if it's offered to you, Sister. It would be great for your résumé, and you've been at Treehouse long enough. How long has it been?"

"Almost three years."

"Mm-hmm," she said. I could see the wheels spinning in her head as she made some sort of calculation. "You arrived at Treehouse too late to get low-priced stock options, and you certainly don't have enough of them to give you any sort of *real* nest egg. Don't get me wrong—you've done well and all, but you could do better. Besides, you know what Silicon Valley says about staying in one job for too long?"

"Employers read that as complacency," my recruiter brother-in-law shouted as he looked over at Audrey for approval. When she nodded and smiled, he looked like a game show contestant who just won the million-dollar jackpot while he flipped a chicken burger on the grill.

Kiss ass.

After dinner, I gently pushed Ava in her swing and found myself comparing Andre to Scott. Both men were geniuses building their legacies—legacies that I wanted to help establish. Scott was improving people's lives through technology and entertainment; Andre was trying to save the planet. Both men were also notoriously difficult, but Scott's kind of difficult—demanding and irrational—had been easy for me to handle. *Thanks, Mom.* He was also overly confident, but knew he needed a trusted inner circle and engaged experts when he wanted to know more. Andre, on the other hand, wanted to do it all by himself. He didn't seem to be the type to listen to others, or even care what they thought. I guessed that Andre held people at arm's length—that he was unwilling to be questioned but willing to be convinced. My analysis seemed supported by the CFOs that each man had hired: Jonathan was a consigliere of sorts to Scott, whereas Rajesh seemed to be only an inexperienced yes-man. Then I told myself I wasn't being fair.

It's way too early for you to pass judgment.

"HELLO!" I SHOUTED after jumping out of the shower to answer the phone.

"Sophia? This is Rajesh Patel from Ion. Andre enjoyed meeting you and he'd like to extend you an offer."

I smirked satisfyingly at the image of Rajesh trying to talk Andre into hiring someone else—some banker Ivy Leaguer—only to be overruled. I was certain Andre's approval of me meant I had a strong upper hand, and that I could use it to my advantage.

"We've done our background checks and we hope you'll start next month."

I did it! I got the job!

It felt incredibly satisfying knowing that I'd made it into one of the hottest companies in Silicon Valley. *Despite* my health, *despite* my lack of an Ivy League education, *despite* everything! My silence must have made Rajesh uncomfortable; his hard and unfriendly voice sprayed cold water all over my excitement as he asked, "What is your salary requirement?"

Game time. Ask for the moon.

I recalled the first time I saw a salary figure that made my eyes pop—it was the day Grant asked me to review one of his clients' employment agreements. I remembered wondering if I would ever make that much money in my entire life. Back then the best I could have hoped for was marrying someone who earned a salary that impressive. Yet here I was, speaking to Rajesh and staring at a VP-level job in a very hot company. I decided to negotiate that same dollar figure for *myself*, but became quickly disappointed when the number I asked for didn't seem to alarm Rajesh.

"That's definitely within our range," he said easily, making me wish I'd asked for more. "We are also offering forty thousand shares of stock options that should add to the appeal of the offer. Our VP of HR will be in touch."

I held my voice steady even though my stomach was doing somersaults. "Um, could we talk about the option grant before you hang up? In my view, much of my role is to generate support for Ion's stock, and it behooves you to grant me more shares so I'm fully incentivized. I'm expecting options more in the seventy-five-thousand-share range," I said.

Rajesh sighed and remained silent for a few seconds; I wondered if I'd pushed too far. It felt like hours before he said, "That's more than I'm comfortable with. Some of our other VPs with actual operating roles don't even get that much."

Did he just offend me?

"None of your *operating* VPs are responsible for your stock price the way I would be."

Another few moments of silence passed before Rajesh said, "It's a fair point and I will pass it on to Andre. Either way, our VP of HR will be in touch because I'm taking my family on holiday for the next two weeks."

I pressed the End button to hang up my phone, then double-checked the screen to make sure the call was disconnected. Slowly, gently, I put the phone on the bathroom counter and took one deep breath. Then another. Suddenly I began screaming—loud and long—as I felt power, strength, and electricity run through me. There was an underlying feeling of dread as I wondered if my new job would mean a permanent end to me and Peter. *Should I call him to let him know I got the job?* No, he said he was busy. *Lie low, Sophia. Give him space.*

I tried to focus on Ion again, on how easy it was for me to ask for what I wanted and the possibility that I could actually get it. Whether I got the job or whether I took it didn't matter. The only thing that mattered was that I felt like I could conquer the world. Like Dad always said, "It never hurts to ask."

"I'M MOVING OUT," I declared over the telephone, figuring it was better to tell Mom and Dad my news while they were overseas. They could threaten and complain all they wanted, but there was little they could do about it *from over there.*

I heard Mom freak out in the background. Dad used his CEO voice. "Excuse me?"

"I'm moving out."

"Over my dead body," Mom shouted into the speakerphone.

"Sophia, please don't upset your mother. We won't allow this."

"Oh *puh-lease*, Dad. I'm not a child. Stop treating me like one."

"You'll *always* be our baby," Dad said.

"Well, your baby is moving out!" I exclaimed with joy. "The lease is signed and I'm moving out!"

"What? She's renting? That's just money down the drain," Mom said, disgusted. "Where does she think she's moving to exactly?"

"San Francisco. The Marina District. It's really safe there," I added, hoping that would help ease their angst.

"Sophia, I will burn down your apartment," Dad threatened. I was certain he believed he actually would take such action, but Mom and I couldn't help but laugh at the ridiculousness of his statement, which softened Dad's voice.

"With who? Kate?" he asked. "No boy roommates, right?"

"Kate's married now, Dad, remember? And no—no boys. I'm living by myself. It's a two-bedroom, so you guys can come visit anytime!"

A *Yes I am, No you aren't* went on for about thirty minutes more. Dad tried to trick me by saying, "Okay, fine. We'll talk about it when Mommy and I get home," then tried to delay me by saying, "Okay, but only when you find a nice roommate."

"Oh no, no, no. I'm moving out next week," I said, patting myself on the back for timing my lease application perfectly with my parents' overseas trip. "I've got to go. Love you and see you when you get back home!"

I hung up even though I could still hear my mother's voice reverberating through the receiver. Seconds later, my phone rang again and (*Thank God for caller ID*) I ignored it. Another few minutes later, it rang again—this time it was Audrey. I laughed because my parents were trying to call in the cavalry, but it was no use.

I'm movin' on up!

THE FEDEX TRUCK caught my attention the second I walked out of Starbucks because I could see that it was blocking me in. While telling myself the driver should be *right back,* I calmly climbed into my car and sipped on my soy au lait, which warmed me that chilly early morning. Minutes passed and I gave myself credit for being so patient; then I pushed my hand vigorously on the horn. When the driver didn't appear, I got out of my car and walked up to the large steel truck; there were keys inside the ignition. *Stupid, stupid driver.* It was awkward climbing into a truck while wearing a knit dress, but I did it anyway and sat on the edge of the driver's seat, as far forward as possible so that my Prada-heeled feet could reach the brake and clutch. I turned on the ignition and put the transmission in first gear, then let up on the clutch so the truck moved forward just enough to block someone else. I turned off the truck and climbed back into my car. *Voilà.* Problem solved.

Back inside my car, I noticed my BlackBerry vibrating. I picked it up and saw the email I'd been waiting for.

To: Sophia Young
From: Ion Human Resources
Subj: Offer letter

Dear Ms. Young,
We are pleased to offer you the role of Vice President of Investor Relations at Ion. Enclosed please find the details of your offer. Please note that they are exactly as you and Rajesh discussed.

  I am also including a full benefits summary for you to review. I look forward to discussing with you, although we are in the middle of moving offices so I will call you next week.

  Thank you.

I opened the attachment and skimmed the first page, stopping only when I saw the salary and stock option figures Ion offered. I wasn't sure whether it was Rajesh or Andre who'd agreed to the terms, but they were indeed the same ones I'd requested. Seeing those figures *in print* with my name attached to them filled me with a sense of ac-complishment. The letter proved that I was valuable, not because of the dollar figure, but because Ion, a highly respected company, went above and beyond *just* so they could recruit *me. Little ol' me.*

I quickly reached for the phone to call Peter. *He'll be so happy and proud!* Then reality kicked in and my excitement turned into disappointment. I slouched over my steering wheel and set down my phone.

He doesn't want to talk to me.

We hadn't spoken since Labor Day, and I allowed myself to ac-knowledge how badly I missed Peter; how much I wished he were there to witness the moment with me. A debate ensued inside my head for the hour-long drive to Treehouse: *he'd want to know* versus *he wants some space.* By the time I arrived, I was kicking myself for allowing a *man* to ruin the moment. *My moment.* I shut my door and called Grant. He'd want to know, and I wanted to thank him again for recommending me for the job.

"Are you going to take it?" he asked.

"I don't know. But it's nice to be asked."

"When do you have to decide by?"

"They didn't say. The HR person is calling me next week, which brings us to the end of September, and I'm due to go to L.A. for a few days the following week so maybe that will buy me some more time to decide." I realized I wasn't really answering Grant's question but rather thinking aloud, so I finally said, "Rajesh originally said October but that's right around the corner. I'm going to try to drag it out."

"This could be a life changer for you, Sophia. But make sure you leave things on a good note with Scott and Jonathan."

"They're really the reason I wouldn't take it," I said. "The idea of changing companies is scary, but what makes me really sad is thinking about leaving the guys and the rest of the team. Regardless, thank you so much for thinking of me, Grant. You've always been good to me."

"You deserve it. Congratulations, Sophia. Not many people can say that they got a job offer from Ion. Either way, you win."

It felt great to be wanted and valued, and I didn't have to make any decisions until Ion's HR person called me the following week. I decided to let the whole thing sit for a few days. I wanted to bask in my glory, first.

chapter 20

ASHLEY'S VOICE ECHOED FROM DOWN the hall of Treehouse's executive suite. Based on what I could overhear, she and Scott were arguing over the hotel arrangements.

"I thought you hated the Ritz," Ashley said.

Scott shouted back, although not nearly as loudly as I was used to hearing, "Not the one at Laguna Niguel!"

"Laguna Niguel is way too far—it will take you over an hour to get to your Samba meeting in Burbank, and that's the hour you need to be dialing in to your staff meeting. I don't want to risk your call dropping during the drive because you'll find some way to blame me for that, so . . ."

"So move the staff meeting to a different time. I want to stay at—"

"Laguna Niguel. Yes, I know. This is totally ridiculous."

"DON'T CALL ME RIDICULOUS! I HATE THAT!"

I stopped walking toward my office, closed my eyes, and listened more intently as though it were music. The shouting coming from down the hall may have intimidated some, but it felt like a cozy blanket wrapped around me—oddly comforting and reminiscent of home. Seconds later, though, I unwrapped myself from the cacophony of discord and hurried to my office so I could call back one or two more investors before Scott and I departed for Burbank; Jonathan and our head of PR—a position Scott finally agreed to fill—were already there. It was time to renegotiate the Samba Studios agreement, and I knew my CEO and CFO were prepared to fight for significantly better terms. Truth be told, there was really no reason for me to attend the meeting at Samba, and I knew how lucky I was to be invited. Witnessing Scott and Samba's CEO argue a new contract point-for-point would prove to be the lesson of a lifetime.

AS SOON AS the seat belt light went off, Scott took off his shoes and pulled at his socks through his jeans. He then pored over the spreadsheets Jonathan had emailed him earlier that morning, just as he'd done during our drive to the airport and again while we waited to board our flight. I knew some of what he looked at were our financials up to the end of our last quarter, September, and the others were perhaps projections regarding *The Amazings* Thanksgiving release that was to take place in just over a month. To say Scott was prepared was to understate the situation by a mile; forty minutes into the flight he finally closed his eyes and took a deep breath, signaling that he was ready for our meeting.

The sound of the flight attendants bustling in the front galley signaled that we were about to descend. I sat in the aisle seat, staring at Scott's hands resting on the armrests. They looked different—wrinkled, frail, and ashen, as though the life had drained from them. I wondered if he'd gone from being vegan to an even more restrictive diet.

"Do you want anything, Scott?" I asked, holding up the tote bag full of snacks.

"No, thanks."

I reached into the snack bag anyway—he might not have wanted a treat, but I did. Inside the familiar bag were *unfamiliar* snacks—the custom trail mix and applesauce were not there. Instead I found individual packets of almond butter and fist-size parchment-paper sacks that were neatly tied at the top.

"What are these?" I asked as I held up one of the sacks and smelled it.

More important, where's the tasty applesauce?

"It's a coconut sweet-potato muffin," he answered.

An alarm sounded in my head. Scott hated coconut, so I knew something was awry. I pondered the snacks, Scott's weight loss, and his softer-than-usual voice, and was lost in my sleuthing when the flight attendant asked, "Is your seat belt fastened, miss?" Even though she was looking right at me, I didn't realize that her question was directed at me. She leaned closer to me and said extremely slowly and loudly, "DO. YOU. SPEAK. ENGLISH?"

Stunned, I didn't say a word. Scott looked at me, then looked back at the flight attendant and responded, "Yes. She speaks English. And yes, her belt is fastened, thank you." The flight attendant, perhaps a little embarrassed, nodded her head and continued down the aisle. When she was out of earshot, Scott turned to me and asked, "What's wrong with you?"

"What's wrong with *you*? You've lost so much weight."

I never was one for beating around the bush and decided we'd have to laugh about the flight attendant another time.

"It's just stress," Scott replied before changing the subject. "I forgot to ask how your appointment with the UCSF oncologist went. What's his name? Are you going to stick with him or go back to Pacific Medical?"

I found his question strange. That appointment was in August. Why was he asking me about it now?

"Dr. Madden. I like him better so I switched to UCSF, but for oncology only. Let's assume I won't need to go back, shall we?"

Scott agreed, but then peppered me with more cancer-related questions: had I spoken to any Stanford doctors, did I need chemo, did they expect it to come back, how long did they think I'd actually had it before they found it.

"Why are you asking all this?" I queried.

Scott tugged at the hem of his jeans before slipping his shoes back on. "I'm interested," he said.

But there was something in the way he acted that made me suspicious—he was muted and more pensive than usual, and his jean tugging had gotten worse while I was on sick leave.

"Scott, what's going on? Are you okay? Something is bothering you. I told you Quince was going to be too much work."

I wondered whether he knew about Ion, whose offer I still hadn't formally accepted.

"No. That's not it," he snapped, but when he saw my concerned look, he softened. "I haven't been feeling well."

"What's wrong? Is that why you've lost all that weight?"

"That has something to do with it. I'm just not very hungry."

"So have you been to the doctor? How much weight have you lost?"

"I have been to the doctor."

"What did they say?"

Scott stared out the airplane's small oval window and remained silent for a few long moments, leaving me waiting for an answer. Then he turned toward me with hard, laser-focused eyes.

"You need to fail, Sophia. You need to *fail* to succeed."

"What? I'm not in the mood for a 'Scott's Philosophy' session."

"You've never failed in your life. Not really," he continued, as though he hadn't heard what I'd just said.

I told myself to give Scott space, fully understanding the desire for privacy. But my natural instinct to help and take care of him was too strong, and I pushed him further.

"We're not talking about me, Scott. Tell me what's going on."

"Listen!" he said loudly as the people across the aisle turned and stared. Scott lowered his voice and took a deep breath. "You had an asshole of a boss at the investment bank, but you were too young and stupid to know better. And Sterling, Rich, they just had you doing grunt work."

"Well, I don't know about—"

"I've taught you as much as I could at Treehouse, and Jonathan has done a great job with you as well. You've honed your negotiating skills, have developed a true understanding of how to deal with Wall Street, and you're showing us signs that you're going to be the leader we have always hoped you would be. We're both extremely proud of you."

"Thank you."

Now I know something is really wrong.

"You're welcome," Scott said, looking satisfied before he took another deep breath. "But it's time for you to go out on your own. To begin your own journey separate from Treehouse."

I should have relished in Scott's compliments. But he didn't offer compliments. Hardly ever, and he didn't sound like himself at all. I should have been relieved that he wanted me to leave Treehouse—it cleared the way for me to accept the job at Ion. Instead I worried that perhaps Scott knew about Ion and was trying to push me out. But if that were the case, he would have been angry about my disloyalty, so I erased that thought from my mind almost immediately. The only other reason that I could think of was that he was ill, but then how could the vegan, meditating, chemical-avoiding Scott could be ill? How could someone who loomed so large be affected by an ailment? Wasn't he untouchable? When I didn't respond, Scott repeated himself, which kicked in my natural instinct to argue.

"Oh, come on, Scott. What happened to that bullshit you always used to say: 'You're exactly where you're supposed to be.' What about that?"

"Don't change the subject. Don't deflect."

"I'm not! But tell me what's going on."

"Are you sitting on your brain? I said I didn't want to talk about it."

Scott's insult made me want to laugh. He could throw them my way all he wanted, so I kept pushing. "Scott, please. You can trust me. Let me—"

"Yeah, yeah, yeah," Scott said, cutting me off just as he'd done a million other times when he wanted me to shut up. Then he continued, "I'm cutting back even more of my time at Treehouse. After this Samba agreement is done, I will still be involved when needed, but it's time for me to focus on Quince and for you to leave."

He's pulling back from Treehouse? Now I know for sure that something is wrong.

"I don't want to leave," I replied in a panicked, high-pitched tone.

With a soft, almost tender voice, Scott said, "You, my dear, are destined for greatness. If you'd smile more instead of pretending to be so curmudgeonly all the time, I could almost guarantee it. I know that whatever you do, whatever it is, it will be truly inspiring. You've learned from the best. But there's not another step up for you here. You've hit the top. So you need to go and find some way to be creative and innovative. Stop fearing failure so much."

"Puh-leeease. I fear failure because if I mess something up, you'll fire me!"

"You know that's not true. You know I don't just fire people for no reason. You still don't have the confidence to know that you'll recover from something that goes awry, which baffles me, because look what you've overcome with your health. It's amazing! But your fear of failing is hard for me to watch, and it's why you're leaving Treehouse in a few weeks."

"What?" I shrieked, leaning forward in my chair wondering if I'd heard him correctly. The shock and fear that something was really wrong caused tears to well in my eyes. "I can't leave! I won't! Not until you tell me what's wrong."

Scott put his hand on mine, leaned in close, and whispered, "I have cancer. There, you made me say it."

I slumped, then straightened immediately, and my moment of weakness disappeared. Suddenly it all made sense—his absence before the Quince news was announced; his shriveling frame. The change in snacks. I wondered when he'd been diagnosed and whether *that* was the reason he was in South America that day he called me in the hospital. None of that mattered, though. What mattered was getting him healed. I jumped into rescue mode, figuring if I'd survived, he could, too. *What are the tricks? How did I do it?* He wasn't the "fat, dumb, and happy" type, but I gave it a shot anyway.

"What? That's not a big deal! You want real problems? I wore my favorite white jeans yesterday and got them dirty. But if I wash them, they're going to shrink, and they fit me perfectly *now*," I stupidly said, trying to make Scott laugh and downplay his illness.

"That's what you get for wearing anything but black," he said in a serious tone.

"So what are we dealing with here?" I asked, not wanting to say the *C* word.

"Leukemia. I've had it for a while—a few months before you were diagnosed."

"Chemo?" I asked. "And I never thought I'd be pushing herbs, but I assume you're taking an integrative approach to all this? Eastern and Western?"

"Yes, Florence Nightingale. I am. Although the chemo isn't intravenous—it's an oral medication that I take. It was working well, but there have been some changes lately so we're making adjustments."

Without knowing anything about his diagnosis—what *kind* of leukemia, in particular—I offered to donate my bone marrow. It would never have occurred to me *not* to do such a thing. In many ways I felt as though this man next to me had saved me; I'd walk through fire for him. I wanted to help him, to save him, just like I saved myself.

Scott looked at me differently now, as though he saw me as a real person and not someone who worked for him. "That is very generous of you. *Too* generous. I can't imagine you'd be eligible to donate your bone marrow given you just went through a major surgery, and my doctors and I haven't even discussed anything like that yet. Regardless, and don't take this the wrong way, but I'm not exactly sure I want your DNA shot into my body, Ms. Diabetic with Cancer."

His comment was so offensive I started to laugh. "Filter, Scott."

"Well, it's the truth," he answered dryly, signaling he was in no mood for fun.

I wanted him to know I was there for him, always. "Look at me, Scott! I am alive and kicking, ready to be a pain in your ass for a long, long time. *We* can fix this. I know we can. This is no big deal. You can't kick me out! I'm staying to help hold down the fort, especially if you're spending more time at Quince."

"No. It's time for you to fly, Sophia. It will be hardest on Jonathan, but believe me, he and Treehouse will be fine without you."

His words hurt my feelings, as though I weren't needed at all. But I knew he didn't mean it that way and that he said those things because he cared about my future. Still, it felt as though I were being fired all over again; as if someone else wasn't giving me *any* choice about my own life. It had happened too many times—men determining my fate! My father, Jack Wynn at Global Partners, Grant at Sterling, Rich. And the person I least expected was doing it, too. I didn't want to argue with Scott, though. It didn't seem to be the appropriate time to do it. So I half agreed and told myself I'd convince Jonathan to let me stay. Although I wanted the Ion job, I didn't want to leave this way. It was supposed to be my decision, on my terms, and certainly not when Scott seemed to need me the most. I did my best to hide my concern for my mentor, my role model, the man who saw me as something greater than I could have ever imagined myself.

Please, please, please let him be okay.

"For the next few days we're going to renegotiate our deal with Samba, and I expect it will be a huge milestone for Treehouse—something that will set up the company for the foreseeable future."

I could tell by the determined look on his face that he had a vision for Treehouse—one he'd been formulating for a long time. This trip to Burbank was step one in his plan to make it a reality, and there would be no plan B. It was now or never. "Amen to that!" I said with a smile, but Scott didn't seem to hear me.

"What did I tell you the first day of our roadshow? When you asked me why I was doing Treehouse?"

"I don't remember," I answered. But that wasn't true. I remembered— I remembered everything.

Scott looked at me disappointedly.

My voice caught in my throat and my bottom lip began to quiver as I held back my tears. "You said that you wanted to leave behind a legacy—a legacy that would entertain families for generations. Or some bullshit like that."

"Do you think I've done that yet?" Scott asked, his eyes pleading for me to say yes.

He looked like a child, waiting for my assurance. Suddenly a strength rose up in me that felt powerful and certain.

"Yes, Scott. Yes, of course you have. Treehouse is the household brand you wanted it to be—the brand you've fought so hard to build. And now you're going to set Quince on the right course. You've done it, you've absolutely done it all," I said.

Scott smiled and nodded. "Technology comes and goes; it's the natural law of the technology life cycle, right? But just think. It's possible that one hundred years from now, our movies will still be entertaining families just like Samba's have been for generations and generations. That's one thing that will *never* change. I take so much comfort in that." I wanted to touch his hand and to tell him that it was okay, to tell him how much he meant to me and how much respect and awe I had for him. But he knew—he must have known. So I left him to his thoughts as he gazed out the window.

THE PLAIN CONFERENCE room felt chilly, but the air conditioner continued to blast, and as I did my best to rub away the goose bumps that ran up and down my arms, I wished I had heeded one of Mom's daily reminders: *Always bring a warm sweater to a meeting.* The room felt tense and unfriendly, exacerbated by the way Samba's team of a dozen positioned themselves along one side of the longest table I'd ever seen. This was their attempt to underscore their status as the eight-hundred-pound gorilla, but little did they know that Scott and Jonathan couldn't have cared less.

This is do or die.

Pages and pages of documents were littered all about, and I did my best to listen, to learn. But all I could focus on was Scott—his arms were crossed and his shoulders were up. *He's cold.* I stood up and walked to the small table just behind me, picked up the insulated stainless steel beverage dispenser, and filled a plain white mug with steaming hot water. To the right was a wooden box full of various teas, and I selected the one I knew Scott liked, rooibos, then picked up a chocolate chip cookie for Jonathan. His favorite. I quietly approached the table and set down the tea and cookie before resettling in my seat next to our head of PR.

Witnessing the dynamic duo of Scott and Jonathan in action was like experiencing the purest form of perfection. Point for point, Scott and Jonathan discussed, debated, then argued with Samba's CEO and his posse of lawyers, and corporate development, marketing, and strategy personnel. As the end of the third day approached, the opposite end of the table looked as though they had been through the wringer; *my guys* had barely broken a sweat. The last topic to settle was the economics; Treehouse lobbied to retain the majority share of its box office and merchandise receipts as opposed to the low double digits the company received as part of the first agreement. Back and forth the two sides went, but none of Samba's protests could stand up to the facts that Scott repeated over and over again: "Your last *five* animated films have had declining box office receipts *and* merchandise," and "Treehouse's two movies are going to produce more revenue in tickets sales and merchandise than your last four movies combined. *The Amazings* toys are already flying off the shelf and the movie isn't even out yet!" When it was all settled, *my guys* showed Samba they were the new game in town. Even Samba's CEO had fallen under the Scott Spell. He and his team bought into Scott's vision for what would elevate both Samba's and Treehouse's success: Treehouse University, led by Dylan, would be accessible to both Samba and Treehouse employees and would foster great storytellers and turn traditional animators into technical ones. Samba's CEO also drooled over Scott's description for a future Treehouse Adventureland, a digitally driven mecca that would reside *within* Sambaland and offer new experiences that Sambaland couldn't offer without the technical expertise of our team in Emeryville.

At five thirty the next morning, a joint Samba-Treehouse press release was distributed over all the world's major wires. I sat in a Samba auditorium where on the stage, just behind the podium, a press conference backdrop filled with the Treehouse and Samba logos was set up. I shook my head at that backdrop, remembering how it had kept me up the entire night thanks to a rancorous argument with Samba's PR team. It had been a ridiculous "whose logo looks bigger" debate, but equal exposure was a requirement of the new agreement, and both teams were there to ensure that equal it would be.

An hour later, my eyelids desperately fought to stay open as I spoke with the Goldman Sachs research analyst who reported on Treehouse.

"Well, investors certainly like the news," Darren said excitedly. He

was the first of the sixteen calls I had to make before the press conference at nine thirty, and I struggled to maintain enthusiasm in my
voice.

To Darren I repeated the exact words used in the press release:
"It's an important milestone for us. It validates our leading position within the entertainment industry." My mind wandered elsewhere—to life after Treehouse—and as our share price climbed
higher and higher, I forced myself to fight my bittersweet feelings
and to focus on the now.

At nine o'clock, members of the press began filing past me to find
seats inside Samba's auditorium. Their energy suggested excitement
over our announcement—a moment few people thought would
ever come. I overheard their conversations and how amazed they
were that there was a serious challenger to the mighty Samba, and
how Scott Kraft must have walked on water. Less than an hour later,
Scott strutted onto the stage, his cheeks ruddy and his face glowing
with pride. The Samba CEO followed, wearing a stoic expression,
like a general who had lost the war but got out with all his men
alive. Perhaps there was a hint of a smile, one that suggested he was
pleased—as though he knew the new agreement would end up being
a positive move. When he stopped at the podium and stood beside
Scott, the *click, click, click* of cameras was almost deafening.

After the two leaders made their prepared statements, Samba staff
roamed both sides of the auditorium's aisles carrying microphones
to the journalists whose hands shot up with questions. Most of them
wanted to hear from Scott—how the deal impacted his long-term
hopes for Treehouse, whether it meant he would be more actively
involved in operations, and more. I stood up and took a seat next to
Jonathan—it felt right to be next to him at this moment. He leaned
over and whispered in my ear, "This is going to dominate tomorrow's
headlines." I grinned, knowing my family and Kate would be proud
of our achievement; I wondered if Peter would feel the same. I had

kept my distance as he requested, but I missed him and wished he were here. He would have made me feel better about Scott's cancer news, and about my uncertain future. *If I could only have a hug, I'd feel better—safe and secure again.*

FIVE DAYS AFTER my return from Los Angeles, Scott appeared just outside my office doorway and said, "You know I don't write recommendations, but I'm sure if you drop my name at Stanford they would let you sit in on classes next quarter." He looked healthier than he had on the airplane—there was color back in his face and he seemed less frail than before.

"I'm going to Ion," I said without enthusiasm. "I accepted a job there."

"What?" he asked, looking disappointed and surprised.

"I'm going to work for Andre Stark."

"Goddammit, Sophia! That is *not* what I told you to do," he shouted. I had read his face wrong—he was neither disappointed nor surprised. He was simply disgusted. "I told you to create a new challenge for yourself, not to take another fucking IR job. And certainly not for *that* man."

I felt my cheeks flush.

How dare he tell me what to do? He's the one forcing me out! So dammit, I'm going to be fucking rich!

"This isn't about you anymore!" I argued, loudly at first, but only whispering the last syllable of the last word because it was just then that I understood why Scott didn't like Andre—he foresaw the changing of the guard and it frightened him.

"I just don't understand why you would take *another* IR job unless you're trying to chase the money," my mentor said, interrupting my thoughts. "And if you are, then we really haven't taught you anything at all."

More calmly now, I tried to explain, "This is all very easy for you to say. You already have more money than you could ever spend and you've had your life's great success*es*." Then I added with more emphasis, "At this point you could fail all you want, but the fact is that you'll always be known as *the* man who changed the world—the man who revolutionized the personal computing and animated film industries."

Scott softened slightly and took two steps into my office. He looked as sentimental as I had ever seen him. "And you can too, but not with an IR job."

My temper flared again, "You and Jonathan *made* me who I am—an IR person! You can't just suddenly say that that's not good enough and act as if, with the snap of your fingers, I'll have some brilliant idea that will solve world hunger!"

Scott's pursed lips and fiery eyes suggested that was *exactly* what he wanted me to do. He wanted me to be an extension of his legacy; not just an evangelizer of someone else's vision, but an executor of my own. He wanted *me* to change the world, too.

"I know you've watched me closely, but watching from the sidelines is no way to live. You've got to get out there, study, and observe, Sophia. Try everything and anything that you find interesting because that journey, as rocky as it may be, will lead you to what you love." Scott touched his lips with his left hand for a brief moment, then continued. "Go after that thing that gives you passion. You may fail at it, but that's just an opportunity to try it again, only better this time." He looked in my eyes for some sign that he'd gotten through, but I was too overwhelmed to show any reaction at all. One of the first things this man had ever said to me was that he didn't explain things, so I'd spent three years at Treehouse trying to decipher Scott. But finally, he was explaining himself. Explaining it all loud and clear. He assumed my silence was a sign of resistance, so he shouted before storming out of my office. "If you take this job, you are not to speak to me for *one* year. I mean it!"

I wrinkled my brows and wondered if Scott knew how ridiculous he sounded. But his words weighed heavily on me. I asked myself what gave me passion and I began to question what I wanted to do or be. *How am I supposed to know? I'm only twenty-seven!* I placed my hand on my stomach. Through my black ribbed V-neck sweater, the skin around my large abdominal scar felt numb. A sense of urgency filled me. *I want to have it all—passion for my work, money, and love.* At that moment, I had to focus on Ion. Who knew? Maybe the passion and money would be found there, and maybe, hopefully, Peter would come around, too.

THREE WEEKS AFTER the new Samba agreement was signed, it was time for me to leave Treehouse. I waited until almost everyone was gone before I left; it was Friday evening, so the office emptied out early. *I can't stand saying goodbye.* Jonathan had gone home several hours ago, but not before he gave me one of his trademark bear hugs and handed me a stainless steel telescope inscribed with the words *Fortune Favors the Bold*. This carefully chosen phrase fueled me with the strength I needed to grab my purse and a small box of my personal belongings. I looked around my office one last time and gently closed the door.

The only visible light in the hallway came from Ashley's office. *Of course she's still here.* Carrying my things, I stopped at her door to give her an armless hug.

"We will miss you," she said.

"Call me if you need *anything*."

Ashley smiled. "He's going to be fine, Sophia. Don't worry."

"Please take good care of him."

"You know I will," she said. Then she turned to the console behind her, picked up a box, and said, "He left this for you. He said you would understand."

I set my things down and chuckled at the sight of the box, which was dark blue with *Patek Philippe* embossed on the top. Inside was a rose-gold watch with a plain cream-colored dial, gold Roman numerals, and a matching pearly beige alligator band. *It's beautiful.*

"Did you pick this out?" I asked, looking at Ashley.

"Of course I did. You know Scott doesn't believe in watches. But he's always felt bad for taking yours so he said to buy you a new one."

"Thank you, Ashley. It's gorgeous. I wonder what he did with mine?"

"He threw it away," Ashley said with raised eyebrows. We looked at each other and laughed. "He's a gem that way, isn't he? Anyway, I thought you'd like this one. There's also something that's been delivered to your new apartment. *That* one Scott picked out himself."

WHEN I ARRIVED home from Treehouse, Audrey's car was parked in front of my apartment. As soon as I opened the front door, I heard Ava's voice singing inside. "Hello?" I called out as I climbed the stairs leading to my flat.

"Hi," Ava shrilled, then Audrey added, "I hope you don't mind I let myself in with the key you gave me."

"No, no problem. What's up? We didn't have plans, did we?"

"No. I just had to open the door for this delivery. Ashley called me a few days ago."

I stepped onto the landing, then proceeded through the wide, arched open doorway into the living room. Against the wall was a huge glass fish tank, and the sight of it sent a shiver up my spine. I heard Ava's feet rush toward me and turned to pick her up; we both peered into the carefully lit aquarium. My niece squealed with delight at the brightly colored fish inside, but I saw beyond the fish. My bottom lip quivered and tears streamed down my face, but I laughed all the same.

Inside swam a small octopus.

chapter 21

"AI-YA, PUT ON SOME LIPSTICK, Mei-Mei. Ladies should *always* wear lipstick. And *please* get your car washed! You must take care of these things," Mom shouted from her front doorway as she examined me walking to my car. Just when I thought she was finished, she threw in one more zinger: "I have no idea why you *rented* your own apartment when we live just ten minutes away from your new office!" Without turning around I waved my hand to acknowledge my mom while kicking myself for deciding to come "home" last night. In doing so I'd traded traffic for my dear, wonderful mother, who'd spent the morning sharing her opinions about my mistakes with Peter and reminding me that I was "no spring chicken." In some ways it was reassuring to see that Mom was up to her old antics, but I would have appreciated a more relaxing morning before my first day at my new job.

Ion's new office was located in a rustic section of Palo Alto ten miles south of my parents' home. It was not an obvious setting for *any* type of company. Slopes covered in tall grass, oak trees, and wild mulberry bushes filled the landscape, yet hidden within was a technology mecca—a place where Silicon Valley stalwarts had set up shop three-quarters of a century ago. A deer casually grazing by the side of the road raised her head as I drove by; feral jackrabbits hopped along to complete the idyllic fall setting.

"I think I'm close, Kate, so I should hang up soon. But when are you finally going to go on your honeymoon? Your wedding was five months ago!"

"I know! But Mark's slammed at work and I don't have a break from school, so we're just doing a quick getaway to Cabo San Lucas for now. You should come with!"

"Ha! Yeah, I'm sure Mark would *love* that!"

Kate's invitation was genuine, and I felt touched by her kindness. I knew she was worried about me because of what had happened with Peter, and she expected that any moment I'd fall into depression. "Let's not forget how you reacted to the Daniel breakup," she said.

"Well, first of all, we haven't officially broken up. He's just busy right now." But it had been nearly two months since I'd heard from my boyfriend, and although I didn't miss him any less than before, I wanted to give him the space that *we* deserved. It was important for Peter to have the time to evaluate whether he could accept all of me—work, health, my batshit crazy family—and to know he could still walk away if any part of me didn't suit him. I also needed to think seriously about the commitment Peter had asked for—I didn't want our relationship to be just another "thing" that I jumped into like I had my jobs. *Nothing is forever* couldn't apply here, and the permanence of it all frightened me.

"So what's going to happen? What are you and Peter doing?" Kate asked.

"I don't know yet, but don't worry about that. Let's call it a holding pattern for now. You two lovebirds go ahead and enjoy. Besides, I should work at least a week or two before I take off," I joked.

"Work is for suckers," she said.

"AMEN!"

Ion's huge parking lot was only half full when I arrived, but something told me that Andre would make sure it was completely full within no time. Ion was in a hiring frenzy—it takes people to save the world—and I felt lucky to be part of what I believed would be an amazing company.

A wide cement path ahead led to a plain, unmarked door, which served as the entrance into a two-story square building (circa 1960s) with dark-tinted windows. Although I'd just been kicked out of my last job, I felt surprisingly confident as I strutted up the path wearing a light gray cashmere dress and black heels. My hair was neatly pressed by one of my most valued possessions—my flat iron.

Ion's plain, dark gray lobby was unfurnished except for a long reception desk that looked like it belonged inside the service department of my BMW dealer. A glass display case ran the width of the entire lobby; inside the case, Ion T-shirts, sweatshirts, and other branded items were on display. I considered buying one for Peter before realizing I was an Ion employee now and that there would be plenty of time for company swag.

"Good morning," said a serious young woman who looked as though she had been hand-selected from a modeling agency catalog.

I considered announcing myself as the new vice president of IR, but it sounded too presumptuous. "Hi. I'm Sophia Young. I was told to ask for Jacob."

"Human resources," she declared, seeming to say this more for herself than for me. "I can't tell you to take a seat because we don't have any chairs yet, but I will let him know you're here."

I nodded and took a few steps to the right, then pretended to peruse the items in the glass case. What I was really thinking about, though, was how my first day would be. A few minutes later, a handsome, fair-skinned man in his forties with curly hair and oval wire-framed glasses sped toward me from the hallway behind reception.

"Jacob?" I asked.

"Hi, Sophia. So nice to meet you in person," he said. "I've heard so much about you."

He looked exactly as a VP of human resources should: friendly, warm, approachable.

"Sorry for the wait," he continued. "I'll give you a quick tour and show you your desk. Then we'll go and find Rajesh."

Oh boy. Rajesh.

I followed Jacob upstairs, which landed us on the hill-facing corner of Ion's office. I was surprised at the scene that unfolded in front of me: more than one hundred people sat behind matching gray workstations. Some stared into their computer screens, while others talked quietly on their phones. Everyone looked busy, but in a robotic and sterile way, unlike Treehouse's lively, creative world. The rigid and formal atmosphere felt foreign compared to the casual and comfortable culture I was accustomed to. The confidence I'd felt walking in just a short while ago faded.

It's okay, Sophia. You just need to get used to it here.

From where we stood on the wide-open second floor, it looked as though Ion was devoid of any individual offices. Cold steel beams and tin-colored exposed HVAC ducts ran across the high ceilings, making statements on their own and adding to the chilly tempera-ture of the office. Most of the desks were lined up in a mazelike configuration in the center of the floor; smaller pods of desks were placed in the far corners. I turned my head slowly from left to right so I could get a complete view of my surroundings. My eyes scanned the open space, looking, hoping for someone wearing a smile—someone I might befriend. There were only a few women visible, and they sat inside the maze; they wore preppy clothing and seemed to be my age.

While Jacob led me approximately seventy feet to the opposite, parking-lot end of the building, he explained Ion's curious layout. "All of our battery engineers and testing are downstairs, and I can bring you down there later, but this is where finance is located," he said. "At twelve, six, and nine o'clock are our top executives: Rajesh is closest to you at twelve; our cofounder and CTO, T.J., is at six; and Andre and his assistant are at nine. In the middle of the office—where the hands of a watch might be centered—is PR, sales, and customer service." When I asked where the marketing department was, Jacob responded, "We don't exactly have a *marketing* department. Andre doesn't believe in that. He believes that PR and test-drive events are the best way to spread the word about the Model A and any of our future cars. To date, that's all we've really needed."

Ion's approach to marketing was interesting to me—nearly all the companies I'd worked with at Global Partners and Sterling, Rich had assigned the biggest budgets to the very department that didn't even exist at Ion. *Is that good or bad?* Even Treehouse relied heavily on Samba's marketing strength. I noted Andre's unique perspective, and filed it away as something I would probably include in Ion's roadshow presentation, then turned my attention back to Jacob.

"Until you get to know who's in which department, you can probably tell the teams apart by what they wear. The guys wearing the Ion polo shirts and khakis over there are our sales guys," he said, gesturing toward a group of men in their late thirties. "And the more casually dressed folks in jeans are in customer service." I examined this team and noticed there was only one woman.

"Is there a dress code for each department?" I asked curiously.

"Ha, no. It may look that way, but that's just how it naturally ends up. Anyway, everyone else over there is PR, and they're led by our VP of communications, Roberto, who I imagine you'll work fairly closely with." Jacob was indicating a group of twentysomething women seated around a tall Latino man.

Jacob stopped in front of a vacant workstation—one among six in the finance corner. He introduced me to my "office mates": Rex, Tom, Ryan, Matt, and finally Miles, who sat back to back with me.

"Hi, we've spoken. I'm Miles, the VP of finance." He looked like a short, skinny weasel with a butt cut. Miles shook my hand and said, "Most of my morning is clear so I can get you up to speed."

Then, nonchalantly, as though it was a regular occurrence, he added, "We'll talk. Unfortunately right now I need to go fire someone who works for me, but it will only take a few minutes."

"Oh dear. What happened?" I asked, not meaning to be nosy, but hoping that I could be sure I didn't make the same mistake.

"Oh, she gave me some wrong stock option figure that ended up in our first draft of the S-1 and we had to tell Andre so now he is pissed. She's our stock administrator, so she really should be giving me the right information."

Yes, but she reports to you, so shouldn't you be the one taking the blame here?

"To be fair, she wasn't given the right information in the first place, but Andre is angry, so Rajesh wants someone's head to roll. I feel sort of bad, but the stock administrator is going to be the one to take the fall," Miles continued before telling me to go ahead and get settled and that he would be right back.

Jacob looked as alarmed as I was, but when he noticed me trying to catch his eye, he smiled uncomfortably and said, "Anyway, welcome to Ion. I'll let Rajesh know you've arrived." With red flags about Miles flying high and my nerves on edge, I repeated what I'd told myself when I was thinking about interviewing for this job: *Nothing is forever unless you want it to be.*

I shook off any thoughts about Miles and pulled from my purse two sets of the IPO checklist I'd printed last night. It was the list that Jonathan and I had used for Treehouse's IPO, and not dissimilar from what we'd used at Sterling, Rich, although I'd tailored it slightly to make it relevant to Ion's business. Then I took a deep breath and walked a short distance toward Rajesh. When he saw me approaching, he said in a saccharine, uptight tone, "Welcome, Sophia. We're glad to have you here. Would you like me to walk you over to say hello to Andre?"

I found Rajesh's offer odd. *Does he think women need to be escorted? Does he think I'm afraid of Andre?* Red flags were raised once again and I quickly concluded that I didn't fit in at Ion, but I was resolved to be myself.

"Thanks, but no," I said to Rajesh in a defiant tone, trying to establish myself as a strong and independent person. "I can walk over myself. Besides, he looks busy right now."

Rajesh peered over at Andre, who was drawing something on a sheet of paper. I thought it would be best if I got right down to business, so I handed my new boss the IPO checklist and asked, "Do you have time right now to go over some things? This would probably be a good place to start."

Rajesh quickly flipped through the document, looking somewhat stunned at its length. "I think the most critical thing for you to do right now is to get our roadshow presentation together. Here's what our investment banker Jack Wynn, Miles, and I drafted, but we haven't gotten sign-off from Andre." He handed me a forty-two-page presentation and sat down at his desk; I could tell he wanted me to go through it with him, but the name Jack Wynn was ringing in my ears.

Oh God. Him again?

"Sophia, do you want to sit down?" Rajesh asked.

"Oh, sure," I said, completely forgetting that I'd told Miles I would meet him at our desks. "This presentation—it's quite long, isn't it?"

"We have a lot of information to get through."

"It's been my experience that twenty slides is the maximum for an investor meeting. We just need to convince them on the investment highlights, not explain every financial detail of our business."

"I'd like to see what you come up with," he said, as if daring me to do better.

"I'll draft an outline and run it by you and Andre to make sure I'm not operating in a silo."

"Andre is a visual person so outlines don't work for him. Drafts are almost worse because he gets caught up in how the graphics look, so we always do our best to show him what we think will be final versions. When do you think you can have this completed?"

"I'm not sure. It will take me at least three weeks to nail down the story, and then the graphic designer will take a few weeks as well. Do we have a target roadshow date?"

"If all goes well, we'll leave for the roadshow mid-January. And what do you mean, graphic designer? Andre doesn't believe in consultants. He says if they're good enough to hire as consultants, they're good enough to bring in-house. I thought you knew how to do PowerPoint."

Andre thinks this. Andre doesn't like that. Does Andre control everything around here?

"I do know PowerPoint. But everything about Ion is sleek, beautiful, sexy, and futuristic. Clip art isn't going to fly, Rajesh. We need a graphic designer."

My boss shook his head with disapproval, but I knew it meant something more. Rajesh was probably afraid of Andre. That was why he let Miles fire the stock administrator, why he didn't ask for Andre's feedback, and why he was resisting a graphic designer. *What's there to be afraid of?* I decided to fight the graphic design battle later, confident I would get my way somehow. I always did. *I just need to figure out how.*

"Is there anything else I should know? What Andre doesn't like?"

Rajesh spent the next five minutes sounding like a child who'd memorized a list of rules: Andre didn't like the color blue; Andre didn't like BMW mentioned in the same sentence as Ion; Andre wouldn't talk about the licensing portion of our business; Andre wouldn't provide a road map for our next cars.

Well, this is going to be a barrel of laughs.

ANDRE WAS ROCKING back and forth at his desk, drawing something on graph paper, when I approached him later that day. He looked halfway between startled and confused when I broke his concentration with a cheerful "Hi, Andre!"

"Uh. Hi," he said in his slight South African accent, continuing to rock.

First I had Mr. Pull at His Socks. Now it's Andre the Rocker?

"It's Sophia. The IR person. We've already met," I said.

"Oh, right. Our new *VP* of IR. Right. Hello. Welcome."

"Thank you," I responded. "How did Burning Man go?"

Andre looked at the floor and mumbled, "Fine," which put a quick end to that part of the conversation.

"I'm working on the roadshow deck right now, so if there's anything you feel strongly about, please let me know," I continued.

"Did you see the first version of it? From the bankers, Miles, and Rajesh?"

"Yes."

"Well, I hate it!"

I assumed you would.

"Hate is a strong word, but let's see if we can fix it. I've gone through it a couple of times now, and I'm going to start all over. The key to making this IPO great is going to be convincing investors that there's really very little risk involved as far as our ability to *manufacture* the cars and to *sell* them. There are a lot of naysayers out there since no one has ever been able to bring an electric car to market before—"

"Not since the golf cart," Andre added proudly. He grinned as though he'd made a hysterical joke.

"Yes. The golf cart. Anyway, I think we should redo this presentation with only three messages in mind. First, we have to show them the cars. Second, we have to show off our management team. The talent you've recruited is really amazing, you know."

"Yes, I know. But we can't bring them on the roadshow. I want them here focusing on getting our car finished."

"I'm not suggesting they come. We can take care of number one and number two through a sizzle reel. We can show the prototypes of our cars along with snippets of each executive talking about all their past professional accomplishments and what they bring to Ion."

Andre nodded. "Roberto has a lot of professional-grade B-roll."

"Great! That's great!" *Never mind that we're going to need a professional to put this film together; I'll deal with that later.* "And I'll script every executive so they say exactly what we need them to say."

"Okay. I like it. What's the third thing?"

"Oh, the third thing is—we have to convince investors we can sell enough cars to make the financial forecasts that the analysts are estimating. Since we are the ones guiding those investors to those numbers, we have total control. Based on what Rajesh tells me our twelve-month forecast will be, we only need to sell cars to less than one percent of the total midsize luxury car market."

Andre sat up. "How did you come up with that?"

"I just looked at the number of midsize luxury cars that were sold last year and divided that by the number of cars we think we'll sell by the end of next year. That's *one* percent. That's it!"

Andre made a note.

"Even better is that I checked how long our reservation for the Model A list is. If only half of those people who are waiting for the Model A actually buy it, we'll easily make our twelve-month revenue estimate," I continued. "Oh, and one more thing. I don't suppose we could take a few Model A prototypes on the road with us?"

Andre smiled. "Speak to Colette in communications—she can organize it. We'll have two or three cars meet us in the largest cities we visit. We can even offer test-drives."

He stood up, looking pleased with himself, then took a few steps toward the Asian woman sitting in front of him. She was talking to Roberto, the VP of communications.

Andre motioned at me to come over.

"Sophia, this is Roberto," said Andre. "And this is Ji-yan, our executive assistant."

"We've spoken on the phone. Welcome to the jungle," said the Latino man whom I'd noticed standing in the PR department earlier this morning. He had dark skin and smoky brown hair that was cut short enough to be professional, but long enough to show his big, loose curls. His athletic, slender body was dressed in a pair of loose jeans and a fitted blue button-down shirt; the look was nicely rounded out by trendy black-rimmed glasses. *Hot rockin' babe.*

Before I could embarrass myself and say something stupid to this beautiful specimen of a man, Andre said, "Roberto, can you show me the latest designs for the new home page? I sketched something out here that I think may work better, but let's have a look." Then he turned to Ji-yan and asked her, "Can you please put Sophia on my calendar for a weekly?" before walking away with Roberto.

Awesome! I wonder if Rajesh gets his own weekly one-on-one, too.

Ji-yan was a pretty, petite-framed woman with long stick-straight black hair and perfectly lipsticked pink lips. She had a very warm, calm energy about her, which made me want to be her friend.

"Hi. I'm Ji-yan. Let me know if you need anything," she said. "Andre works out of our Hawthorne office most days and is generally only here Tuesdays and Wednesdays. His days here are really packed, though, so do you mind heading down to Hawthorne on Thursdays?"

"Sure, I'll go. Where exactly is Hawthorne?"

"Southern California. Andre's other company, Stark Aerospace, is there, and our design and engineering teams are in a building on the same property. A small group of our battery engineers go down every week, so you can just catch a ride with them tomorrow."

"Oh! Do we have a corporate jet?" I asked excitedly.

"Ha. No, no." Ji-yan smiled. "Only Andre flies in a private jet, and that's *his*. The head of our battery team has his pilot's license and a small propeller plane. People who need to work with the design team fly with him from Palo Alto Airport. I'll tell him you're coming—be there at seven thirty tomorrow morning."

On my long drive back to my new apartment in San Francisco, my mind swarmed with all the tips I'd learned from various coworkers I'd met that day, all of them falling under the topic of "Things Andre Doesn't Like." It certainly wasn't the fun, warm, embracing culture of Treehouse, but I was excited all the same. Maybe IR wasn't what Scott wanted me to do, or what I loved—but I knew I was energized by everything around it: the chase of the IPO, the thrill of bringing exciting products to market, and advising these powerful visionaries. I knew Ion wasn't my be-all end-all, but it was exciting enough for now.

JUST BEFORE I reached over my nightstand to turn off the light, I checked my BlackBerry one last time. An email had arrived from Ji-yan.

To: Sophia Young
From: Ji-yan Chen
Subj: Tomorrow

Hi Sophia,
Andre's brother was badly injured while sledding in Colorado this evening. He's going to be okay, but Andre is on his way to the hospital in Colorado so tomorrow's meeting with him is canceled. You're still welcome to fly down to meet the design team located in L.A., but Andre won't be there.
Thanks, JY

chapter 22

THE RECEPTIONIST LOOKED TERRIBLY FRAYED when I walked through Ion's front door the next morning. She was on the telephone and other lines were ringing. There was a frantic air about our empty lobby, although I couldn't quite put my finger on why. As soon as I set foot onto the second floor, though, panic rose up inside me. The eerie scene in front of me made me feel something was going on. Ion's second floor was completely deserted, even though our parking lot was as full as it had been the day before. The space was silent except for the drone of unanswered ringing telephones and Ji-yan's soft voice in the distance. Sure, the empty office could have meant free bagels downstairs, or perhaps an emergency meeting, but I walked toward Ji-yan to find out. She was speaking to someone on the phone when I approached; when she looked up, her eyes were wet and her expression was grave. What felt like hours but was only minutes later, she hung up and said, "Oh, thank God you're here! I wasn't sure whether or not you decided to go to Hawthorne after all. Roberto is at the crash site dealing with the press and Jacob is there working with the police investigators."

"Wait. What crash site?"

Ji-yan didn't hear me, she just spoke into the floor, seemingly to herself. "The guys in Hawthorne won't be any help. Rajesh should be here, but I can't find him anywhere. He's not answering his home or mobile phones."

"Ji-yan," I said more loudly. "What crash site? What happened?"

She looked at me as though I'd startled her awake, then said, "I'm sorry, but you're the only VP here, so you're in charge and you need to handle the incoming calls."

"What is going on? What crash site?" My thoughts went straight to Andre. *Oh God, no.*

"There was a plane crash this morning. The one you were supposed to be on. No one survived," Ji-yan whispered, although there was no one around to hear.

Suddenly I was having trouble breathing. *I was supposed to be on that plane.* But Ji-yan's sobs forced me to focus; I walked to her side, leaned down, and wrapped my arms around her shaking shoulders.

"I just spoke to all three of them last night," she said. "I needed them to take some samples down to the designers."

Her phone rang and then a second line rang a split second after. "Where is everyone?" I asked.

In one fell swoop Ji-yan answered both calls and asked them to hold before she informed me that everyone was in the downstairs kitchen watching the breaking news coverage of the crash. "I'm going to ask reception to forward all crash-related calls to you. Oh, and Roberto says we can't release the names of the passengers until the coroner arrives, so keep that in mind."

Martin, John, and Joe were their names. I had met them only yesterday.

My phone was already ringing when I sat down at my desk. I rushed to grab it, although I wished I hadn't. The voice on the other end of the call sounded shaken, and pleading.

"Uh, yes, hello. I'm calling to ask whether my son was on the airplane that just crashed. His name is Martin Moore and he works on your battery team."

My hands trembled as Mrs. Moore continued. She pronounced her words very slowly, as though she were trying to sound out a scrambled word. "He—flies—down. He—has—an—airplane." I sat at my desk, stunned and unsure of what to say. Although I didn't really know Martin, tears began crawling down my face.

Ring, ring, ring.

"Mrs. Moore, my name is Sophia. I don't have any information at this time. I'm so, so sorry." I wanted to reassure her, to take her anguish away and tell her it would be okay, but it wouldn't have been appropriate. The only thing I could do was listen to this grief-stricken mother as she searched for some speck of hope that her worst fear hadn't come true. Minutes later, over the din of the ringing telephone, Mrs. Moore abandoned complete sentences entirely and alternated between sobbing and screaming into the receiver.

"Tell me! Please! Alive? God, please," she cried.

I let my tears fall onto my desk and thoughts began racing through my head: how lucky I was that it wasn't *my* mother sobbing to a stranger; what I could do for this poor woman; where the hell Rajesh could be; and didn't Ion have a crisis communications plan? *I'm not qualified to handle this.*

Finally I said, "I'm really sorry, but I don't have any information. Can you please give me your phone number? I'll be sure someone calls you back as soon as we know more details. I promise."

That wasn't a lie. At least, I hoped not. My line lit up with another call. Then my telephone display showed me a call was waiting. *Ring, ring, ring.*

Mrs. Moore choked out her telephone number and begged me once more to give her news. I apologized again, then had no choice but to hang up. Ji-yan was waving at me to get my attention, and when she got it, she shouted, "I'm transferring Jack Wynn to you. He's asking about Andre."

I picked up the phone. "This is Sophia Young."

"Sophia, it's Jack Wynn."

No "Hello, how are you holding up? Is there anything I can do?"

My former boss simply asked, "Was Andre involved in that plane crash?"

"Andre wasn't on the plane," I said.

"What about the men who died? Are they key employees?" Jack was all business and no sympathy.

"I'm not allowed to disclose who was on the plane," I said.

"I need to know if the passengers were working on projects critical to the *on-time* delivery of the Model A. If we announce a delay, our IPO will be shot."

"Everyone here is important, Jack! If you don't need anything else, I have to go. I have calls to take here." I hung up without wondering if I should have been more professional. There was no time to be pleasant, though, especially to assholes like him, and quite frankly, I didn't have any idea what *exactly* the three men on the airplane were working on.

Ring, ring, ring.

For the next thirty minutes I fielded calls from various members of Ion's board of directors, as well as the venture capitalists who'd funded Ion from the start. They all wanted to know about the IPO—or in other words, when they were going to be able to cash out and get their money. I despised them for being so insensitive and greedy until I realized that *I* actually played a huge role in helping these rich men get richer.

I was slumped over in my chair when Ji-yan shouted from her side of the floor, "Transferring Roberto to you."

Before the phone finished its first ring, I picked up the receiver. I was anxious to hear what was happening and to speak to someone who could relate to what I was going through. "Hey. It must be chaos over there. Are you doing okay?"

Roberto shouted over sirens and loud voices, "I'm okay. The coroner just arrived and the police are notifying the families. Don't talk to the press—just say 'no comment' and forward them to my voicemail. I'll deal with them later."

"I've already told some people that Andre wasn't on the airplane. Is that okay?"

"Yeah, that's fine to say. But that's it. Gotta go."

"Wait! One more thing. Have you touched base with Andre? Everyone is asking about the IPO."

"I spoke to Andre—the IPO is still on track, but . . ."

"I will need to give insiders a little more, Roberto. They all want to know what roles the crash victims played and what their absence means for the completion of the Model A."

Roberto was silent, which gave me time to think. Suddenly I burst out with an answer that I knew was the right one, but which felt wrong all the same. "Hey, how about I tell the insiders that Ion's teams are broadly trained and deeply structured, and that we do a lot of knowledge exchange internally, so we still anticipate having the Model A out on time?"

"Great. That sounds good. Now seriously, I've got to go."

Click.

As I hung up the receiver I became slightly sickened at how quickly I put a positive spin on such a terrible tragedy. I wondered whether I was any different from the Jack Wynns of the world, and felt disgusted with myself that I'd made my decision to come here because I was chasing the money.

When my phones were finally silent, I listened to the messages on my cell phone. The message indicator had been blinking for hours.

"Sophia, this is Dad. Please call us back and let us know you are okay."

"Hey, lady, it's me, Kate. I heard the news on the radio and just want to be sure you're okay. Call me."

"Sister. Please call me or Mom and Dad as soon as you can. We're really worried."

"Sophia, it's Ashley. Please call us back. You know the numbers."

"Sophia, it's Sissy. Please answer the phone."

"Grant here. What the hell? Call me back."

"It's Peter. Please answer the phone. I've been calling all morning. Are you okay?"

The sound of his voice enveloped me like a warm, safe embrace and I quickly covered my mouth to choke back a wail. All morning I'd done my best to be strong and calm, but the sound of Peter's voice weakened me. My chin tilted down to my chest and I whispered quietly to the man I loved, as though he could hear me, "God, I miss you." Suddenly, I sat up straight and looked around me to make sure no one had witnessed my moment. *Shake it off, Sophia. Now isn't the time.* I then picked up the phone to call my parents.

"*Ai-ya*, Mei-Mei. You had us so worried. Are you okay?"

"Yes, I'm fine. Sorry I didn't call earlier. It's just crazy here. Can we talk later?"

"Of course. Get back to work. I will tell Daddy."

"Okay, bye. Love you," I said.

"Just one thing before you go. Have you spoken with Peter?"

At a time like this? Only my mother.

"No, Mom."

"This is one of the reasons you guys broke up. You're too independent. Too bossy. Your father and I have both told you—'Don't be so bossy.'" Mom sighed. She'd already forgotten about the plane crash and was now blaming herself for not fixing my bossiness problem sooner. "You've been like this since you were a little girl."

"Mom! Listen! That's not it. I have to go."

"Okay, okay. But if that's not it, is it because he doesn't think you're a virgin? I *told* you not to use those tampons! The boys are going to think you've been to bed with lots of people if you use those tampons."

Jesus H. Christ.

"Mother. I'm at work and I am surrounded by people," I lied. "Can we *please* talk later?"

"Fine. Just be aware that you spend most of your day with extremely important people, Mei-Mei, and it's not wise to hold the bar that high for your husband. Those men count on *you* to take care of *them* and your life will be much easier if you marry someone who will take care of *you*."

I rolled my eyes and nodded. "Okay, Mom. Yes. Okay. And don't forget it's also those men who fired me!"

I hung up and called Audrey, Ashley, Grant, and Kate to give them updates. All the important people. Well . . . all but one. I debated whether to call Peter, knowing that if I heard his voice I would crumble, and he would come running to save me from this nightmare. *But what good would that be for us? Or worse yet—what if he* doesn't *come running?* My stomach filled with dread as I imagined all the different ways a conversation with Peter could play out. I decided it was safer to email him instead, so I drafted a message, then redrafted it at least a dozen more times before pressing the Send button.

To: Peter Bruce
From: Sophia Young
Subj: Your voicemail

Peter, thanks for the voicemail. It meant a lot. It's chaos here, but I'm fine. I hope work is okay and that you can come up for air soon.
Love, Sophia

I sat back, questioning whether I should have written something different. *Maybe I shouldn't have signed it using* Love. Then Mom's words crept back into my head. "Those men count on *you* to take care of *them*," she'd said. "It's not wise to hold the bar that high for your husband." I questioned again why I'd hesitated when Peter asked me about our long-term plans. *Is it that I'm afraid I'll have yet another person depending on me? Or is it that I'm afraid he'd be yet another man telling me what to do, or worse, that he'd "fire" me?*

FOUR WEEKS AFTER the crash, our office lobby looked like a sprawling, colorful shrine that wound all the way up the stairs to the second floor. Mixed in between the lovely rainbow of flowers were notes of sympathy and cards of encouragement—all from strangers who were cheering us on. I was surprised by the country's outpouring of emotion, and took a moment to wonder what it all meant: so many supporters who had no affiliation with Ion whatsoever were going out of their way to let us know they were thinking of, and rooting for, us. I stood at the base of the lobby stairs, gazing into the sea of colors, feeling as though the country was begging us to make it proud. A sudden rush of patriotism caught me off guard as I realized Ion wasn't just about profits and losses, stock options and employment agreements. It was about solidifying America's position as a leader in the automotive industry by bringing the world's first electric car to market. The image of myself as a hero elicited a chuckle, and I ignored my desire to strike a superhero pose. Instead I began climbing the stairs, and any concerns I'd had previously—about becoming like the money-hungry, merciless Jack Wynn—fell away.

We're going to make history.

As they say, the show must go on. Literally. I scurried up the remaining stairs to toil away on the perpetual bane of my existence: the roadshow presentation. I thought I'd gotten it nailed down that first day that I spoke with Andre, but the state of my personal work area was a good indicator of my progress: stained coffee cups from the kitchen downstairs were stacked around my computer stand, Post-it notes were stuck to my telephone and my pen-marked desk, and my trash can was overflowing with crumpled balls of paper. I took a deep

breath and sat on the gray exercise ball that two weeks ago had replaced my Herman Miller Aeron chair (according to tie-dye-wearing
Gordon from Ion's "Healthy Workplace" team, it would force me to
use my core). I was ready to attack the blessed presentation again.
The only things I had going for me were the graphic designer and
film director I had surreptitiously recruited. The designer was the
one Roberto had hired to build our website—the same one that Andre'd already approved. If Andre liked this designer's style, it made
sense to use the same person for our roadshow graphics. When our
controller, Rex, informed me I had signing authority on anything under ten thousand dollars, I convinced the graphic designer to take on
my presentation project for $9,999, even though he'd normally get
paid four times that amount. For the sizzle reel I recruited an Oscar-
winning film director whose name I had spotted on the Model A's
waiting list when I was reviewing it my first day on the job. Yet even
with all this talent, Andre still hadn't signed off on either project, and
I was still unsure why.

After several hours, I saved the sixty-fourth draft of the presentation and said to myself, *This is it! The final!* Then, before turning my
attention to scripting out the slides for Andre, I checked my email.

To: All
From: Andre Stark
Subj: Moving on

Today we will be unveiling a memorial dedicated to our peers who
we tragically lost four weeks ago. Please meet us at two o'clock this
afternoon at the newly landscaped area on the far end of our parking
lot (where the asphalt ends and Palo Alto's hiking trail begins).

I thought a lot about this memorial—about what it should be and
what it should stand for—and selected a hand-carved sandalwood
bench that contains a natural fragrance that will last for decades.

Though the scent won't last forever, our memories of our colleagues will. Martin, John, and Joe were an important part of Ion's success and it's up to us to make them proud.

I hope the bench will be a place of reflection for many of you, and that it brings some peace to us all.

—Andre

I stopped reading the email and thought about how beautiful and generous a gesture this was. *Qualities of a great leader.*

I CONNECTED MY headphones to my computer so I could do the next-best thing there was to observing Andre on a roadshow: I watched every past interview Andre had given and noted his body language, his voice tones, his language and cadence. When I finished watching all the videos I could find, I listened to Andre's radio interviews with my eyes closed, hoping to permanently embed his words in my head via osmosis, if there was such a thing. I replayed certain phrases my CEO liked to use, then quietly repeated them to myself. Two hours later, at noon, a tap on my shoulder startled me from my psycho-transmission. I opened my eyes and flipped around; Rajesh stood behind me, motioning for me to remove the headphones.

"What are you doing?" he asked. He sounded less than friendly. "Are you listening to music?"

"I'm listening to interviews of Andre."

"Why? You look like you're sleeping. We can't have that in our office. This is a place of business, Sophia. And by the way, I think you should stop smiling so much in meetings. You know, men can interpret that the wrong way, and, well, I find it unprofessional."

"Excuse me?" I stood up quickly, which sent my exercise ball flying toward Miles. "First of all, I'm not *sleeping*, Rajesh. I'm listening to Andre's interviews so I can hear how *he* tells the story," I defended myself. An awkward pause passed before I decided to drive my point home harder: "Since the way *you* and Jack wanted to do it didn't resonate."

Rajesh's stunned expression concerned me for a moment, but I decided I didn't care. I had to set boundaries with this asshole. The two of us stood at my desk, staring each other down, and just when I thought Rajesh would fire me, he nodded with approval. "That's smart."

Of course it's smart!

"And if you're suggesting that my smiling is flirting, I don't agree. This place needs to lighten up a little, don't you think? Shouldn't we be having some fun here?" My boss looked surprised at my reaction, and I doubted myself for a moment before remembering that Rajesh was the last person qualified to challenge my professionalism. I decided to passive-aggressively address how he treated me, "I'm really trying my best, Rajesh. I would sincerely appreciate some guidance about how to do my job better, and it would be terrific if you could give me a bit more feedback on this presentation. I feel as though I'm flying blind. Isn't that a better use of our time instead of etiquette lessons? If you have problems or concerns about *my work,* perhaps a three-month review is appropriate."

"There's no need for a quarterly review. You're doing fine. Just fine. I have no concerns at all."

I nodded and looked at the clock. *Meeting time.*

"Glad to hear it," I told Rajesh as I slipped by him. "We have *your* finance meeting now, so I'll see you in the Einstein conference room. I just want to get some coffee before I head down." This would be my first meeting with the broader finance team—until then it had been only smaller meetings between me, Miles, and Rajesh—and I had a feeling it would be death by spreadsheets.

Unlike Treehouse, Ion *loved* meetings. Spread throughout my day were investment banker meetings; status meetings with the entire executive team; meetings with battery engineers so I could grasp the proprietary nature of our technology and translate it into something understandable for our investors and research analysts; sync-ups with Roberto's PR team, who, bless them, wanted to make sure that any PR messages they sent out that week wouldn't jeopardize or conflict with any of my planned IR messages. To be fair, I *asked* to be invited to all these meetings when I started, because I knew it would be the fastest way for me to learn Ion's business. But on that day, carrying my coffee into Ion's largest conference room and seeing the complicated spreadsheet projected onto the large white wall screen, I regretted sticking my nose into every department's business.

As I eased myself into one of the conference room's cushy brown leather chairs, the men seated around the large black lacquer table swiveled in their seats to see who had arrived to the meeting. I looked at the clock and noted I wasn't late, but clearly they were all waiting for me. *Note to self: arrive early to Rajesh's meetings.* My boss's glare sent chills up my spine—he looked like I had walked in twenty minutes past start time, like he thought he owned me and I'd disobeyed him in the worst possible way. I diverted my eyes toward the screen and swiveled my chair to face it, all the while feeling sorry for his wife, and daughters, who had no choice but to deal with Rajesh's very same glare.

The weight of the room was heavy, even though the sun shined brightly through the wall of sliding glass doors that led to our office's large back patio. Everyone looked fairly casual in their button-down shirts and khakis, but their straight-backed seated postures and quiet voices suggested a much stiffer environment. My casualness stood out among my peers—even my clothes screamed *trendy* while theirs whispered *conservative*. I questioned at least a dozen of the calculations that were presented, while everyone else in the room, including Rajesh, seemed content to assume that what was presented was flawless. Their passivity, particularly Rajesh's, made me nervous, and I wondered whether he had a good grasp on these financial matters.

If he did, he'd be asking many more questions. *Or maybe it's me that isn't understanding.* When the meeting was over, Rajesh announced, "This is Jason's last day, so after work the team will be meeting at the bar downstairs to wish him well."

Finally! Some fun!

"Rajesh is buying!" I shouted happily, trying to lighten up the mood. The roomful of men seemed to *want* to cheer, but no one could miss my boss's daggered glare. *Oops. Not funny?*

THREE WEEKS LATER, my phone rang at the end of the day. I considered not answering it because I was so tired. I could barely lift my chin to check the caller ID; when I saw Grant's phone number flashing, I picked up the handset.

"How's it going?" he asked.

"Good. I felt good today. I finally nailed the presentation and can proudly say that Andre has signed off," I cheered, feeling a brief injection of energy. "What's going on over there? Are you guys *still* trying to get that lease negotiated in Orange County?"

"It's a living nightmare. Andre picked a real winner. The manufacturing site is riddled with environmental issues, permitting issues, and a landlord that is anything but cooperative. The joke of the year will be, 'How many lawyers does it take to negotiate a lease?'"

"Rajesh is worse! That guy is so uptight that I think he may break," I said.

"It's a tough culture over there for sure. It doesn't help that Rajesh is so green and that Andre is never there."

"Yeah, so if Andre is never here, that means Rajesh is setting the culture, which, quite frankly, seems fear-based to me. I don't know who I can trust here!"

"Trust no one," Grant advised in a rather serious tone. "No one."

I nodded in agreement and told myself to just get through the

IPO, before changing the subject altogether. "Hey, do you know why our in-house counsel quit last week?" I asked. The timing of his departure was very sudden and suspect. "I liked that guy."

"Only he and Andre know the reason, or reasons. I think it has something to do with this new facility, though. Andre isn't a fan of lawyers."

"No offense, but most people don't like lawyers," I said, defending Andre a little while delivering a friendly jab to my old mentor. I listened to Grant complain for a few more minutes about Andre and Rajesh, chiming in with my own "Oh I know! He did that to me" statements once in a while. I realized how lucky I was that he continued to watch out for me and hoped that Scott would, too. I wanted the same relationship with Andre that I had with Scott and Grant. But Rajesh? Not so much.

A call from Kate lifted my mood even more. She rang to tell me about her trip to Mexico.

"We had a great time. A really great time," she said. I noticed how much more mature she sounded, more like a real adult than the echo of the crazy college roommate I always knew and loved.

"Yeah? What did you do?"

"Nothing! We snorkeled, slept a lot, ate a lot, and read books on the beach."

"And drank margaritas, I hope!"

"Well, no. I wasn't drinking."

I thought to myself for a moment: *Kate. Not drinking. Relaxing and sleeping. Doesn't sound like her.*

"You're pregnant!" I shrieked.

"Yes! Can you believe it? We haven't told anyone yet but I'm delighted, although it's going to be rough raising a kid during law school."

"You can do it. I know you can. And I call dibs on being the godmother!" I said, feeling genuinely happy and excited for her.

"Uh, no doubt! I'd force you to do it even if you didn't want to."

We both laughed and shared more details about our weeks. I told her about work and how Ji-yan and Roberto were the only two people I connected with.

"Roberto sounds cute," Kate said. "Any jewelry?"

"Unfortunately, yes. A very cool silver ring. His wife is probably gorgeous, smart, and hip," I responded.

In the late hours of the evening, I went through the same drills that I did at Treehouse: reviewing stock exchange proposals, revising Ion's S-1 registration statement for our next filing with the SEC, and more. It was during those late hours, when the office had mostly cleared out and I was alone, that I wanted to call Peter the most. In my head I counted the exact number of days since Peter left me that "I'll call you in three months" message—the fate of our relationship should be decided any day now—and I noticed that it felt like it had been way longer than three months. It felt as though it had been forever. I wanted to see Peter, to go out to dinner with him, to laugh with him, to feel his comforting embrace, but I could only assume the worst. I forced myself to think about something else, fearing I'd become sad. I reached for the phone to call my parents, but then stopped and grinned when I saw the email that had just arrived in my personal email inbox. *It's from Scott.*

> To: Sophia Young
> From: Scott Kraft
> Subj:
>
> "Sophia Young reported directly to the world's 'penultimate' marketer"? Did you write that? E.S.L.
> SK

It was the first communication I'd had from Scott since I left Treehouse, and imagining his reaction to my bio that was posted on

Ion's website made me laugh. Roberto had pushed me for it when I first started the job, so I'd drafted it very quickly and sent it off before rushing to a meeting with investment bankers. I brought up the Company Management section of Ion's website and read my bio to see if I'd made a mistake. Then I looked up the word *penultimate.*

Oops. I thought penultimate *was like the supreme ultimate. Not "next to last."*

To: Scott Kraft
From: Sophia Young
Subj: Re:

1. Oops. Yes. Fixed. BTW, I win the "no talking" contest.
2. Congrats on the launch of the Q-phone. I want. If I buy twenty, may I have a discount?
S

To: Sophia Young
From: Scott Kraft
Subj: Re: Re:

1. You still can't write.
2. No.
SK

chapter 23

THE HOLIDAYS PASSED WITHOUT ANYTHING close to a Viennese Waltz party . . . or a call from Peter that was now officially overdue. Instead Rajesh declared that Ion Palo Alto would be treated to a self-serve sushi platter in the kitchen downstairs, and thoughts of Peter gave way to the piles of work that should have been easy, but instead took twice as long to finish because of the amount of premeditating, planning, or straight-out changing of directions that needed to occur to get Andre's approval. The graphics in PowerPoint weren't good enough for him, so we had to change to a different graphic design program. He didn't like how our logo's color looked in the S-1, so we had to have a new one designed. And on and on. In addition, somehow I became the middleman between my CEO and his nemeses: the lawyers and bankers. Nearly every issue related to the roadshow required careful steering, and I seemed to be the only one who could handle Andre. Perhaps it was because of my gender, perhaps it was because Scott and my mother trained me well, but working with Andre wasn't an issue for me—I knew his type. My trick—although I believed Ji-yan did the same—was to refrain from telling Andre what he *couldn't* do. Instead, I spent an inordinate amount of time figuring out why he objected to something, then offered a solution I knew he would accept.

For example: the bankers strongly suggested that Andre wear a suit on the roadshow or else the investors, particularly in Boston, would find him disrespectful.

Andre said, "Fuck them. We don't need them." To which the bankers responded with a simple, "We're not taking you out on the road then."

Now, now. Let's not be hasty.

My solution to steer Andre in the right direction was to identify a piece of acceptable clothing that I knew he loved (loved, loved) to wear. I said to my CEO, "Hey, how about that *really cool* blue suede sports jacket of yours—with an Ion T-shirt?"

Mission accomplished. Queen of compromise.

Or, the lawyer said the IPO would be put on hold if Andre stopped in the middle of the roadshow to make an appearance with Stephen Colbert on *The Daily Show.*

Andre, always one to fight for what he wanted, said stubbornly, "I'm doing it anyway." To which I responded (knowing it would take months to organize), "How about we get you a *60 Minutes* interview instead? That's more our target car buyer."

AS THE PLANE'S wheels hit the tarmac at Los Angeles International Airport, I opened my eyes from my hour-long nap and looked at the watch Scott had given me. *Nine o'clock.* I stretched my arms upward and yawned before unbuckling my (economy class) seat belt (even though passengers were supposed to wait "until the plane comes to a complete stop"). As I groggily dragged my feet off the airplane, I realized my nap was the best sleep I'd had in weeks. I was thankful for the respite. *It's going to be a long day.*

I stepped off the airport curbside and into the taxi, reminding myself there were only two weeks remaining before Ion's road-show kicked off. I should have been excited, elated even, just as I'd been before Treehouse's IPO, but the only thing I felt was mentally exhausted—I was homesick for Treehouse, for Jonathan and Scott, and was hardly enjoying myself anymore.

The taxi ride to Ion's Hawthorne office took only minutes—

minutes that I used to psyche myself up for the day ahead. That afternoon I was to host a group of research analysts—the very same ones that were lined up to write public reports about Ion once the company went public. The timing for the event wasn't great (there was still so much to do) and I'd already spent hours conducting "teach-ins" with them. But despite my efforts to get the analysts excited about our business and Andre's vision and, more important, to get them to believe that we'd actually be able to do what we said we would do—build *and sell* luxury-level electric cars—they simply weren't drinking the Ion Kool-Aid. Hence, the afternoon's dog and pony show: Ion's chief designer, VP of engineering, VP of manufacturing, and Roberto—after having been carefully scripted by me—would spend six hours boasting about their vision, their progress, and their experience. The analysts would be allowed to see, touch, feel, and actually test-drive our Model A prototypes before ending the day dining with Andre (at his steak house, a magnet for Hollywood's Who's Who, of course). Before their arrival, though, I was due to meet Andre for his final sign-off on the sizzle reel.

Fingers crossed!

Ion's Hawthorne office—our design center—was extremely different from the company's headquarters in Palo Alto. Instead of the Toyota Priuses, Volkswagen diesel Jettas, and other gas-efficient vehicles parked at headquarters, the latest Porsche, Maserati, and Ferrari models adorned Hawthorne's lot. Our chief designer and VP of engineering each had access to generous budgets—budgets that would have paid for one thousand graphic designers (yet I had to kick, scratch, scream, then beg to get just one)—that were earmarked for these luxury brands under the guise of "competitive research" and "testing." *Testing, my ass.*

Small square windows lined the entire perimeter of our remarkably white design center's one-story building. Its skylight-dotted roof sent light streaming into the modern space, which was decorated with elegant gray and black Herman Miller workspace furniture. Each time I visited, I felt a twinge of office envy. Palo Alto was obviously the red-headed stepchild; even more appealing to me, however, was this office's casual, inspired, creative culture. Most likely the culture differences were because Andre spent most of his time at Hawthorne; unfortunately Rajesh's formal and strict personality had shaped Palo Alto.

I sat on one of the eight white leather chairs surrounding a long glass table inside a narrow, stark white conference room. The tasteful steel borders of the room's five glass windows added a pop of contrast to the otherwise whitewashed setting. It all looked very L.A.

While waiting for Andre, I played the sizzle reel one last time. *Thank God he already signed off on the presentation.*

And thirty minutes after we were scheduled to meet, Andre stormed in with a man in tow and said, "I'm really busy today. What do you need?"

I tilted my chin toward the strange man and mouthed the words, *Who's that?*

"That's my new bodyguard," Andre said, as though having a bodyguard were a normal occurrence. "Now what's up?"

"I need you to sign off on the sizzle reel. We need to get it finalized because the lawyers and bankers have to have time to review it."

"Fuck them," Andre said, still standing. He responded to my annoyed expression by adding, "Fine, just email it to me."

"But—"

"I'm really busy, Sophia. I don't have time for this. If we don't make the launch this week, I'm not going on the roadshow," Andre threatened.

He was referring to his other company, Stark Aerospace, and its

first-ever rocket launch. A lot was riding on the launch's success because if it worked, NASA would sign on as Stark Aerospace's first
customer, which meant the company would win the contract to manage all shipments to and from the International Space Station. The
launch had been delayed for weeks, first because of bad weather, and
then due to a technical issue. I tried to be sympathetic to the unbearable pressure Andre must have been feeling, but I resented the fact
that his space company distracted him from what *I* needed him to
do. He was making my life, and the lives of everyone else involved
with the IPO, very difficult.

"Please just watch it once. It's thirty seconds," I begged while
fumbling around on my laptop to bring up the video. In my opinion, the sizzle reel did exactly what I wanted it to do, and I was
certain it would make investors sit forward in their chairs. As the
video began, Andre, still standing, folded his arms and let out a
frustrated sigh.

Four seconds into the reel, Andre said, "I don't like the music." His
eyes were glued to the door and he started to pace back and forth like
a caged animal, anxious to break free from the confines of me and
the conference room.

"What type of music do you want?" I asked.

"Not that kind."

That's very, very helpful. Thank you.

"You've said that twice now," I said patiently. "The film director
and I have tried slow-paced music, fast-paced rock, and even a blend
of rhythm and blues, but you don't like any of them, so perhaps you
could be more specific?"

Andre flashed a rabid look my way, stomped his foot, and shouted
as he stormed out of the room, "I don't have time for this! I have to
launch the fucking rocket!"

Okay, then. That went well.

To: Ji-yan Chen
From: Sophia Young
Subj: Music

What music does Andre like?

To: Sophia Young
From: Ji-yan Chen
Subj: Re: Music

Ibiza disco house music.

When I received Ji-yan's response, I immediately took to the Internet to figure out what she meant. As I searched for the term *Ibiza*,
I wondered, *What in the hell is that?*

FOR THE NEXT three hours, I listened to Ibiza disco music while I
waited for Miles and my six research analysts to arrive. When they
finally did, I ushered them into our scheduled meetings, where our
executives wowed them with computer-animated designs that sim-
ulated aerodynamics tests, detailed drawings of the Model A, and
explanations about how those designs translated into the working prototypes of the car. Our visitors were also shown a Power-
Point presentation of the cars' step-by-step manufacturing plans
and schedule, and they were shown photos of the manufacturing
facility we'd recently acquired, which, incidentally, was *not* the one
Grant and his team had been trying to negotiate for months. Our
new plant was purchased only one week ago—the day Andre and I
toured the 5.3 million-square-foot former car manufacturing facility in Fremont, California, that had recently closed. The plant was

so large that we took a trolley to get to the middle of it; we climbed out and walked around for only a few minutes before Andre turned to me and said, "I want it." Satisfied, he'd climbed back into the trolley and driven off, leaving me standing alone and responsible for, what else—buying an entire factory. In a week.

At the end of the day, the whole group was caravanned off to Andre's popular restaurant on Sunset Boulevard, where, upon arrival, I immediately noticed the Kardashians dining in one booth while Reese Witherspoon and her husband sat at another. The analysts didn't seem to care or notice the Hollywood stars, though—they were too starstruck by Andre. Three hours later, I signaled for Andre to wrap it up (which he ignored), and when the analysts were finally safe in their taxis, I grabbed Miles and raced to the airport. By the time we arrived, it was too late. The last flight to San Francisco had departed.

While Miles stood at the airline desk trying to find a different route home, I called Rajesh to let him know that his VP of finance and VP of IR would likely have to spend the night in L.A.

"We missed our flight. Dinner ran long," I said, sounding exhausted and regretting my high heels.

"Oh no. That's terrible. I feel very badly for Miles. He has a family at home," Rajesh said.

"They'll be okay. His wife is home," I said, glancing over at Miles to see if there was any sign of progress.

"Yes, but he has children and, well, it's always better for a man to be home with his family."

I wanted to lie—to tell Rajesh that *I* had a family waiting for me at home, too. It was clear he didn't care at all that I was stuck in L.A. with no toothbrush or change of clothes. Instead I passive-aggressively said, "Oh, don't worry about me. I don't have any of my insulin, but I'll be fine." Exhausted and homesick, I thought of Peter. I'd be spending the night in L.A. by myself, and no one would be missing me.

Later, as I stepped into my room at the Hyatt Regency near LAX, I thought of that day more than three years ago when I opened the door to the Presidential Suite at the Four Seasons Hotel. How silly and naïve was I to be excited about something like that? Now, staring at yet another empty hotel room, I questioned whether I was exactly where I was supposed to be. It certainly didn't feel like that anymore.

chapter 24

RAJESH, ANDRE, THE BANKERS, AND I spent the next two weeks getting ready to kick off the IPO. We were on a high after the successful rocket launch, a triumph for Stark Aerospace, for Ion, and most of all for Andre. After so much loss—the plane crash and the failed launches—we really needed a win. Stark Aerospace's milestone lightened the mood, and Ion's usual tense atmosphere changed to a *nothing is impossible* energy that made everyone feel proud. For me, the best part was finally having Andre's undivided attention, which was sorely needed to kick off the roadshow. At long last, we were almost there.

The sizzle reel, with the Ibiza background music, was finished. All the graphics, scripting, and messaging were approved. *Thank God!* The last thing we needed to do, at the bankers' request, was to finish rehearsing the Q&A with Rajesh. The bankers and I had already completed three rehearsals with him, and he had not "shown" well.

IT WAS TWO o'clock in the morning on the day we were scheduled to leave for the roadshow. Six bankers, two lawyers, and I sat around a conference table at Ion and drilled Rajesh as though he were on trial. I felt a little sorry for him as he slumped in front of us looking exhausted and defeated.

"Rajesh, maybe this will help," I said. "Put yourself in an investor's shoes. You're trying to shoot holes through someone's business plan. You're just looking for some reason to *not* invest. The CFO's job is not only to answer the questions, but also to put a positive spin on them."

Rajesh glared at me and I recognized his familiar *shut up* look. The room got quiet until Jack Wynn asked, "Would you mind giving him an example, Sophia?"

Stunned that Jack actually asked *me* for *my* opinion, I stuttered slightly as I answered, "Well, uh, for example, if investors ask about why our employee turnover is so high, you can say that we take only the top one percent of the thousands of résumés we receive each day."

"That's not actually answering the question," Rajesh complained.

"No, it's not. But I guarantee the investor will *think* that's an answer. And even if he doesn't, he will be impressed and take note that we are hiring the best of the best in a very competitive hiring environment."

Rajesh pushed back. "I understand. But—"

"No buts," said Jack. "Sophia is right. She's not telling you to lie to the investor, but don't give them any cause to worry." He shot me a look of approval and a crack of a smile.

The man who was often wrong but never in doubt—the man who'd refused to listen to *any* of my opinions when I worked for him at Global Partners—finally said that I was right! *I've gained his respect. It's about time.*

Jack looked at his watch and said, "We can practice more on the airplane tomorrow. The plan is to meet at Andre's jet at seven in the morning. Don't forget that we're going straight to the Global Partners offices for an afternoon sales force teach-in in New York."

We collected our things and I stood at the conference room door waiting for Rajesh.

"Don't worry," I said. "You're going to do great."

Rajesh scowled at me and I wasn't sure why. I wondered if it was because I'd tried to give him advice. Had I embarrassed him in front of other people? But wasn't I just doing my job? I turned my eyes toward the floor and walked silently away, too tired to care.

MY HAIR WAS still wet but there was no time to dry it. A ponytail had to do. The black sedan had arrived five minutes ago and was waiting outside on Greenwich Street.

My phone rang as I closed the front door to my flat. I hesitated to answer the call, but when I saw that it was Rajesh, I picked up.

"Hi, Rajesh. I'm on my way."

"Where are you?"

"I'm just leaving the house. The car is here. Why? What's wrong?"

"Oh, good. You haven't left. I asked Ji-yan to book you on a flight out of SFO, so you'll just meet us all in New York."

"What? Why?" I asked.

"Just meet us there. I think Ji-yan said she booked you on American. The details should be in your email."

"Hang on. That doesn't make any sense at all. Why wouldn't I just fly with you guys on Andre's jet?"

"Just get on that flight."

I had no idea what was going on, but I had a suspicion it was because of our rehearsal the night before, or rather, earlier that morning.

"Is this because of the prep session? Really, Rajesh, it wasn't personal. I was just doing what you hired me to do—get you ready for the IPO. Investors are going to question everything you say. It's their job to shoot holes through our business."

"No. That's not it."

Bullshit.

"Well, then what is it?" I asked.

"I just don't like you and I don't want you to fly with us," Rajesh responded quickly.

There was a short silence. I could hear a blue jay squawking in the maple near the door. I took a breath and adjusted the phone against my ear.

"Well, I can work on whatever it is you don't like, but we're about to kick off the IPO of the decade. I'm getting on that jet, Rajesh."

"No, you're not."

"What if I promise not to say a word during the entire flight?" I asked, shocked and disappointed at myself for even suggesting such a thing. *What the fuck are you doing, Sophia?* It was only then that I realized—*I can't work for this man.*

"Just get on the American flight. This isn't a negotiation."

"We don't operate on the caste system, Rajesh. I'm not taking a different flight than everyone else when there's a perfectly good seat for me on the jet."

"Sophia." His tone was cold and hateful, and I hated him for putting me in this position. But he'd backed me into a corner.

My voice cracked when I said, "I will not get on the commercial flight. You are going to have to fire me."

"Okay, fine," Rajesh said. "You're fired."

"What?!"

Shit. He actually did it!

But there was no response; the line was dead.

"Miss, we need to go if we're going to stay on schedule." I stared at the driver, who was now standing on the curb in front of my flat, his hand closed around the handle of my suitcase. With surprising speed I yanked it out of his grasp, wheeled around, and returned to my front door. I unlocked it with shaking hands.

"Miss!"

But I couldn't speak; I just slammed the door in his face. Then I turned the dead bolt, slid to the floor, and tilted my head back against the door. I held my breath, waiting for tears, but they never came.

You deserve better than that. Scott's words. He'd said them to me a dozen times, and he'd say them again now. I knew that I had stuck up for myself and that I had done the right thing. But I felt awful. I took a deep breath, then another, and then lifted my head, confident that Andre would call. *He'd better.*

THIRTY MINUTES LATER, Andre's name appeared on my caller ID.

Andre shouted, "What the fuck are you doing? You're ruining this whole thing!"

"Talk to Rajesh!" I screamed back. "I didn't do a damn thing."

"I don't give a shit what he did or said. Get your ass to New York."

"Well, he fired me. Didn't he tell you?"

"Oh Jesus." The phone crackled. I could practically see Andre rolling his eyes and pacing. "Why can't you just make it work with him?"

"It's not me, Andre. The man has hated me since the day I started." I ran a hand over my tightly pulled-back hair. *I'll handle this better than I handled Rajesh.* "Look, I'm not coming to New York. I don't work for Ion anymore. If you want me back, I want to report to only you, not Rajesh."

Andre paused. "You know that's impossible," he said, his voice softening. "I can't just pull the IR function away from my CFO. What will it take for you to come to New York and finish out this road-show?" That's when I realized. *He doesn't care about me at all. He only cares about the IPO right now.*

I narrowed my eyes and pursed my lips. *No more Ms. Nice Guy.* It took me only seconds to decide what I wanted; I visualized it the way Scott would have wanted me to. His voice played in my head: *"Ask for everything and more."*

With my heart in my throat, I took a deep breath. And I asked. "I want six months' severance, eighteen months' *paid* health care, and *all* my stock options accelerated so they're vested and exercisable."

"I don't think we can accelerate *all* your options, but we could certainly get you one year's worth," Andre said. "Consider it done.

Call Jacob and tell him what's going on. And I'll send the jet back for you after we land, but you're going to miss the bankers' sales force teach-in and I'm very unhappy about that."

"Wait! *And* I want Rajesh to walk behind me at all times while we're on the road. I don't want him anywhere near me."

"Sophia . . ."

"I'm not kidding, Andre. I despise that man. It's nothing different than what he just asked me to do. He's a complete pig—a misogynist!"

Andre didn't disagree. He knew the man he'd hired was a lawsuit waiting to happen, so he simply said, "Fine. Just get over here."

I hung up the phone, my entire body shaking. I leaned against the wall, slid to the floor, and began to cry.

chapter 25

"HERE WE GO," I SAID, offering Andre a bottle of water. He grabbed it from my hand, took a sip, then gave it back. We were just steps from the side door of the Grand Ballroom in the Pierre New York. Nearly two hundred potential investors were inside, gathered to hear Andre tell them why they should buy Ion stock. As Andre had promised, Rajesh walked several feet behind me, and there were three bankers between us. It was the last day of our road show and I was physically and mentally exhausted.

I swung open the gold-painted door and Andre strode through. Round tables of ten were spread throughout the ballroom with neatly plated breakfasts placed in front of each attendee.

I followed Andre up the three steps leading to the stage, then hung back at the edge as he took his place behind the dark wood podium. *Touchdown.* I glared at Rajesh as he walked past me and took a seat behind the podium, knowing that that was as far as he would *ever* get: sitting behind someone, waiting for his turn.

With the spotlight shining brightly on him, Andre took a moment to absorb the sight of the crowd. He held his hands up and said, "Good morning! Before we get into the presentation, I'm going to show you a video featuring some of our executive team . . . and real footage of Ion's brand-new Model A. It is a true technology velociraptor!"

What the hell is a velociraptor? Shit, he's veering away from the script!

The room erupted into cheers and I heard the audio-visual technician behind me whisper into his walkie-talkie, "Cue sizzle reel." As the Ibiza music began to play, I looked to the three large white screens projecting the video that was *my* vision—the beautiful cars and the carefully scripted words that I wrote. Although the room was dim, I could see the well-dressed audience; they were sitting forward in their chairs just as I'd hoped. I smiled at the investors' blissed-out expressions. I took a slow, deep breath and looked down to the floor. *We did it, Sophia. We did it.*

AFTER BREAKFAST, ANDRE and I sat in a stretch limousine facing forward; Rajesh sat alone on the seat that ran sideways. I'd traveled nine days with these two. From time to time Andre looked from Rajesh to me, then back; he knew we didn't speak to each other, but it didn't seem to bother him whatsoever. As we drove to our next meeting— our last—I looked out the window at the joggers in Central Park. The rain that had just begun to fall didn't appear to bother them, and I wondered what those people did for a living, thinking how nice it was that they had the luxury of exercising in the middle of the day. The sound of the windshield wipers brushing against the glass woke me from my daze. I glanced around the limo; Rajesh and Andre were checking their phones. I pulled mine out, too. Voicemails. Two of them.

Message 1: "Sophia, I was hoping to catch you in person. It's Eric McCabe from Chaussure.com. I'm funding a new company called Lasso and I want you to be one of the founders. Give me a ring, or better yet, get on a plane to Seattle. I need you here the day after tomorrow." Then, before Eric hung up, he laughed and said, "Working there is going to be like working at the Champs-Élysées."

Message 2: "Hi, baby. It's me, Peter. Listen, I know it's been a long time—more than I had intended—but I needed the time for self-reflection and to understand how I fit into 'us.' The truth is—and we both know it—that you truly don't *need* me. I had to figure out if I could be happy with that. But I know you want me in your life, and I am one hundred percent certain that I want you in mine. I miss you and would really like for us to talk. Please call me back. I love you."

I gripped my phone tightly, as though daring it to tell me that this was all a joke. Eric McCabe wanting *moi*? A man who was willing to love and support me just as I'd do for him? Before I could ask myself what had caused Peter's change of heart, or what had inspired Eric to think of me as his next business partner, I stopped the questions dead in their tracks. I knew the answers. Finally.

It's me. Unfiltered me.

Andre and Rajesh were still pecking at their phones when the car stopped at the next red light. I knew it was crazy, but there was some force building inside me, some wild energy that wouldn't let me sit there on these fancy leather seats one second longer. I'd had enough.

I grabbed my purse and opened the car door.

"Hey!" Andre exclaimed, his head whipping up from his new Q-phone. "Where are you going?"

"You don't need me anymore," I said as I climbed out of my seat. "The company is going to do great. I promise." I slammed the car door just as the light turned green.

The window rolled down, and Rajesh leaned past Andre to shout something at me, but his voice was drowned out by the honking yellow cab behind the limo. I caught one last glimpse of Andre as I stepped back and let the limo pass. He didn't look *too* angry; he looked perhaps even understanding.

Thank you, I mouthed.

I hailed the next taxi, slid into the back seat, and said, "Take me to the closest airport, please."

There was no time to think twice. No time to second-guess myself. As Jonathan said, "Fortune favors the bold," and that's exactly how I liked it. I was living my life *my way* from here on out—not Audrey's, my parents', my doctors', Peter's, or any other way. *There's no "supposed to" anymore.* I rolled down the taxi's window and stuck my head out so the rain and wind pelleted my face. For the first time in way too long, I smiled. *I am exactly where I'm supposed to be.*

epilogue

SAN FRANCISCO'S SECOND STREET LOOKS uncharacteristically clean. Gone are the clouds that brought rain pouring down on the city last night; in their place are clear skies that suggest spring has finally arrived. On this early April morning, the pedestrians I pass seem to be walking slower than usual. Their faces are turned up toward the bright shining sun, soaking in the warming rays and replenishing winter-depleted vitamin D reserves. On a different day, I might be doing the same. Instead, I am racing toward the entrance of a nondescript five-story building that is easily dwarfed by taller ones on either side of it.

Inside a small, empty lobby, the elevator's Up button is already lit. I press it again anyway—urgently and repeatedly—believing that doing so will get me to the fourth floor faster. When I finally reach our office's closed front door, I push it with such force that it flies open and breaks through the drywall behind it. A dozen or so heads turn to see me storm through our doorway. *I've arrived.*

"What the fuck happened?" I ask, my face flushed with anger.

A sturdy, Eastern European–looking man wearing a thick red-and-black flannel shirt tilts his head and shrugs his shoulders. His name is Adam Kalezic—my Lasso cofounder—and I'd hoped he would have more information by now.

"We were robbed," Adam says.

Doing my best to maintain a neutral tone of voice, I take a deep breath and respond, "Yes, you told me that this morning. Did you call the police like I asked you to?"

"No, not yet."

"Why not?" I ask, furrowing my eyebrows. Adam's technical genius might be unmatched, but he's always left *everything else* up to me.

"I forgot."

Bygones, Sophia. Bygones. Everyone has their own talents.

I dig my Q-phone out of my purse and dial 911. After providing the details to the dispatcher, I hang up and face the dozen or so employees who are scurrying about.

"Who was the last person out last night?" I ask.

"I was," says Viktoria, an engineer and a significant contributor to our company's product—software that automatically backs up data. "Not sexy, but definitely in demand" is how Eric McCabe described it to me just over a year ago as I sat at JFK waiting for a flight home. So much has happened since then; this isn't something I would have ever imagined.

"Did you lock the doors when you left?" I ask, completely prepared to fire her because I'm certain our predicament could have been avoided.

"I did. I didn't leave until about two A.M. and I'm sure I locked both the front door and the one off the kitchen that leads to the stairwell."

My gut reaction is to play detective and solve this puzzle myself, but surveying the damage is much more important. I look around the office—monitors are still sitting on desks that look untouched. "What did they take?"

"Umm," Adam mumbles, but before he goes on, I hold up my hand to stop him because I already know what he's going to say, and I can't bear to hear his words out loud.

They took our laptops.

My stomach drops. I feel faint as I think about all the proprietary software code stored on those laptops—all of it lost, fifteen months' worth of work down the drain. I want to blame someone, or at least to berate the team for leaving their laptops at the office.

How many times have I warned you to take your laptops home? Now what are we going to do?

As I play the dialogue through in my head—how to explain this to Lasso's shareholders, to Christine Kraft, Jonathan Larsen, Grant Vicker, and of course, Eric McCabe—Adam says with a proud grin, "The good news is that we just tested our product last night so all our work is backed up! Lasso works!"

"What?"

"We tried Lasso for the first time last night. Or technically, this morning. It works! We have our data!"

Oh, thank God. Thank God! Thank you!

Adam hands me a piece of paper that lists the information for all the stolen laptops, then tells me he and Viktoria are going to Best Buy to purchase replacements. I hand the list to our receptionist and ask her to file an insurance claim with our provider. It's only then that I notice what she—an Ivy League graduate—is wearing: a tight pink cotton sweater whose V-neck drops so low that one has to make a serious effort not to look. Her midriff is slightly showing and I'm certain she can't breathe in her tight jeans.

I lean toward her and whisper, "Tomorrow let's try not to look like we're fishing for a husband, shall we?" I kick myself for sounding like a mix between my mother and Scott Kraft, but I feel as though it's my duty to give her some styling advice. *God, I miss him. He would have been so proud.*

Back at my desk, I plug in my laptop and call out to our newest member of the marketing team, "Hey, new girl! Draft a press release announcing the robbery. Title it: 'Data Company Loses Its Data.' Got it? We pitch it like that to get people's attention and then go on to explain what really happened."

There's no such thing as bad press.

"Why would we want to do that?" asks our new employee as she walks toward me. I can see she's eager to learn, a quality I appreciate.

As I'm about to answer, my monitor's screen saver turns on and I watch an octopus swim gaily through a colorful, breathtaking coral reef. Bittersweet memories of Scott flood through me and I close my eyes to acknowledge just how much I miss him. When New Girl is seated across from me, I glance past the framed photo of Peter and me that sits on my desk, then lean in toward her to respond to her question. "Are you stupid, or fucking stupid?"

acknowledgments

This story would never have been shared had it not been for the team: Katie, who gave me the confidence to start this journey; the Dijkstra Agency, who believed in me; and Rachel, who saw potential and put in hard work to make it happen.

A huge thank-you to my family, for their unconditional love and support; to Adam, Alan, and Steve for helping me breathe easier; and to the Reading Group—our laughs carried me the whole way through.

Also, never-ending gratitude to all my mentors and friends who provided the inspiration behind the story. As Nora Ephron said, "Everything is copy."

about the author

Anna Yen has been an executive at a wide range of tech and media companies. She lives in San Francisco with her dog.